AT GUNPOINT

He waved his gun toward the dock. "The two of you," he said. "On the dock."

"Why?"

"Jesus Christ, Ruby. Will you just do what I say?" He raised his gun, pointing it directly at her head and Ruby helped Jesse stand, placing the cane in Jesse's right hand.

"Come on, sweetie," Ruby crooned. "Come with me. It's okay."

"All the way to the end," he said.

The aluminum boat floated high on the water before them. Ruby scanned the shore for hunters or week-enders, anyone who might spot them and be alarmed by the tableau.

"Forget it," he said, guessing her thoughts. "No one's paying any attention. Hunters sure as hell aren't stalking deer in the lake. Even if they looked right at us, what do you think they'd see? A nice little family enjoying their dock."

Ruby supported Jesse as they crossed the broken dock board and stopped three feet farther. How could the water be so calm, the trees so bright and colorful beneath the autumn-blue sky? It should be storming, the lake wind-lashed, lightning on the horizon. . . .

Savage Cut

Jo Dereske

A DELL BOOK

Published by
Dell Publishing
a division of
Bantam Doubleday Dell Publishing Group, Inc.
1540 Broadway
New York, New York 10036

ISBN: 0-440-22221-4

Printed in the United States of America

Published simultaneously in Canada

November 1996

10 9 8 7 6 5 4 3 2 1

OPM

For my brother Ray, who knows the woods

Many people generously shared their time and knowledge with me and I am exceedingly grateful. Any errors in this book are completely my own. I would especially like to thank: Ken Ford, John Blum, Jerome Miller, Rod Burton, David Drobnicki, Walter Robertson, Barbara Bell, Margaret Ziegler, Tom Dereske, Kip Winsett, and the sawmill operators of western Michigan. To Ray Dereske I am grateful beyond words.

Estimates made in 1836 gave the amount of pine then standing in the northern two-thirds of Michigan as 150,000,000,000 feet. The present estimate of the pine standing in the whole state is 35,000,000,000 feet.
—Charles Sprague Sargent,
Report on the Forests of North America (1884)

So deep a silence, so complete a calm prevailed in these forests that one might say that all the forces of nature, were, as it were, paralyzed.
—Alexis de Tocqueville,
A Fortnight in the Wilds (1831)

Chapter 1

It was uncommonly warm for late September, sultry even, when Ruby Crane returned to Waters County. A haze more appropriate to July hung over the still-green trees, diffusing the bright sunlight.

Waters County, Michigan, had three things going for it. First, one slanted edge of the county dipped into Lake Michigan, meaning there existed at least a slender strip of highly desirable real estate within its borders.

Second, it had an abundance of inland lakes that lured tourists who didn't have enough money to vacation on the "big lake" itself.

And finally, 70 percent of Waters County was still forested—not by virgin timber, *that* was long gone—but by second- and third-growth hardwoods and less valuable Civilian Conservation Corps–planted red pine plantations. Logging trucks were too common to be noticed; chain saws, only background noise.

The county was divided into two strata: the Lake Michigan shoreline—miles of dunes and pale beaches, touristy and expensive—and the remainder of the county, where the trees flourished and real estate could be bought for one-fifth the price. During summers and deer season, the population of Waters County doubled, although its year-round population was 16,000, 120 souls less than in 1872.

Blue Lake, locally renowned for its perch and bass fishing, lay twelve miles inland from Lake Michigan and a mile north of the small town of Sable.

Inside the oldest log cabin on the southeast shore of Blue Lake, Ruby Crane cut open a cardboard box marked "kitchen stuff," raggedly tearing the brown tape with the rusty point of a beer can opener she'd found hanging on the cabin wall.

But when she pulled away the crumpled pages from the *San Francisco Chronicle*, instead of "kitchen stuff" there lay a jumble of aspirin bottles, face creams, thermometers, Band-Aids, and other detritus from Ruby's Palo Alto medicine cabinet.

"You can't tell the difference between kitchen and bathroom?" Ruby asked herself aloud, tossing the newspaper back into the box. That's what she got for taping the boxes closed before she labeled them.

Her words didn't exactly echo in the log cabin, but they remained in the air, buoyed by the silence. Ruby tipped her head, listening: no traffic, no sirens, no heart-thumping rock music. Grasshoppers whirred. A bird called a long looping note. She remembered its voice but not its name. It had been too long: nineteen years.

She gazed at a stand of oaks crowded outside the kitchen window, running her hands through her reddish brown hair, a habit during moments of frustration or uncertainty. Her mother had gone completely gray by thirty, but Ruby, at thirty-seven, had found only a few silver strands, and those she hadn't bothered to remove.

The leaves of the oak trees were fading, beginning to curl and droop as the sap drew down before autumn. Beyond the oaks, the south arm of Blue Lake shimmered and Ruby could just make out the red roof line of a boarded-up cabin on Strawhill Point.

She lugged the wrongly marked "kitchen stuff" box from the kitchen through the main room toward the tiny bathroom. Even the interior walls of the cabin were built of logs, and in the morning sun, they glowed golden in reflected light. As she set the box in the bathtub to unpack later, her toe wedged sharply against the tub's claw foot.

"Damn!" She rose and glimpsed her tense face in the medicine cabinet mirror. The mirror had been cracked in the lower corner forever. Hadn't she done it herself with her cousin's b.b. gun?

Ruby traced the crack with her finger. She was edgy, making too many motions for the simplest tasks. Clumsy and jumpy.

She slipped the rusty can opener into her shorts pocket, pointy edge out, and returned to the kitchen. The ice in the Coleman cooler had melted and she chose a Diet Coke from the water, dropping onto a box promising "books."

During the night something had bitten Ruby's left ankle, leaving an itchy red welt she couldn't stop scratching. Old voices in her head scolded "Keep on scratching it like that and you'll only make it worse." Ruby ignored them.

She tugged her sticky T-shirt away from her underarms, feeling gritty. It wasn't that the log cabin was that dirty, despite having sat empty for three months. Mostly the grime came from wrestling with travel-dusty boxes in the unusual-weather-for-this-time-of-year heat.

"You okay, sweetie?" Ruby called. She raised herself to peer over the boxes into the cabin's main room where her daughter Jesse lay on the couch beneath an uncreased summer quilt, each and every light brown hair in place, eyes closed and pale face expressionless, her lips slightly parted.

"Five boxes unpacked and I'm already a dishrag," Ruby continued, giving Jesse a play-by-play, as had become her habit during the past three weeks. "We should have sold this stuff instead of dragging it across the country." Ruby rebanded the hair at the back of her neck and came away with a pewter tangle of cobweb.

She sat down again and wiped the gray threads on her dusty shorts, noted her broken thumbnail, and leaned against the wall. "Or given it away." She thought a moment, then added, "Or burned it."

The log wall rounded into her back, fit the curve of her neck, smelling of hardened varnish and a confusing mishmash of past summers. The wood was warm and she rubbed against it like against a muscled arm.

Ruby bent the tab top on her Coke can back and forth until it broke off, then slipped it on her pinky like a ring. Tomorrow she'd arrange for new locks on the doors. "I don't know nothing about no keys," Nolan MacIntosh, who'd overseen the arrival of their belongings, had shouted into the phone as if he had to physically make his voice heard all the way to California. "Probably got lost thirty, forty years ago. Might never been any."

Ruby had inherited the cabin and fifteen acres across the road three years earlier from her mother, the only possession of her parents she'd truly longed for. It was a surprise in more ways than one, not only that her mother had withheld the property from Ruby's father but that her silent and restrained mother had realized how much Ruby had loved the cabin on Blue Lake. At the time Ruby had never intended to live in the cabin. She'd just relished owning it: her "property back east."

But there was that old saying about never saying never. She'd had trouble in California and, in times of trouble, people went home. Sable, Michigan, was all Ruby had left that even remotely fit the definition of home.

It was this place, this cabin, this lake that Ruby considered "home," not the town of Sable itself, not the gray house a block off the main street where she grew up. She tapped her foot on the wooden floor, mentally constructing a twelve-foot wall around the cabin, *her* cabin. She was a woman who longed to be an island.

The cabin had come down through her mother's

family, bought cheap during the 1920s. Rumor was it had been built for a gangster gunned down in a south Chicago alley before the builder was paid off. As children, Ruby and her sister Phyllis had poked and dug around the cabin for years, searching for gangster treasure.

There was a single bedroom downstairs and a loft above supported by beams of flawless white pine. A fieldstone fireplace filled one wall of the main room, but everywhere else was wood: worn oak floors and log walls and wooden doors and casements. Ruby stroked the sleek log wall behind her, thinking she must have descended from tree dwellers. Nowhere did she feel as content as she did when she was surrounded by wood.

The telephone jangled the silence and Ruby jumped, sloshing Coke on her leg. *She* didn't even know her own number yet and she'd requested it be unlisted, so who on earth was calling?

On the floor behind a box marked "Quilt tops, 1910–1925," sat a black rotary telephone, the old heavy kind with a receiver that weighed more than most modern phones. "We're not equipped for push-button service yet," Peggy Dystix at Sable Telephone, one of the last privately owned phone companies in Michigan, had told Ruby when she called from Palo Alto to connect the service. Ruby would have preferred no phone at all, but with Jesse, a phone was a must.

"Hello?" Ruby answered warily, glancing again at her daughter, who lay exactly as before. Sleeping Beauty, Snow White, the Ice Princess.

"Ruby? This is Fran at Paulas's Drug Store. How are you doing out there?"

Ruby closed her eyes, the cool receiver to her ear, picturing Fran at Paulas's Drug Store: overweight, thick glasses that magnified eyes already protruding with curiosity. Because Fran had graduated from high school when Ruby was still in eighth grade, Ruby remembered Fran as being from another generation, reigning behind the soda fountain, concocting cherry Cokes and ordering Ruby and her friends to "Either buy that comic book or put it back." After nineteen years, Fran still worked at Paulas's Drug Store?

"We're fine, Fran. Still unpacking."

"Well, welcome home. I never thought you'd be one to come back to little old Sable. We must be small potatoes after big-city life in California."

Ruby hadn't anticipated being on the defensive so soon. She rubbed her temples. "It's a beautiful day, isn't it?" she said carefully. "What can I do for you?"

"Dr. Doyle called us to make sure we kept lamotrigine on hand. He said it was for your daughter?" Fran paused on the upbeat, giving Ruby time to fill in the blanks.

"Yes. She's been ill."

"Her last name's Crane, too? Did Dr. Doyle have that right?"

"That's right. *Do* you carry lamotrigine?"

Fran's voice definitely cooled. "This has been a full-service drug store for nine years, ever since Bill and I bought the place and saved it from being run into the ground by Harry Bonet's wife. It's hard work but you know what they say about hard work . . ."

"It makes Jack a dull boy?" Ruby supplied and squeezed her eyes closed at the way words slipped out sometimes.

Fran paused. "No. A little hard work never hurt anybody. We don't usually get a call for lamotrigine—so I wanted to verify it."

It was Dr. Doyle who Fran should have verified the prescription with, not Ruby, but Ruby said evenly, "That's thoughtful of you, Fran."

"Just part of our service. I heard you slept at the cabin last night. Dolly Johnson cleaned it up after the renters left, you know. She said that bathroom looked like they birthed pigs in the tub. Are you going to stay long?"

"We might." Go ahead, Ruby thought. Be generous. "It'll be a quiet place for my daughter to recover."

Fran tch-tched into Ruby's ear. "Poor little thing. She's fourteen, right?" Without waiting for a response, she went on. "Sure hope it's an easy winter. Blue Road drifts shut at the first blow. Always has, always will. You and Mrs. Pink'll be the only ones out there by December. And those Chinese, but I don't count them."

"Mrs. Pink is still alive?" Ruby asked. Mrs. Pink had been old when Ruby was a girl.

"Mm-hmm. Worries everybody just sick. She refuses a phone, but the Lutherans installed a gas furnace so she'd stop cutting her own firewood. Used an ax at her age, can you believe it?" Fran paused and Ruby pictured her on the other end, eyes sharp as a crow's, calculating how much return she was likely to get for pressing. "Your coming back is like the Prodigal, isn't it?"

Ruby's hands were damp with sweat. She balanced the phone between her chin and shoulder and wiped her palms against her shorts. "How did you get our phone number?" she asked. "It's unlisted."

"Peggy Dystix at the phone company gave it to me. She figured you didn't mean for it to be unlisted *locally*. Have you seen any of your old friends yet? You probably heard about—"

"My daughter needs me now, Fran," Ruby interrupted. "Thanks again."

"Oh. Well, you're welcome. Stop by next time you're in town. See how Sable's changed."

Fran stretched out the word Sable the way the locals did when they finally got around to correcting tourists. Sable was pronounced "Sobble," like "hobble," and it had always been a minor local sport to see how long outsiders ignorantly pronounced the town's name like "table." A smug little pinch of resistance to the tourist invasion.

Ruby replaced the receiver and nudged the phone against the wall with the toe of her sneaker. She didn't want to hear Fran's gossip about the drug store business, her old friends, or Sable. The past had no place in her current life. There was room for only two: Ruby and her daughter.

They'd passed through Sable in their rental car at dusk the evening before. Ruby had slowed down, noting the boarded-up Ford dealership, the scattered cars parked on Main Street. No pedestrians in sight except for two teenagers in a clinch beneath a burned-out streetlight. She'd recognized every landmark, noting it by what she'd done or seen or experienced at that very spot, as potent as memories of Christmas past.

The windows and door facing the lake were open to air the cabin, and Ruby stepped onto the screened-in porch that stretched across the front of the cabin, pushing aside one of the green metal lawn chairs that had managed to survive the intervening nineteen years.

Beyond the porch the rough and sandy lawn sloped to the cattailed shore of Blue Lake where the old wooden dock advanced tipsily into the water.

The Crane cabin, as it had been called for forty years despite having been in Ruby's mother's family, not her father's, sat on a one-acre peninsula that jutted into Blue Lake. Behind it, the driveway passed through a small woods and across a narrow swamp to Blue Road, and on the other side of Blue Road lay Ruby's fifteen acres of trees.

She stood behind the screen watching a fat red squirrel undulate across the front yard. Seven-year-old Ruby had been tricked into believing Billy Doyle's pet rat was a squirrel with a shaved tail. Now whenever she saw a squirrel, all she could see was a rat with a fluffy tail.

Ruby briefly considered the landscape covered in snow and ice, shuddered, and went back inside the cabin. She perched on the arm of the couch beside Jesse's head, scratching her ankle with one hand and stroking her daughter's hair with the other. "Your name's Jesse Crane now. What do you think? You can bet Drug Store Fran will put an interesting spin on *that*."

Jesse's hand twitched and Ruby knew her daughter was rousing from deep sleep. Ruby leaned over and kissed her cool cheek.

Ruby's ex-husband had done this to Jesse three weeks ago. It was an accident. Ruby constantly reminded herself: an accident. Jesse had been the single saving grace in their wretched marriage, and she and Stan had both felt awe that, together, two people so unsuited could produce such a loving and loved daughter.

Ruby would probably never know what had happened when Stan drove off Highway 1. The autopsy showed he'd been drinking but he wasn't drunk. Had there been another car? No one admitted to witnessing the accident. A passerby spotted Jesse lying by the side of the road, the car—with Stan still buckled inside—a crumpled heap a hundred feet below.

Jesse always fastened her seat belt. Had clever quick Jesse, alarmed by something in Stan's face, unbuckled her belt and jumped from the Audi? Maybe Stan, during a long sickening struggle to keep the car on the highway, managed to unbuckle Jesse and push her out of the car. He might have had the time.

Jesse's only visible injuries were abraded knees and palms. The other, her head injury, was still the mystery, the enemy, the great unknown. There *had* been change, dramatic change; from coma, to stupor, to erratic awareness and response. Now Jesse shifted between fairy-tale sleep and intense wakefulness when her forehead wrinkled like an old lady's and she studied her surroundings as if each object had materialized from Mars.

Ruby had noted well the other head injury patients in the hospital whose recovery ranged from not at all to complete. She told herself she was prepared for anything.

"Could I interest you in a lovely chicken dinner ground to a pleasant beige mush and a bowl of delightfully smooth applesauce?" Ruby asked her, gently tweaking Jesse's nose.

She was sure her daughter heard her and even more sure that someday soon this newly compliant Jesse would rise up and remind her mother that applesauce made her gag and she didn't, under any circumstance, eat dead animals.

Chapter 2

Ruby finally discovered her own telephone number when Dr. Doyle's office called to report Jesse's records from the physical therapist hadn't arrived, and then she had to beggar it from the doctor's receptionist.

"I tried calling the Sable Telephone Company's office but there's no answer," Ruby told Georgia.

"Well, it's unlisted," Georgia told Ruby doubtfully.

Ruby ran her fingers through her hair, unloosing it from the band, which dropped to the floor behind her. "But, Georgia," she said. "It's *my* number."

Georgia was one of the Beckets. For generations, the Beckets had occupied tidy farms on three adjacent corners east of Sable. Beckets died instead of divorced. They were sturdy folk with solid bodies, big hands, and wide faces; the boys played football and the girls rose to leadership in 4-H. No matter whom a Becket mated with, their children were born sturdy, wide-faced Beckets.

"I guess it's okay to give it to you then," Georgia finally conceded.

Ruby jotted the number on her hand with a Bic pen and gratefully asked, "How's your brother Bruce?"

When she was sixteen, Ruby had attended the Sable High School Autumn Dance with Georgia Becket's older brother Bruce, whose idea of walking on the wild side had been to attend the Autumn Dance with Ruby Crane.

There was the slightest hesitation. "Bruce is fine. He

does most of the farming now. He put both the south and north corners into corn this year."

Ruby's attention wandered as Georgia went on to explain some oddity about the dreaded corn smut becoming a desirable gourmet fungus, "like those truffles foreign pigs root around for."

All Ruby knew of farming came from her father's romanticized tales of tilling the land "back when life meant something," which wasn't how Gram had described *her* years on the farm at all.

"Dr. Doyle said you were looking for somebody to take care of your daughter," Georgia was saying, bringing Ruby back.

"Do you know of anyone? I need somebody with head injury experience."

"My sister, DeEtta," Georgia said in a rush. "She's good, really good. She was a nurse's aide at the Shadows Nursing Home before they had that staph infection. Her husband . . . well, DeEtta's alone so she'd be available at night, too." Georgia stopped to catch her breath, then continued, "There aren't very many people around here who know as much as DeEtta." Ruby heard another phone ringing in the background. "She can do food tubes and enemas and everything. And she knows CPR and the Heimlich maneuver, you know, for people who are choking."

"Thanks, Georgia. Ask her to call me in a day or two."

Ruby hung up the phone, then studied the inky number on her hand, thinking of Todd in Palo Alto. They'd been seeing each other the past year, both of them divorced and making cautious headway.

Their parting had been strained, overly polite. Following the accident, Todd had practically moved in with Ruby, sitting with her in the hospital, making sure she ate, picking up her mail. After her decision to take Jesse to Michigan, Todd had continued to help, but without the tenderness, more like a well-mannered friend. "If you leave, you'll never come back," he'd said, and Ruby had laughed, shocked such a ridiculous idea had occurred to him.

Quickly, before she had second thoughts, Ruby dialed Todd's number, knowing he wouldn't be home yet. "It's me," she told his machine. "We're here, playing *Little House in the Big Woods.* Jesse's fine. The sun is shining and here's our phone number."

She hung up—the next step was up to him—and transferred her new phone number from her hand to her address book, then moistened her thumb and rubbed her skin until only a smudged shadow remained.

The kitchen was unpacked, right down to Jesse's cat clock hanging over the cupboards. The coffeemaker sat on the counter, a half pot of fragrant coffee on the warmer. Like other times she'd moved, once the kitchen was in shape, the rest was a breeze.

She mopped up dust and dead flies from the built-in bookcases between the kitchen and the main room and shelved her books.

Ruby was twenty-five when she picked up a torn copy of *Gone With the Wind* from a yard sale free! box, the first book she'd ever read for pleasure, shocked at the wealth of mere *words*, how they made her feel. In Palo Alto, she'd prowled used bookstores, ignoring the new ones because she had so much catching up to do. A book waiting to be read filled her with a hunger that was almost physical. What would her old teachers say: Ruby Crane a *bookworm*?

At one o'clock, Ruby washed off the worst of the grime, arranged Jesse in her purple wheelchair, and pushed her out onto the front lawn, maneuvering by foot, elbow, and hip with all the awkward grace of a mattress mover.

The sandy lawn caught at the wheels. Ruby put her back into it and pushed Jesse to firmer ground beneath the oaks.

"Here we are," Ruby said, surveying the way her land projected into Blue Lake. The water surrounded them on three sides, and if she considered the little swamp the driveway crossed from Blue Road, it *was* almost as if they were protected by a moat.

Jesse frowned intensely at a distant point in the lake. Ruby followed her daughter's gaze and saw only the blue water, too riffled for reflections.

"It's wet," Jesse said, still frowning at the water.

"The lake is wet," Ruby agreed, smiling. Little triumphs.

Ruby locked the brake on Jesse's chair and did Jesse's range-of-motion exercises with her.

"Not ready for any long-distance jaunts yet, eh?" she asked Jesse as she manipulated her legs, concentrating on the left side, her daughter's weakest. Back and forth, up and down, flexing and pointing, Jesse watching in mild interest.

It wasn't labor; it was a dance of movements Ruby knew by heart and performed with ever more grace and flair. A form of prayer, only this prayer actually delivered results.

"How about a good old-fashioned show of pissed-off teenage stubbornness with this crap?" she suggested to Jesse as she pushed the girl's thin leg toward her chest.

Jesse, whose face had once mirrored every tumultuous teenage thought, now frowned, gazing through Ruby. "Crap," she said softly. "Crap, crap, crappy."

"Exactly," Ruby agreed.

Jesse's left side was too weak for her to stand alone more than thirty seconds. Her eyes either dreamily followed movement or stared to bore holes, and occasionally flashed in the old awareness. When she was prompted, she spoke in slow wonder as if an invisible being were dealing words back to her one at a time.

"She's young. Anything is possible. We know too little about head injury," the doctor had told Ruby. "She mainly has right brain injury, but some of the actual injury is too minute to see. Microsheer."

"What's that?" Ruby had asked.

"To put it bluntly, that's when tiny brain cells are damaged as the brain is sloshed back and forth inside the skull. It's called coup and countercoup."

Ruby had swallowed hard. *Sloshed.*

"There *will* be improvement; we just have no idea how much. Anything is possible, anything."

"I can take care of her," Ruby had told the disapproving doctor. "I'll take her home," she added, surprising herself when she realized that, by home, she meant taking Jesse to Sable, not their apartment on Pioneer Court.

"Jane Fonda would be proud," Ruby said when a sheen appeared on Jesse's forehead. "That's all till next time." She wiped Jesse's face, smoothed her clothes, and sat on the ground beside her chair, her head against her daughter's knee.

"Ruby Crane?"

Jesse flinched and Ruby raised her head from Jesse's knee, whispering to her daughter "It's okay, it's okay" before she turned toward the lake and whoever had called her name. She was disoriented, feeling as if she'd been attacked from the sea when all her guns were pointed landward.

A green fiberglass canoe pushed on shore, its keel scrunching through sand. The man splashing into the shallow water and hauling his canoe toward her was big and blocky, but not fat and not young. He wore work boots and work pants and a green shirt torn off at the elbows, exposing arms tanned to cordovan.

"Welcome home, Ruby," he said in a smoker's husky voice. "Remember me? Silas Shea."

Ruby rose and met Silas on the little scallop of beach. "Of course I remember you. How are you, Silas?"

Silas Shea had been a friend of Ruby's father, and probably still was; she wouldn't know. Ruby hadn't seen Silas in twenty years, and she searched beneath this older, heavier face for the younger Silas Shea who'd once whirled her in a polka around the VFW hall when she was eleven, a dance so wildly exhilarating she'd measured every dance since against it.

"I'm good," he said, grinning at her. Behind him, Blue Lake sparkled, fading leaves stirred in a sudden breeze that smelled of fresh water. "I was out on the lake and saw you'd made it. Just wondered if you needed any help."

Silas was an outdoors man, grizzled to agelessness. He'd run his family's sawmill when Ruby was young and she guessed from his powerful looks that he ran it still. His eyes were pale blue, almost milky, the corners wrinkled from a permanent squint. Duplicating the curved tip of his ear, the white worm of a scar was visible through the buzz cut of his gray hair.

"Thanks, but I think it's coming together," Ruby told him, waving a hand toward the cabin. "How did you know we were here?"

"Word gets around as fast as it ever did," he said, kneading the inside of his elbow as if it ached. The tips of the two smallest fingers on his right hand were missing, the blunt ends puckered flesh.

He took a step toward Jesse's wheelchair. "Is this your girl?" he asked softly. "I heard she was sick."

"Her name's Jesse."

Silas Shea bent close over Jesse's pale face. He gently touched one finger to her hand. Her delicately curled fingers looked like a newborn's next to Silas's dark and scarred workman's hand. "Hello, Jesse," he said softly. "I hope you're feeling better soon."

It was a totally unselfconscious act, without pity or expectation, and Ruby bit her lip to keep back California-ish words of gratitude that would embarrass Silas.

Jesse stared at Silas, the two deep frown lines appearing between her brows. "Hello," she said, then squeezed her eyes closed.

Silas straightened and turned back to Ruby, his pale eyes shiny. "So how does it feel to be back in Sable? Are you caught up on all the news?"

"We just arrived last night. I haven't been into town yet." She flinched at the word "into," one of the midwesternisms Stan had teased her out of using. "Can you come up to the cabin for a cup of coffee?" she offered.

"No thanks," Silas said, absently rubbing his stomach. "Had to give up coffee: ulcers. The wife has me drinking that hippie herbal tea. Saw your aunt and uncle Edwards the other day. They're doing good, glad you're coming."

"Uncle Mack's slowed down a little, I think," she told Silas.

"A man has to after a while."

Silas was sizing her up; Ruby could feel it, judging her as an adult now instead of a child and speculating what she'd become. He rocked back on his feet, looking up into the oak leaves between quick appraisals of her and Jesse.

"Are you still running the sawmill?" Ruby asked.

"You bet. There are only three sawmills left in the county now. Northern Timber's the big boy. Corbin Turmouski and I hunt and peck for the little stuff."

"You're not cutting trees out of the national forest anymore?" Ruby asked.

"The government doesn't let us cut trees off public

lands much now. We all have to find little mom-and-pop forests and dicker with the owners to cut down their trees. Northern Timber can afford to buy big chunks. Turmouski and I, we bid on an acre here, an acre there, paying owners top dollar so they can send Johnny to college or pay for Suzie's braces." Silas's face was glum. "It isn't as easy as it used to be, but nothing is, is it?"

"Not that I've noticed," Ruby agreed. The sawmills in Waters County had always been all-purpose operations: buying trees, cutting them down, then sawing up the logs in their sawmills.

Jesse's eyelids fluttered but remained closed, the frown intensifying. Ruby knew Jesse was listening but if she added sight to the equation she was likely go into overload, when too much stimuli became unbearable and she rocked herself or withdrew completely.

"Maybe the era of small sawmills is ending," Ruby suggested. "Just as it has for other small enterprises."

"Only the poorly run sawmills get winnowed out," Silas said with a touch of defiance. "There's room for us little guys. We just have to be faster on our feet: go out and find the trees ourselves and cut them down, haul them home to our mills, and saw them up for lumber or sell the logs to one of the big outfits down south for finish wood or veneer."

"Are you that flexible?" Ruby asked politely.

"You bet. Most of the time I only have two or three guys working for me. You take Northern Timber; they don't do much more than I do, just on a bigger scale. What I do myself, like cutting down the trees, they hire a crew to do. They make plenty but it costs them plenty."

"You didn't come here to ask me about cutting the trees on my fifteen across the road, did you?" Ruby asked.

"No," Silas said too quickly, glancing away, out over

Blue Lake. "But you've got some nice red oak in there. If you need to make some good money . . ."

"No," Ruby said. "Definitely not."

"I didn't think so; but expect to hear from a timber buyer or two. There's a lot of prime timber in the county right now, and the competition's hot to cut it. The hardwoods are most valuable: oak, maple. Softwood—the pines—are generally going for pallet wood."

Silas's voice wound down, losing its earnest timbre like a car salesman who knows he's lost his sale.

"So now tell me what you're going to do in Sable," he said, shaking a cigarette from a pack of Camels he pulled from his shirt pocket.

"Give my daughter time to recover," Ruby told him. "I'll find a part-time job."

"You came back where you knew the lay of the land," Silas said, nodding in approval and lighting a kitchen match with his thumbnail. "That's smart when you need to lick your wounds, come back where you don't have to figure out anything new."

"I'm not hiding out," Ruby said, bristling a little.

"Didn't say you were. I heard you did real well in California."

Ruby wondered where he'd heard *that*. "It was all right," she told him.

"Somebody said you were a detective. Handled big cases."

"They were exaggerating," Ruby assured him. "I was the receptionist for an agency, that's all. Nothing very glamorous."

"You can't help learning the ropes wherever you work. Enid used to answer phones and write bills at Tony's Electric, but I tell you, if our TV goes on the blink, Enid can tear right into it."

"How is Enid?" Ruby asked warily about Silas's perpetually meddling wife. One summer when Ruby and Jerry Sitkas had parked by the river behind Silas's mill, they'd returned from a romantic wrestle on the bank to discover that Silas's wife Enid had left a Bible and a dozen chocolate chip cookies on the hood of Jerry's car, along with a note begging them to nibble cookies and read the Good Book rather than "amuse yourselves with cheap pleasures of the flesh." Ruby had always wondered how long Enid had watched them and whether a dozen cookies was payment enough.

"Getting by," Silas told her. "She had gallbladder surgery this summer." He pulled a watch with a broken band from his jeans pocket and glanced at it. "I'd better be going. Let us know if we can do anything for you."

Ruby walked with him to his canoe. Frogs jumped from the shallows into deeper water among the reeds, leaving lines in the water like jet trails.

"It's been a real pretty summer," Silas said as he pushed his canoe into the amber water. "We'll pay for it this winter; see if we don't."

"I haven't seen snow in years," Ruby told him. A breeze stirred the humidity, cooling the air.

"Always comes too soon, you can count on that," Silas said. "So will you set up a detective shop?" he asked, his voice teasing, his eyes not.

"My only interest right now is my daughter," Ruby told him. She glanced at Jesse, who appeared to be dozing, and stepped onto the silvery faded dock. A board was missing. Tilting or not, the dock felt solid beneath her.

Silas shoved off with his paddle, then raised it in farewell. "Never thought you'd grow up to be such a beauty, Ruby. Don't forget. Call me or Enid if you need anything."

"Thanks."

Ruby stood on the old dock and watched Silas Shea swiftly and efficiently paddle into Blue Lake, heading toward the public boat ramp across the lake. She wondered what Silas had been doing on the lake. There was no fishing gear in his canoe, no gun, and his heavy boots weren't that practical for boating.

Ruby walked gingerly to the end of the dock, testing each board before she gave it her full weight. She gazed into the amber water, recalling that the water here was over her head.

Silas was nearly to the boat ramp, resting his paddle across the canoe's gunwales and drifting toward shore. Ruby wondered if everyone in Sable was as well informed as Silas about her life in California.

For six years following her divorce, Ruby had been employed by Kilgore, Inc. Ron Kilgore had failed the California Bar exam so many times he'd finally given up and opened a detective agency instead. At first he'd advertised in the backs of magazines, and his clients were mostly women who'd finally left their husbands and were searching for old boyfriends and true romance. Ruby began by answering his telephone for minimum wage, taking the job—no, *pleading* for it— because at the time she didn't even have a high school diploma and her only other option was waiting tables.

The office of Kilgore, Inc. was run from a post office box and occupied a two-room apartment not far from the campus of Stanford University.

During slow times, Ruby had walked around the campus, at first in a strange soup of timidity and defiance, in awe of the golden buildings and the confident students. Their clothes were sloppier than hers but it was the *way* they wore them, their casual boldness.

Ruby coveted the students' knowledge and smart mouths, their proud irritability at having to study so much. One thing led to another. She copied their clothes, their hair, shyly drank coffee with them, then joined them on the quad and, finally, sat in on classes that interested her—and most any of them did. As long as she looked right and the classes weren't too small, no one noticed.

There were moments when she forgot she was illegal and, in feverish elation, argued over the Second Amendment's rationale or biological evolution or what Flannery O'Connor meant by the wooden leg, sometimes even winning.

It was at Stanford that Ruby saw an exhibit of Emily Dickinson's handwritten manuscripts and became so intrigued by those chameleon lines of penmanship that she'd tried, like a cheap artist, to copy them. Not just copy, duplicate. Searching for the heart of the woman who felt and thought and conjured such heated emotion. Heart to hand. Pen on paper.

Ron Kilgore, seeing her doodles as she played at copying clients' signatures on checks, stepped in and sent her life in another direction.

Forgery. Not to produce but to detect. He arranged for her apprenticeship with Barker Thompson and bought her a beat-up stereoptic microscope and a mercury arc lamp. It didn't matter that she had no college degree. She fell in love with the whole process: spotting every forger's telltale slip-up; matching papers and inks; studying another's penmanship with graph plates and magnifying glass, getting to *know* the trickster. Heart to hand. Pen on paper.

She was "damn sharp," Ron Kilgore said, and with surprise and wonder, Ruby had realized he was right.

Chapter 3

Ruby turned with resignation at the grumble of a vehicle approaching on her long driveway through the trees.

She glanced once more at Silas Shea reaching shore in his canoe and retraced her steps along the dock, wondering as she stepped across the missing board, who could fix it. Be radical, she thought. Do it yourself.

A red, fairly recent Ford, pocked with rust, the driver's door eaten through along the lower edge as if a can opener had been taken to it, stopped next to the cabin.

Out stepped a sturdy young woman in her twenties. She wore an impeccable white uniform with white stockings and gleaming white shoes. Her short brown hair was coiffed the way Ruby's mother used to wear hers, shiny with hairspray. When she saw Ruby and Jesse, she smiled, exposing bright white teeth, her wide face rounded like a pumpkin.

"I'm DeEtta Gre—Becket," she said as Ruby met her halfway between Jesse and the cabin. "My sister Georgia called from Dr. Doyle's office and said you needed somebody to look after your daughter."

DeEtta Becket's skin was paler than Ruby remembered Becket skin to be, spattered with freckles and four moles in a row across her left cheek. DeEtta had the wide-shouldered body of a big-breasted woman but in fact had the small high bosom of a young girl.

"Jesse was injured three weeks ago," Ruby told her.

"She was in a coma for three days and she's wobbly, but she's recovering."

DeEtta's eyebrows raised and Ruby wondered exactly what information Georgia Becket had passed along to her sister.

"Well," DeEtta said gravely. "My experience has been that patients in that condition need a fair amount of stimulation, consistent schedules, frequent physical therapy, and patience." She took a breath and fingered the strap of her oversized shoulder bag. "Neurologic changes can be rapid and dramatic or subtle and barely perceptible."

DeEtta stood well postured in her nurse's uniform and spoke in words stiff from memorization. The woman was trying to bluff Ruby and, for some perverse reason, Ruby liked that. She tried to imagine DeEtta's mad flurry after she received her sister Georgia's call in order to stand before Ruby in such knowledgeable nursing splendor.

"Dr. Doyle still has to make recommendations for therapy and nursing," Ruby told her.

"I've got excellent references," DeEtta assured Ruby. "You can call them, everybody I worked for."

"It's not that. It's . . ." Ruby considered the eager young woman in front of her. "Would you like to meet Jesse?"

DeEtta's cheeks dimpled as she held back her smile. "It would give me a better idea if I can help out."

Ruby led the young woman to Jesse's wheelchair, and DeEtta knelt on the sand, murmuring quietly. She placed a palm on Jesse's forehead and took her pulse, then peered in Jesse's mouth and lifted one of her eyelids. Jesse sat in her chair unresisting, too accustomed to being prodded and poked to care.

DeEtta pulled a blood pressure cuff from her bag and there on the shore of Blue Lake efficiently fastened it around Jesse's slender arm while Ruby tried to keep a straight face.

"Your daughter appears very healthy," DeEtta pronounced with the authority of a grudgingly surprised head nurse. "She's obviously had excellent care."

"And I intend for Jesse to continue having excellent care," Ruby told her, unlocking the wheelchair's brake and pushing Jesse toward the cabin.

DeEtta nodded absently, walking beside Jesse, one hand hovering near her shoulder. "How many hours a week will you need me?"

"That depends on how soon I find a job," Ruby told her. "For now, two to three hours every day to give Jesse and me a break from each other."

"I think," DeEtta said after she helped Ruby bring Jesse into the cabin, frowning and speaking deliberately as if she'd given the matter hours—days—of thought, "that I'll take the position. I'll need a list of her meds. You can show me her physical therapy program and then we can work out a schedule."

DeEtta described her favorite arm exercises, vitamin therapy, and miracle recoveries: "worse cases than this," she'd seen attributed solely to exceptionally fine nursing care.

The telephone rang and Ruby excused herself to answer it, trying to remember a day in Palo Alto with as many interruptions as this first day in the remote countryside.

"Ruby?" a woman's voice hesitantly asked. "Is that you?"

"This is Ruby Crane," Ruby answered, not recognizing the voice. Across the room, Jesse had opened her eyes and DeEtta spoke to her in a low voice.

The voice on the telephone grew stronger. "Ruby. You really came back. This is Mina."

"Mina," Ruby said, leaning against the table behind her. Then again, stupidly: "Mina. How are you?"

"Can you come see me?" Mina asked. "Please."

"Of course," Ruby told her. "We only arrived last night. Maybe in a few . . ."

"Today?" Mina asked. Her voice rose unsteadily. "Can you come now?"

Ruby glanced around at the boxes still to be unpacked, at Jesse and the cabin, which she hadn't yet made completely her own. Tiny, vivacious Mina had been Ruby's best friend from fourth grade until Ruby left Sable the night before her eighteenth birthday. They hadn't exchanged so much as a Christmas card in the past nineteen years, but Mina held a complicated position in Ruby's past. Ruby briefly closed her eyes as Mina said, "I need to talk to you," aware she would do whatever Mina asked.

"All right," Ruby told her. "Where do you live?"

"Do you remember where Silas Shea lives? On Bell Road? We're almost directly across the road." Mina hesitated. "I'm married to Corbin Turmouski now."

The last Ruby knew, Mina had been married to Ford Goodlight, her high school sweetheart. She tried to remember Corbin Turmouski, whom Silas had mentioned as the other small sawmill owner in Waters County. Corbin was older than Ruby and Mina by ten or fifteen years. He limped. Polio, she thought, remembering how people had said what a shame it was, how much worse it was for a boy than a girl.

"I'll be there within the hour," Ruby told Mina before she hung up, setting aside her curiosity about Ford and Corbin, recalling what she owed Mina. Jesse had fallen asleep again. Recharging, the therapist had called these frequent naps.

"And I don't always wear a uniform," DeEtta finished as if their conversation hadn't been interrupted by Mina's phone call.

"I wouldn't expect you to. As long as you're here," Ruby suggested, "why don't we give it a trial run? I'll shower and drive to a friend's. I won't be gone more than an hour."

"I'm up for that, and I'll do it at no charge."

Ruby lightly slapped her forehead. "Wages. We haven't even discussed wages yet."

DeEtta smoothed the lap of her uniform. "I could live in." She glanced around the cabin as if searching for a corner to spread her sleeping bag. "I'd be willing to trade room and board for most of the pay."

"No," Ruby said more forcefully than she intended. Seeing the flinch at the corner of DeEtta's mouth, she explained. "I'm sorry. Right now we need privacy. What kind of wages would you expect?"

DeEtta looked out toward Blue Lake. "I'll think about it. Can we discuss it when you come back?"

"Are you sure?"

"Positive."

When Ruby returned to the main room after her shower, DeEtta was sitting on the end of the couch, Jesse's socks slung over her shoulder, rubbing Jesse's bare feet. "They like this," DeEtta said, thumbs circling the girl's arches.

"Well, I know *I* do."

Ruby knew this would be more than a trial run, that she'd already decided to hire DeEtta. She suspected the young woman's nursing costume was just that: a costume. DeEtta would do whatever worked for Jesse. Ruby didn't care about the medical texts or the doctors' opinions or established routines. Whatever worked was all right by her.

And if DeEtta didn't make good, Ruby wouldn't think twice about getting rid of her, either.

"Everybody's curious about you," DeEtta said. "They're saying all kinds of things: that you're running

away from an insane husband who tried to kill you, and
that you're a rich detective."

"Sable has always been filled with overly curious
people," Ruby said, deliberately not requesting or providing the details.

"You're telling me!" The words exploded from
DeEtta's lips and she ducked her head, blushing.

"Don't listen to them. I never did."

"They say that, too." A mischievous look brightened
DeEtta's wide face and Ruby laughed.

In a week, Ruby was scheduled to return her rental
car. She was reminded of that two miles before Mina
Turmouski's house when she spotted an aging black
Buick beside a cottage near the river. Grass grew
around its tires and the windows were speckled with
dust. FOR SAIL CHEAP a hand-lettered sign on the
windshield read.

The land was hilly at this end of Waters County,
rising up and down in long forested swells. It was deer
hunting country, and the roads traveled through a mix
of meadows and forests.

Ruby passed squared stands of red pine forests
planted on national forest land by the CCC camps in the
1930s, thanks to Franklin Roosevelt as a scheme to put
young city men to work and reforest the countryside.
Row after unnatural row of dark and crowded narrow
pines, planted too close together all those years ago,
their branches mingling and struggling for sunlight.

Between the CCC plantations grew forests of oak
and maple, beech and aspen, mixes of whatever grew
in the changeable soil: sand or loam. On logged-over
acreage, thickets of aspens sprouted like wild grass
among the stumps and slash.

Few people lived so far out, mostly those who didn't
want to be bothered by neighbors or life's amenities

and who cherished walking their land with rifles balanced in the crooks of their elbows.

Just as she was thinking how sparsely populated the area was, she passed a man walking along the opposite side of the road, clad in faded jeans and a T-shirt darkened with sweat, a blue shirt bunched and swinging from his hand. His face was shiny with perspiration. She stopped her car and backed up, abandoning her policy of never stopping for strangers. This was Waters County and here was a man, she was sure, who wasn't walking for pleasure.

"Car trouble?" she asked through her open window.

"That's right," he said, grinning in an uncheerful fashion. "You could definitely say I had car trouble."

His features weren't recognizable as belonging to any Sable family's, and he clipped his words the way inhabitants of upper Michigan did.

He stood at the edge of the road, wiping his neck with his shirt. Over her car engine, Ruby heard the buzz of grasshoppers in the drying grass. He was in his late thirties, wiry-bodied, his brown hair longer than average. Tan like Silas Shea, with paler upper arms. Ruby took in the long jaw and cynical grin, his sharp eyes, and asked, "Can I give you a ride? The Turmouskis and Sheas live behind you about a mile. You've got a good three miles in the direction you're walking before you reach a phone."

"Thanks but no thanks. The walk gives me time to cool off."

"You look pretty warm to me," Ruby said.

"Exactly." He waved to Ruby. "I'll tell you about it sometime." And he resumed walking toward Sable, blue shirt switching against his leg.

"You're welcome," Ruby called after him, watching him in the rearview mirror as she put her car in gear.

The gravel road stretched emptily in front of her so she drove down the center where it was least rutted.

Emerging from a shaded stretch where the oaks touched overhead, she slowed her car, catching sight of a huge black shape in the sky, soaring in circles above the trees, then another one wheeling toward it, their circles overlapping.

Turkey vultures, their ugly red heads plainly visible from so far away. She'd forgotten those unpleasant birds and their vigilant, broody circling while they scanned the forests for carrion, riding the currents and rarely flapping their wings, as if they had no need for such commonplace propulsion. Turkey vultures were the only bird whose young she couldn't imagine.

The road curved and she left the birds behind, her thoughts turning to Mina, wondering what she needed to urgently discuss with a friend she hadn't seen in nearly twenty years.

Ruby was bound to Mina by more than friendship. Mina had seen Ruby at her worst, her most cowardly, and, Ruby believed, Mina had never told anyone, nor had she ever mentioned it again to Ruby.

Pull it out and look at it, she told herself, repeating the only words her counselor had ever said that made sense; it'll never go away so make it your own.

One night, long ago, there'd been an accident. Two teenagers on a lark doing one of those stupid things that seem perfectly logical at the moment: Mina and Ruby illegally climbing the Sable water tower on a mutual dare, falling together from halfway up the steel ladder as neatly as if they'd been roped ankle to ankle. Through some freakish twist of her body, Ruby'd been uninjured and she'd panicked.

She'd run away, leaving Mina writhing on the ground at the foot of the tower. She'd deserted Mina, trying to outrun herself, down Sable's streets and alleys until she sprawled headlong over a curb and regained her reason, horrified at having abandoned her friend.

So she'd run back to the tower, except this time her steps were the leaden gait of nightmares.

"You came back," Mina had whispered, the only time she would ever refer to the incident.

No one else knew how long Mina had lain there before help arrived. If Gram had still been alive, Ruby would have confessed her cowardice to her and explained why she'd run away. "We learn our lessons best when we hurt somebody else," Gram had said once in her heavy Lithuanian accent. "People truly do die for each other's sins."

It was years before Ruby allowed herself to remember the incident and even more years before she understood what she'd learned: not to turn her back, especially on a friend.

She topped a rise that overlooked the shallow valley where the only two residents for miles lived almost directly across from one another: Silas Shea and Corbin Turmouski.

Both men ran sawmills on their property. Sawmills on the West Coast were multimillion-dollar affairs, occupying acres of land, operating around the clock with troops of employees who punched time clocks and wore regulation hard hats.

But here in Waters County, there was only one sawmill that approached West Coast standards: Northern Timber on the north end of the county. The two other mills operating in Waters County lay before Ruby: Silas Shea's and Corbin Turmouski's. These small mills were run by two or three people, pay frequently went under the table, and mechanical repairs were completed with spit and hope.

But all three mills bought timber off forested land, cut it down, sawed it up, and sold it. Northern Timber might contract with loggers to cut down trees, while Silas and Corbin cut the trees themselves and hauled them to their mills to be sawn into boards.

Either way, the three mills competed with one another for trees to cut and the best prices for the boards they sawed, or for the logs they sold to bigger mills for veneer and furniture wood.

Ruby first passed Silas Shea's sawmill on the left. A long building with a rusty and sagging tin roof housed his saw. The never-painted boards of the building had gone gray, and here and there they were replaced by newer slab wood with wavery edges of bark still attached. Logs were piled to one side of the saw mill, square stacks of golden boards to the other. Heavy vehicles were parked haphazardly in the mill yard.

On the same property stood Silas's two-story house, with its wide front porch and gabled roof, built by Silas's father before the turn of the century. Behind Silas's house stood a sagging unpainted barn and a bladeless windmill.

The white curtains in a front window moved, pulled aside a few inches. Ruby waved and the curtains dropped.

Fifty yards ahead on the opposite side of the road, set farther back, was Corbin and Mina Turmouski's land. Ruby turned into the wide driveway and drove through the trees to the tidy green ranch-style house.

There were no flowers or lawn ornaments, no pots of flowers beside the front door. Ruby had expected evidence of children—scattered toys or swings—but there was none. A black-and-white collie slept in a patch of sunshine in the driveway.

Across the driveway, centered in a sandy lot, was a low wooden building similar only in shape to Silas Shea's. Corbin Turmouski's sawmill was arrow straight, walls painted a handsome barn red, roof of shiny tin. Heavy yellow vehicles were parked side by side, wheel to wheel. The effect was of control, hard work, and no unnecessary frivolity. The buildings, including the house, were all fairly new, built with the past ten years, still straight-angled and solid, not settled and softened like Silas's.

Ruby pulled her car alongside a gray Pontiac, turned off her engine, and climbed out. Neither sawmill was operating and the silence was as deep as around her cabin. For a brief moment, she longed for the comforting familiarity of sirens and honking cars. As Ruby walked past the collie, it stood, growling, lips quivering over its teeth.

"Sit," Ruby tried, holding out one hand palm up.

The dog walked stiff-legged toward her, its teeth still bared. Ruby reached slowly behind her for her car door handle.

"Quiet, Pepper. Go lay down," a girlish voice called. The big dog immediately lost interest in Ruby and dropped to the ground.

If Ruby hadn't known Mina lived here, she wouldn't have recognized the tiny woman scolding her dog.

Mina was prematurely gray. Not just her hair, *all* of her. There'd been a flash and spirit to Mina, more identifiable than her looks. Not even the bright pink sweatshirt she wore could dispel the dullness of her skin. Mina, whom they'd called a firecracker, a mouth for all seasons, whose presence in a room could be felt before her fast-moving tiny frame, seemed to have shrunken into herself.

"Ruby," Mina said, holding out both her hands, her wide smile dampening her eyes. "You turned out gorgeous."

Ruby took Mina's hands and then dropped them, and they embraced, laughing for no reason.

"Come in," Mina invited.

Ruby followed Mina into her kitchen and felt like Alice who'd nibbled from the wrong side of the toadstool. The cupboards and counters had been built to suit Mina's size and reach, and Ruby felt even taller than her five foot six inches.

The room was as stark as the front yard. No knick-
knacks, no frills, nothing distinctive. The tablecloth was
plain, the same pale green as the exterior of the house.
This was the home of Mina, who'd gotten away with
ruffles and fringes and mixing loud colors, who'd once
dyed her hair to match a red coat.

"Sit down," Mina said, pointing to the table. Her
smile faltered and dimmed and her shoulders sagged as
if greeting Ruby had drained her. She tugged at the
hem of her sweatshirt. "Would you like a cup of
coffee?"

"That sounds good," Ruby told her.

But instead of making coffee, Mina sat down at the
table opposite Ruby and folded her hands on the tablecloth. Her nails were chewed; a thin line of blood
stained the quick of her left thumb. She smiled shyly at
Ruby. "It's good to see a friend," she said.

Ruby folded her own hands, suddenly awkward with
this woman she'd once known as well as herself, whose
birthday was two days before her own. "You remarried,"
she blurted, then rolled her eyes. "Oh, God. Open
mouth, insert foot. The last I knew, you and Ford
Goodlight were . . ."

Mina smiled the quick familiar smile that made the
years and grayness fall away. "Class couple, right? We
were way too young to know what we were in for." She
shrugged with a touch of sadness. "To make a long story
short, we fooled around on each other. But I got
caught, by Alice Rolly, who runs the Sable Wak 'n Yak,
remember? It took about ten minutes for all of Sable to
hear the grizzly details." She sighed and twisted in her
chair. "End of story."

"But Corbin?"

Mina relaxed. A soft helpless smile appeared on her
face. "Corbin's who I was caught with. That's him," she
said, pointing to a framed black-and-white photograph
hanging near the doorway: a middle-age man raptly

studying a tall oak tree, chain saw in hand, every bit the lumberjack except for the off-kilter stance, the pants leg hanging on a withered left leg. "Mabel Parker took it."

"It's an arresting photo," Ruby said. And, she didn't add, somehow disturbing, the emphasis on body, his face in shadow.

"Some people are disappointed we don't have a miserable marriage." Mina opened her mouth as if she were about to say more, glancing at Ruby in a beseeching way, then closed it and looked at the wall clock. "You really were my best friend. Where did you go?"

"To the West Coast, eventually. I was in Portland for a while and then I moved to California."

"Did you get in trouble?"

"Mostly I tried to stay out of it."

"I wondered about you but I didn't worry," Mina said. "I always knew you'd be okay. I missed you, though."

"I couldn't write," Ruby told her. "I needed to leave all this behind."

"Because of the accident?" Mina asked softly.

"Partly."

"It wasn't your fault," Mina said, leaning across the table toward Ruby, her voice low. "I probably would have run away if it had been me."

"Your legs were broken," Ruby pointed out.

"Details," Mina said, waving her hand in dismissal.

Ruby looked down at her hands, a sudden memory of that soft summer night, the stars so bright and reachable, the pounding of her heart.

"Don't remember the past worse than it actually was," Mina told her in a quiet voice. "We were good kids. You had a tough time after your grandmother died, that's all. Now they'd send you to a counselor or"—Mina's voice sharpened—"give you pills to make you nice and pleasant and forgetful."

"What's going on, Mina?" Ruby asked. "Why did you need to see me so urgently?"

Mina pressed her lips together, then with both hands, smoothed back her silver hair, holding it flat to her head. "I can't discuss this with anyone else around here," she said, taking a deep breath and letting her hair fall back around her face, resting her elbows on the table. "I was so glad to hear you'd come home. I need to talk about Corbin."

"Is he sick?" Ruby asked, remembering the polio, an article she'd read on relapses.

"No. He's fine. But he works himself into the ground. Building up the sawmill is his dream. He had a smaller mill on the other side of the county before this one, before we got married. I wish he made his living another way. I hate the sawmill." Mina's mouth drew down in distaste. "I won't go inside it. I hate the sound of the saw running and everything about the business."

"He and Silas Shea must compete with each other."

"That's an understatement. They chase all over the county trying to beat each other to a dozen or so trees on little chunks of property. Last week Corbin drove thirty miles to cut down six oaks in somebody's backyard."

"So you're worried about how hard he's working?" Ruby prompted, watching the range of emotions playing across Mina's face: hesitancy, concern, doubt.

"Do you remember how we're all aware of each other's business around here?"

"Definitely."

"But at the same time, people overlook what's going on right under their noses?"

"I'm not sure."

The collie in the yard began barking, not in warning but greeting. Mina rose from her chair and pulled aside white café curtains as a yellow pickup—the same color as the machinery parked by the mill—pulled to a stop behind Ruby's car.

"It's Corbin," Mina said. Then she shook her head and laughed shortly. "I forgot to make the coffee, didn't I?"

While Mina poured water into her coffeemaker, Ruby watched Corbin haul himself from his pick-up, moving laboriously, his face grim as he balanced himself against the truck door and rubbed his shrunken left leg.

Corbin was at least ten years older than Mina and Ruby. His hair had receded and his head was partially tanned the way a man's was who usually wore a hat. His shoulders were broad, a man who'd worked all his life at physical labor.

Corbin took three sluggish and awkward steps toward the house, then, glancing toward the door, he straightened his back, raised his head, his gait suddenly firm with only the hint of a limp. It was an impressive—and wrenching—display of self-control and willpower.

Mina turned at the click of the kitchen door opening, touching her hair and smiling.

Ruby felt herself reduced to the invisible observer as Corbin and Mina kissed and then Corbin fondly squeezed his wife's shoulder. Corbin's face was square-jawed, his blue eyes intent.

"This is my oldest and best friend, Ruby Crane," Mina told him. "You might remember her; she's from Sable."

"Good to see you," he said, eyes turned on her in quick appraisal, then drawn back to Mina.

"You couldn't find him?" Mina asked Corbin.

"I found him all right," Corbin told her, shaking his head in disgust. "Too hung over to get out of bed."

Coffee ran from the machine and Mina adroitly switched the glass pot for a mug, filled it from the stream, and handed it to Corbin. "Then you'll put it off until tomorrow?"

He blew on the coffee, then shook his head. "Can't. This is a rush job. Lyle's picking that oak up tomorrow morning."

"You'll saw it alone?"

"I've done it before. No big deal, kiddo," he said, lightly touching Mina's chin. "I'll take this with me," he said, raising his coffee cup. "Thanks." He nodded to Ruby and left the house.

"See what I mean?" Mina asked, looking at the door as if Corbin were still there. "Danny Greenstone, his off-bearer, the guy who pulls the sawn lumber off the belt, has been flaky lately. His wife left him and it's getting worse; he's hardly ever on time and then, today . . ." She sighed. "I don't know why Corbin doesn't just fire him."

Ruby glanced at her watch. She should go home. What if DeEtta was having problems with Jesse?

Mina caught Ruby's glance and said, "Don't go yet. Here, now we can have coffee."

From outside came the roar of Corbin's mill starting up. Mina tipped her head, listening until the roar smoothed to the rumble of a well-maintained engine.

"Were you married?" Mina asked, her previous intensity now turned into polite good manners.

"Yes," Ruby said.

The saw of Corbin's mill screamed as it cut through a log. Mina's head moved slightly and on her face Ruby caught the same close attention that mothers gave their young children: caution, awareness of any unusual sound. The saw screeched again and again, regularly, rhythmically, and they raised their voices to compensate for the outside noise.

"We divorced," Ruby told Mina, leaving out what came after.

Mina raised her coffee cup in a toast. "We all deserve at least one practice marriage; it should be erased from our records when we find true love, the way they delete a juvenile's record when he reaches twenty-one."

"I'm for that," Ruby agreed.

"Do you remember ..." The rhythmic sawing stopped and Mina quit speaking at the same time, tipping her head to listen. Ruby heard only the steady drone of the saw's engine. They sat silently, waiting for the log-cutting to resume.

And waited. Mina brought her eyebrows together in a questioning frown and turned to look at Ruby.

"What's wrong, Mina?" Ruby asked.

"He stopped. Why did he stop?"

Ruby rose from her chair and pushed it neatly against the table, remembering what Mina said about hating to enter the mill. "I'll check. You wait here."

The sawmill's engine ground steadily on, a single-noted roar. Without the whine of the blade through logs, the machine grumbled with impatience.

Ruby closed the kitchen door behind her and walked across the driveway and the rutted sandy yard to the sawmill. Sunshine glared from the mill's tin roof. The black-and-white collie turned in agitated circles near the door paying no attention to Ruby.

A hand touched Ruby's arm and she gasped and spun around, meeting Mina's white face and panicked eyes. Mina spoke but Ruby only made out the word "happened."

Ruby gripped Mina's shoulders, squeezing the narrow bones to emphasize her words. "Don't move," she shouted close to Mina's ear. "Stay here."

Mina nodded and Ruby took two long strides toward the sawmill, assaulted by the deafening sound of the engine. She swept her eyes across the scene. The still-whirling circular saw blade, the piled logs and freshly cut lumber, comprehending without allowing herself to actually *see* the man she had just met, who five minutes ago had stood in his kitchen, looking adoringly at his wife, now ripped apart by the spinning saw.

She turned back to Mina who stood where Ruby had left her, a tiny figure holding her hands in fists at her sides. Ruby was struck by the resignation on Mina's face. Resignation and heart-breaking sorrow, but not shock.

Chapter 4

While Ruby and Mina waited in the kitchen for the police, the sawmill engine continued to run, buzzing and humming like a horde of giant bees, blotting out every other sound.

Mina sat at the table, frozen-faced and dry-eyed, all her attention on her old friend as Ruby heated a pan of milk. Ruby stirred the milk with a wooden spoon, concentrating on flame and liquid, not the relentless drone of the mill.

She was placing a cup of warm milk in front of Mina, who now swayed back and forth in her chair like Jesse did when she was overstimulated, when she spotted two police cars followed by an ambulance pull into the driveway. She'd expected sirens and gyrating lights and vehicles careening around corners, but they approached sedately. No hurry, which Ruby supposed was appropriate and practical.

"The police are here," Ruby told Mina, hunkering down beside her, noticing how only the toes of Mina's feet reached the floor.

"Stay with me," Mina said, turning dull eyes to Ruby.

"I'm not leaving, I promise."

Ruby opened the kitchen door and watched the authorities through the screen door. Instead of stopping at the house, they drove directly to the mill, one of the sheriff's cars parking sideways as if to bar hordes of ghoulish onlookers.

Six men stepped from the vehicles, four in brown

uniforms, two in plain clothes with EMT jackets. One of the uniformed men carried a camera. Ruby couldn't make out any of their faces. The six men formed a huddle, heads bent as they exchanged words, then straightened their clothing and shoulders before they disappeared into the sawmill.

"I should have never let him run the saw alone," Mina said. She'd wadded the edge of the tablecloth into accordion pleats and absently worked and reworked the folds.

Ruby pushed the warm milk closer to Mina. "You couldn't have stopped him," Ruby assured her. Mina didn't answer.

The engine in the sawmill was finally switched off and Mina gasped at the shock of silence. Perversely, now Ruby longed for its drone. She heard the birds, the distant sound of men's voices, and felt they'd been dropped into an even stranger situation: horrible death in the midst of normalcy.

She removed the folds of tablecloth from Mina's hands and gave her the warm mug, wishing she'd been able to find alcohol in Mina's cupboards. She yearned to rock Mina in her arms the way she sometimes did Jesse, but when Ruby touched Mina's shoulder, her friend stiffened until Ruby pulled away her hand.

After a while, one of the uniformed men left the sawmill and walked slowly to the house, reluctance in every step. He was thin and nearly bald, with the upright bearing of a man who'd served in the military. A sheriff's badge gleamed on his uniform shirt pocket. Pausing before Mina's door, he took a deep breath before lightly tapping on the door jamb, squinting inside through the mesh.

When Ruby opened the screen door, he nodded, saying without surprise or introduction "Hello, Ruby. How is she?"

Ruby was momentarily confused. A younger version of

Sheriff Carl Joyce, who'd been the sheriff when she was a child, stood before her. Physically very like him, yet softer, without the power and authority she recalled.

"It's Carl Joyce, Jr.," he said, seeing her confusion. "Call me Carly; everybody does."

"Carly," she acknowledged, remembering the boy two grades ahead of her who'd been best known and least liked for being the sheriff's son. "Come in. Mina's . . ." She waved a hand toward the table where Mina was concentrating on drinking milk from her mug as if it were the most important task in her life.

Carly stood awkwardly for a moment, then pulled a chair close to Mina and sat down, gently removing the mug and taking her hands in his own narrow ones. "Mina, honey," he said softly. "Corbin's gone, sweetheart. Can you tell me what happened?"

It was several seconds before Mina answered. Carly didn't move a muscle, just sat close to the bereaved woman and held her hands.

"He was sawing oak," Mina finally whispered. "It was a rush job."

"He was working alone?"

Mina nodded. "Danny was supposed to help him but . . ."

Carly sighed and nodded as if he already knew *that* story.

Another vehicle pulled into the driveway, and Ruby heard the slam of a car door and hurried footsteps.

"That'll be your mother, Mina," Carly said. "I called her. I hope that's okay?"

"Thank you," Mina whispered.

Fay Asauskas, in blue jeans and a sweatshirt, pushed past Ruby without seeing her, her eyes seeking only Mina. With Mina's silver hair, the two women could have passed for sisters instead of mother and daughter.

Mina collapsed into her mother's arms, going limp but still without tears. Fay lifted her from the chair, guiding her toward the living room and the bedroom beyond. "I'll take care of her," Fay said without glancing back at either Carly or Ruby.

When the two women were gone, Carly sat in Mina's chair, slouching, his face sagging. A clock ticked from somewhere.

"Goddam," Carly said in a low, harsh voice. "Just double goddam it to hell in a handbasket." He stretched his head back, looking up at the ceiling, then turned to Ruby. "You were here, Ruby? What happened?"

"I don't know," Ruby told him. "Mina and I were visiting here in the kitchen when Corbin came home and said his off-bearer was hung over and he'd have to run his sawmill alone."

"Yeah," Carly acknowledged, glancing in the direction Fay had led Mina. "Did you hear anything?"

"Only the sawmill operating. I heard the saw cutting through the logs. And then it stopped. After that only the sound of the engine."

"Why did you go out?" he asked. Carly's hands were clasped behind his neck and he regarded Ruby steadily, rarely blinking.

"Mina asked me to." Ruby stopped and thought. "No, she didn't really ask me to, but she was worried and I . . ."

"You suspected something was wrong?" Carly asked, eyes narrowing at her, his forehead tightening.

Ruby shook her head. "No, but Mina was afraid. She said she hated the sawmill."

Carly nodded. "So you walked over to the mill. What did you see?" Over Carly's shoulder and through the door, Ruby caught sight of the EMTs opening the back of the ambulance and removing a gurney.

She glanced down at her hands. "I didn't look. Not really. Only enough . . ."

Carly's voice dropped to the same soft level he'd used when he spoke to Mina. He bent closer to Ruby. "Do you remember anything else, Ruby?" he asked. "Did you see any movement in the trees or by the road? A person? A car maybe?"

Ruby opened her eyes and regarded Carly in surprise. "Are you asking me if I spotted a possible murderer?"

He leaned back, frowning as if in pain. "Now that's not what I asked at all, Ruby. I like to be thorough in any investigation I make, study every angle."

"I didn't see anyone else," Ruby told him. "What do *you* suspect happened?"

"It's too soon to say. Deaths and maiming happen too often around sawmills; they're damn dangerous."

"From what I've heard, the sawmill business itself may become extinct."

"That's blasphemous talk around here." He stood up from the table, more relaxed as the first shock of Corbin's death receded. "It sounds out of place under the circumstances, Ruby, but welcome home."

"Thanks. I was expecting to see your father. Did he retire?"

"Dad died six years ago and I was voted in as sheriff last election."

"I'm sorry about your dad," Ruby told him. "He was a powerful force in this county."

"People expect me to be Dad all over again, but . . ." Carly shook his balding head, regretful. "I understand you're involved in the law, too."

"Who told you that?" Ruby asked.

"It's my business to know," he said with a touch of pride.

"I see. Then you must also know I'm involved with the law on a very peripheral level."

"It doesn't matter. The right side's the right side. What do you hear from Phyllis?" he asked, his expression slipping into wistfulness. The ambulance sedately drove around the police cars and past the house. The EMT on the passenger side was eating a banana.

"Phyllis is still in New Mexico as far as I know," Ruby told him.

The last Ruby had heard from her older sister was when they'd exchanged obligatory Christmas cards, Phyllis's name dashed off in large letters, with an angry slash at the end. Ruby had taken care not to betray any emotion in her own signature. She was too knowledgeable to give herself away like Phyllis had.

"A woman engineer," Carly said with admiration. He shook his head, moving a step to the left, blocking Ruby's view of the departing ambulance. Was he trying to distract her? "I knew I should have held on to that girl."

The way Ruby remembered it, Phyllis had lost interest in Carly before their first date had ended. He'd been one forgettable entry in the long parade of her sister's boyfriends.

"Well," Carly said as he pushed against the screen door. "You know what they say, it doesn't matter where you start out; it's where you end up."

Ruby refrained from mentioning the obvious: that here they both were, right where they'd started.

Ruby slowed on Blue Road at the turnoff to her cabin, then sped up, following the soft sandy road around the lake, giving herself a few more minutes to collect herself before she went home to Jesse.

She breathed slow and deep, driving fifteen miles per hour past the cottages that edged the lake on one side of the road and the forests of oak, beech, and aspen on the other. A few new summer homes stood out among the humbler cottages, with quantities of glass and cedar decking. Upscaling had begun, even on little Blue Lake. A motorcycle passed, zipping around her car, both rider and bike in black, a flash of chrome.

She rounded a curve and braked in the middle of the road. "What the hell?" she said aloud.

To her right, where she expected to see the tall oaks and maples of Fox Woods, the forest opened to a jagged landscape of broken and downed trees. She turned off the engine, staring. Treetops lay on the ground, their leaves dead and dried, clicking together. Fox Woods was devastated; a few trees stood bedraggled and damaged, all bones. Flat-topped stumps squatted among the debris.

Ruby got out of the car, taking in the pathetic remains of the woods where she'd built a clumsy tree house with her cousins, drank her first beer, and lost her innocence. Several hundred yards ahead she saw the dark high wall of trees where the forest became whole again, as if a razor edge had been laid down.

"Ruby Crane," a gravelly voice said from the cut-over land, and Ruby gasped. She turned, searching the debris, light on her feet and ready to run for her life.

A small dark figure sat on a stump beside the road, her white hair in a rough bun.

"Mrs. Pink?" Ruby asked.

"*Ja, ja.* Who else would it be?"

Ruby stepped closer and Mrs. Pink leaned back as if fearing Ruby might touch her. Mrs. Pink had always walked. Up and down the roads, around the lake. A solitary old woman everyone suspected of spying. And Ruby knew it was true. She, too, had spent hours walking and brooding and had seen Mrs. Pink sitting in the shadows, her still figure peering in windows or hanging back in the trees, watching.

"I didn't think you'd still be . . ." Ruby began.

"Living or walking?" Mrs. Pink asked and then laughed, a gargly laugh that ended in a wheeze.

"Both," Ruby told her, and Mrs. Pink's wheezing progressed to coughing.

"I'm still here," Mrs. Pink said, wiping at her eyes

with her sleeve. "I move more slow but I end up where I'm going."

Mrs. Pink had to be in her mid-eighties by now. She'd aged to delicate bones, her wrinkled face a fine pale skin clinging to her skull.

"What happened here?" Ruby asked, waving a hand toward the remnants of Fox Woods.

Mrs. Pink spat on the ground. "Cutting. Turmouski cut it because he was a madman. Snip, snip, and no more home for the birds."

"He's dead," Ruby told her.

"*Ja.* I heard that already. Elanor Becket is out spreading the news. Cut in half. Snip, snip."

"Did you know Corbin Turmouski?" Ruby asked.

"*Mein* Frank said Turmouski is a brute. Ripping up all the good trees." Mrs. Pink jabbed the air with her finger.

"*Mein* Frank" was Mrs. Pink's husband, who'd died in Germany before she came alone to America. For over fifty years, Mrs. Pink had claimed to converse with her dead husband, and until that moment, Ruby had never thought anything odd about it. We get used to anything, she thought.

"It was a terrible accident," Ruby said.

"Maybe."

"Can I walk you home, Mrs. Pink?"

The old woman raised a walking staff of gnarly wood from the ground where it had been lying at her feet. "I don't need help. *You* go home. That Becket is a nosy one. She'll go through your underwear."

"Come visit me sometime," Ruby invited.

"I already *see* you when I want to," Mrs. Pink said.

Ruby stood in the road until Mrs. Pink disappeared around the next bend, her pace slow but even, matching her staff to her measured gait.

o   o   o

When Ruby's car tires rumbled across the wooden bridge over the little swamp at the end of her driveway, she consciously tried to put Corbin and Mina from her mind. It was an impossible task, she knew that, but she was determined to keep as much of the world away from Jesse as she could.

She'd been gone three hours instead of one—although it felt like she'd left the cabin days ago—and when she emerged from the trees to the welcome sight of her cabin, she spotted DeEtta watching from the kitchen window. Five seconds later and DeEtta was striding across the yard to meet Ruby.

"Is Jesse all right?" Ruby asked, seeing DeEtta's solemn round face.

DeEtta nodded. "She's listening to that tape you had in the machine, the one about the lion in the wardrobe." She bit her lip. "Peggy Dystix from the phone company called to tell me about Corbin."

"Bad news has wings," Ruby said.

"Were you there?" DeEtta asked.

"Yes, I was."

DeEtta stared at Ruby, her expression a mixture of dread fascination and awe. "I heard he died in his sawmill. Was he . . . Did you see him?"

"I don't care to discuss it now, DeEtta," Ruby told her wearily. "I'm sorry I'm late."

"Does Carly know who did it?" DeEtta persisted, stolidly blocking Ruby's entrance to the cabin.

"It was an accident," Ruby told her.

"Did he say that?" DeEtta's voice rose and cracked.

Ruby studied DeEtta's round face, seeing more than simple curiosity. DeEtta was more concerned about the means of Corbin's death than the fact of it. DeEtta stood in her white uniform, hands clasped, waiting for Ruby to answer, and Ruby could have sworn she was holding her breath.

"He implied it was an accident," Ruby said,

feeling some crazy need to reassure DeEtta. "He's still investigating."

DeEtta nodded her head once and looked down at her nurse's shoes.

"I appreciate it that you were here, DeEtta," Ruby told her. "Are you ready to discuss your salary?"

DeEtta shook her head. "I can't think about money right now. Next time, please?"

"Can you come back tomorrow afternoon?"

"I can be here whenever you need me," DeEtta said fervently. "I'll stay all night if you want me to."

The sun had set and Ruby stood on the cabin's screened-in porch, watching mists rise on Blue Lake and waft across the water out of the cattailed shores. The clear evening had turned cool, autumn sharp. From the east, a whippoorwill twice gave its tender cry and shivers rose along Ruby's neck. She'd always loved the whippoorwill's call, but now it sounded too lost and mournful.

She hoped Mina wasn't alone. Her parents lived in the county, and there were brothers and sisters. And Corbin's family. Whatever it was that Mina had wanted to discuss with Ruby would now have to wait. Maybe she would never know.

A flurry sounded in the oak leaves to the left of the cabin and Ruby jumped, knowing it was only birds settling in for the night. Still, she wasn't accustomed to the night sounds anymore and she went inside, locking the door behind her.

A Vivaldi concerto played on the tape player. Ruby owned a lot of Vivaldi. "That figures," Stan, her ex-husband, had chided her. "Vivaldi's simple, uncomplicated. A favorite of the common man."

But by then, Stan's criticisms had lost their power

and Ruby had shrugged, saying without concern "It's okay. I'm not a very complicated person."

She drew the dilapidated mesh screen in front of the fireplace, feeling its heat. The wood was dry and the fire burned hot, sparks and flames rising into the chimney. Jesse was already asleep for the night.

Boxes still waited to be emptied in the main room and bedroom, but for the moment, she'd lost her drive to unpack. Ruby's own things, including her lab, she intended to move up to the loft and give Jesse the only bedroom downstairs.

Being a floor above Jesse didn't concern Ruby. After she pulled Jesse out of the hospital, Ruby had regained the mother's ears, that child-specific and almost supernatural sense of hearing. If Jesse so much as sighed, Ruby awoke, already upright in her bed.

There wasn't a television and Ruby was too restless to read, her mind always turning back to Mina, so she searched through the boxes by the bedroom door until she found the cardboard box she'd marked with "Quilt in Progress." She carried it to the couch and opened it.

From the time Ruby was six, when her parents began leaving her at Gram's house, her grandmother had kept her occupied with cloth and needle. Ruby sewed like some people doodled, hand-stitching figures and designs and displays of scenery on leftover pieces of cloth. "You should be a painter," Gram had said. "Is so beautiful."

Gram's passion had been arranging pieces of fabric into intricate, exotic, beautifully designed quilts. But once she'd fitted all her squares and triangles and diamonds into a quilt top, Gram had lost interest, leaving the top unfinished, without backing or batting, folding each one away into boxes, too eager with new ideas and new colors for the next one to finish the old one.

Ruby wasn't interested in quilts. She didn't understand the subtleties of the interplay of colors, the infinite possibilities of shape. Together they'd sat in Gram's living room in easy companionship, the mantel clock ticking, each of them sewing her own projects, Ruby's heart at rest. She'd loved Gram with all her heart.

Her grandmother died when Ruby was sixteen and willed her quilt tops and sewing materials to her granddaughter. Ruby had left the whole mess with her parents. When she was twenty-five, her father cleaned the attic and shipped the boxes to her in California without comment.

Opening those boxes had been a revelation. Besides finally understanding that Gram's quilt tops were works of art, Ruby could smell Gram's house on each one. She closed her eyes and caught the scent of the hand soap Gram used. It was as if a balm had eased her heart, as if her scattered mind had suddenly been gently caught and contained yet at the same time, set free. From that day, her life began to change.

One by one, Ruby began to put the quilts together, basting a cotton batting between Gram's quilt top and a muslin backing. Then on Gram's old quilt hoop, she stitched the three layers together in designs that flowed across the quilt, in their own way as intricate and creative as Gram's sense of color and shape.

And so she and Gram were bound in a strange partnership. Ruby estimated there were enough quilt tops to put together to last into her own retirement, that, in some way, she'd have Gram with her until she herself died.

The fire had burned down to lava-red coals when the telephone rang.

"It's Todd," the voice on the phone greeted her. "Want me to come get you? In ten minutes I could clear my junk out of the spare room for Jesse."

"It would definitely save me from having to unpack here," Ruby told him.

"Seriously, Ruby . . ." he began, his voice dropping to softer tones.

"We're fine," Ruby said, gently cutting him off. "I'm emptying boxes and running into old ghosts."

"Live ones or dead ones?"

She hesitated, then decided against telling Todd of Corbin Turmouski's death; she wasn't prepared to reduce the event to mere words yet and, besides, Todd's life was the city; he had no concept of sawmills or the Midwest.

"So far only live ghosts," she told him. "The cabin's in better shape than I expected. And there's a heat wave. Hot days and cool nights."

They exchanged news and Todd asked, "Does it feel like home?"

Ruby looked around the warm log walls, the worn floor and peeled rafters, the glowing fire. "The cabin does," she told him.

"Your boss called and left a message."

"Ron?" Ruby asked, picturing the burly near lawyer making one of his lightning-swift phone calls.

"Yeah. He sounded frantic, as usual. I bet the place is falling apart without you. He wants you to call him yesterday."

"Typical. I will in a few minutes."

"I miss you," Todd said as he signed off his end of the conversation.

"Thanks," Ruby said, gently replacing the phone on the cradle. Did she miss Todd? There hadn't been time. She was too involved in settling back into a place where she'd once vowed she'd eat dirt rather than spend a single night.

Before Ruby left Palo Alto, Ron Kilgore had been thrown out of his third wife's house and moved into the second room of his two-room office. So when his answering machine greeted her, still bearing her own voice, Ruby said, "This is Ruby, Ron. If you're there, pick it up."

Ron Kilgore came on the line so fast he must have been hovering over the phone. "Ruby! I need you. Why in hell did you have to move back to that island?"

"Michigan's not an island, it's a peninsula. The state motto is 'If you seek a pleasant peninsula, look around you.' I can even say it in Latin."

"Yeah, yeah. Might as well be an island on Mars. I've been trying to call you all day. Some fruit named Peggy Dipstick wouldn't give me your number."

"It's Peggy Dystix and my phone number's unlisted although you're probably the only person she hasn't given it to."

"Lucky me." He took a breath, revving up. "Two things: First, your local sheriff, Somebody Junior, called me."

"Carl Joyce, Jr. Why?"

"Checking up on your lost years, I gathered."

"What did you tell him?" Ruby asked.

"That you were a damn good receptionist."

"That's all?"

"That's all. You can parcel out the details, if you want. Any trouble back there?"

"A friend's husband was killed today," she said, telling him what she couldn't tell Todd.

"Accident?"

"I think so, but there are a couple of oddities."

"When you're ready, tell me about the oddities."

"I will," Ruby said. "What's the second matter?"

"I've got a rush job for you."

"Ron," Ruby said patiently. "We arrived here last night. I haven't even unpacked my socks. I'll give you my phone number and you can call me next week."

After working a week for Ron Kilgore, Ruby had figured out why he'd repeatedly failed his bar exams. Life was an emergency to Ron. Whatever he did he couldn't do fast enough. He paced during phone conversations, twisted his chair and tapped his fingers when consulting with a client; he grunted impatiently as he skimmed newspapers and couldn't stomach idle conversation. "Get to the point" was one of his favorite phrases. Ruby doubted he'd been physically capable of sitting through the hours-long bar exam. His gift was instantly sizing up people and situations and knowing when to cut his losses.

"It can't wait," he said now, and Ruby pictured him turning on his heel at the end of the phone cord like an animal at the end of its leash. "I'll give you a 90 percent cut on this one. The guy's in a hurry. No, he's in a panic."

"Next week," Ruby repeated. "Ask Mike Callendar."

"He's not as good as you."

"Well, thank you but save the compliments. The answer's still no."

Ron heaved a sigh. "Too late, Ruby. When I couldn't get your number I shipped it via FedEx. You'll get it tomorrow." He paused, then asked, "They do have FedEx back there, don't they?"

"Some people even have computers."

"That's a relief," he said seriously.

"What are you sending me?" Ruby asked.

"Mama's handwritten will. Her son's—"

"Don't tell me any more," Ruby warned. "What are the standards?"

There was a rustle of paper. Then Ron read off "Social security application, a handwritten recipe for carrot cake, her handwritten minutes for the meeting of some group called The Ceramic Queens, and a letter to her granddaughter. Two done within a year of the piece in question, one three years ago and one five, just the way you like them."

"Okay," Ruby told him in resignation. "I'll do it, but it's going to cost you 95 percent."

Ron sputtered and Ruby said, "Or I can send it back and you can give it to Mike."

"Aw, Ruby. You've got me by the balls. Ninety-five percent, it is. Just this once."

"That's okay because I'm only doing a tricky rush job like this just this once."

"How's my girl?" he asked, his voice going gentle.

"She's more alert," Ruby told him. "This place is very quiet; it'll be good for her."

"It better be. Call me if you need anything; I mean it. And get that job back to me by Thursday, Friday at the latest. All the usual reports."

"That's not giving me much time," Ruby protested.

"For 95 percent it is."

As usual, Ron Kilgore hung up without saying good-bye. Now Ruby understood how Sheriff Carly Joyce figured she was on the "right side" of the law. Had Carly then shared it with all of Sable?

She *wanted* Ron's job. Her lab was still to be unpacked but, frequently, the only equipment she needed was a magnifying glass and good light, sometimes just light. Her favorite jobs involved handwriting, when she began to "feel" the honesty or culpability of the executor. She was good at papers and inks, too, but those were "cooler" projects, like jigsaw puzzles or paint-by-number pictures.

In the past year she'd spent more time on forgery than her original secretarial duties; her reputation was solid, her opinions respected; she'd testified in three court cases and written reports for dozens more. She could have gone on her own but she was loyal to Ron Kilgore, the way he'd hired her before she'd even completed her GED and how he'd sponsored her in forgery detection.

Ruby filled a glass with water and turned off the

kitchen light, ready for bed. As the room darkened, through the window she caught sight of a dark shape outlined by moonlight: a person backing into the trees. She gasped and dropped her glass, which bounced harmlessly and splattered water up her legs.

She leapt to the kitchen door and jerked it open, not thinking that someone was spying on her but more that someone had dared to invade her sanctuary.

"Who's there?" she shouted into the silence. "What do you want?"

The leaves rustled, a breeze stirred. Above her, the Milky Way shone like poured glitter and a pale half moon cast a silvery strip across Blue Lake from shore to shore, illuminating the mists. Water lapped quietly against the little beach, a faint sound that would be lost in the city.

Apparent serenity. Ruby swallowed and peered into the trees, one hand still on the doorknob. "Mrs. Pink? Is that you?"

There was no answer, no movement, and finally Ruby returned to the cabin, locking both doors and placing chairs beneath the knobs before she went to bed.

Chapter 5

The morning sun cast a wavery light on the log walls and Ruby snuggled deeper into the tangle of blankets she'd been too tired to turn into a bed.

She'd stayed up until two in the morning, lugging boxes up the steep stairs, unpacking and arranging her lab in the loft, duplicating the arrangement that had fit her so perfectly in Palo Alto: two tables forming an L and holding her lamps and light table, the locked metal cabinet where she kept her records and stereoptic microscope. All she needed was an outlet strip and for FedEx to deliver Ron Kilgore's job; she was ready.

She remembered Corbin's death and every other thought fled her mind, except Mina. She got up, buttoning her shirt as she went downstairs to Jesse's room, making plans to call Mina later in the day.

Jesse lay in bed awake, her frown severe, staring around her room. She tugged rhythmically at the hair on the right side of her head, her left arm lying limp on the blankets.

"Hi, Mom," Jesse said, her gaze now brilliantly intense on Ruby's face.

"Good morning, sweetheart," Ruby answered.

Such a simple thing to fill Ruby with so much gratitude. Hi, Mom.

Ruby helped Jesse dress while she explained every step of the process, pausing to allow her daughter time to comment or absorb. Since her accident, Jesse had been most intrigued by the sight of socks going over her bare feet, and today she wiggled her right toes as Ruby pulled on a blue anklet, smiling.

"It's good to see you give me a rough time," Ruby told her.

"Okay," Jesse said.

Jesse's left side was especially weak when she first woke up, so Ruby began her day by transferring her to her purple-webbed wheelchair, which had been a parting gift from Ron Kilgore.

Jesse's eyes widened; the frown deepened as Ruby wheeled her through the cabin; then she closed her eyes as if it were all too much to absorb.

Rapping sounded on the cabin door and Ruby jumped, the events of the day before flooding over her. Now who? Mina?

It was DeEtta, impeccable in another crisply ironed white uniform, holding her oversize bag in both hands, her face shiny and determined.

"I wasn't expecting you until this afternoon," Ruby told her.

"I thought you might want to go into town or something," DeEtta told Ruby.

Actually, Ruby did. She hesitated though, unwilling to allow this eager young woman to determine her schedule.

DeEtta's mouth remained in a forced smile even as she spoke. "I was supposed to visit friends but it got canceled," she continued in a rush. "So I figured . . . well, here I am." She leaned into the cabin, calling. "Hi, Jesse."

Ruby reluctantly opened the door all the way. "All right," she said. "But next time, please call first, would you?"

"Okay," DeEtta said, already sidling past Ruby toward the cupboards to prepare Jesse's breakfast.

As Ruby pulled her purse from the peg behind the door, DeEtta said, "I heard the sheriff's probably going to declare that Corbin Turmouski's . . . you know, was an accident."

"That makes sense to me," Ruby said.

"Does it?" DeEtta asked, turning with a box of Raisin Bran in her hand, her eyebrows raised, a flicker of hope in her eyes.

"Why does that surprise you?" Ruby asked.

DeEtta shrugged and turned her attention to opening the box of cereal. "Did you sleep okay?" she asked.

"Actually, I thought I saw . . ." Ruby began, then remembered Jesse, who sat in her chair at the table, her attention caught by the leaves outside the window. Ruby could never be sure how much her daughter understood. "Never mind," Ruby told DeEtta, who was regarding her thoughtfully, lower lip between her teeth. "I'll really be home in an hour this time."

Ruby drove slowly through Sable's familiar two-block downtown, noting the few changes in the 150-year-old town. Sable had never experienced growing pains. Photos of the downtown had to be scrutinized to discover exactly which quarter century was being depicted.

The town's commercial buildings were mainly plain red brick of two stories with wooden front doors set up from the sidewalks by concrete steps. Paulas's Drug Store had a remodeled entry with a steel-and-glass door. The bakery sported a bright yellow awning. And where the Montgomery Ward catalog store had burned, the vacant lot held three wooden benches and a concrete pot of marigolds.

Signs announcing the upcoming Color Festival hung on lampposts and in store windows. The Color Festival was Sable's biggest and oldest annual event: part carnival, part fair, cunningly paired with the first weekend of whitetail deer bow-hunting season to bring in the most revelers. Every year during high school, Ruby and Mina had cut school on the first day of the Color Festival to spend hours screaming on carnival rides, flirting with boys, and dodging anyone in authority.

Near the parking spot Ruby angled into, a knot of mostly older men stood in front of the hardware store, involved in serious discussion. She was sure of the topic: Corbin Turmouski's death.

Out of habit, as Ruby got out of her car, she fished in her purse for change and then realized Sable still hadn't got around to installing parking meters.

One of the men separated from the group and came toward her, smiling, his hand out. "Ruby," he said. "I heard you were back."

Before her, dressed in a light gray suit and red tie, stood Wally Kentner, former friend and classmate. He'd been closer to Mina than to Ruby, but she'd once snuck into the Crane cabin with him on a winter night after her parents had closed it up for the season. They'd drunk sloe gin, gotten high, and made love in the loft—if that's what you could call their rough and clumsy coupling.

She felt herself blush as she shook the hand of this slender and successful-appearing man. "Wally," she said. "It's good to see you."

"Ditto." His blond hair was thinner and stylishly cut, and except for the creases at the corner of his green eyes, he'd hardly changed. He flashed the lopsided grin that had infuriated teachers and thrilled the girls, and Ruby suspected the same memory as hers had crossed his mind.

"Do you have time for a cup of coffee?" he asked. "Maybe a few mintues of catch-up?"

"I'd like that," she told him.

"Let's stop by the office first," he said, waving his hand toward a small office next to the hardware store. A sign in the window read: KENTNER REAL ESTATE & INSURANCE.

A second man, in his fifties, separated from the group and called to Wally, "See you Thursday then?"

"Noon," Wally said and introduced him to Ruby, "This is Glenn Wister, Ruby. He works for Northern Timber. A pillar of the community. If you want something done, Glenn's your man."

Glenn Wister shook his head and waved his hand in a self-deprecating way. "With me you get somebody to blame, anyway."

As Ruby walked beside Wally to his office, the smile switched off and Wally's face grew serious. "This thing about Corbin has everybody shook up. I heard you were there." He looked at Ruby sympathetically. "You doing okay?"

"I think so. But Mina . . ."

"I know. I talked to her mother this morning." Wally held his office door for her. Ruby was assaulted by 1973. Wood paneling, orange shag carpeting, a clock inside a fake brass sunburst. The dark-haired woman at the desk looked up and smiled.

"Ruby Crane," she said.

They were close in age but Ruby couldn't spot a familiar feature. She was plump, her face smooth and pink-cheeked. Pretty in a bland way yet with a firm line to her jaw. It was easy to picture her with her mouth closed tight and her chin stubbornly pushed forward. Finally, it was the scar on her chin that tipped off Ruby. A scar made by Ruby's own ice skate when she was eight.

"Mary Jean Hannah?" she asked.

"Very good. It's Mary Jean Scribner now. Most people don't recognize me if they haven't seen me since I was a kid."

Ruby could understand that. Skinny, quiet Mary Jean who Ruby probably *wouldn't* have remembered if she hadn't run over Mary Jean on frozen Blue Lake during

Ruby's eighth birthday party. That much blood tended to make a person unforgettable.

"We're going for coffee," Wally told Mary Jean. "Hold off Ralph if I'm late getting back, would you?"

"Sure," Mary Jean said, and to Ruby: "Let's get together, okay?"

People said that all the time and didn't mean it, just like they said "How are you?" so Ruby answered, "Give me a call," all of it meaningless conversation.

"It looks like Sable agrees with you," Ruby told Wally when they were back in the warm sunshine.

"I thought I'd have to leave town to make a living, like you did. But here I am." Wally spread his arms. "Local success story." He shrugged. "Sable's still a good place to live."

They walked a half block to the Knotty Pine restaurant, where there was no knotty pine, inside or out. The painted pale blue walls were hung with local art: stiff oils of lighthouses surrounded by static waves, dumbly staring puppies and kittens, a crosscut saw painted with a moonlit snow scene. Handmade rag clowns sat beside the cash register with a sign that read TAKE ME HOME.

In the dark varnished booth where they sat, paper placemats touted the charms of Waters County. Every attraction listed was along Lake Michigan. Nothing over a mile inland.

"Did you know Corbin Turmouski very well?" Ruby asked.

"Pretty well." Wally gazed over Ruby's shoulder. "You remember I was good friends with Mina and Ford before and after they were married. When she and Corbin had that affair . . . well, the talk was pretty harsh. But after they were married, Corbin and I got along. I didn't want to lose Mina's friendship."

In high school, Wally hadn't bothered to hide his infatuation with Mina, which had slowly developed into a close friendship. Back then Mina's notice of other boys had begun and ended with Ford Goodlight.

"Carly asked me if I'd seen anyone around Corbin's sawmill when he died," Ruby said. "Is he suspicious about the death?"

"If he's not, everybody else in town is," Wally said. The waitress topped off the coffee in their cups and Ruby emptied three plastic thimblefuls of cream into hers, diluting the taste of canned grounds.

"Why?"

"People have a damn hard time accepting that mean accidents happen," Wally told her, straightening his tie. "They want reasons: enemies and murderers. You start believing a death that horrible is a simple *accident* and the next thing you know it might happen to you."

"*Did* Corbin have enemies?"

"Sure he did; don't we all? The righteous were pissed over his affair with Mina. He and Silas Shea had an out-and-out war going over their sawmill businesses. And you can bet Corbin probably screwed *somebody*, either buying trees off their land or selling cut lumber."

A man in a checked shirt got up from the lunch counter and headed for the door. As he passed their booth, he and Wally nodded to one another, but he paused and smiled at Ruby. "Thanks for the offer yesterday," he said. "I'll see you sometime."

It was the man she'd seen walking along Mina's road and offered a ride, who'd had car trouble. Ruby watched him walk leisurely across the café and out the door. He wasn't local; she could see that more clearly now. Nothing definable, more the way he carried himself: separate, without the weight of past or family. After all these years away, did Ruby carry herself that way, too? She hoped so.

"A friend of yours?" Wally asked.

"No. Who is he?"

"His name's Hank Holliday," Wally said, looking

toward the café door. "He blew into town last spring. He's all right but he stirred up the whole county, especially the sawmill owners."

"Corbin and Silas, too?"

"That's right. He's what they call in polite society a consulting forester."

"With the Forest Service?"

Wally shook his head. "No, on his own. One of your loose-cannon types. Before Holliday came along, a sawmill owner like Corbin or Silas would approach a farmer or a homeowner who owned several acres of trees and offer him an amount of money to cut down the trees."

Wally snapped his fingers. "And it was done. Just like that. The trees were cut down and everybody was happy. But now, along comes Hank Holliday, the consulting forester. He waltzes up to the tree owner and convinces the poor sap to let him *manage* his forest. So instead of a nice clean sale between the sawmill owner and the landowner, you've got Hank Holliday kerplunking himself in the middle and pissing everybody off. He decides which trees can be cut, how they're going to be cut, and then stands there like a mother hen while they're being sawn down."

"Is that so awful?" Ruby asked. "Wouldn't you at least have some trees left instead of a disaster like Fox Woods near my cabin? Corbin Turmouski butchered Fox Woods."

"Who told you that?"

"Mrs. Pink."

"Well, she's right. I admit, some of the logged sites are pretty ugly. We've grown into a prime timber area in the past couple of years. I've got a list of out-of-state clients begging for timbered plots. They'll buy anything with trees on it." He shrugged. "Or even without trees. Property here looks cheap to outsiders, but by local standards, if you're not wealthy, there are certain areas off limits, like along Lake Michigan." Wally leaned toward her across the table. "Now *your* place, on that little peninsula like that. You could sell it for a nice nest egg."

"I'm not interested in selling, not for any amount of money."

"You never know. Keep me in mind. I can give you an appraisal any time."

"Did Hank Holliday and Corbin tangle over any forested property?" Ruby asked, ignoring his offer. First Silas eyeing her trees, now Wally coveting her land.

"Constantly. The first thing Holliday did when he came to town was take over an eighty-acre woodlot that Corbin thought he had in the bag. I heard they exchanged a few words, maybe some blows over it." Wally glanced at his watch. "Have you seen your father yet?"

"No," Ruby told him.

"Are you going to?"

"No."

"I didn't think so. I guess your sister Phyllis pays to have somebody come in every day, but she hasn't visited Sable in three or four years herself."

Ruby didn't answer and Wally whistled through his teeth. "Nothing's changed since you left home, huh?"

"This is the way he wanted it," Ruby said.

"And you're determined he's going to live to regret it, by God," Wally said, his voice teasing. "Take-no-prisoners Ruby Crane."

On the edge of Sable, among brick and wood-frame houses, Ruby parked in front of a single-story white house with a no-frills addition jutting from its side. The sign in front of the separate entrance read PARKER POR-TRAIT STUDIO.

Mabel Parker's husband had built the addition

twenty years ago to give his wife the means to finance the type of photography she loved best. Mabel skulked the streets and byways of Sable with her camera, so common a sight no one paid any attention to her. Always in her brimmed hat and fisherman's vest, loaded with equipment, reducing everyone and everything to a photographic possibility.

"Hello, Ruby," Mabel said when Ruby walked in the door of her cluttered studio, as if they'd seen each other yesterday. She was bent over a set of proof sheets with a magnifying glass. "Take a look at this and tell me what you see."

Ruby took the magnifying glass and studied the frame Mabel pointed to. "I see a heron sticking its head out of last summer's cattails."

Mabel smiled. "Very good." She was thinner, more wrinkled, her gray hair cropped close to her head. Around her were piled stacks of folders, proof envelopes, and unopened mail. Scraps of paper and receipts littered her desk, some with safety pins through them.

"I'd like to work for you," Ruby said, knowing that to keep Mabel's attention she'd better skip the small talk and get right to the meat.

"Doing what?"

Ruby waved her hand around the chaotic office. "I'd clean up this mess, help with your shoots, answer your phone, do your billing, make coffee, chase away solicitors and creditors."

Mabel slipped the magnifying glass in her shirt pocket and blew lightly on the heron photo. "I could use help; everybody keeps telling me that. Bill's dead: heart."

"I'm sorry. He was a nice man."

"The best, but it was fast at least. I'm not busy enough to hire you full time."

"I'm not interested in full time."

Mabel shrugged. "Okay, we'll try it. I always liked

you, Ruby. I'm glad to see you're not dead in some gutter."

"I always liked you, too," Ruby said. "I'm surprised to see you're not in New York at some magazine."

"Touché. Can you start tomorrow?"

"I'll be here. One o'clock."

Chapter 6

Ruby drove around the curve of her driveway and nearly crashed into the front end of a green tractor with a tinted cab, slamming on her brakes and shimmying to a stop inches from the monstrous machine.

The driver was looking over his shoulder as he backed a small blue-and-white travel trailer between the trees, definitely positioning it next to the pump house across the driveway from *her* cabin. DeEtta Becket stood in the cabin's kitchen door, her arms crossed, blandly watching the whole intricate operation.

Ruby leaned on the horn and stuck her head through her window. "What's going on?" she shouted against the engine.

DeEtta shook her head and pointed to her ears. Ruby leaned on the horn again and DeEtta waved her arms at the tractor driver, cutting her hand across her throat.

Ruby jumped out of her car and jabbed her finger toward the tractor's cab. "Get down out of there! What is this?"

The side of the cab opened and a lanky figure casually emerged, dressed in green coveralls and a baseball cap pulled low. DeEtta ran forward, still wearing a nurse's uniform but her gleaming white shoes now replaced by beat-up sneakers.

"It's my brother, Bruce," she shouted into the silence. "I asked him to do it. It's my fault."

"What's your fault?" Ruby demanded. "This is private

property. Get that trailer out of here. And this damn tractor, too."

"Oh," DeEtta moaned, wringing her hands. "It's mine."

"The tractor's yours?" Ruby asked, knowing that wasn't what DeEtta meant at all.

"No, the trailer." DeEtta's freckles stood out on her pink face. "I—I thought you'd be gone longer," she stammered.

"And you'd have it in place when I got home? I'm not running a trailer park."

Bruce stepped forward. "Go keep an eye on the girl, DeEtta. Ruby and I'll talk."

Ruby turned her attention to Bruce Becket as DeEtta fled without another word, her professional confidence gone, her shoulders hunched as if she expected blows.

Bruce's wide face was in contrast to his thinner, angular body. The expression of clarity, that awareness that he was out of step with the rest of his classmates but he was in the right so it didn't matter, was gone. Bruce appeared tired—and older and, yes, a little bewildered and worn. He looked down at Ruby from beneath the brim of his cap.

"Ruby Crane . . ."

"Don't say 'welcome home,' or I'll scream."

"Your daughter reminds me of you in high school."

"Only a little less animated," Ruby said, pleased at the shocked narrowing of Bruce's eyes. "And don't start any of that innocent local yokel talk. I'm from here, remember? What in hell is this operation?" Ruby waved at the trailer and tractor.

"Let's walk down to the water," Bruce said, motioning toward Blue Lake.

"No thank you. Just kindly climb back in that monster and pull that trailer out of here."

Bruce looked up at the pale sky and put his hands in

the pockets of his coveralls. "DeEtta's not getting along too well at home right now."

"That's not my problem." Ruby took a deep breath, tamping down the spluttering near the surface. "I'm looking for somebody who can take care of my daughter, not somebody else to add to *my* list. My agenda is *full*, do you understand?"

"DeEtta doesn't need taking care of. Her being here will be a solution for everybody."

"For *everybody*? Is that a fact? How?"

"She'll be more on her own, have a chance to get over a heartache and get back on her feet. You'll have a nurse . . ."

"Nurse's aide," Ruby corrected.

". . . nurse's aide right outside your door you can call in the middle of the night if you need to, but DeEtta won't get in the way of your privacy. And you'll save money because DeEtta will take all her wages in rent."

"*All* her wages?"

Bruce's eyes shifted and Ruby suspected he was making this up as he went. "Let her have a few groceries. You'd have a top-notch nurse . . . nurse's aide for practically free."

"She needs the crinkly stuff," Ruby pointed out, rubbing her fingers together. "Real greenbacks. She owns a car, has expenses. I can't support her."

"DeEtta gets a monthly allowance from the farm. That'll get her by."

"Why didn't DeEtta ask me?" Ruby asked, pointing to the little hump-topped trailer.

"She thought you'd see the advantage once everything was in place."

Ruby scuffed her sneakers in the dirt. The money-saving argument was potent. She hadn't faced her money in actual numbers yet but she knew it wasn't good. DeEtta *would* be close by; that could be reassuring, she thought, remembering the shape she'd seen outside the cabin the night before.

"I don't know," she told Bruce. "I don't like the way this was done." Now she understood why DeEtta had avoided talking about her salary; she'd had other plans.

Bruce grinned at her. "It's not much different from the way you used to operate a few years back."

"I was young."

"So's DeEtta. What do you say we try it? I'll set up the trailer beside the old pump house and, if it doesn't work, call me and I'll yank it out of here the same day." He raised his right hand. "Scout's honor."

The trailer wasn't any longer than DeEtta's car. It wasn't really an eyesore. There *were* advantages to the plan. But Ruby's privacy, her fantasy twelve-foot wall ... She absently pulled out her hairband and rebanded her hair. It was Jesse she had to consider. Jesse's health and future.

"If ..." she began. One corner of Bruce's mouth raised. "This is only a trial," she warned him. "I'll make that clear to DeEtta. And I'll hold you to your promise."

"You can count on it."

They shook hands and Bruce swung back up to the tractor's cab, already intent on the complicated maneuvers ahead.

Ruby found DeEtta exercising Jesse's fingers, her back to Ruby, singing "This old man, he played one" in a sweet low voice. DeEtta didn't turn while Ruby unpacked the groceries and Ruby didn't speak to her either.

"Knickknack paddiwack," echoed in Ruby's mind as she left the cabin and Bruce's machinations behind her and walked down to the lake.

She walked to the end of the dock, stepping across the broken board and gazing into the dark water over the dropoff. She'd come to Blue Lake for solitude, for Jesse's recovery, and now she'd taken in a young woman who "wasn't getting along too well at home." Her closest friend had pleaded to speak with her, to share a problem she was reluctant to tell anyone else, but then her husband had died practically in front of Ruby's eyes, a death the sheriff was hesitant to declare accidental.

"Ruby?"

It was Bruce Becket. He held his cap in his hands. "I just wanted to say thanks, Ruby. This will really help DeEtta. Her marriage went sour, and you know how our family is about staying married come hell or Hades. Mom's been pretty hard on her."

Ruby held up her hand. "This is only a temporary situation."

He looked over Ruby's shoulder, a touch of wistfulness in his eyes. "I know. DeEtta needs to get out of Sable. Maybe getting acquainted with you will help her make the move."

"There's no wall around this place."

"She's scared, I guess. She should have gone right after high school. Like you did."

"You're forgetting I didn't finish high school," Ruby reminded Bruce. "And here I am, back again anyway."

"We come back for different reasons than we leave." He waved toward the blue water. "You and Mrs. Pink and the Vietnamese are the only people wintering on this side of the lake."

"The Vietnamese?" Ruby asked, stepping from the dock to the sandy ground.

"There's a family in Capistan's old place. The Congregational church sponsored them."

Ruby leaned down and pulled a piece of tufted grass from its stalk. She chewed on its sweet end. "What about you?" she asked. "Didn't you leave Sable?"

"Just for college in East Lansing. Agriculture. Half of what I learned I had to unlearn and listen to my dad's farming theories. That tickled him for sure."

"Silas Shea stopped by yesterday. That's the way he talked about forestry," Ruby told him.

Bruce shook his head. "Silas," he said, half to himself.

"That sounds like you're omitting the words 'poor bastard,' " Ruby told him.

"I guess I am."

"Why?"

"Some people suspect him in Corbin Turmouski's death. Those two had a battle royal going between them. Who would be more comfortable using a sawmill as a murder weapon than another sawmill operator?"

"You don't really believe Silas killed Corbin, do you?" Ruby asked. "The sheriff hasn't ruled the death a homicide."

"Not yet. Not officially. He will, though. If we're talking about murder, Silas had as much reason as anybody."

"Including you?" Ruby asked, growing irritated with the way Bruce Becket so easily passed judgment.

"Including me," Bruce said calmly. "Somebody's going to tell you sooner or later that Corbin screwed me out of thousands of dollars when he bought the timber off my forty acres behind the old Valley School."

"Then why did you sell it to him?"

Bruce shrugged. "I didn't know how much the trees were worth. Hank Holliday, the forester who came to town a few months ago, filled me in after it was a done deal." His mouth hardened. "Which only made me feel stupider. Corbin knew I was desperate for the money, too, but I guess that wasn't a problem of *his*."

"Couldn't he have made it up to you?" Ruby asked. "That would have been the decent thing to do."

Bruce snorted as if Ruby were being very naive. "How's Mina doing?" he asked.

"I haven't talked to her since . . . yesterday."

"She's kept to herself the past few years. She could use a friend."

"Mina and I hadn't seen each other in two decades, but I never stopped considering myself her friend."

"That's good." He smiled. "Did you know in high school we used to call you two the Dynamic Duo? You're looking good, Ruby," he added without a trace of the clumsy shyness Ruby and her friends had made fun of. "I'm sorry about your daughter."

"She'll recover. She's better every day." When Bruce didn't respond, she asked, "What about you? Do you have a family?"

"You could say that." Bruce flicked off a grasshopper that clung to his pants leg. "I'd better finish leveling that trailer before it gets dark."

"Don't make it too permanent," Ruby told him.

Bruce palmed his cap back on his head and headed toward his tractor. Ruby watched him, noticing his rolling walk, like a movie cowboy's. He stopped near the stand of oaks and turned.

"You might think about a dog," he called back to her.

"A dog?"

"Yeah. Way out here. It's not a bad idea. A watchdog."

"And does DeEtta already have a dog? Is it maybe inside her trailer even as we speak?"

Bruce laughed. "Nope, but I could find one for you. Bet your daughter would like a dog."

"I'll think about it."

"This arrived while you were gone," DeEtta said hesitantly to Ruby, holding out an oblong FedEx package.

Ruby had forgotten about the handwriting job for Ron Kilgore. Her agreement to analyze the will and standards felt as distant as Ron himself.

She broke the sealing tape with a kitchen knife and carried the package to her lab in the loft where she donned disposable gloves before she removed the handwriting samples. Each sample was sealed in a separate plastic envelope, protected by foam core sheets. Ron was a stickler at protecting evidence, saying "I follow the big boys' rules."

Ruby's technique was to take a quick glance at a job before she actually analyzed it. Analysis was cumulative, not just comparing styles or one letter matching another. She developed a feel for the shape and truth of a document from her first glances, like spotting hidden figures in "Magic Eye" pictures, which Ruby always saw immediately. Sometimes in overall, slightly unfocused studies she caught an oddity of spacing or placement she wouldn't see during intensive magnified study.

The documents belonged to Mrs. Andrea Lowell, deceased, and the document in question was a handwritten will. Ruby didn't read the pages, just observed the shapes and lines and rhythm of the words.

The will was written in badly deteriorated—or cleverly disguised—penmanship. From the slant, perhaps written lying in bed. Penmanship deterioration wasn't due to age but to illness. No matter how much of a tremor or change in slant, certain subtle characteristics always remained.

Ruby glanced through the papers one more time, then replaced the documents carefully in the FedEx box, locked them in her metal cabinet, and removed her gloves. She wouldn't look at the documents again until tomorrow. By then her initial glances would have jelled in her subconscious and she'd launch into her examination with confidence.

Ruby, holding a glass of scotch, stood at the cabin window looking out at the night and seeing, in the lighted trailer across the driveway, DeEtta's shadow passing in front of the drawn blinds. A thick black extension cord ran like an umbilical cord from the side of the trailer to the outlet outside the cabin's back door. Bruce had taped the cord to the outlet with silver duct tape, tugging at it twice to be sure it was secure.

Ruby sighed and turned away. "I hope you like her," she told Jesse, who stared intently into the snapping fire in the fireplace, the frown lines deep. "because you'll be seeing a lot of her for the next little while."

Jesse jerked her head as if a fly had buzzed too close and continued watching the flames.

"Is Mina there?" Ruby asked the woman who answered the telephone. "This is Ruby Crane."

"Oh, Ruby. It's Fay, Mina's mother. The doctor gave Mina something to help her sleep. She was awake all night. I'll tell her you called, will that be all right? Everybody's calling. They all want to know . . ." Fay Asauskas's voice faltered. Ruby heard men speaking quietly in the background.

"That'll be fine, Mrs. Asauskas. Thank you. Just tell Mina I'm thinking of her and I'll call later."

Ruby struggled awake, frantically clawing her way out of a nightmare about Stan and the car accident. Even in her dream, she knew the outcome of the long swerve and struggled to rewrite history and free Jesse from the doomed automobile.

The sun had barely risen and Ruby heard voices, unsure at first whether she was still dreaming. She raised her head, pushing back her hair. The voices came through the window she'd opened a few inches last night. A man and a woman, speaking low, but the tones grabbing her attention as if the couple were screaming. The man pleaded, on the edge of desperation; the woman, cold with anger, denied him whatever it was he was asking.

Ruby pulled one of the blankets from the bed and draped it across her shoulders as she silently moved around her lab to the window, the wood floor beneath her feet like cool marble. The voices grew more heated, though no louder.

She pressed close to the window, peering sideways down into the yard, the scenery distorted in her long view through the old slumping glass.

She could only see half of DeEtta Becket's figure, her back stiff, her head held high. Her shoulders moved as if she jerked her arms in emphasis. Their words were incomprehensible except for DeEtta's now-wavering "No, I won't."

Ruby reached for a clean pair of shorts from an unpacked cardboard box. The quarrel had nothing to do with her and Jesse, but here it was, spilling over into her home, directly outside her window. Was this DeEtta's "trouble" that her brother Bruce had referred to? She zipped her shorts and slipped her bare feet into sandals. It was none of her business, but she wouldn't tolerate the complications of DeEtta's life spilling over on Jesse.

The voices abruptly went silent, followed moments later by the closing of the kitchen door, then the kick start and rumble of a motorcycle.

DeEtta was in the kitchen making coffee, her movements tight and angry.

"DeEtta," Ruby said, and DeEtta jumped, knocking over the coffee, spilling dark grounds across the counter and onto the floor.

"Ooh," DeEtta cried, scooping up the bag and holding it to her body, smearing grounds across the front of her sweatshirt. "I was making coffee for you. I'm sorry."

"No, I'm sorry I startled you," Ruby told her as she took over brewing the coffee herself and DeEtta began cleaning up the mess. "Whatever's going on, I'm not interested. But don't let it get mixed up with taking care of Jesse."

"I won't," DeEtta said. "He has a new bike and he wants—"

Ruby held up her hand. "Don't tell me, please. Just don't."

DeEtta nodded and swallowed. "Okay," she said as Ruby left the kitchen.

From the main room, while the coffee brewed, Ruby looked out at the still lake, the morning mists caught against the northeast shore. Not a leaf moved. But gliding toward her dock was a green canoe and Ruby recognized the paddling figure as Silas Shea.

She slipped outside through the front porch and down to the dock, dew wetting her ankles. A few feet offshore, Silas sat in his canoe with the paddle balanced across the gunwales, his face turned toward her. He was dressed in the same work clothes as the day before, with the addition of a faded blue cap that bore the insignia of the USS *Nimitz*. Dark circles bagged under his eyes and he needed a shave.

"Good morning," Ruby said when she was ten feet away. "You're out early."

"I was fishing for bass."

The fishing pole was propped in the canoe, a wormless hook dangling above the water. "Enid baked some bread for you but I left it in the car," he said.

The words hung in the moist morning air, the silence emphasizing his lie. Ruby couldn't imagine Enid baking a loaf of bread for her, not unless Enid suspected Ruby was up to no good, and then she would have delivered it herself in order to sneak a peek.

"Have you heard how Mina's doing?" Silas asked.

"I talked to her mother last night," Ruby told him. "Mina was sleeping. She might welcome a visit from you."

Silas shook his head. "No, she wouldn't. There's talk.

Some people suspect I had something to do with Corbin's death."

"What's the sheriff saying?"

Silas rolled the paddle on the gunwales, back and forth. "He still hasn't made an announcement. I'd swear it was an accident. Corbin was trying to reset the guide pins without turning off his saw. That happens."

"I don't know what that means," Ruby told him.

Silas lifted his hands from the paddle and pointed his two index fingers at one another, leaving a half-inch space between them. "These are guide pins," he said. "Picture a circular saw spinning between them. The guide pins keep the saw spinning straight and steady. When they're set correctly, you get a true cut. When they're not, you can get crooked boards and a worn blade."

"But you're supposed to turn off the saw when you reset the guide pins?" Ruby asked.

Silas nodded. "A guy gets to thinking he knows his sawblade the same way he thinks he knows a woman."

"And Corbin was confident of his skills in his sawmill?" Ruby asked.

"He was."

"I saw the way Corbin butchered Fox Woods," Ruby told him. "Did he always leave such a disaster?"

Silas shook his head. "Corbin and I didn't agree on much but I respected the way he cut his trees. He usually left a clean forest behind him, not a mess of slash and damaged trees like that."

"Did somebody local own Fox Woods?" Ruby asked. Two mallards flapped over them, then came back and neatly landed in unison fifty feet behind Silas.

"No, the owners are from out of the area. They'll probably never see the mess Corbin left—and wouldn't care anyway—but you can bet they've already spent their check." The canoe began to drift and Silas dipped the paddle once, steadying it. "I was curious, do you need to buy a car?"

Had that got around Sable, too? She didn't even have to say it, only think it?

"I have to return my rental in a couple of days. Why? Do you have one for sale?"

"As a matter of fact, I do. It's in mint condition and I'll sell it cheap. It belonged to my sister in Arizona. She was a librarian. Stop by tomorrow and take a look at it."

When Ruby hesitated, Silas said, "Enid plays bridge at ten."

"I'll stop by after I visit Mina."

"Stop before Mina's. You can drive it over, try it out."

"Thanks, Silas."

"You're welcome. I see you got help for your daughter."

"I hired DeEtta Becket."

"She moved in," he said, nodding toward the little trailer just visible in the trees.

"It's temporary," Ruby said.

"Anything the Beckets do temporary they try to make permanent," Silas warned. "DeEtta went to school with the granddaughter we raised. She got mixed up with the middle Greenstone boy and has been paying for it ever since."

"I don't know what DeEtta's story is," Ruby told him. "I'm making it a point to stay out of other people's business."

Silas snorted. "That'll be a saintly trick. Beckets are hard workers, though."

Naming someone a hard worker was probably Silas's highest compliment.

"At least she's out from under Danny Greenstone's thumb," Silas went on.

"Danny Greenstone?" Ruby asked. She'd heard the name recently, but couldn't place it.

"Corbin's off-bearer," Silas explained. "He was supposed to work for Corbin the day of the accident. Didn't show because he got too snockered up the night before."

"DeEtta was married to Danny Greenstone?" Ruby asked.

"She still is, as far as I know."

Chapter 7

When Ruby stepped into the kitchen, the first thing she saw was Jesse, her wheelchair pulled up to the table, gray blobs of oatmeal down the front of her T-shirt, oatmeal crusted on her cheek and a sludgy wad stuck in her hair. DeEtta sat on her right side, encouraging Jesse, who held her spoon in the fist of her left hand.

"What are you doing?" Ruby demanded. "Jesse's left side is too weak to feed herself."

"But she's left-handed, isn't she?" DeEtta asked calmly. "She has to relearn."

Ruby felt the tears at the back of her throat. Since the accident she'd helped Jesse feed and dress herself, kept her daughter clean. And now, here Jesse sat, frowning over a bowl of oatmeal as if it were a mathematical problem, digging a spoon into the bowl like a dagger, sometimes bringing up oatmeal, sometimes not, sometimes getting it to her mouth and often missing completely.

It was what Ruby had wanted, wasn't it? To see Jesse progressing in a two-fisted manner? But she'd failed to envision Jesse filthy or failing. She'd imagined one smooth tidy step at a time. Ruby squeezed her eyes closed and lowered her head. For the first time, Jesse looked damaged.

"I'll clean her up," DeEtta said softly. "Clean as wax, like my mother says. She'll be feeding herself in a few days, you'll see."

° ° °

While she waited for Jesse to take a nap so she could talk to DeEtta about Danny Greenstone, Ruby returned to the loft, unlocked her metal cabinet, and removed the FedEx box and her stereoptic microscope, then spread the five standards and the questioned will on the table.

Mrs. Andrea Lowell. The papers lay in chronological order, from carrot cake recipe through the letter to her granddaughter and the minutes of the Ceramic Queens to her handwritten will. Firm Spencerian handwriting deteriorated at the end to tremulous scratches and broken lines.

Barker Thompson had drilled into Ruby that handwriting examination was a science and had absolutely nothing to do with graphology: the analysis of a personality through handwriting. Ruby didn't confuse the two, but over the years, because she found any handwriting fascinating, she'd come to recognize certain traits and personalities apparent in handwriting samples.

Mrs. Andrea Lowell, Ruby guessed from the smooth connections and rhythm, had been a practical woman, orderly.

First, in every standard except the questioned will, Ruby listed the characteristics consistent in each sample: size and slant, closed os and ds, spacing, the upward stroke of word endings, the odd little hook at the turn of each h, the way her ns and ms had sharp arches forming deep gullies between the humps.

Ron had said Mrs. Lowell suffered from severe arthritis, and the last two documents, most notably the will, reflected her illness: larger writing, laborious lines, heavy pressure, and the loss of smoothness.

She examined the tremor through her microscope. Frequently forgers were inconsistent when copying a tremor, forgetting the quaver in a loop or connection, or even trembling *too* consistently.

Mrs. Lowell's tremor was mainly horizontal, and although the letters were patched, the pen lifted and then restarted to form a continuous line—which was also a frequent indication of copying—the patching was obvious, with no attempt at concealment. Even with the tremor, the hook and the deep gullies were still apparent; so was the now-exaggerated but proportional spacing.

When she'd finished her examination and her report was roughed out, ready to be typed on the typewriter Ron Kilgore had lent her until she could afford a computer, Ruby finally read the documents that she was convinced had been written by Mrs. Andrea Lowell, every one.

Please give your father my love, she'd written to her granddaughter, Patricia, in an otherwise mundane grandmotherly letter. *I hope he will someday remember happier times.*

She then read the labored will, which listed Andrea Lowell's few effects, the largest being her home, which she left to her grown granddaughter, Patricia. *To my son, Dominic, I leave the photograph albums.* That was all. Ruby didn't know but she guessed it was Dominic who had challenged the deathbed will.

Practical Andrea, who'd probably baked a fine carrot cake and made colorful but useless ceramic figurines, had exacted a gentle revenge on an indifferent son. Ruby sighed and rotated her shoulders, thinking how often wounds were inflicted beyond death and resolution. "Unresolved issues" was the buzz term. Not unresolved, but buried—six feet under.

She stripped off her gloves and dropped them in the trash, then returned to the world of the living, conscious for the first time of the spicy odor of baking wafting through the loft. She'd always possessed the ability to shut down every other sense while she concentrated. It had angered her father, amused her mother, irritated Stan. "I'm a laser beam," she'd told long-ago friends.

"Were you keeping it a secret that you're married to Danny Greenstone, Corbin Turmouski's off-bearer?" Ruby asked DeEtta, who was sliding a pan of cookies from the oven.

DeEtta paused, then set the pan heavily on the stove top. "You said you weren't interested in my personal life," she accused Ruby with a touch of sullenness.

"You're right; that's exactly what I said," Ruby conceded. "Can we meet halfway? Was that Danny you were arguing with this morning?"

DeEtta nodded. "He wants me to come back to him," she said in a flat voice.

"But you're not divorced?"

"Not yet. He drinks."

"Is that really why he didn't show up for work the day Corbin died?"

DeEtta tapped the edge of the hot pan with her finger as if testing its temperature. "Danny came home at three in the morning; he didn't even take off his boots. I couldn't wake him up at six." She twisted the dish towel she'd used as a hot pad, her face drawn. "I'd already told Danny I was going to leave him and he said that was why he drank too much, because I'd hurt him so bad. We lived behind my parents and after Corbin died, Bruce threw Danny out."

DeEtta sat down at the kitchen table and neatly folded the dish towel into a square. "We had money problems."

Why was it, Ruby wondered, when money was lacking for the basics of life, there was always money available to drink too much?

"Was Corbin planning to fire Danny?" Ruby asked.

"I don't know. *I* would have." DeEtta looked up, her eyes troubled and shiny with tears. "Danny *did* drink more after I decided to leave. If Danny had gone to work, Corbin might still be alive." DeEtta's voice caught. "Danny said it was partly my fault Corbin died."

Ruby leaned across the table and gripped DeEtta's shoulders, resisting the urge to shake her. "No, DeEtta," she said firmly. "Corbin's death has *nothing* to do with you. Don't let anyone else blame you, either. Not anyone."

DeEtta lowered her head, her face still doubtful, and Ruby patted her shoulder and leaned back, surprised such a seemingly strong young woman could be convinced she was guilty for her husband's actions.

"I don't want Danny coming to the cabin," Ruby said. "If he starts hanging around, I'll ask Bruce to move your trailer out of here," she warned. "I have to think of Jesse."

DeEtta nodded. "I don't want him here, either, but if I tell him that . . ."

"If I see him, *I'll* tell him," Ruby said, realizing she didn't have a clue what Danny looked like; she'd only heard the timbre of his voice through her bedroom window.

Ruby stopped at Sable's brick post office before her first afternoon of work at Mabel's studio. As she got out of the car, a Northern Timber semi rumbled past towing a double load of pine bolts. Shreds of bark dropped onto the street and twirled like falling leaves. The logs were all identical in size, probably from the CCC plantations.

Ruby laid the package containing Mrs. Andrea Lowell's will on the counter. "I'd like to send this by registered overnight mail, please."

"It must be important," the clerk said.

He laid the paperwork for her package smartly in front of her. "You've got general delivery mail waiting for you, from California. I was going to put it in your dad's mailbox if you didn't come in pretty soon."

"Now that I'm here you won't have to."

He nodded. "He was in here about an hour ago. Old Albert Conley brought him in." He snorted. "Talk about the blind leading the blind. Don't forget to sign right there."

The clerk gave her a key to her mailbox and a letter from beneath the counter. It was from Todd. Under the clerk's attentive gaze, she slipped the letter in her pocket and left the building, conscious of the clerk still watching her.

Two men stood talking beside a planter of fading petunias outside the post office, both dressed in dark suits. Ruby was about to pass by when one of them said, "Hi again."

Ruby stopped and regarded the handsome smiling man in front of her, then recognized Hank Holliday, the forester she'd offered a ride. "Hi," she said. "I didn't recognize you in . . ."

"In civilized clothes?" he finished. "So clothes really *do* make the man?"

In a way, Ruby admitted to herself, they *did* make a difference. Before she could respond, Hank held out his hand. "Don't answer that. I'm Hank Holliday."

"Ruby Crane," she said, shaking his hand. His hands were large, his handshake firm.

"This is Glenn Wister," he said, nodding to the man beside him.

"Wally Kentner introduced us yesterday," Glenn Wister said, smiling, not offering to shake hands. He was a small man, jovial looking with a brush mustache.

"I remember," Ruby said. "You're with Northern Timber."

Incredibly, on the plate-glass window behind him, just to the left of his shoulder, hung a poster advertising the Color Festival. In the lower left corner was a photograph of Glenn Wister, the words beneath his picture reading OUR GRAND MARSHAL, GLENN WISTER.

"You're the grand marshal of the Color Festival parade?" Ruby asked, nodding to the poster. "I thought only the mayor received such an honor."

Hank Holliday made a sweeping gesture toward Wister. "Meet the man who's responsible for Sable's new football field, the new ambulance, and the repair of the clock on city hall. Local hero."

Wister actually blushed. "It's an honor," he said. "I'd better get going. Nice to meet you, Ruby."

When Wister was out of hearing range, Hank said in a low voice, "It's an honor, all right. Profits must be running high at Northern Timber."

"Does he own Northern Timber?"

Hank shook his head. "No, but he's their wheeler-dealer timber buyer. Probably works on commission." He shrugged. "You have to appreciate somebody who spreads the wealth, though, don't you? Even if he does make it off the backs of the ignorant." He grinned at Ruby and asked, "Can I walk you wherever you're going?"

She pointed to her car in the parking lot. "It's not far. Do you have an office in town?"

He frowned, then said, "Oh, you mean because of the suit? No, I just came from Corbin's funeral lunch."

In shock, Ruby realized she hadn't considered attending Corbin's funeral. Not once had it crossed her mind.

"You okay?" Hank asked.

Ruby nodded. She hated funerals, but the lunch; why hadn't she gone? "I thought you were on the other side of the fence from the timber people like Corbin and Glenn Wister?"

"I am in philosophy, but that doesn't have anything to do with life and death, at least not usually. You've been talking about me."

"You have come up in conversation," Ruby said.

"So have you." He shook his head sadly. "I'm sorry you were there when Corbin died, but if Mina had been alone . . . She's a fragile woman." He paused. "Corbin's death has everybody spooked. If the sheriff would declare it either an accident or a murder, the talk would die down."

"Carly's cautious," Ruby said.

"Yeah, I know. There probably hasn't been a murder here in years, and he'd like to solve one of his own." He opened her car door for her. "I'm parked beside you," he said, pointing to a dusty four-wheel-drive Cherokee parked half out of its parking space.

"Then you had your car repaired," Ruby said.

"Luckily I have two vehicles. Auto number one is in a garage in Pere. I did say I'd tell you the story sometime, didn't I?"

"You did. The garage in Sable couldn't fix it?" She got in and he gently closed the door.

"Wouldn't, not couldn't," he said, giving an exasperated shake of his head, loosening his groomed hair. He leaned against her car. Closer, she could see that his eyes were hazel, his lashes thicker than she attained with a mascara wand.

"What was wrong with it?" she asked.

"Sugar in the gas tank."

"Oh. So you've been in town long enough to make enemies?" Ruby asked.

"That's an even longer story. It might take an evening over dinner to tell it to you."

"Call me," Ruby said. "My phone number's unlisted but just ask Peggy Dystix at Sable Telephone Company. She'll give it to you."

Ruby drove through town to Mabel's, noting more

citizens on Sable's streets dressed as if they'd just come from church. Why hadn't she considered attending the funeral of her oldest friend's husband? Did she believe herself too much of an outsider to have the right?

Mabel stuck her head through the black curtain at the back of the office and said, "I'm shooting the Patronases' sixty-fifth anniversary. Go ahead and perform your promised miracles."

Ruby surveyed the piles of paper, the tipsy stacks of magazines, the green bean carton of proof folders blocking the file cabinet, dirty glasses, and Little Debbie cookie boxes. Color Festival raffle tickets were thumbtacked to the bare walls, slips of paper stuck to the phone, notes attached to notes. All of them in Mabel's vertical printed hand, with slashes replacing loops, undotted *i*s, and hastily crossed *t*s.

Ruby began by mining the heaped desk, burrowing toward the desktop and liberating the telephone, finding along the way an appointment book Mabel hadn't used since January 21, nine months ago.

Mabel ushered out the elderly couple, Mrs. Patronas leaning on her husband as he bent over a spider-legged aluminum cane, both of them frail, parchment-skinned.

They halted beside Ruby and Mrs. Patronas said in her fading voice, "Your mother, God rest her soul, was a saint."

"She was, Mrs. Patronas," Ruby said politely. "She was a martyr."

Mabel closed the door behind the Patronases and, when the hanging bell had subsided, said to Ruby, "She was, wasn't she? Your mother, I mean. A martyr. I wonder if she intended to be . . ." Mabel's voice faded away as she drifted into deep thought. "I wish I'd taken a picture," she said, and wandered off to her darkroom.

Ruby sorted through pages of portrait proofs Mabel

had never filed or even organized into folders, many of them faces she recognized, marking all their life's events: births, marriages, anniversaries.

"Mina Asau ... Turmouski showed me the black and-white photograph you took of Corbin," Ruby told Mabel when she paused to marvel over Ruby's progress.

Mabel nodded as she unwrapped a box of film. "That poor kid. Corbin always fascinated me: his powerful body and withered leg, making his living destroying powerful trees. Lots of diametrics to catch in a photo."

"And you captured them?"

"As much as he would allow." She tossed the film wrapper in the trash, saying "Live by the sword, die by the sword."

"What kind of a man was Corbin?" Ruby asked.

Mabel shrugged again, frowning. "Determined. Adored his wife, I think. He took his limp too seriously, and I got the impression he spent a considerable amount of time looking over his shoulder. How should I know, Ruby?" she asked in irritation, taking a step toward her darkroom. "I'm a photographer, not a psychologist. Dig up the proofs if you want. Read his obituary. Ask his wife. Don't ask me."

"Can you take a break for a short walk?" Mary Jean asked, phoning from Wally Kentner's real estate office.

Ruby hadn't really expected Mary Jean to call and it took her a second to picture the dark-haired woman with the scarred chin. She glanced at her watch. She'd been straightening Mabel's office nonstop for two hours. "Sure. I'll meet you at Wally's office."

Ruby paused at Porter and First to watch a pickup drive past, pulling a farm wagon. Three teenage girls sat on the wagon, holding down incomprehensible wood–and–chicken wire structures, waving like festival queens from the nascent Color Festival float.

"Wally's out showing property," Mary Jean told Ruby as she tucked a folder in her desk drawer, pushing back her curly dark hair.

"Can you still go for a walk?"

"Sure." Mary Jean scribbled *Back at 3:30* on a piece of paper and taped it to the office door.

"Aren't you going to lock?" Ruby asked.

"If anybody comes in, Fran at the drug store will see them," Mary Jean said, waving across the street toward Paulas's Drug Store.

Mary Jean was a serious walker: long purposeful strides, arms swinging. They passed the gas station, the Wak 'n Yak, and followed the looping road around the high school.

"How long have you worked for Wally?" Ruby asked.

"Two years. I'm studying for my real estate license."

"Wally seems successful."

"He needs a little competition." Mary Jean grinned and pointed her finger into her chest. "Me. He sells a lot of property to buyers out of the area, advertises in big city papers, hunts buyers down. I plan to concentrate more on local transactions."

They slowed near the high school, and the only changes Ruby could see was an addition to the parking lot; it was filled to capacity.

"So what do you think of the news?" Mary Jean asked Ruby.

"What news?"

Mary Jean raised her eyebrows. "You haven't heard? Carly announced he's investigating Corbin's death as a 'possible homicide.'"

"*Possible* homicide?" Ruby asked, pausing midstride. "Why?"

"Nobody knows. I mean, nobody's told *me*. The

town's burning down with rumors. Some people claim Carly's just trying to get attention. But . . ."

"What?" Ruby asked.

Mary Jean rolled her eyes. "This is completely gossip but it's too good not to tell. You make the connection if you want to. Carly made the homicide announcement this morning. When his wife went home for lunch, guess what she found on their front porch?"

"Probably not a congratulations note," Ruby ventured. They parted around a young woman pushing a stroller.

"A dead turkey vulture," Mary Jean said with a touch of glee. "Gross, huh?"

"Definitely. I wonder if Mina's heard Carly's decision."

"I guess Carly told Mina's mother right after the funeral."

Boys in team shirts grunted through calisthenics in the new football field.

"Did you talk to Mina at the funeral?" Ruby asked.

"Briefly," Mary Jean said, shaking her head sadly. "She sleepwalked through it."

At five o'clock, the bell on Mabel's door jangled and Sheriff Carly Joyce, Jr., entered the studio.

"Can I talk to you for a few minutes, Ruby?" he asked, smoothing down the shirt of his uniform.

"Sure," Ruby told him. "I was just about to head home."

Carly looked around the office, then out the window toward his patrol car. "Maybe someplace more private," he said.

Mabel stepped into the office from her darkroom. "For God's sake, Carly, stay and talk to her here, not in your car like she's some kind of criminal. I'm going to eat supper now, anyway. Lock the door when you leave,

Ruby." Mabel left through the door that connected the studio to her house, closing it behind herself with a sharp click.

Carly sat in one of the straightback waiting chairs. He wasn't a big man but in his uniform and solemnity, he seemed too large for the chair. He looked at the door Mabel had closed and shook his head. "That woman still makes me nervous."

"Mabel?" Ruby asked.

"When I was a kid she took a picture of me with my finger up my nose. Sent it to me in a congratulations card when I was elected sheriff. It makes you worry what other pictures she has tucked away to spring on you."

"I'll let you know if I find anything too incriminating," Ruby teased.

"Thanks," Carly said seriously.

"Is it true you're declaring Corbin's death a possible homicide?"

Carly uncrossed his legs and leaned forward, resting his elbows on his knees, his hands clasped. "Yes, it is."

"Why *possible*?" Ruby asked. "What makes you suspect a murder? I was there."

"You were in the house," Carly corrected.

"I thought there was evidence Carly was adjusting guide pins without turning off his saw."

"That's one possibility."

"And what's another possibility?" Ruby asked. She set aside the Johnson baby's baptismal proofs.

"That's what I'm here to talk about." Carly removed a ballpoint pen from his shirt pocket and turned it in his hands, clicking it.

"I've only been in Sable a few days," Ruby told him. "What could I possibly know about Corbin Turmouski's death?"

Carly removed a folded piece of typing paper and jotted a few words on it. "It's about Mina."

"Mina?" Ruby repeated. She got up from the desk and sat in a chair beside Carly. It was a strategy Ron Kilgore used when he was wheedling the details from a client: trust me.

"She came to my office about a week ago," Carly said. "She was troubled about Corbin but ended up not telling me a damn thing. She changed her mind in the middle of a sentence." He pulled his chair closer to Ruby, and she wondered if he was employing the same closeness-breeds-trust tactic she was attempting. "I've talked to her since Corbin died but she's not willing to continue that conversation."

"Maybe it's too soon," Ruby suggested. "Or maybe whatever she had to say doesn't matter now that Corbin's dead."

"That could be," Carly said. He shifted on his chair. "I'm aware you two are close friends. Did she mention any fears about Corbin to you?"

Ruby considered the question. "She did say she was worried about Corbin," Ruby told Carly. "But Corbin came home and we didn't finish the conversation. She thought he worked too hard, trying to make his sawmill successful."

"He was that," Carly said. "But that's not a subject she'd bring to me. What she had in mind was more serious."

"Are you basing your suspicions of murder on an unfinished conversation with Mina?" Ruby asked.

"You sound like . . ." Carly began and then stopped, scratching his chin.

"I sound like who?" Ruby asked, jumping on what Carly had left unsaid. "Is somebody pressuring you to declare Corbin's death an accident? Who's leaning on you? I heard about the turkey vulture."

He shrugged his shoulders without looking at Ruby. "Don't jump to conclusions, Ruby. People always want definitive answers," he said. "But only the answers that suit their theories. If you say the word homicide, people begin pointing fingers."

"At Silas?" Ruby asked. There was a thump against the wall and Ruby turned to see the paper boy crossing Mabel's yard.

"He and Corbin were always at each other's throats," Carly said. "Corbin was a fool to build his sawmill right across the road from Silas's."

"When did he do that?"

"Five, six years ago. Corbin read in some hot-shot business magazine if the same kinds of businesses situated themselves in the same area, they all drew in more customers."

"It sounds reasonable for clothing stores and car dealerships," Ruby questioned, "but sawmills that far out in the country?"

"Exactly," Carly agreed. "They ended up like two little nations aiming their warheads at one another. Bell Road was their line in the sand. One other thing I'd like to ask you."

"Sure."

"Do you remember what Corbin said about the job he was doing?"

Ruby thought back, remembering Corbin gently reassuring Mina that he could run the sawmill alone. "Only that it was a rush job for somebody who was planning to pick up the wood the next day."

"Who?" Carly's face was still, his attention completely on Ruby.

"Lyle somebody."

"Zander?"

"He didn't say. Who's Lyle Zander?"

"A builder in Pere."

Carly's face was closed, expressionless, but still, Ruby caught the alertness there. He was on to something.

"There was no order for a rush job, was there?" Ruby guessed. "And that, combined with Mina's unfinished conversation, is why you declared Corbin's death a homicide, right?"

"You're jumping to conclusions again, Ruby." He looked at her in entreaty. "But I'd be grateful if you didn't feed that bit of information to the gossips."

"I won't," she promised, repeating the name of Lyle Zander in her head, memorizing it.

Carly clipped his pen to his pocket and gathered himself to rise. "I'd never ask you to rat on your friend, Ruby, but if Mina *does* say anything to you, will you encourage her to come talk to me?"

"I will," Ruby promised.

Ruby drove slowly between the rows of shade trees that lined the narrow lane through the cemetery. Chestnuts spread like the poem over granite tombstones.

She didn't glance at the familiar surnames on the headstones. She hadn't planned to come here; she'd left Mabel's, intending to stop somewhere quiet to read her letter from Todd.

Halfway through the cemetery, beside the ravine that bisected the grounds, Ruby stopped her car. There was a new grave across from Gram's: ALICE MARY CRANE, the plain marble stone read; he hadn't even allowed her her maiden name on the tombstone, marking her as his from birth to death.

That one glance was enough. Ruby removed Todd's letter from her pocket, smiling at the careful straight penmanship on the single folded sheet.

"You'll figure out my deepest secrets from the way I loop my *h*s and cross my *t*s," he'd said.

He missed her. He offered airfare without strings. Work was hellacious. It was a determinedly cheery letter that made Ruby's heart ache. She closed her eyes and sat awhile, her head against the headrest, smelling the musky scent of autumn.

The sound of a car engine behind her disturbed her reverie. She peered into her rearview mirror and saw a large brown automobile stopped behind her. Two men sat in the front seat, both wearing old-fashioned felt hats, the driver's head barely above the steering wheel. She recognized the passenger, even in shadow, the way he sat so ramrod straight, the hawked nose. It was her father.

The motor of the big brown car was switched off and silence covered the cemetery, interrupted by the *pings* of the cooling engine.

Ruby sat up and reached for the ignition key. She forced herself to smoothly, slowly drive away without looking again in the rearview mirror, thinking her father was still a hypocrite, no matter how often he visited her mother's grave.

"Did you finish it?" Ron Kilgore demanded.

"It's in the mail," Ruby assured him. "Overnight delivery."

"Couldn't you FedEx it?"

"Their office is twenty-three miles away."

"Of course it is." Ron sighed and Ruby heard the tap-tap of his fingers against his desktop. "Are you back in the small-town saddle?"

"It's more complicated than I remember," Ruby said.

"No it's not; you're just older."

"Remember when I told you my friend's husband had died?"

"Yeah. Men do that."

"He died in his sawmill."

"Ouch." He paused. "It wasn't an accident and you're getting mixed up in it, am I right?"

"Only by association." She related Sheriff Carly's visit to Mabel's studio and his questions about Mina.

"She's hiding something," Ron said. "Find out how

heavily this guy was insured. Maybe you just showed up at the wrong time and there weren't supposed to be any witnesses."

"No, she really loved him, I'm sure of it."

"Love of money is stronger than love of man, I guarantee it."

"Well, I don't intend to become involved," Ruby told him again.

Ron snorted and Ruby pulled the phone away from her ear, but she still heard Ron Kilgore say, "I know you better than that, Ruby Crane."

Chapter 8

After Ruby confirmed her visit with Mina, she timed her arrival at Silas Shea's to inspect the car he was selling for ten-fifteen, hoping Enid had kept her bridge date. The garage doors stood wide on an empty stall and she took that as a good sign.

Glossy Rhode Island Red chickens scratched in the yard, scattering huffily when Ruby opened her car door. A tabby cat lay curled on a stack of burlap sacks on the back porch.

Silas Shea opened the back door to Ruby's knock, his hair mussed and his eyes red as if she'd interrupted his nap. "Ruby," he said, glancing over his shoulder at the kitchen clock. "Come on in while I get the keys to the car."

Ruby stepped into Enid's kitchen, a large harvest kitchen. One end of the long room held a console television and easy chairs.

"I'll be right back," Silas said. "Make yourself at home."

A lighted picture of the Last Supper hung over the couch, the bulb behind Christ's head forming an electric halo.

Ruby perused a row of videos: *The Littlest Rebel*, *Bright Eyes*, *The Little Princess*. All Shirley Temple movies.

"Here we are," Silas said, returning to the room and holding a set of car keys. He'd combed his hair and washed up. "It's in the barn."

A white Pinto station wagon sat in the barn beside the remains of a hayloft. At first glance it appeared in perfect condition, without rust or dents, just as Silas had promised.

"My sister was a stickler for oil changes and tune-ups. Since she was a librarian, she did it all by the book, if you know what I mean. Runs like a champ."

"What about parts if it breaks down?" Ruby asked. "It's twenty years old."

"Nothing to it. The junkyard's full of Pintos. Go ahead and drive it around awhile."

Ruby took the car keys from Silas and got in. "If you don't mind, I'll stop by Mina's on my way back."

"Take your time. I'll be at the mill." Silas waved in the direction of his sawmill. He bent down and pulled a thistle from the ground with his bare hands. "Would you mind doing something for me?" he asked casually. Ruby's hand froze as she reached toward the ignition key.

"If I can," she said, just as casually.

"Could you take a quick glance at something in Corbin Turmouski's mill for me?"

"I doubt if Mina and I will tour the scene where her husband died."

Silas's face was dead serious. "I'd do it myself, but Mina'd take it wrong coming from me. You've heard the talk. What do you think would happen if she saw me poking around the sawmill? It'd only take you a second. I'll pay you."

"If you're offering to pay me, Silas, there's more involved than a 'quick glance.'"

"Not for you," Silas said fervently. "You've had experience."

"Can't you ask somebody else?" Ruby asked him, choosing not to explore what kind of "experience" Silas believed she had.

Silas shook his head. "Not around Sable."

"Mina's my friend," Ruby told him. "I won't do anything behind her back."

"I promise you, this has nothing to do with Mina. In fact, it might put her mind at ease. In exchange, I'll bring you enough firewood to get you through the winter. You could heat your cabin for free. Won't cost you a red cent."

"I won't do this for pay, Silas," Ruby said. "Keep your firewood. If the opportunity comes up, I may look. If it doesn't, I won't. I'm not turning a visit to a friend into a sleuthing fest."

"Understood. I appreciate it. Now let me explain what I want you to look for." He paused. "I mean if you get the chance."

The Pinto felt low to the ground, heavy and steady. Ruby could change her own oil when money was tight or fix a flat in an emergency. Beyond that, she wasn't interested. A car either ran or it didn't run, period.

She drove to the south, then turned around in front of a sloping field thick with pumpkins, brilliant orange globes among dying leaves and vines, and headed back.

As she turned into Mina's wide shaded driveway, she saw Corbin's mill standing still and silent, the huge doors rolled closed. A green garbage bag lay in the mill's sandy yard, its edges fluttering.

Mina stood by her kitchen door, her arms crossed, a small figure in baby blue, her hair pulled back in a tight knot. Ruby got out, warily looking for the black-and-white collie, but it was nowhere in sight.

She embraced Mina and, for a moment, Mina clung to her, her arms tight. "I'm sorry," Ruby said.

Mina took a step back and nodded, smiling slightly. "Everybody is," she said. "Come in. I remembered the coffee this time."

The rooms were cool and as silent as Corbin's mill.

No dirty dishes or music. Ruby had a sudden urge to walk over and lay her palm on the television to test if it was warm, the way her father used to do to discover if she and Phyllis had been wasting their time watching TV. Except in Mina's case, Ruby hoped she *had* been watching TV, anything to take her out of herself for a little while.

Mina carried a tray into the living room that held two cups of poured coffee and a glass plate of cookies and chocolate cake. "My freezer's full of food," she said. "Enid Shea brought over a carrot cake; she said she knew it was Corbin's favorite—isn't *that* weird?"

"Not from Enid," Ruby said.

Mina laughed a single note and handed Ruby a cup. "I guess not. I've had an offer to buy the sawmill already, and my mother's asked me to move in with her. I think she hopes Randy will come back."

"Randy?" Ruby asked.

"My son. Mine and Ford Goodlight's. He's fifteen. Randy and Corbin didn't get along too well. Nothing serious but Randy got to be a handful for us. Ford owns a gun shop over by Cadillac. Definitely more exciting than living in the woods and sawing up logs." Mina tipped her head. "Although *being* sawed up made Corbin more interesting than Ford to Randy for a couple of days."

Words dropped from Mina's mouth as if they'd been dammed there. Ruby imagined Mina sitting in her Spartan house alone after the funeral and everyone had gone home, the words rising behind clamped lips, waiting to spill out.

"The funeral was packed," Mina told her. "It was an open casket."

Ruby felt a prickle along her arms. She listened, reluctant but undeniably enthralled.

"They just put him back together. In a suit jacket,

and the way the casket lid comes up to here, you couldn't tell. People feel cheated if it's a closed casket."

"Oh," Ruby couldn't keep herself from saying. Mina blinked and looked into Ruby's face curiously. Her eyes were dry, her pupils wide and black.

"Does that make you sick?" Mina asked Ruby.

"No. Well, maybe a little."

"I've been reading the papers, looking for people who've died worse deaths," Mina said. "Corbin's was fast, I think. I read about a woman who died in a car fire; that probably took a long time. For a little while it made me feel better about Corbin. Don't you think Corbin died fast?" Mina asked Ruby.

"I'm sure it was very fast," Ruby assured her, not saying she believed that everybody, in those last milliseconds, knew what hit them. Her mother had known. Stan knew. She touched Mina's corded wrist. "Mina, do you have someone you can talk to: a counselor?"

Mina shook her head. "I couldn't *pay* somebody just to talk."

"In California everybody and his dog sees a therapist. I have. It helps, I promise." Ruby sipped her coffee. It was cold, as if it had been poured hours ago.

"Oh no, I couldn't," Mina said, shaking her head and pulling back into herself, pressing against the back of her chair.

"Are you going to stay here?" Ruby asked, leaning forward to counter Mina's pulling away. Come back.

Mina looked out the window toward the long red building. "I'll sell the sawmill. Sometimes at night I think I hear it start up."

"Then get rid of it. It's too lonely out here. Move into Sable, or even Pere."

"Maybe. It's complicated."

"It only seems complicated right now."

"And this too shall pass?"

"Exactly."

Mina's hands twisted over one another and then abruptly went still. She made fists and pressed them against her hips.

"Mina," Ruby said firmly. "You can't stay out here alone. I'll drive you to your mother's, or you can stay with me on Blue Lake."

Mina shook her head. "Not yet." She took another sip of her cold coffee. "Do you remember when we used to hang around the junkyard and sit in those cars?"

Ruby hadn't thought of that in years. They'd been ten or eleven, immortal. The junkyard was behind the Shell station on the edge of Sable, and sometimes, after fatal accidents, she and Mina would sneak through the fence and sit in death vehicles, deliciously trying to imagine. Pondering the crumpled windshield, the missing back-seat, wondering why the steering wheel was gone. Sometimes they'd find things, like buttons or marbles under the seats, a letter, once a flashlight that still worked, and they'd take those macabre items home as souvenirs. Strangely, Ruby couldn't recall ever seeing any blood. But there must have been. Perhaps their imaginations wouldn't allow the intrusion of that much reality.

"We didn't understand what we were seeing," Ruby said.

"Yes we did," Mina protested. "Children are too inexperienced to have compassion for death. When I recover from this," she said, one corner of her mouth raising, "I'll have more compassion than God."

"If you feel like visiting or talking," Ruby said, "call me. Any time. I mean it."

"You would come rushing to my rescue?" she asked.

"If I was able," Ruby assured her.

"What are people saying?" Mina asked. She picked up a wafer cookie, then broke it into pieces on a napkin without eating it.

"Not much," Ruby told her.

Mina snorted. "Bull. Who do they blame? Tell me."

"Some people have mentioned Silas."

Mina nodded and her eyes went blank, staring over Ruby's left shoulder.

"What was it you wanted to tell me the other day, Mina?" Ruby asked softly. "About Corbin?"

"It doesn't matter now."

"Did it concern Corbin's death?"

"He and Silas . . ." she began. "No, it really doesn't matter now."

"I already know they were competing against each other for timber property."

"Not just for trees to saw down, but in every phase of the business. It's cutthroat—" She stopped and closed her eyes.

Ruby asked, "Is that why some people think Silas was responsible for Corbin's death?"

"Silas wouldn't be my first choice," Mina said.

"How about Enid?" Ruby offered without thinking.

Mina's eyes widened and she burst into giggles. Ruby joined her. Finally Mina wiped her eyes. "Enid could slice you to ribbons with her tongue; she doesn't need a saw." She sobered. "Enid . . . she tries. At the lunch after the funeral she told me it was a shame I'd already gone through two husbands when I wasn't even forty. 'It doesn't look good,' she said."

As Mina walked Ruby to the kitchen door, she said, "I heard you met Hank Holliday."

"How did you hear *that*?" Ruby asked.

"He stopped by last night. He was trying to be subtle but even in my self-absorbed grief I could see he was interested. Are you?"

"I've only met him once," Ruby told her. "Did he and Corbin work together?"

"Not together, not if they could help it. When Hank first arrived in Waters County, he stole a forest from

Corbin, to manage it instead of cut it. Hank and Corbin had words." Mina shrugged. "But I liked him."

Outside the door, Mina said, "Oh, I have something for you. Don't leave yet," and she turned and hurried back into the house.

Ruby glanced at Corbin's sawmill. "Just one peek," Silas had said, and here, clearly being offered to her, was the opportunity to look for the metal contraption he'd described.

Ruby swiftly crossed the driveway and mill yard to the building that held the saw. The ground was rutted from heavy machinery, bare of plant life.

A single door gaped open on the narrow end of the closed building and as she walked toward it, a sickly sweet smell and a flash of silver next to a stack of cut boards caught Ruby's attention.

Thrown together in a rotting jumble were flowers: in foil-wrapped pots, in vases and baskets, a wreath with a black ribbon. Wrinkled and stained sympathy cards were still attached to the withering plants.

After one long look, Ruby left the detritus of Corbin's funeral and slipped through the door into the shadowy sawmill.

What hit her first were the odors of sawdust and fuel, held captive inside the mill. The sawing device stretched in front of Ruby, an alien contraption of pulleys, belts, rollers, levers, and mechanisms. One of those machines, Ron Kilgore would have said, that "you need a penis to understand."

She walked the length of the machinery, moving deeper into the dim building, her hands held close to her side, her footsteps on the sawdust-softened concrete floor silent and wary.

A square log sat on the carriage in preparation of going through the saw. At the opposite end, freshly sawn boards lay haphazardly, half off the rollered track.

This was the wood Corbin had been sawing when he died. The rush order.

The round saw blade stood out prominently, like an evil rising moon. The steel blade was as big as a tractor tire. Ruby stepped closer to its circle of hooked teeth, drawn by the blade's size and shape, its motionlessness. What had it done?

Just as Silas had described, there were two levers near the saw blade and a grated platform where the operator stood. The platform was shockingly close to the blade with its teeth hooking forward, spinning toward the operator.

Ruby balanced herself with her hands on the oily platform and peered down low into the oncoming blade. She spotted the guide pins like two fingers against the blade, unable to imagine reaching in to adjust them while the saw revolved.

But the guide pins weren't what she'd come to see. "Near the tallest lever," Silas had instructed, "the one that rises in front of the platform, look for a metal brace like a small church kneeler, only the padded part is at thigh level." Then he'd added as if he were giving road directions, "You can't miss it."

Well, either it wasn't there or Ruby *could* miss it. Even in the gloomy building, Ruby was sure if the brace existed as Silas described it, it would be unmistakable. But she didn't see it. It wasn't there.

She backed away from the saw, straightened, and permitted her eyes to see the dark stains beside the saw blade, the splatters, wondering. It was too dark to tell. A late-summer fly buzzed sluggishly past her and disappeared into the gloom.

Ruby reached a hand toward the blade and gently touched one jagged tooth with the tip of her finger, feeling the cool curve, the thicker point. The iron teeth were smaller than she expected, closer together. They curved delicately like rows of quarter moons. She was surprised by the amount of rust on the blade.

No, it wasn't rust. She jerked away her hand and stepped backward, two steps, four, six, bumping into the hanging door behind her, sending it rocking and vibrating in its track like thunder.

"Oh, shit," she whispered, heading for the open door where the sunlight shone while the hanging door still shuddered behind her.

As she stepped gratefully into the autumn afternoon, Ruby glanced toward Mina's house. Her friend was at the screen door, pushing it open with her shoulder, but for no reason Ruby suspected Mina wasn't stepping out of the kitchen at that moment, that she'd been standing there behind the screen, waiting for Ruby to leave the sawmill.

Mina offered a foil-covered plate to Ruby. "It's Enid Shea's carrot cake. I can't eat it."

Ruby protested but Mina said, "Please. I'd like you to have it. Enid's a good cook."

"I know. She left me chocolate chip cookies once," Ruby said, taking the plate. "Thank you. My daughter will love it."

"Oh, Ruby. I've been so overwhelmed, I've never even asked you about your daughter. How is she?"

"She's better," Ruby told her. "Why don't you come over for dinner on Sunday and meet her?"

"It's silly, I know," Mina said, "but I can't think that far ahead. Can I call you?"

"That's fine. Call me anytime, please. I mean it."

Glancing in her rearview mirror as she turned onto the gravel road, Ruby saw Mina's small figure standing in her driveway, but instead of watching Ruby's departure, she'd turned to face the sawmill where her husband had died.

Chapter 9

Ruby parked the Pinto near her rental car and walked to Silas's sawmill. She swallowed as she approached the mill, hearing the familiar scream of a circular saw cutting through logs.

Silas stood in front of a lever similar to Corbin's, his complete attention on the operation. At the other end of the machinery a stoop-shouldered man, Silas's off-bearer, pulled freshly sawn boards off the rollers and stacked them in various piles. Both men wore ear protectors. Ruby felt the grumble and scream of the machinery in the bones behind her ears. The air was fragrant with fresh-cut wood.

Silas pulled a lever and a log rolled onto the carriage. Three steel devices clamped down on it, securing the log so that when Silas pulled the upright lever in front of him, the carriage rolled forward on narrow-gauge train rails. With a high-pitched whine, the log rode through the spinning circular saw, which sliced off a slab of wood with dread ease and efficiency. Sawdust flew, the new board slid forward, and the carriage moved backward. Silas released the devices holding the log and, using the smaller lever and his hip, turned the log and reclamped it. Another whine of the steel and another board shot forward. The skinny man at the end grabbed for the new board as it came at him.

The whole operation was blindingly fast. Forward, slice. Back. Rhythmic and hypnotic. The blade turned with such speed the hooked teeth were invisible. Silas moved like a man performing a mechanized dance, matching his speed to the machine, his eyes intent on the procedure.

After three logs had been turned into raw boards, Silas's off-bearer made a hand motion and Silas pulled a switch. The engine died down but the blade continued spinning, whistling like a strong wind.

"You ever seen a sawmill up close before?" Silas asked, turning when he saw Ruby. He pulled off his ear protectors.

"Only Corbin's," Ruby told him.

Silas briefly closed his eyes. Dirt speckled his sweaty face. Sawdust yellowed his hair. "Yeah," he said. He waved to his off-bearer. "Take fifteen, Ron, then deliver that chain to Johnson's. Enid left a coffee cake on the porch."

He turned back to Ruby. "Can I show you how it works?" he asked, waving his hand toward the saw. "I'm cutting boards for the new VFW booth at the Color Festival."

"I think I got the general idea. Shouldn't you turn off that blade?"

Silas laughed. "It *is* off. It stops in its own time; I don't rush it." He tipped his head, listening. "Hear that?"

"What?" Ruby asked.

"How it turns so smooth it sounds like a breath? When your blade saws, it talks to you. A good sawyer can tell if there's a tooth out of alignment, if he's gone too long between sharpening, if the blade's beginning to wobble."

"What does it say?" Ruby asked.

"When it's happy, it hums when it cuts. If a tooth goes, you'll hear it ticking. It changes pitch depending on whether it's sawing hardwood or softwood, or if it cuts through a knot. And . . ." He paused.

"And . . . ?" Ruby prompted.

Silas held up his right hand with its two shortened fingers, "When it cuts through flesh, it doesn't make a sound. It's silent."

Silas watched her closely. Ruby held her expression neutral.

"You had the presence of mind to listen when you cut off your fingers?" she asked. "Or did you have another occasion?"

"Only once," Silas said calmly. "That was enough."

"I read a line long ago about a mouse appreciating the softness of a cat's paw between strikes," Ruby told him.

"Something like that. What do you think of the Pinto?"

"I'll buy it."

"Good decision. Did you get a chance to look inside Corbin's mill?" Silas asked, his voice more relaxed than his eyes.

"Explain why I was looking before we discuss it any further."

Ruby could see him thinking, considering. He leaned against a peeled pole that supported the tin roof over his mill. "I don't want to get you messed up in this, Ruby."

"Isn't that exactly what you've already done?"

Silas shook his head. "No. No, I haven't."

Ruby faced him, crossing her arms. "Tell me why I was nosing around in Corbin Turmouski's mill."

"You know Corbin had polio when he was a kid?"

Ruby nodded, although his illness had been before she was born, before the Salk vaccine.

"One of his legs shriveled. He wore a brace for years," Silas said. "The leg gradually strengthened and he quit wearing the brace, but his leg was never strong. He got tired quick."

"And?"

"In his mill"—Silas spoke slowly, as if he knew by telling this to Ruby, he was crossing a line she didn't comprehend—"Corbin rigged up this support he could lean against when he ran his saw. There's a lot of standing in the work we do . . . he did."

"When he worked the lever?" Ruby asked, remembering the slippery platform in front of the lever, how close it was to the saw blade.

Silas nodded. "It moves the carriage back and forth. The log is clamped on the carriage and rides it through the blade, just like you see here on my mill. Corbin hooked up a support so he could stand longer on his bad leg."

"I couldn't find any device that resembled your description."

"You're sure?"

"Unless I misunderstood you. A steel brace with a padded section about thigh high, right?"

"That's right." Silas's jaw tightened. He hit his fist into his palm. Once, twice. Behind him, the big saw blade gradually slowed and Ruby could make out the saw's individual teeth.

"When was the last time you saw Corbin leaning against that support?" Ruby asked.

Silas gazed over her head. "Actually, it was three or four years ago. We haven't talked much recently."

"Maybe he quit using the support during that time. Ask Mina."

"No," Silas said emphatically. "Mina stayed out of the mill, even in the beginning. No sense in bringing it up to her."

"If there really *was* a support and if for some reason it was gone," Ruby said, "it would be easy for Corbin to fall into his saw blade."

"That's right."

"Do you know Carly's calling Corbin's death a possible homicide?"

Silas stiffened. "The fool," he began.

"I don't understand. Why is he a fool?" Ruby asked, counting off on her fingers. "You think Carly should declare Corbin's death an accident, yet you suspect the missing support is an indication Corbin was murdered."

Silas shrugged and brushed sawdust from his hair. "I'm just not thrilled about facing a lynch mob some dark midnight. Carly should have waited until he had *proof* there'd been a murder." He kicked at a shred of bark. "But I can take it, I guess. A man can't roll over and die every time something goes south."

"Supposing Corbin *was* adjusting the guide pins while the saw blade was spinning," Ruby said. "I saw the guide pins. What was the evidence?"

"There's a wooden platform beside the saw," Silas said, showing her with his hands. "It's called a table, and it works as a cover for the guide pins. You lift it up so you can reach the pins."

"And that table was raised when Corbin's body was discovered?" Ruby guessed, thinking if a woman had designed the saw mechanism, she would have designed the blade to stop turning when the table was raised, the same way a washing machine stopped spinning when the lid was lifted.

"That's what I understand."

"Then tell Carly about the missing support," Ruby advised. "It's evidence, Silas. Tell him so he can follow up on it and remove the suspicion from you."

"Maybe."

"Is Carly a good sheriff?" Ruby asked.

Silas laughed. "Carly doesn't exactly fill his old man's shoes. He missed out on getting Carl's toughness, so he tries to please as many people as he can. There's no job security in having an elected position. If you get too many folks mad at you, you're out of work. But, yeah," Silas went on. "I guess he's pretty fair."

"But who would want Corbin Turmouski dead?"

Silas pointed toward the house. "Let's walk that way. Corbin pissed off . . . sorry, angered, a few people around here, and grudges run deep. Maybe a logging deal; could be over something his grandfather did. Who knows?"

Ruby noted the way Silas's eyes didn't meet hers. Ron Kilgore would have a few succinct comments about *that*.

"I heard Corbin didn't always pay landowners fair value for their trees."

"It's a business, Ruby. Like any business, you try to make the most advantageous deal you can."

"That sounds like an excuse for both of you," Ruby said.

"You show me a businessman who runs his business any different and I'll show you a man in bankruptcy," Silas told her.

"I'll have the car waiting for you when you return your rental car," Silas said, handing her the Pinto's title.

"You're giving me a generous price, Silas," Ruby said as he walked her to her rental. "Does your generosity have anything to do with my father?"

"Do you mean, did he ask me to keep an eye on you?"

Ruby nodded and Silas's expression slipped from teasing to gentle sadness. "No, he didn't, Ruby. Sorry. Even when you were a little tyke, you had a grit about you that my own girls never had. I just want to help out, that's all."

At the corner, where the gravel road met paved asphalt, a Cherokee four-wheel-drive blocked the right lane. Ruby braked behind it while a pickup passed from the other direction, rattling on the washboard road.

A man in jeans and a sweatshirt stepped from the woods to her right and jumped across the ditch. She recognized Hank Holliday and lightly tapped her horn, waving out her window. He frowned, then grinned and came around the driver's side of the car.

"Out for a drive?" he asked, glancing inside her car, at her bare legs, and back to her face.

"I was visiting Mina."

His grin faded. "Glad to hear it."

"She said you visited her last night."

He picked a fuzzy burdock from his shirt sleeve. "Yeah, but I'm a stranger, not as good as having a friend or relative around. I'm finished here; how about a cup of coffee?"

"In town?" Ruby asked.

"I've got a Thermos in the car and half a package of fig bars." He pointed toward the trees. "If you don't mind jumping across the ditch, there's a nice patch of grass beneath those sugar maples."

"I've got a carrot cake," Ruby offered.

"Bring it and let's forget the fig bars." Hank opened the back of his Cherokee and rooted around in the jumble until he pulled out a Thermos and two mugs. He rinsed the mugs under water from a jug, inspected them, then handed one to Ruby. "Good enough?" he asked.

"Good enough," she said without glancing inside. "What about our cars?"

"We'll be close enough to see them. Come across over here," he said as he stretched his legs across the ditch. "You'll miss the nettles."

The ground was spongy, thick with last year's rotted leaves. In the shade beneath two tall trees, the soft grass was smoothed down like a fragrant cushion.

"Are these really sugar maples?" Ruby asked, looking

up into the three-lobed leaves where pale winged seed pods prepared to twirl off into the world.

"Yep. *Acer saccharum.* Or hard maples they're called, too."

"But nobody's tapped them for maple syrup, have they?"

He poured coffee into Ruby's mug. "Good thing. These will bring top dollar for veneer wood." He closed the Thermos and gave the gray trunk of the closest sugar maple a friendly pat. "Sapstreaks lower their value."

"Are you going to cut these trees?" Ruby asked.

"Not me, but I'm recommending a few be cut. They're prime right now. We'll let a little sun in here."

Ruby unwrapped the dense carrot cake; Corbin's favorite. It was covered with a thick cream cheese frosting. "Do you have anything to cut this with?"

"Sure." He pulled a pocket knife from his hip pocket and opened it for her.

She sliced two generous pieces off the square cake. "I know you're a consulting forester, but what does that mean exactly?"

"I try to make a living, like everybody else. Consulting foresters are a fairly new breed of animal," he said, taking his piece of cake and setting it on his pant leg. "It used to be, most of the sawmills cut their trees from federal and state lands. Now the government realizes we really *can* use up our renewable resources and they're cutting off—ha-ha—access to public timber. Over eighty percent of the trees that end up in sawmills now come from private lands."

"By private lands you mean . . ." Ruby waved her cup at the forest surrounding them.

"You got it. The land owned by your grandpa, your uncle, and your next-door neighbor. So you might say I'm working for the common man. Say your grandpa has forty acres out behind the house forested with oak and maple trees, maybe a few beech and aspen. Before me, if he needed a little extra cash, he'd sell off the trees to a timber company like Northern Timber or a smaller sawmill like Silas's. The sawmill company would hand Grandpa a check and cut down all the best trees because that's all they'd be interested in, right?"

"To saw up the logs for lumber, you mean?" A sparrow landed on a branch fifteen feet away, its black eyes fixed greedily on their cake.

"Right. Or to sell the very best logs to one of the finish mills downstate for furniture lumber or veneer. Your grandpa probably doesn't know the worth of his trees so he takes whatever amount he's offered, even though their actual value might be ten times the check he's already cashed. And he's left with forty acres of brush and trash, all the best trees logged off, and a forty-acre chunk of land that'll take another couple of generations to recover."

"So you advise the landowner not to sell to the sawmill owner?"

"Not at all. I'd advise *which* trees to sell and make sure he gets a good price. Then I'd be the avenging angel watching over the actual cutting down of the trees to make sure it was done right. The object of the whole exercise would be to retain enouh of the best trees so you've got a healthy forest left and another harvest in ten or fifteen years. I like to think I'm doing some long-range planning for the benefit of the woods. Not to mention the owners."

"Then you're an environmentalist," Ruby said.

"I'm no tree hugger, if that's what you're asking. I get my ten percent when the timber's sold. And of course I get the best prices for our fictitious grandpa and make sure he doesn't get screwed."

Hank wiped frosting from his mouth with the back of his wrist. "This is great. Did you make it?"

Ruby shook her head. "Enid Shea did. She gave it to Mina Turmouski."

"Funeral food."

"Does it still taste all right?"

"Worth dying for." He hit himself in the forehead with the heel of his hand. "God, I didn't mean that."

"I know you said you and Corbin were on opposite sides of the fence, but what was your opinion of him as a man?"

"A maniac for his sawmill. He was a wizard with a chain saw, too. He come up through the ranks as a logger first and could drop a tree within inches of any spot he wanted."

"I saw how Corbin cut Fox Woods, near Blue Lake," Ruby said.

Hank frowned. "He did that last month. I wasn't involved with that job. The owner lives out of the area and just wanted the most bucks for his bang. But something went wrong on that cut. I hadn't seen Corbin make such a mess—cutting down every standing tree whether it was valuable or not and leaving a scarred wasteland—but I'm a relative newcomer so I asked around and nobody else had ever seen Corbin cut a woods like that, either."

"What do you think happened?"

Hank shrugged. "Maybe he was making a statement against absentee landowners. A lot of people get pissed when outsiders come in and buy up land they themselves can't afford."

"Wally mentioned that."

"Kentner, the real estate agent? He should know. He courts buyers from out of the area, I understand, whoever'll give him the most money."

"Aren't *you* from out of the area?" Ruby asked him.

Unconsciously, Hank raised his right hand toward her the way Michiganders did, pointing to a crease on his palm which, when matched with the mitt-shaped map of Michigan, would correspond to the northern end of Saginaw Bay.

"I was working on the other side of the state with a forestry consulting business but I wanted to go on my own. A friend of a friend asked me to inspect his property here in Waters County. Once I got here, I saw all this prime timber and only three sawmills working it. I knew a gift horse had landed in my lap and I decided not to look up its nostrils." He grinned. "Of course, I didn't start out so well."

"What happened?"

Hank Holliday thoughtfully chewed his cake, swallowed, and said, "The property that belonged to the friend of my friend? Corbin had already made an offer and thought he had it in the bag."

"I'm beginning to understand your unpopularity," Ruby told him. "Bruce Becket mentioned you claimed Corbin hadn't paid him enough for his trees."

Hank winced. "Another mistake. I should have kept my mouth shut. Nobody likes to hear they've been taken."

Ruby pulled a twig from beneath her that was digging into her hip. "*Did* Corbin cheat Bruce?"

"Cheat may not be the right word, but Corbin definitely paid Bruce several thousand dollars less than those trees were worth." Hank shook his head. "Yeah, then a guy from out of town shows up and starts telling people how to conduct their business and how their neighbors are screwing them over and naturally their hackles rise."

"But somebody seriously wishes you'd leave or they wouldn't be vandalizing your vehicle," Ruby said. She finished her piece of carrot cake and brushed the crumbs from her shorts.

"It's not my charming self they dislike; it's that I'm

messing up local standard practices. Cut *and* save your woods; novel idea. So you're a local? You have frosting on your chin."

"Semi," Ruby told him, wiping off the frosting and licking it from her finger. "I grew up in Sable and left when I was seventeen; I couldn't get out of here fast enough. But my mother willed me a cabin and land on Blue Lake, and my daughter's ill . . ."

Hand nodded. "So you came back. Are you married?"

"No. Are you?"

"I've been wounded but never legally."

"And now Waters County is your home?"

The Thermos was empty and Hank swallowed the last of his coffee. "Charming Sable itself."

A truck growled down the road toward them. Ruby recognized the red flatbed that had been parked beside Silas Shea's mill. The truck pulled behind her car and momentarily stopped. Silas wasn't alone. His wife, Enid, sat in the passenger seat, avidly peering out the window at Ruby and Hank in their sugar maple bower.

Ruby would have recognized Enid anywhere. She wore her gray hair in the same style as the year Ruby left Sable: cut short with little sausage curls around her face as if she'd taken out bristled rollers and not combed them out. Her mouth was prim, her jaw set, her eyes eagerly searching for indiscretion. "She keeps Silas on a short leash," Ruby had heard her father say once, and she bet Enid still did.

As the truck pulled around Ruby's car, Ruby smiled and waved.

Enid leaned out the window and called over the truck's shifting gears, "You didn't even come home for your mother's funeral, Ruby Crane."

Hank looked after the departing truck, his mouth open. "Subtle," he commented.

"Enid's always spoken her mind," Ruby told him as she dumped the last of her coffee in the grass.

"It was good cake, anyway," Hank said.

Ruby nodded and folded the aluminum foil over the remaining cake. Her hands were shaking.

Chapter 10

Ruby hit her fist against the steering wheel. Within ten seconds of seeing her, Enid Shea had managed to jam in the blade and jiggle it around in her gut. Like old times.

Ruby *hadn't* come back for her mother's funeral. She could have: she'd had money for airfare. But her mother was *gone*; what was the point in being closed in a room with a casket, her father, and her sister Phyllis?

Ruby firmly believed her mother had begun dying the moment she stepped away from the altar on her father's arm. "Keep busy," Ruby's mother had always advised, making it her own credo. Keeping busy had kept Alice Crane from noticing her own gradual disappearance from the land of the living.

Ruby was too angry to go home yet, and she drove from one side road to the next, not noticing the scenery, letting the motion and hum of the car engine gradually soothe her. When she finally did notice her surroundings, she laughed aloud. Just as wilderness books described the lost wandering in futile circles, she'd driven in a circle and was again passing Mina Turmouski's and then Silas Shea's.

She briefly noted the maple trees she'd sat under with Hank and then the abundance of wildflowers. She'd forgotten how many wildflowers saved their blossoms until autumn.

Goldenrod, Queen Anne's lace, and asters bloomed along the road, and Ruby spotted a bright patch of wild sunflowers at the edge of a small meadow. Jesse responded to bright colors the same way she responded to strong shapes or odors or sounds: as if she had to relearn the most primary aspects before she was allowed to comprehend life's subtleties.

Ruby pulled her car off the road and climbed out. She'd pick a bouquet for her daughter.

She jumped across the ditch, pushing through the tall grasses that were drying to gold. Shiny deer droppings were scattered across a patch of British soldier moss. Sunshine filled the meadow, but surrounding it, the trees formed a gloomy darkness, thick with underbrush. Ruby couldn't see more than a few feet into the woods.

The sunflowers were at their peak, each crisp petal bright yellow, the knobby centers light brown. Ruby's hands quickly grew tender and stained from breaking off the tough hairy stems. She'd gathered a respectable bouquet when suddenly she heard movement, the snapping of twigs, in the woods behind her. She turned, narrowing her eyes and peering into the murky shadows beneath the trees.

Nothing moved, and she heard no unusual sounds as she turned in a circle, scanning the woods. But at the edge of the meadow, she caught a glimpse of black and white in the tall grass.

She approached cautiously, holding the bouquet of flowers to her heart. The dark shape didn't stir.

An animal lay crumpled among the dying ferns. At first she thought it was a raccoon, but when she stepped closer, she discovered a black-and-white collie.

It was Mina's watchdog, Pepper. Had it been hit by a car and then dragged itself from the road to the meadow to die?

"Poor thing," she said aloud.

Ruby raised her head. Nearby an engine roared to life and she heard the spray of gravel as a vehicle sped away. She ran to the road, but by the time she jumped across the ditch, all she saw was a collapsing tornado of dust heading north.

Back in the meadow, she slowly circled the dead dog. Blood matted the white fur at the back of its head. She bent lower to inspect its body.

The blood had come from a small hole behind the collie's left ear and the blood was still liquid, not even congealed. Mina's dog had been shot.

When Ruby walked into the cabin, she found Jesse propped up by pillows on the couch next to DeEtta who was playing a piccolo, the notes soft and clear. Jesse's eyes were closed and her face peaceful.

Ruby motioned to DeEtta to continue playing and went directly to the telephone, stretching the cord to the farthest corner of the kitchen and laying the sunflowers in the sink as she passed it, before she dialed the sheriff's telephone number.

"Carly's gone for the day, but this is George Moore, his deputy. What can I do for you?"

"Is Carly at home?" Ruby asked, keeping her voice low as DeEtta continued playing. "I can call him there."

"He went to Muskegon and won't be back until late. Some kind of meeting. What do you need?"

"I just found Mina Turmouski's dog shot to death about two miles from her house," Ruby told the deputy. "It hadn't been lying there for very long, either."

"And?" he asked.

"It was her watchdog," Ruby said patiently, her earlier anger resurfacing. "Mina is alone and her husband just died and somebody killed her watchdog."

"The dog was probably in the woods running deer," the deputy said mildly. "It happens."

"Can you please check into it?" Ruby asked.

She thought she heard a muffled snort on the other end of the phone and then the deputy said, "We don't usually investigate dead dogs. Big livestock sometimes. You know: cows and horses. Somebody was killing cows and cutting off their ears a few years ago. We never did solve that one."

"I'll talk to Carly when he returns," Ruby told the deputy in frustration. She hung up and returned the phone to its stand.

DeEtta's melody wound down and she pulled the piccolo away from her mouth and shook its end against her pants leg. Her face was rosy from exertion.

"That was nice," Ruby told DeEtta, and asked Jesse, "Did you have fun today?"

The frown appeared and Jesse's eyes slipped into concentration.

"If you move a little more to the right, she'll see you better," DeEtta said.

"Jesse doesn't have vision problems," Ruby told her.

"Try it."

Ruby walked to the caned straightback chair to Jesse's right and sat down. "Hi, Jesse," she said.

It was as if Ruby had materialized out of the mist. Jesse smiled. "Mom," she said.

"How did you know?" Ruby asked DeEtta.

DeEtta pointed to the built-in bookcases. "I've been reading one of your books about head injury. It said with a right brain injury sometimes things on the left side just don't compute."

Ruby had read her books about right brain injury, too, but there was so much to absorb, too many variables when what she searched for was one basic answer: Was Jesse going to get better or not?

"We'll talk about it later," Ruby said, realizing she was doing what she'd sworn not to do: discuss Jesse in front of her, to reduce her daughter to an object. "Did anyone call?"

"A man who said he was your boss."

"Ron Kilgore?" Ruby asked.

"That's right. Are you doing detective work here?"

"I'm *not* a detective, DeEtta. You've been listening to rumors."

"Mmm," DeEtta murmured, not appearing convinced. "And Mrs. Pink was down by your dock a while ago. She kept looking up here but Jesse and I stayed in the cabin. She's probably still hanging around out there."

"She's harmless."

"I know, but it's creepy."

It was early evening when Mina phoned.

"Ruby, this is Mina."

"Are you all right?" Ruby asked, instantly thinking of the dead watchdog.

"Yes. Do you remember the time we stole all the history tests from the backseat of Mr. Wickler's car?"

Ruby searched her memory, caught off guard. It was one small incident in a long line of more interesting trespasses. "Was that the time neither one of us had studied so we thought we'd level the playing field?"

"Yes!" Mina said triumphantly. She chuckled but there was a hysterical edge to her voice.

"But then," Mina went on in an unsteadily animated voice, "I chickened out and confessed to that counselor. What was her name, Sherbet? Sherwin? And you nearly killed me?" She laughed again, her voice ending in a high cackle. "We didn't speak for a month, at least."

And Mina lapsed into silence. End of story. Was she sitting at her plain table in her plain house, worrying over her life like a dog with a bone? "I remember," Ruby said lamely. "But we made up." She paused. "Please, come spend the night here. I have a fairly unlumpy couch and I make great coffee."

"No, I want to be here, at home, Ruby. Really."

Ruby sat down at the table and tucked her legs

beneath her. "Then let's talk awhile," she said, searching for the ordinary, the mundane in conversational subjects. "Do you sew? Remember my grandmother's quilts? I'm putting them together now. I'll give you a quilt top to work on if you enjoy quilting."

"Wally brought out a benefit check from Corbin's life insurance this afternoon," Mina said as if she hadn't heard Ruby. "He pulled strings to have it paid so fast. All the money was wrapped up in the mill and I was low, especially after paying for . . ."

Wally brought Mina the life insurance benefits? Then Ruby remembered Wally's card and sign: Kentner Real Estate and Insurance.

"That's good, Mina. Then you'll be able to look for another place to live."

"Maybe."

"I watched Silas run his mill," Ruby said carefully. "There's so much movement involved. I'm curious how Corbin managed to stand for so long."

"What do you mean?"

"With his weak leg. It must have been tiring."

"Oh. He built a metal-and-cushion affair beside the operating lever."

"He braced himself against it?" Ruby asked.

"He used to. But a year ago he went back to wearing a leg brace, one of the new lightweight kinds that lock. He said it was safer."

So Silas Shea had been wrong. Corbin himself had removed the support from his sawmill.

"That's right," Mina was saying, almost to herself. Ruby listened to her steady breathing. Then Mina went on: "We had a perfect marriage."

Jesse was in bed asleep and Ruby was writing a letter to Todd when she heard shouting, followed by the slamming of a door. More shouting.

Her heart pounding, she dropped her pen, grabbed a carving knife from the knife holder and threw open her kitchen door.

Two people stood in front of DeEtta's open trailer door, light framing their figures. The man leaned forward, threatening. DeEtta stood her ground but Ruby could tell she was weakening, leaning backward, one hand to her cheek. They were both so involved in their confrontation that neither noticed Ruby.

"What's going on?" she demanded.

"Nothing," DeEtta said weakly.

"Cut the crap, DeEtta," Ruby ordered. "Go in the cabin."

DeEtta ran past Ruby as the man backed away toward the shadows.

"You must be Danny," Ruby said to the man who was only an inch or two taller than she was, his face sharply featured and petulant, pitted acne scars on his chin. She held the knife to her side. "Don't run away yet."

"I'm not running away from an old broad like you."

"Well, it might be the wiser course."

"Huh?" He grunted.

"Listen, asshole," she said. "I've seen you around here for the last time. If DeEtta won't make a complaint, I will. What you do elsewhere, no matter how despicable, isn't my concern. But if you step one foot on my property again, day or night, I'll hit you with everything I can."

She took a step closer to the seething young man. "And I don't just mean whatever happens to be legal, either."

"This is none of your business," he said, raising a fist to waist level.

"You've made it my business."

"DeEtta's still my wife."

"That doesn't make her your property."

"You talk smart but you aren't," Danny Greenstone snarled. "You're stupid. And you ask too many questions."

That made Ruby pause. What questions was he referring to? "If you mean Corbin Turmouski's death, maybe I should ask you a few. You were supposed to work for him the day he died, weren't you?"

"Shit happens."

Bumper sticker mentality.

He snorted, emboldened. "You come in here like you own the place, sticking your nose everywhere. Into my life and my wife's . . ."

"Don't set foot here again," Ruby warned him. "Now get out of here."

He walked twenty feet toward the shadowy outline of a motorcycle before he turned and said, "Nobody around here will listen to you, lady. If you start looking for trouble with me, you'll find it. You don't poke me and walk away. So drop dead, you and your weirded-out kid."

Ruby walked back to the cabin, turning the knife in her hand, hearing the kick-start of Danny's bike. This was how murders happened. Crimes of passion.

DeEtta sat at the table, crying. One cheek was red and swelling, and she rubbed her shoulder. Ruby picked up the heavy rotary phone and set it in front of DeEtta. "Call the sheriff."

"I can't," DeEtta said.

"Then I will."

DeEtta bit her lip and Ruby asked, "How long has this been going on?"

"What?"

Ruby jerked out a chair and dropped into it. DeEtta flinched. "How long has he been hitting you?"

"He didn't at first. Just joking around, maybe, but then once I came home late from being out with my girlfriends and he was worried . . ."

"DeEtta, there's no legitimate excuse on this earth. None."

"He wants me to move back with him. We're still married."

Ruby picked up the receiver and held it to DeEtta. "Call Carly."

"He'd kill Danny if he knew."

"Better he do it than me," Ruby told her. "And I wouldn't hesitate, I promise you."

DeEtta sniffled. "I just can't, because . . ."

"Because why?"

"Carly's married to my sister Georgia."

"Dr. Doyle's receptionist?" Ruby asked. "Carly's your brother-in-law?"

DeEtta nodded. Between Carly and Georgia, Ruby thought, they had every illness and scandal in Sable covered.

"No excuse," Ruby said. She took back the phone and dialed the sheriff's number.

"All right," DeEtta whispered, and held out her hand for the receiver.

Ruby gave it to her and stood. "You tell him however you want. I'll check on Jesse and when I come back I want to talk to him so don't hang up."

She left the kitchen and stood inside Jesse's room, her back against the wall, breath slowing to match Jesse's rhythmic sleeping breaths, feeling the comfort of this semidark room that held the most precious person in her life.

Only once had Ruby been physically hurt by a man. She smiled, barely able to remember the night in an Oregon bar when she'd pummeled a man who'd grabbed her, one hand to her breast, one to her crotch. He might have finally flailed his arms in self-defense. Ruby came out of it with a sore ear. He had a broken tooth and a bloody nose. Stan would have never hit her; he'd prided himself on bringing a person to his or her knees without lifting a finger.

When Ruby's breathing effortlessly matched Jesse's, she returned to the kitchen where DeEtta was hunched over the phone, nodding and saying "Okay." She glanced up at Ruby and said into the mouthpiece, "Ruby wants to talk to you."

"Make a written report on this, Carly," Ruby said.

"Do you really think that's necessary? Those kids . . ."

"I'm sending your office a letter detailing the incident, with a copy going to a friend in California, just so there's a record."

"Why go to all that trouble?"

"Because there needs to be a history if he shows up again. I warned him."

"What will you do, shoot him?"

"It depends."

"Come on, Ruby. He's just a hot-headed kid."

"I'm not responding to that comment, Carly. And don't pretend you haven't known this was going on."

She heard him sigh. "All right," he said wearily. "I just came home from Muskegon. I'll get a bite to eat, then write it up. I'll talk to Danny tomorrow. Okay?"

"Okay. Did your deputy tell you about Mina's dog?"

"Yeah, he did. I'll look into it."

"Thank you," she told him, and when she hung up she said to DeEtta, "Sleep on the couch tonight. I'm going to bed."

Ruby sat at the end of the dock, her feet dangling in the cool water, watching light play across the lake. As much as she loved Blue Lake, she'd rarely swum in it, even as a child. She wasn't a strong swimmer; her shoulders tired too quickly.

Ruby's sister Phyllis had been the family swimmer,

spending every summer as a lifeguard on Pere's Lake Michigan beach, tanning to a deep gold, collecting boys.

Ruby checked her watch; it was almost time to head for work at Mabel's. She'd promised Mina she'd bring Jesse for a visit tomorrow morning, but first she intended to talk to Carly again about the shooting of Mina's dog. Unless she pressured him, she knew the dog would be forgotten, become just "one of those things."

In the distance, she heard the high-pitched whine of a motorcycle on Blue Road. Ruby stood, listening, following its whirring sound as it passed from north to south, noticing how long it took to pass, as if the rider had paused at the end of her driveway and then ridden on.

When Ruby returned from work, a red Toyota was parked beside the cabin. On the edge of the lawn facing the lake where grass surrendered completely to sand sat Jesse, DeEtta, and her brother Bruce. A dog lay stretched on the ground, a gold and brown shepherd mix.

"I came to see DeEtta," Bruce said, grinning fondly at his sister. "Everything going okay?"

Ruby caught the imploring look on DeEtta's face and said, "So far."

Blue Lake was tranquil; on the opposite shore, a curve of autumn color bloomed by the public boat ramp. Ruby didn't recall seeing those yellows a few hours ago.

Bruce stood and hiked up his pants over his narrow hips. "I guess I'd better get back to work then. Let me know if you need anything."

The dog raised its head and watched Bruce walk away but didn't make a move to follow him.

"What about your dog?" Ruby asked.

"She's staying," Bruce told her. "She's your watchdog for as long as DeEtta's here and for as long as you want her after that."

"I didn't request a watchdog," Ruby said. The dog laid its head on its paws, eyes shifting between Bruce and Ruby, as if it sensed it was being discussed.

Bruce stepped closer to Ruby and said quietly, "Do me a favor. Keep the dog for now. Not just for you, but . . ." He glanced over at DeEtta straightening Jesse's shorts and Ruby wasn't sure which of them he meant. "You won't regret it."

"What's her name?"

"Spot. She won't run off as long as DeEtta's here. In two days she'll believe she owns you, and you'll have a first-rate watchdog. Just keep her close in when bow season starts."

Spot didn't have a leash; her throat ruff of fur held no impression of having known a collar.

"Do you like Spot?" Ruby asked Jesse. The dog wagged her tail when she heard her name.

"She's pretty," Jesse said slowly. "Like in my old dog books."

"That's right." Jesse could remember more clearly what she'd read years ago than what she'd done yesterday.

Chapter 11

"Where are we going?" Ruby asked Hank. She sat sideways, her seat belt loose so she could see Jesse in the backseat.

Hank had arrived during dinner, offering to show her and Jesse a forest he was managing. "See the woods up close and personal," he'd invited. "Escape all the speculation about Corbin for a while."

They drove along the western side of Blue Lake, past closed and shuttered summer cabins with chains across driveways. The yards were empty of anything that might tempt thieves over the winter: garden hoses, lawn furniture, wooden planters.

"I'm consulting on sixty acres across from Tony's Point," Hank told her. "There's an area I'd like to show you."

"So not everyone in Sable is plotting to sabotage you if you're being hired locally," Ruby said.

"Money talks. Word's getting around that I can get owners bigger bucks on their back forty and leave them with a decent forest besides. Most people need the money but they hate to see the woods they played in as kids reduced to trash, and it's my pleasure to tell them it's not necessary. It's the timber buyers who wish I'd shut up and leave town."

"Because you tell the owners what their trees are really worth?"

"Right. And telling the loggers which trees to cut and watching like a hawk while they do it makes me the fly in their ointment, the sand in their gears, and, you might say, the sugar in their gas tanks." He looked over at her and grinned. "And I like it like that."

"A rebel," Ruby commented. "Did you miss the sixties?"

"I was born too late to make my mark. But these are better times. Less competition."

They passed Mrs. Pink's house. It nestled beneath the largest oaks on the lake, knotty old trunks and crowns spreading like children's book illustrations. A split-rail fence zigzagged down to the shores of Blue Lake. The house had a closed-up air, the windows tightly curtained and the front door closed. Was Mrs. Pink asleep, resting up for her next nocturnal outing?

The yard was studded with birdbaths, gaily painted bird feeders and bird houses, many on poles, dense like pictures Gram had shown Ruby of a shrine in the old country: a hill so studded with crosses, paths had to be constructed between them.

"Do you know the old lady who lives there?" Hank asked.

"Mrs. Pink? She mostly keeps to herself."

"I've seen her walking. She refused a ride from me."

"Don't take it personal. She doesn't accept rides from anybody. She looks in people's windows sometimes."

Hank's eyebrows raised. "Bedroom windows?"

"Maybe. It bothers the summer people but nobody else pays any attention."

"Local color," Hank commented.

Hank turned into an overgrown two-track through tall trees, downshifting into first gear. The Cherokee groaned and entered the woods, which closed densely behind them. Bushes growing too close scraped the sides of the vehicle, screeching like nails on a blackboard.

"Okay back there, Jesse?" Hank asked.

"Okay," Jesse answered.

Ruby braced herself with one hand on the dashboard. Bracken ferns had turned yellow, the fronds curling in on themselves like useless hands. The brilliant reds and golds of changing maples flashed out among the green trees.

"Not much farther," Hank said. "There's a rare piece of property in here you'll like."

"Is this a valuable forest?"

"Very."

"I don't see any pines."

"The white pine days are long gone. It's the hardwoods that are most valuable. Especially oak and hard maple, furniture wood, veneer. Pine's a softwood. The red pine you see growing in rows on plantations from the CCC plantings during the Depression is mainly sawn up for landscape timbers, telephone poles, even pallet wood. Worth bucks but not big bucks like the hardwoods."

Hank stopped his Cherokee in the middle of the two-track. "Here we are," he said, shutting off the engine. "It's a short hike from here."

Ruby glanced at Jesse, who sat patiently—no, uncaring, her gaze through the windshield on leaves riffling in the breezes.

Hank got out and pushed his seat forward to reach Jesse. "I'm going to unfasten your seat belt, Jesse," he told her. "You and your mom and I are going for a walk." To Ruby he said, "Can you grab that blue daypack?"

Ruby helped Hank position Jesse on his back. He clasped her legs around his waist with one hand and with the other held both her hands around his neck. He did it so adroitly, Ruby asked, "Do you have children?"

"Not that I know of." He smiled and looked at Ruby, then his smile faded and he said, "My little brother had cerebral palsy. I used to carry him like this. He died of pneumonia several years ago."

"I'm sorry."

"Actually, he lived years longer than anybody expected." Hank paused a moment, then readjusted Jesse's weight and said, "Ready? I've walked over the acreage once. I like to get a first impression and then come back and do a detailed inventory."

It reminded Ruby of the way she studied handwriting. They walked side by side, Ruby keeping one hand free in case Jesse slipped or grew agitated.

But Jesse turned from side to side looking. After a while she laid her head against Hank's back and closed her eyes.

Within three minutes, Ruby had no idea which direction they'd come from. Following Hank blindly, wearing his daypack, she heard only the sounds of their own passage and the whisper of leaves above their heads.

"This is a beautiful forest," she said. "Does the owner really want it cut?"

"Managed," Hank said. "It's at its peak but it's too crowded in here for the up-and-coming trees." He stopped and pointed out a cluster of trees. "See how close together those maples are growing? If we thin out a few, he'll get a good price for them but the best trees will be left standing. They'll really gain in size—and value—during the next five to ten years."

"You're still cutting down the trees," Ruby said.

"What's the alternative?" Hank asked, turning to her. "Let it be highgraded? Or lambasted like Fox Woods?"

"What does 'highgraded' mean?"

"It's sometimes called 'take the best and leave the rest.' You cut every valuable tree, say over eighteen inches in diameter at chest height. It's not an unusual practice, just an increasingly outdated way of cutting timber. It takes forever for the forest to grow back and what does isn't worth Shinola, financially or botanically."

"Why cut these trees at all?" Ruby asked.

"The owner needs the money. It's his property and his right, and this is the best solution I can see." Ruby heard the irritation in his voice, the weariness of having attended this same argument before.

"In an ideal world," Hank went on, stepping around a silvery stump, "the population wouldn't increase, we'd live on nothing but air surrounded by majestic trees that lived long lives and died natural deaths to be replaced by equally majestic new trees. But this isn't an ideal world. The virgin forests are gone. Nothing stays the same. People die, trees die. Idealism is dead. The only solution is to manage what we have left."

"You're cynical," Ruby said.

"Realistic," he corrected.

A sudden sharp odor reached Ruby: a vinegary smell that made her eyes water. She covered her nose. "What is it?"

Hank nodded to a pile of reddish orange pulp beneath a tree. "Cider press squeezings to attract deer."

Hank peered up into the trees. Ruby followed his gaze and saw a rough wooden structure, a bow-hunter's deer blind.

"Somebody's thinking ahead. Bow season opens in a week."

Ruby contemplated the clear shot from the blind to the apple squeezings, and noted all the deer tracks around the rotting vinegary remains, thinking it was as sporting as shooting a cow in a field.

"Do you carry a compass?" she asked Hank.

He shook his head. "My dad swore I had a piece of iron in my forehead. I can always find north." To demonstrate, he turned to the left and pointed straight in front of him. "There it is," he said, as if she should see a sign reading NORTH: THIS WAY planted among the trees. "I bet I can bring us out of here within a hundred feet of my Jeep."

"I'm game. What'll we bet?"

"Dinner. If I'm way off, I'll buy; if I'm on the money, you cook."

"You'd better pray you're off by a mile, then," Ruby told him.

She pointed to an oak smeared with a brownish mass that had once been viscous. "Gypsy moth nurseries," she said. "When I was a kid we used to rub those off the trees with sticks."

"Go ahead," he said. "You might save a few leaves."

Since the 1960s and '70s, the gypsy moth caterpillars had reared up in destructive masses every few years to defoliate the trees. Three consecutive ravaging episodes and many trees died, too weakened to resist disease and pests.

During one particularly ruinous year Ruby had stood in the woods across from the Crane cabin and listened, not moving a muscle. What she'd heard had sounded like the gentle patter of rain. But it had actually been the sound of gypsy moth caterpillars defecating as they ate their way through the forest canopy.

Now she picked up a stick and vigorously rubbed away the brown mass of eggs, reveling in childish satisfaction.

Fifty feet farther and Hank's face changed, opening like that of a young boy who anticipated a gift. His stride increased, and Ruby had to stretch out to keep up with him. "Almost there," he said.

He stopped and nodded toward the trees to their left. "See those? All that scrub oak, those popples and hawthorn? Most of them are worthless. Poor sandy soil. Glaciers brought in the soil, and every once in a while you hit a section of good soil with clay banding to hold the water."

"I suspect you're about to show us a section of good soil," Ruby told him.

"That's right. Do you trust me?"

"Not yet."

He laughed and shifted Jesse on his back. "That makes sense. But try to for a minute. Close your eyes and hold on to Jesse's leg. I'll lead."

Ruby closed her eyes and placed her hand lightly on Jesse's leg while Hank talked her through the woods. "A little more to the right. We're walking through some slippery leaves. A short incline."

Ruby didn't peek. She had never peeked during hide-and-seek or tried to see beneath the blindfold during any game, as a child or an adult. She relished the disorientation of darkness, aware she held the power to end it at will but anticipating more the sensations of touch, the surprise when she finally did open her eyes.

"Okay," Hank said, halting. "You can look."

Ruby opened her eyes and turned in a slow circle. "Where are we?" she whispered.

Surrounding them were the thick straight trunks of trees that reached fifty to sixty feet toward the sky before branches began. It was prehistoric, a fantasy. Sun filtered and streamed through the still-green distant treetops, slanting onto the forest floor that was clear of brush, open as far as she could see, only trunk after trunk into the distance. It was primeval, as de Tocqueville had described: *Everywhere, the forest seems to walk in front of you.* "Is this virgin forest?" she asked Hank.

He shook his head. When he spoke, his voice was low, respectful. "It was logged in the 1800s but somehow it's been overlooked during the past hundred years. Good soil, perfect conditions. I've rarely seen a stand of red oak like this, and there's a hard maple in here that's the biggest I've ever laid eyes on. Whenever you see oak and hard maple you can bet it's good soil."

"These trees are all so straight."

"A tree needs a little competition to grow straight; otherwise it spreads out. That's why an oak standing out in the middle of a field looks like a different species of tree from an oak growing in the woods."

Ruby wrapped her arms around the nearest tree trunk. She couldn't even reach halfway around. She laid her cheek against the rough bark, breathing in its woodsy odor. "This is a red oak?"

"Right. There won't be oak forests like this again for generations."

"Why not?"

"Look around you." Hank rebalanced Jesse, leaned over, and brushed his hand across the inches-high seedlings that carpeted the forest floor. "These are all maple seedlings. They can tolerate shade but oak seedlings need a lot of sun. Better yet, they like a good forest fire to burn out the competition, then the stems pop up from acorns that fell years ago and spent that whole time establishing a root system while waiting for just the right conditions. In another hundred years, there will be a few oaks left in this woods but the maples will have taken over."

"Is that bad?"

"No. It's just the natural succession of the forests. Like I said, nothing stays the same." He nudged a broken branch away from the base of an oak tree with his foot. "If you spread the blanket that's in my pack, we can sit here awhile before we head back."

Ruby slipped off Hank's daypack and pulled out a green wool blanket, then helped Jesse down. She stood unsteadily, leaning against her mother. Hank shook out his arms, raised them above his head, and stretched, his face toward the treetops, smiling.

"It's so quiet," Ruby said. "No birds. Where are the animals?"

"It's too shady in here for good forage. Except for the acorns. The turkey and deer eat them."

"You're not recommending this forest be cut, are you?" Ruby asked.

"Not really. This would be a very sensitive, very selective job. Like that dead oak over there, while it's still valuable, before it falls and damages the nearby trees. I might have that beech removed to release the oak next to it. A good logger can drop a tree exactly where he wants it. Corbin could have done it easy. I wouldn't let an amateur in here."

"What does 'release' mean?"

Hank dropped on the blanket the other side of Jesse. "Let the sunshine in. You have to be careful. Too much light causes epicormic sprouting—a mass of branches growing up and down the trunk. It lowers the grade of the wood. Too much light can even shock a tree and kill it."

Ruby placed a fig bar from Hank's pack into Jesse's hand. Jesse looked at it with disinterest. "Go ahead and eat it," Ruby encouraged her. She understood why people with head injuries sometimes grew thin and slipped into ill health; they simply lost interest in eating. If Ruby stopped feeding Jesse, she'd probably never ask for food.

"What happens after you decide which trees should be cut?" Ruby asked Hank.

"I have a contract with the owner, everything in black and white. Then I put out a request for sealed bids and when the highest-bidding loggers get into the woods, I keep an eye on them to be sure it's done right."

"That's when loggers like Silas Shea and Corbin Turmouski bid to cut down the trees?"

"Right. And buyers for bigger mills, like Northern Timber, too. Sometimes the high bids are two to three times as much as the low bids. It can be a real crap shoot."

"You *are* Tree Man," Ruby said.

Hank laughed. "That's the way *I* work. There are stinker foresters just like there are stinkers in any other field."

Jesse gazed at the surrounding trees, her lips moving. The fig bar lay on the blanket, forgotten.

"Did Silas or Corbin ever threaten you?"

"Do you mean trying to scare me out of the county?"

He shrugged. "I wouldn't use the word 'threaten.' Of the two of them, Corbin had the least fondness for me. I guess it doesn't matter now."

Hank picked up an acorn and unscrewed the tiny cap. "People still suspect Silas killed Corbin, you know. Picture those two: crippled Corbin and grizzled Silas, slugging it out in Corbin's mill while you and Mina sit in the kitchen, until Silas finally gets the upper hand, flips the switch, and tosses Corbin into the screaming blade, then raises the table by the headsaw to make it appear Corbin was adjusting his guide pins."

"How did you know Mina and I were sitting in the kitchen?" Ruby asked, so surprised she didn't notice how Jesse had fastened her attention on Hank.

"Isn't that the social center of houses around here?" Hank asked.

"I guess, but you don't really believe Silas could have killed Corbin?"

"I think Silas looks out for number one, but he's no killer. Have you seen their mills?"

Ruby nodded.

"Different philosophies. Silas could squeeze a dime out of a nickel, and Corbin would spend a dime to make a nickel."

"Then do you believe Carly was right to declare Corbin's death a possible homicide?" she asked.

Hank shrugged. "He may as well check every angle, but there are a lot of men with missing body parts from trying to mess with guide pins while the sawblade's turning. Anybody who could deliberately saw a man in half . . ." He reached for another fig bar. "The next thing you know, he'd pour sugar in gas tanks."

Ruby grimaced. "Don't say that."

"Okay," Hank agreed. "So tell me what you did in California."

"I worked for a detective agency."

"Ouch. There's no connection between that and Turmouski's death, is there?"

"No. I started out as a receptionist," Ruby told him. An ant trekked across the blanket beside her leg and she set her finger in front of it, watching it march up and over it without pausing.

"What did you end up as?"

"A questioned documents examiner. Forgery detection."

"Like the fake Hitler diaries?" Hank leaned closer, regarding Ruby, his hazel eyes wide. "You can detect that kind of forgery?"

"I'd love to have a case like that. That forgery was easily detected once a top professional examined it. Diaries are simpler to crack than a lot of other forms of forgery: if you write in a diary every day for years, you use different pens; sometimes you sit at a desk or in a chair and that changes the slant of your writing; so do your moods. But mostly I examine signatures on documents, handwritten wills, anonymous letters. Not too thrilling."

"It sounds pretty thrilling to me." Hank leaned back, grinning. "My diabolical mind is toying with the possibilities: checks, fame, and fortune."

"No possibility is too outrageous," Ruby assured him. "And it's most likely been tried."

"What's your favorite case?"

"It's a silly one, really. And simple. A risqué note to Marilyn Monroe signed by President Kennedy. The owner was planning to sell it to the tabloids."

Hank whistled. "How'd you crack it?"

"The examiner before me couldn't positively declare it a forgery. It was perfect in every way: natural variations in the handwriting. A couple of his unique strokes."

"But?"

"I held it up to the light and the paper had a water-mark introduced by the stationer in 1965."

"And Kennedy was assassinated in 1963."

"Exactly. You might say the other examiner couldn't see the forest for the trees."

Hank groaned. "*You* might. But that case wasn't broke by forgery detection."

"That's why we're called questioned documents examiners. It's often something besides the handwriting that gives away the criminal: paper, misused language, wrong pens or inks for the time."

"Do you go to court?"

"Sometimes. Most of my work is written reports. I don't say with certainty whether a handwriting sample is a forgery or not, only make statements of likelihood."

Beside Ruby, Jesse began to rock back and forth. Ruby placed her hand on her daughter's shoulder and the rocking increased, becoming more forceful and rhythmic.

"Is she all right?" Hank asked, reaching a hand toward Jesse.

"She does this sometimes. It's sensory overload."

Suddenly a crack sounded through the silent forest, followed by the distant sound of breaking glass. "Damn it," Hank said, jumping up. "Stay here. Don't leave the blanket. I'll be right back."

"Where are you going?" Ruby asked, turning so she could take Jesse into her arms.

"I'll be back," he said, and was gone.

Ruby watched Hank run away from them in his heavy boots, clueless as to which point of the compass he was running toward. She listened to the fading sound of his feet and finally nothing, only the stillness beneath the trees where the breezes didn't reach. Above them, the leaves formed a green roof that tinted the air lime; the overstory, Hank had called it.

Ruby held Jesse, but not too tightly, and matched her

rocking to her daughter's, each sway and pivot identical, pressing Jesse's head against her heart and gradually slowing them both, repeating the lullaby, "Bye Baby Bunting, Daddy's gone ahunting, to catch a little bunny skin, to wrap his baby bunting in."

The crack had been a gunshot, a light rifle, maybe a .22. As a girl, Ruby had heard and shot enough to judge that higher-pitched, lighter sound. And the breaking glass. Were they near a cabin or a house?

Jesse finally went lax and Ruby lay her down on the blanket, resting on one elbow beside her. On watch, scanning the woods. Whoever had fired the shot would be long gone by the time Hank reached the damage.

Ruby fantasized never leaving this deep woods. She'd build a house of sticks at the foot of this giant oak and eat roots and berries and dedicate her life to making Jesse strong again. They'd stay here until she returned to Jesse all that was lost, living lives so pure of heart no power would dare interfere.

The sun slanted through the canopy of leaves onto their blanket, rippling light and shade. Jesse held up her right hand, intently watching the shadows cross and recross her flesh.

Ruby heard Hank before he came into sight, the movements of humans so telltale and ungainly. His face was grim. He hunkered down beside the blanket and balanced his elbows on his knees.

"Another visit from the Sugar Brigade," he told her. "They shot my Cherokee."

"Oh! But isn't it back that way?"

Hank shook his head. "Don't ever go into strange forests by yourself, Ruby." He pointed in the direction he'd just come. "It's about a quarter mile that way."

"Is your Jeep damaged?"

"They shot out a side window and wrote a love note on the windshield suggesting I perform an anatomical impossibility. They also invited me to leave town."

"Tell the sheriff," she advised.

He looked at Ruby seriously. "If you don't want to see me again, I understand. There's no romance in ducking potshots on a date. Hanging out with me could be dangerous and it won't exactly endear you to Sable."

"I make up my own mind."

He reached out his hand and touched her shoulder, smiling. "I'm glad."

Chapter 12

Ruby stood in her kitchen, holding the phone to her ear and looking out at the faintly glowing light in DeEtta's trailer.

"Does Mina have any idea who shot her collie?" Carly asked.

"She doesn't know the dog's dead and I don't think you should tell her, either. But I *do* believe you should investigate it."

"I said I'd look into it, Ruby, but it may not accomplish anything. Pepper probably wandered into the woods and an idiot with the meanies took a pot shot at him."

"Mina's by herself, Carly. Pepper's been her only protection and now she's truly alone. If someone trespassed on her property, she wouldn't know it."

"I'll radio Don and tell him to drive by Mina's tonight. I've only got three deputies to cover four hundred square miles."

"Thanks. And thanks for talking to Danny Greenstone."

Carly heaved a sigh. "Yeah. I called Wally Kentner's brother in Phoenix to ask if he'd hire Danny on his construction crew. I'd like to get Danny away from DeEtta permanently."

"Are you making progress investigating Corbin's death?" Ruby asked.

"Not as much as the community thinks I should be making," Carly said edgily. "Do me a favor. Get together with Mina's mother and convince Mina to move into town. Being alone isn't good for her now."

"I'm visiting Mina tomorrow," Ruby told him. "I'll do my best."

"Thanks, Ruby. I appreciate it."

Ruby hung up and for a few minutes considered calling Mina to be sure she was all right, then pulled her hand away from the phone. Tomorrow. There was no sense startling Mina with a phone call just as another long night began.

In the main room, Spot balanced on her hind legs against the window, ears perked forward. She didn't growl but neither did her tail wag.

A figure stood twenty feet back from the screened porch. Ruby gasped, her first thought that Danny had returned, then recognized the hunched shoulders, the head thrust forward. It was Mrs. Pink.

Ruby opened the front door, stepped onto the porch, and unlocked the screen door. Mrs. Pink remained motionless.

"Come in," Ruby called, staying back, remembering how Mrs. Pink had pressed away from Ruby when she'd come upon her near Fox Woods. "I'm making coffee for us."

And she turned on her heels and entered the cabin, leaving the doors standing open to the night air.

Ruby filled the pot, measured out grounds, and set out sugar and milk without glancing toward the open front door.

When she finally turned to set two cups on the counter, the front door was closed and Mrs. Pink sat in the straightback chair by the rocker, her staff lying at her feet and Spot sitting squarely in front of her, regarding her solemnly.

Mrs. Pink wore black from head to toe. Her dress was dotted with the remnants of a black bead design at the neck. Her head was covered by a black beret worn like a stocking cap.

"Do you take sugar in your coffee?" Ruby asked Mrs. Pink.

"One lump, please."

Ruby emptied a spoonful of sugar in one cup and none in the other. "Are we the only ones left on the lake?" Ruby asked her.

"*Nein*. But you and me, we are our own closest neighbors."

"Then we'll have to look out for each other," Ruby told her.

"*Ja, mein* Frank, he watches." Mrs. Pink nodded to the quilt hoop and the quilt Ruby was working on. "That's your grandmother Sofia's work. I remember."

"I'm finishing it. Did you know Gram very well?"

Mrs. Pink smiled. "As well as I know you."

"You mean you watched her through the windows?"

Mrs. Pink laughed as if Ruby were very clever, and Spot wagged her tail. "That's what I did. We would have been good as girls together, your grandmama and me. She was a fine lady."

"I know it."

Ruby filled the cups with coffee and carried them into the main room.

Mrs. Pink's fingers were too swollen to hold the cup by the handle, so she cradled it in both her hands. Ruby watched the cup warily, wishing she hadn't poured it so full.

"Do you knit or crochet?" Ruby asked Mrs. Pink. "What do you do during the winter, when it snows?"

"I use snowshoes."

Ruby couldn't decide whether Mrs. Pink was teasing or not. The lower rims of the old woman's eyes sagged outward, exposing pink flesh. Tears perpetually brimmed there.

"From now on," Ruby told her, "whenever you come

here, I'll expect you to come inside and have coffee with me. I'll put on the pot the instant I see you."

Mrs. Pink studied Ruby. "I couldn't stay long. *Mein* Frank would worry."

"You don't have to stay long," Ruby assured her. "We'll just check each other, like good neighbors should."

"I'll think about it." Mrs. Pink shifted uncomfortably on her chair. "What's wrong with your girl?"

"She was hurt in an automobile accident."

"That's why I walk," Mrs. Pink said smugly. "It's not so dangerous. You see a car coming and you take two steps out of the way. But your girl will get better."

She was just a nosy old woman who peeked in windows, but Ruby's heart rose gratefully to hear those words spoken with such certitude. "It'll take a long time."

"Then she needs to live a long life. Everybody's always getting better from something." Mrs. Pink slapped her leg and a little coffee sloshed unheeded onto her hand. "You can always say to people 'I hope everything will be better soon,' and you've said the right words." She laughed softly.

"Do you know Mina Turmouski?" Ruby asked her.

"I knew Mina Asauskas when she became Mina Goodlight but not when she became Mina Turmouski." She paused. "Except once."

"When?" Ruby asked.

Mrs. Pink shook her head. "It's none of your business."

"Somebody shot her dog."

"Maybe it was a bad dog."

At the words "bad dog," Spot's gaze shifted uncertainly from Ruby to Mrs. Pink.

"You know people here. Who would shoot Mina's dog right after she lost her husband?"

"Why ask me?" Mrs. Pink asked sharply. Her face

puckered into a frown, and she thumped her half-full coffee cup on the end table and reached for her walking stick.

"I'm only old. Old doesn't make me any smarter about people because I've lived so long I see every stupid thing humans do." With her walking stick and one hand to the back of the chair she awkwardly pulled herself up. "Seeing people be stupid doesn't make me wise; it makes me sick."

Ruby stood, too. "Come back again, Mrs. Pink. You can meet Jesse."

At the door, Mrs. Pink gently nudged Ruby with her stick. "At least you don't apologize. That's to your good."

"I don't have anything to apologize for," Ruby told her.

Mrs. Pink's raspy laughter hung on the air after she'd faded into the darkness. Ruby stood in the doorway, feeling the moist air, the heavy silence that had weight and texture, like warm water, picturing Mrs. Pink treading through the night like a slow swimmer, her senses blunted and altered to fit her own vision.

The old-fashioned metallic bell jangled through the cabin and Ruby hurried down the loft steps, half awake. She gasped at the sounds of movement coming toward her from Jesse's room and then remembered Spot.

"Yes?" she asked breathlessly, snatching up the receiver at the same time she flicked on the kitchen light. The cat clock read 1:30.

"Ruby, it's me, Mina. I have to talk to you."

Ruby dropped into the kitchen chair and Spot leaned against her leg. She'd *told* Mina to call anytime, day or night, hadn't she?

"What's wrong?" she asked. "Is someone there? Are you all right?"

"I need to talk to you about Corbin. It's important." Mina's voice ran high and fast. "Wired," the pre-accident Jesse would have described it.

"I'm right here, Mina," Ruby said. Night was the worst time for the devils, Gram always claimed; Ruby knew that firsthand.

"No. I have to *see* you. I have something to give you. Can I come over?"

"Can't we talk on the phone? You could drive over in the morning. It's too late to be on the road."

"It's important," Mina insisted, her voice rising. "I lied to you about Corbin and our marriage. And about the sawmill. Please help me. I'm coming over right now. Will you be up?"

"Of course. Drive carefully, Mina."

Ruby suspected this would be a long night. As she waited for Mina to arrive, she made a second pot of coffee.

Chapter 13

By two-thirty, Ruby had quilted a panel of Gram's quilt in a modified leaf and feather design, moving her needle swiftly beneath the high-intensity lamp she'd brought down from her lab, her thoughts on Mina. It had been an hour since her friend's distraught call. The full coffeepot waited on the warmer, the fire Ruby had rebuilt in the fireplace had collapsed into coals.

It was, at most, a twenty-minute drive from Mina's house to Ruby's cabin. Mina might have been in her nightclothes when she phoned; it took time to change. She may have had car trouble.

Ruby set aside the quilt hoop and laid two more logs on the fire. Sparks snapped and rose up the chimney like fireflies. She kicked an errant ember back inside and closed the mesh screen.

She moved to the window and squinted toward the long driveway for a few minutes, willing the headlights of Mina's car to emerge from the woods. Hi! Sorry I'm late. Spot stretched on the rug beside the fireplace, head on paws, ears twitching each time Ruby moved.

Mina had asked, no: begged for Ruby's help; she claimed she'd lied about her marriage to Corbin and the sawmill. Her perfect marriage? Ruby swore there was real love between the two of them. And what about the sawmill? And what was she bringing Ruby? Ruby rubbed her arms and crossed the cabin to the telephone. Mina's phone rang ten times before Ruby hung up.

Supposing Mina had just left her house, Ruby would

allow her another twenty minutes. She poured herself a cup of coffee and sat at the kitchen table with a pencil and paper. First she wrote a cursive alphabet in the Palmer method, connecting all the letters like one long word, then she did the same in Spencerian and Zaner-Blouser methods, her equivalent of doodling, listening for the sound of a car arriving on the sandy driveway.

Three o'clock came and went. Ruby put on her jacket and crossed the driveway to DeEtta's faintly glowing trailer. It was cool, the night predawn dark.

"What?" DeEtta cried out before Ruby's second rap on the metal door. "Who is it?"

"It's Ruby."

A light switched on behind the blinds and DeEtta opened the door. Barefoot, in a long flannel nightgown. Her eyes were wide, frightened. "What's wrong?"

"Can you come over and sleep on the couch? I'm leaving for a while."

The questions came in an indignant barrage. "Why? Is there trouble? Where are you going? It's the middle of the night."

"Mina Turmouski couldn't sleep," Ruby told DeEtta. "She was coming here, but that was two hours ago. I'm going to drive out that way and see if she's stranded with car trouble."

"Call the sheriff," DeEtta said. "Don't go alone."

"I won't be gone long. If her car broke down, I'll bring her back to the cabin."

"I can call Bruce," DeEtta offered.

"If I don't find her, we'll call the sheriff," Ruby promised. "But I'll check the roads myself first."

"I don't think you should do this, but just a second." DeEtta stepped back inside her trailer and in a moment returned in her robe and slippers, a hefty metal flashlight in her hand. "Take this with you," DeEtta said. "You never know."

●   ●   ●

Ruby drove slowly, scanning pull-outs and ditches, her headlight beams on high, her doors locked, moving farther and farther from her cabin without finding a trace of Mina's car. The roads were empty of vehicles.

Houses stood dark and closed. There were no twenty-four-hour grocery stores or all-night gas stations. Her headlights pierced long beams through the dark, and beyond her beams, she occasionally caught glimpses of gleaming eyes and unfocused movement.

But she didn't find Mina's car. Mina, in her unsteady state of mind, might have gone back to bed. Ruby braked on the bridge over the Sable River and rolled down her window, hearing the fast rush and babble of water, checking for skid marks or broken rails.

The other side of the river, Ruby spotted approaching headlights and breathed a sigh of relief. It must be Mina. She pulled over and blinked her lights, signaling for the driver to stop.

But as the car drew near, the driver switched on the high beams, blinding Ruby and racing past her at such speed, she felt her car rock as if a semi had passed. In her rearview mirror, she watched the car's rectangular red taillights disappear. When they were out of sight, she pulled back onto the road, continuing toward Mina's.

A hundred yards before the pavement turned to gravel, at the last turn onto Silas's and Mina's road, Ruby spotted another set of headlights shining through the trees. She couldn't tell which road the car was approaching from, gravel or paved, and she unthinkingly turned on her windshield wipers as if that could help clear her view.

But the headlights didn't draw any nearer. In fact, they appeared to be stationary, pointing upward into the trees. Ruby turned onto the gravel road, her fears momentarily soothed by the ordinary crunch of gravel beneath her tires.

Ahead, off the right side, weakening headlights beamed at a slant, highlighting a misty column of light. A car had run into the ditch. Ruby pulled up beside it and turned off her engine.

A Bonnie Raitt song about good men and women poured from the car in the ditch, reverberating between trees. The doors were closed but the driver's window had either been rolled down or broken out.

"Mina?" Ruby called. Her voice cracked and she called again, louder. "Mina! Are you there?"

There was no answer. It was definitely Mina's car: a gray Pontiac sedan. One front wheel was partly out of the ditch as if the car had spun and slid off the road backward. Ruby swept DeEtta's flashlight beam across the gravel, seeing a long curve of dark tracks dug into the stone and sand leading directly to the ditch.

Ruby slid down to the car, bracing herself against the fender. Holding her breath, she raised her flashlight and aimed it into the car's interior. Mina wasn't there. She didn't spot a purse or wallet. A peechee, a folder like they'd used in school, lay open on the seat; it was empty. Maybe Mina had climbed out and walked home. Ruby wrenched open the driver's door and leaned inside, switching off both the tape player and the lights. The sudden silence was as shocking as unexpected noise.

"Mina?" Ruby called again, standing stone still, straining to hear any sound.

The bottom of the ditch was soft and mucky, sucking at Ruby's shoes. Burdock clutched at her pants. She climbed out of the ditch and worked her way along the narrow level of ground between the gully and a drooping barbed wire fence, every little while calling "Mina?"

She saw Mina's small hand first, palm up, fingers

delicately curled as if she'd just released something very fragile. She lay on her back in the long grasses, partly beneath the old fence, her face and hair streaked with blood. Ruby knelt beside her and touched her wrist. She couldn't find a pulse beneath the cool skin. "Oh, Mina," she whispered. "I'm sorry."

Ruby was still kneeling beside Mina's body, transfixed by the motionless figure, when she grew aware of approaching headlights. Stop that car, she told herself. But what she desired most was to lie down beside Mina and weep.

But the car stopped anyway. Lights on the roof gyrated and a spotlight swept across the scene. Ruby stood and raised her hand.

It was Sheriff Carly Joyce. He jumped across the ditch, paused briefly by the car, then joined Ruby, his light playing across Mina's form and face.

"Oh, shit," he said.

"She's dead," Ruby told him.

He nodded and knelt to feel Mina's neck. "Did you see anything?" he asked Ruby.

"Only what you see here. The tape player and headlights were on. I turned them off. Why are you here?"

"DeEtta called and told me you'd gone out looking for Mina. Don was tied up with a domestic so I drove out." That explained his jeans and a sweater. His feet were barefoot inside his sneakers. He looked down at Mina and hit his flashlight against his palm. "Sometimes . . ." He shook his head. "I'll go make a couple of calls. You can sit in my car. I've got a Thermos of coffee."

Ruby shook her head. "I'll stay with her a little longer."

Carly nodded and left Ruby standing in the damp grass by Mina's body, thinking she should do or say something meaningful. Gram would have lit a candle or said a prayer. Ruby had no candles and she didn't pray.

When the crackle and buzz of Carly talking on the radio was silenced, he stayed by his car, drinking coffee and jotting notes on a clipboard. There was a subtle lightening of the sky; it wouldn't be long until morning and the day was given back.

Carly tossed his clipboard onto the front seat and joined Ruby, carrying a dark blanket, which he tenderly spread over Mina's body.

"What do you think happened?" Ruby asked him.

"She swerved. We've got an overabundance of deer this year and they're starting to yard up. She wasn't wearing her seat belt and was thrown from her car."

"But both her car doors were closed," Ruby pointed out.

"That might have happened when the car came to a stop. It's not unusual for car doors to pop open and close during an accident. This is a damn, damn shame. Do you know why she was on her way to your cabin?"

"She wanted to talk."

"In the middle of the night?"

"Her husband hasn't been dead very long. Nights are the worst and she was afraid to be alone." Ruby thought a moment. "She was agitated."

"Agitated?" Carly asked, gazing down at the blanketed figure.

"Upset. She said she had something important to give me concerning Corbin."

"It was about Corbin? You're sure of that?"

"Yes."

"I'll check the car," he said. He left Ruby and shone his light through the windows into Mina's car. Then he climbed inside and examined the interior, including the glove compartment and beneath the seats. He finally backed out of the car and closed the door, empty-handed.

Another car approached from the direction of Mina's house. It stopped beside the sheriff's car and Silas Shea hurried forward. "I saw the lights," Ruby heard him say. "That's Mina's car. What happened?"

"She swerved and went into the ditch. She didn't make it."

Silas groaned. "Not Mina too." His voice broke and Ruby heard his harsh breathing. "What in hell was she doing out here in the middle of the night? She should have known better."

"She was on her way to Ruby Crane's," Carly said. "Ruby found her."

Silas stepped across the ditch and stood beside Ruby, looking down at the blanket-covered body. "Poor little thing," he said. "This'll kill Enid." After a minute's silent tribute, he asked Ruby, "Why was she coming to see you in the middle of the night?"

Something was in the air. Ruby felt it overlay her sorrow for Mina; it hung in the sad but careful tone of Silas's voice. Sheriff Carly stood on the road looking toward the north, the direction the coroner would come from. Was he listening?

"She couldn't sleep. I told her to call me when she needed company," Ruby told Silas.

"She took Corbin's death hard," Silas said.

Ruby stepped away from Mina's draped body and Silas, and crossed the ditch to the sheriff. "Shouldn't you be protecting the scene?"

"It's protected."

"What about the road?" She pointed to Silas's car parked directly on top of the swerving tire marks.

"I already know those tracks mean she fishtailed into the ditch. We'll check her alcohol level, drugs maybe." He raised his hand. "Don't fly off, Ruby. I'm not saying Mina was on illegal drugs. The doctor probably gave her a prescription to help her through the worst."

That made sense. It could also account for Mina's agitation on the phone. Ruby told Carly about the vehicle that had sped past her near the river.

"You didn't recognize it?" he asked, jotting on his clipboard.

"No. All I saw was its high beams. It had rectangular taillights."

"Most taillights are rectangular. Anything else?"

"No. You can't actually believe Mina's death is an accident," Ruby said.

"I don't know, Ruby," Carly said. "Weird things happen sometimes. We'll investigate it thoroughly, I promise."

"And what about the dog? That wasn't an accident. If I were you I'd check its wound. Match the bullet with a gun in this county."

"Do you know how many guns are in this county?" Carly asked. "It would take months."

"What about Mina's dog?" Silas asked. "Do you mean Pepper?"

"I found him in a meadow a quarter mile down the road," Ruby told him. "He'd been shot in the head."

Silas fingered the scar over his ear. "It's like the whole family is being destroyed."

His words hung in the air. A moth fluttered into the light, then landed on the sheriff's headlight and dropped to the ground.

"Don't talk crazy, Silas," Carly said.

"I'll take a look," Carly said gently. "Go on home now, Ruby. I'm sorry you found Mina. Get some sleep."

"Come on, honey," Silas said, putting his arm around her shoulder. "I'll drive you home. Or you can stay at our house."

"No thank you," Ruby said. "I can drive."

"I'll walk you to your car then," Silas replied.

Birds chirped and called from the trees around them, softening their overloud footsteps on the gravel road.

Beside her car, Silas said softly, "If you haven't already told Carly about Corbin's missing support, I'm going to tell him now."

"I didn't," Ruby told him. "But Mina said Corbin removed it himself a year ago."

"She did?" Silas asked, staring off into the trees while Ruby got into her car. He was still staring into the distance as Ruby started her car and headed home.

As Ruby drove off, she passed the ambulance and another police car approaching in the silvery dawn as silently as they had after Corbin's death.

Ruby wanted to believe Mina's death was due to a sudden swerve as helpless as Stan's, but she didn't. With Mina's watchdog dead, had someone been secretly observing her, waiting for the right moment to engineer an accident?

And the atmosphere at the scene among Silas, Carly, and herself. They'd said the right words: shock and sorrow and cursing fate. But there was another level of awareness, the unsaid.

Corbin was dead and now Mina was dead. Lightning striking twice. But lightning was random, without logic. There was logic in these deaths, a purpose. Simple chance was not a factor in either Corbin's or Mina's death. Ruby knew it, but she didn't know what to do about it.

Chapter 14

Ruby sat on a lawn chair with its front legs set in the lapping edge of Blue Lake, her bare feet in the cold water. If she narrowed her eyes, she could imagine her chair floating on the lake, surrounded by blue water. Behind her and far away lay the rest of the world.

She'd left Jesse with DeEtta and dozed, her head back against the cool metal, but her sleep provided no rest. Her body felt trembly. When she blinked, her eyes scratched and burned.

"Hey," Hank said softly. He knelt beside her chair and gently touched her shoulder. Ruby leaned forward and into his arms, welcoming his hands at her neck, smoothing back her hair. A brief refuge. The tears were unexpected, a relief.

"I'm sorry about Mina," he said, pulling away, his hands still holding her shoulders.

"She was on her way to my cabin," Ruby told him. "I told her I'd listen if she needed to talk."

"You were a good friend," he said, wiping her eyes with his shirt sleeve.

"I didn't have time to be. She said she'd lied, that she had something to give me, but I don't understand what she meant. She pleaded with me to help her."

"Shh," Hank said. "It doesn't matter now. Let her rest."

Ruby wrapped her arms around herself. "Who told you?"

"I had breakfast at the Knotty Pine. I detected a healthy amount of guilt mingling with the shock."

"There should be. After she left Ford for Corbin, people didn't bother staying in contact; they just let her go."

Hank nodded. "That's what we're most guilty of: the good things we don't do."

She thought Hank was about to say more but instead he smiled and rose to stand behind her and massage her shoulders. "The trees are looking good," he said. "See that red one by Mrs. Pink's? I think it's the Burning Bush. Do you feel like going for a ride? No place special. Driving just helps sometimes."

They drove slowly, aimlessly, from road to tree-lined road, once following a yellow grader smoothing gravel. "They're dressing the roads for the hunters," Hank commented as he closed his window on the dust.

Hank slowed by property covered mostly with smaller aspen trees. An orange machine with a huge claw at the end of a mechanized arm was systematically pinching off trees just above the ground, then dragging them to the maw of a chipping machine. The chipper shrieked and, from a chute at the other end, a confetti of pale wood chips spewed into a waiting trailer.

"What are they doing?" Ruby asked. "They're cutting everything."

"It's a chipping operation," Hank told her. "Sometimes it's called whole tree harvesting, one of those mind-lulling terms. Totally mechanized. These guys can go to work in sandals and tank tops and grind up acres without ever having to actually touch a tree."

"But why? Who wants all this?"

"Paper companies. You can chip a woods clean, aspen will grow back like weeds, and chip again in twenty or thirty years, but after two harvests, you wipe out eighty percent of the soil's calcium. We haven't had the technology long enough to know what happens after three or four chippings."

A man in clean and casual clothes walked past. He

waved and walked a few yards closer, squinting into the Cherokee. Then he gave Hank the finger and walked away.

"What can I say?" Hank asked wryly. "I'm a popular sort of guy."

When they were back on the road, Ruby said, "I keep wondering if Mina's lie about Corbin had something to do with the mill or Silas. Even the support."

"His support? How could she lie about that?"

Ruby turned on the seat. "You saw his support?"

"On his sawmill, you mean, by his operating lever? Sure. His leg bothered him more than he let on."

"When was the last time you saw it?" Ruby asked.

"About a month ago. No, I can't actually say I *saw* it then, but I took it for granted it was still there. Corbin was proud; it wasn't obvious how much he used it. Why? What about the support?"

Ruby briefly related her conversation with Mina, excluding Silas's role in requesting she inspect Corbin's sawmill for the support.

Hank frowned. "I saw him wearing his leg brace now and then but it's odd she'd claim he removed the support a year ago. I haven't been in Sable that long and I've seen it several times. He didn't explain its use, but it didn't require a genius to figure it out."

"Maybe Mina continued the charade of claiming he was stronger than he actually was," Ruby suggested.

"Maybe," Hank said. "And you have no idea what she was bringing you?"

"No." Ruby remembered the empty school folder, the peechee, in Mina's car. "It was paper, though, information written on paper.

"There was a note, Ruby."

"A note from who? What are you talking about?"

At his end of the phone, Sheriff Carly cleared his

throat. "Mina left you a note. We found it this morning on her kitchen table."

"What does it say?"

"That the pain was more than she could stand."

"Do you expect me to believe Mina left a *suicide* note?" Ruby asked incredulously. "I'd like to see it."

"It's going in the report."

"Can I have a photocopy?"

Carly hesitated and Ruby prompted, "Only a photocopy. The note *is* intended for me, isn't it?"

"All right. I'll bring it out later."

"No," Ruby said, forestalling a change of mind or giving Carly any more time to talk it over with his cronies. "I'm coming to town right now. I'll stop by and pick it up."

Fifteen minutes later, Ruby stepped through the plate-glass door of the brick building between Sable and Pere that housed the county jail and the sheriff's office.

Carly himself stood at the photocopy machine behind the reception desk. "I'm copying the note for you now," he said. "Come on in my office."

Carly's office wasn't plush. No misuse of taxpayers' funds here. A calendar of Michigan scenes hung behind his desk. September's was a night shot of the graceful Mackinac Bridge, its towers and cables holiday bright. On Carly's desk, a photograph of his wife and two daughters sat beside a ceramic Model T. Ruby glanced at the three wide faces, recognizing the familial similarity to DeEtta.

"Your daughter's one of the Color Festival contestants," Ruby said. "I saw her photo at Mabel's."

"Rachel," Carly said. "God help us if she loses."

Carly slipped a phone pad–size slip of paper into a folder and handed Ruby a photocopy, the smaller slip centered neatly on the page.

The note was a good photocopy, clear and detailed. It said simply "Ruby, this pain is too much. I'm sorry."

"It's not signed," Ruby noted aloud.

"Yeah, but it's her handwriting. Harold Rogers confirmed it."

"Isn't Harold the coroner?"

"He knows forgery. He's good at animal bites, too. Last year he matched a bite on Frank Young's arm to Mrs. Step's Rottweiller."

"Oh." Ruby was surprised the news that she specialized in forgery and questioned documents still hadn't reached Carly via DeEtta; could the nurse's aide be practicing surprising discretion? Ruby didn't see any reason to mention her expertise yet.

"Why would Mina leave me a note when she was on her way to see me?" she mused aloud.

Carly sat back and held his hands so only his fingertips touched. "On the opposite side of the road from where you found her car is that concrete culvert the road commission planned to install about ten years ago. That stretch turns into mud every spring, but the county used up its allocation. Typical. Anyway, they left the culvert sitting on end beside the road. It's a hazard."

"And you believe Mina intended to drive her car into the culvert?"

"If we had freeways like where you lived, she would have chosen an overpass. She changed her mind at the last minute and couldn't straighten her car out in time. She was depressed, wasn't she?"

"It would be unnatural if she wasn't. Her husband was murdered a few days ago."

Carly nodded. "Mina was the key. I thought I'd have more of a case by now."

"Mina *was* the key," Ruby agreed. "That's why she was killed. She was bringing me evidence that proved who murdered Corbin, I'm certain of it. Whoever ran her off the road removed it."

Carly stared glumly at his hands. "If only she'd been open with you or me. She sat in the chair you're sitting in and then clammed right up."

Ruby bit her lip, thinking of Corbin's missing support. She had one thing to do before she told Carly. "Have you talked to Mina's mother?" she asked.

Carly nodded. "Nothing."

"When she phoned, she said she'd lied about her marriage."

A look of understanding flashed across Carly's face and Ruby persisted. "*You* know what that means, don't you?"

Carly closed his eyes. "It's gossip, Ruby. I'm not going into it. They're both dead; it doesn't matter. But I do know that discussing the state of her marriage isn't the reason Mina came to talk to me." Carly looked pained. "Mina isn't the first or last wife who decided to end her life after her husband's death."

Ruby filed the fact that gossip existed about Mina's marriage in the back of her mind. "I've gone over and over what she said on the phone and I believe she was bringing me something, Carly. There was a folder in her car, just like the ones we had in school, with the pockets, remember? It was empty. Whatever she was bringing me was in that folder."

"I saw the folder," Carly said. "It could have been there for months. Maybe she kept grocery coupons in it. There were loose coupons in the car."

"What about Mina's autopsy?" Ruby asked.

Carly chose another page from the folder on his desk. "Alcohol *and* antidepressants. Not a lethal amount of either, but together . . ."

"The cause of death?" Ruby asked.

"Trauma to the head."

Ruby nodded and stood, holding the photocopy by the edges. Trauma to the head. A head injury. "Thanks, Carly," she said, reaching out her right hand to him.

"Sure." He shook her hand awkwardly, not used to the spontaneous glad-handing Ruby had grown accustomed to on the West Coast. "Are you going to the funeral tomorrow?" he asked.

"I'll go to the lunch at the VFW Hall, but I just can't attend the funeral. I never could stand them."

"I know what you mean. Well, I'll see you at the lunch."

Ruby laid the photocopied note flat in her backseat. She needed to compare it to a standard. Mina hadn't been in a state to suddenly jot off a suicide note to Ruby and then drive her car down the road to commit the act. Why not just take too many pills? She had them in her possession. Or start up Corbin's saw? Ruby winced, taking back the thought, standing with her hand on her door handle until the wave of grief passed.

No, on the telephone Mina had been raging to talk to Ruby, to *see* her and explain her lie, to bring her information, not to hint she was about to commit suicide.

She stopped at Mabel's studio. Mabel emerged from her darkroom, a visor pulled low on her forehead, holding two black-and-white photos. Two elderly women sat facing one another on a bench, both with open mouths, talking spiritedly at the same time.

"Which one do you think is better?" Mabel asked.

"They look identical to me," Ruby told her.

Mabel pulled away the two photos. "Then you're not paying attention, Ruby. You're not here to work today, are you?"

Ruby shook her head. "I'd like to use your photocopier and take the afternoon off."

"Go ahead. The whole town should take the afternoon off. Mina didn't deserve this."

"Did Mina send out thank-you notes after Corbin's funeral?" Ruby asked.

"She didn't really have time, did she? If she sent any, I didn't receive one. I had the Flower Hut deliver daisies."

Ruby thought of the rotting flowers behind Corbin's mill. "Do you know anyone who received a note from Mina?"

"If you're asking if Joe Shmoe called me up and said 'I got a pretty little thank-you card from Mina Turmouski today,' no, he didn't."

"The funeral's tomorrow," Ruby said.

"I don't attend funerals." Mabel stopped. "Except Bill's. He made me promise not to embarrass him. So I went." She shrugged. "It wasn't much."

The cabin was fragrant with the odor of baking. Two browned apple pies sat cooling on the counter and two more were in the works under DeEtta's hands. She was rolling out the pale pie crust with a wine bottle when Ruby walked in.

"They're for Mina's lunch," DeEtta told her. "We'll need a lot of food."

"Where's Jesse?" Ruby asked.

DeEtta nodded toward the window. Ruby turned in alarm. Jesse sat on the chaise longue facing the lake, a pair of sunglasses perched on her nose. "You left her out there alone?"

"I'm watching her. She said she wanted to get a tan. I told her there weren't many tanning rays left in this sun but she didn't care. It's good for her to be outside."

Ruby walked out the front door and sat in the webbed chair opposite Jesse. "I hear you're getting a suntan."

Jesse lifted her right arm. "Is it nice?"

"Beautiful."

They sat together, looking out at the water. Ruby sang, "Row, row, row your boat," and Jesse contributed an appropriate word to the rounds every now and then, spoken, not sung.

As thoughts of Mina and the past slipped through Ruby's mind, the answer came to her: her high school annuals. Mina had written in Ruby's yearbooks. The annuals from her two and a half years of high school had been shipped to her by her father along with Gram's quilts. Otherwise Ruby would have thrown them out years ago. They were still in the bottom of Gram's scrapbag.

As soon as DeEtta finished her pies, Ruby dug out her old yearbooks, dusty with fabric lint. She leafed through the ancient pages, ignoring the photographs and glancing at all that childish penmanship, aware the keys, the roots of each person's adult handwriting already existed at ages fourteen and fifteen and, usually, much earlier.

She found Mina's entry at the back of the first annual, on an end page, which was good, no background interference. "Stay out of trouble. Like sure, ha ha," Mina's entry concluded.

Ruby carried the two annuals and the five photocopies she'd made at Mabel's to her lab in the loft. The young Mina had been experimenting with her capital letters, adding curls and extra sweeping lines, but in the body of her high school entry, the capital *T* was plain, almost printed, the same as the suicide note.

The handwriting on the note was larger than that in the yearbook entry, which was curious. Frequently, during depression and often in a suicide note, handwriting was *smaller* than normal, while during a state of elation, writing was frequently larger and expanded. The writing in the suicide note was more consistent than Ruby would expect from a woman who was depressed or under the influence of drugs.

Ruby turned on her light table and placed one of the

photocopies she'd made at Mabel's over Carly's copy, moving letter on top of identical letter: *t* over *t*, *s* over *s*.

Ruby, This pain is too much. I'm sorry.

The letters were identical, no matter their position in a word: the *m* in "much" with the *m* in "I'm, the *s* in "is" and "sorry." Very unusual. It was common to change letter formation depending on the letter's position within a word.

Although the letters were similar to the yearbook entry, the spacing between the words was cramped for the size of the penmanship.

Ruby jotted notes as she worked, as she would for any job, until she'd filled two pages that pointed to Mina's suicide note as being a probable forgery. She needed a recent sample of Mina's handwriting to be certain.

"Hank," Ruby said into the telephone. "Explain to me again what the guide pins do."

"They're a safety device. A spinning saw blade is like a gyroscope. It tends to stay in a straight line but several situations: dirt, hard knots, maybe dull teeth will push it out of alignment. The guide pins hold the blade in place so you get a straight cut."

"How are the pins adjusted?"

"Set screws hold them in place, ideally about four-hundredths of an inch from the blade, although most sawyers eyeball the space between the pin and the blade. If the blade touches the pins for very long, it heats up and the tension changes. Not good."

Ruby jotted Hank's description on the pad beside her telephone. "How often are the pins adjusted?" she asked.

"Depends on the sawyer. Definitely whenever the cut starts to go crooked." He paused. "What are you up to, Ruby?"

"I was curious, that's all. I've heard terms this past week that I'm not familiar with."

"This sounds like more than curiosity."

"Are you attending Mina's funeral tomorrow?" Ruby asked.

"The luncheon. You'll be there?"

"Yes."

"I'd like to get together again after . . . in a couple of days."

"So would I," Ruby told him.

"One thousand one, one thousand two, one thousand three." Thunder cracked, then rolled like timpanies over the cabin and away across the lake. Lightning strobed through the loft and Ruby grabbed her sweater off the floor and ran barefoot down the loft steps, one thought uppermost: Jesse.

Thunder crashed and rumbled, stereophonic turned up too loud; the windows vibrated in their casements.

"Jesse?" she whispered, feeling frantically along the wall for the light switch. "Don't be frightened." She flipped the switch. Nothing happened. Where had she left the flashlight?

She touched the end of the bed and worked her way toward her daughter, bending low and murmuring Jesse's name.

Lightning flared, followed immediately by a peal of thunder and from somewhere the unmistakable rip and crash of a falling tree.

By lightning's glow, Ruby could see that Jesse lay asleep, her lips slightly parted, her right hand outside the covers. Ruby perceived it all in an instant, in a camera flash burned behind her eyes. But she couldn't believe Jesse was peacefully sleeping during this racket. With pounding heart, she lowered her face close to

Jesse's until she felt her daughter's breath on her cheek. Steady, warm, the slow intake and release.

In the next flash of lightning, Ruby caught sight of Spot standing in the driveway between the cabin and DeEtta's trailer. A wan light flickered in the trailer. The poor dog was soaking wet.

Ruby unlocked the kitchen door and opened it to the wind and rain. "Here, Spot. Here, girl."

Instead of Spot bounding into the dry house, Ruby heard a low warning growl.

"Spot?" she called again.

Two bolts of lightning cut the sky and Spot crouched ten feet in front of the kitchen door, facing Ruby, teeth bared, rain dripping from her matted fur. The whites of her eyes shone. She looked demented. The dog gave one low and meaningful bark and Ruby slammed and locked the door.

At daylight, the storm had passed, leaving behind a gray and dripping morning. When Ruby opened the kitchen door, Spot sat on the low stoop, wagging her tail, tongue lolling and her toothy mouth tipped up in a smile.

Ruby cautiously stepped toward the dog and Spot stood to greet her, turning in a happy circle.

"What are you?" Ruby asked. "Canine Jekyll and Hyde?" Spot leaned against Ruby's leg, then gave a happy bark and ran toward DeEtta's trailer.

That's when Ruby noticed the cleaved maple tree, one seared shard standing like a broken tooth, the remainder toppled into the trees, luckily away from the house.

The tree had to be sixty feet tall. The trunk and leafy crown felled like a giant cut off at the ankles.

DeEtta emerged from her trailer, combing her hair. "I heard it come down, did you?"

"Yes, but I didn't realize it was this close."

The gray clouds still hung low above them, and from all around came the sound of dripping water; water puddled in the driveway and in every concave surface.

DeEtta circled the treetop with Spot close by her left leg. "They take up a lot more room when they're on the ground," she said, and pulled off a leaf, absently tearing it to shreds.

Chapter 15

At eight o'clock on the morning of the funeral, Ruby drove the long way around to Mina's house, approaching from the south to avoid passing Silas and Enid Shea's property.

The roads she traveled were little-used farm roads, winding through trees in every stage of autumn color. In the late 1800s land in this area had been sold by mail to unsuspecting immigrants. The soil was too sandy but the immigrants put their all into it until they died or lost their mortgages. Now the land had mostly gone back to oak savanna and forest, dotted by stone foundations and sudden gnarled orchards.

A half mile from Mina's, she pulled far enough into an abandoned two-track that her car couldn't be spotted from the road, switched off the engine, and got out.

Ruby kept to the edge of the gravel road, jumping across the ditch and ducking into the trees when Silas's house came into sight. She stepped on a cluster of brown puff balls that shot greenish brown spores into the air, spores she'd once believed were mustard gas.

Mina's house felt abandoned and brooding. The sawmill and all the vehicles were intact, parked as they'd been the first time Ruby had visited. Mina's Pontiac was gone; had it been towed to the junkyard behind the Shell station?

Ruby took a steadying breath, looking both ways before she crossed the driveway to the sawmill yard, her stride self-conscious, as if eyes watched from the close-faced house.

The sliding doors of the sawmill were locked and Ruby approached the closed side door, childishly crossing her fingers behind her back as she turned the knob, certain it would be locked, too.

But the door opened soundlessly into the gloomy sawmill. This time she'd come prepared with a penlight in her pocket, adequate enough to illuminate her way to the light switch.

When the row of bulbs over the saw flicked on, ruffling sounded above her head. She ducked instinctively, then spotted the round eyes of a barn owl gazing through her from its perch on a roof beam.

Ruby had already seen all she wanted to of the circular saw blade. Instead, she concentrated on the operator's platform where Corbin's support had supposedly stood.

She stopped. The support was there, a narrow metal stand bolted to the side of the platform. At hip height was attached a padded leather cushion, dark with perspiration and oil. Ruby reached out and gripped a metal side, tugging. The support didn't move. It was solid.

How could she have missed it? She stepped back and studied the metal-and-leather device. Even being unfamiliar with a sawmill, she should have seen it.

"It *wasn't* here," she said aloud. She crouched beside the platform and shone her tiny light beam on the bolts that held the support to the platform. The bolt heads were caked with grease like the rest of the machinery, as if they'd been in place for years. Then Ruby leaned farther down and shone her light beneath the platform, on the nuts and washers that held the bolts.

Amid the grease and sawdust under the platform, the nuts were scratched and shiny as if a wrench had been taken to them recently.

Ruby rose. Corbin's support had been removed and

replaced. If it had never been removed or never reappeared, she'd doubt her own suspicions. Had Mina known?

Ruby would inform Carly, show him the tampering on the bolts. There must have been photographs taken when they removed Corbin's body. Those would prove the absence of the support.

But why? Why remove the support and then carefully bolt it back to the platform, even dirtying the bolts to disguise its temporary absence?

Unless the murderer had been sloppy. Maybe the murderer knew Mina avoided the sawmill and hadn't expected to be interrupted by Ruby investigating the silent saw. And luckily for the killer, in the horror of his crime, no one had noticed the missing support. Then, because Ruby had asked questions, the killer had bolted it in place again. But why had Mina lied to her about the support, saying Corbin no longer used it?

Ruby brushed off her hands. There was one more thing to check. She moved to the end of the roller where the last three boards sawn on Corbin's mill still lay askew, waiting to be stacked on one of the neat nearby piles.

Using the span of her hand as a guide, she judged all three boards to be eight feet long, one inch thick, and six inches wide. She pulled the first board off the roller and laid it on top of a stacked pile of one-by-sixes near the door, lining up its edges with the board beneath it. The board was perfectly straight. When she turned it sideways and peered down its length, she could see no change in thickness. She pulled the next board off the track and checked it: The edges were even, straight as a ruler's.

When Ruby reached for the last board, a sliver jammed into the fleshy part of her thumb. She ignored it and gently swung the board around, laying it on the stack, measuring and eying.

Finished, she stepped back and leaned against the wall, working at the sliver with her teeth while she thought.

If Corbin had been adjusting his saw's guide pins so hurriedly he hadn't turned off his saw, it was because his saw was out of alignment and the blade was producing crooked boards. If that was true, why were these boards perfectly straight? Shouldn't they have some waver to their edges, a bulge of thickness, an obvious sign that the saw was going out of true?

He hadn't been adjusting the guide pins. Add that to the disappearing support Corbin had braced himself against and this was proof Carly wasn't dealing with a *possible* homicide but an actual murder. The killer had raised the wooden cover by the guide pins, making it appear that Corbin had made the fatal mistake of adjusting the guide pins while the saw was running. Find whoever killed Corbin and Mina's death would be solved, too.

Ruby froze, hearing a car approach, wary until it had driven past without reducing speed.

But she'd forgotten one other thing: the rush job that Carly claimed wasn't actually a rush job. She tried to remember the name. A contractor in Pere, Carly had said. Xandau. Zander, that was it. Lyle Zander.

She drove back to Blue Lake the way she'd come, and it wasn't until she was teasing Jesse into holding still while she combed her hair that she suddenly realized she'd forgotten to turn off the lights in Corbin's mill.

Ruby was one of the last to arrive at the VFW Hall for the luncheon, right behind the funeral party.

She'd briefly considered returning to the mill to switch off the lights while most of Sable dressed for Mina's services and then talked herself out of it. No one had seen her; why risk being spotted now? She couldn't be linked to the lights; whoever discovered them burning would simply turn off the switch and forget it.

The day was crisp, colors heightened by low humidity and the autumn sun. As Ruby parked her Pinto behind Mina's parents' car, she noted the way each leaf on the maple in front of the building stood out, the sharp clarity of Fay Asuaskas's gray hair, every wave distinct. Oblique light. Barker Thompson had told her that not only handwriting but the whole world was more revealing when light was cast on it from an angle.

"There are more people here than at Corbin's lunch," DeEtta commented from the backseat.

Ruby pushed Jesse into the room filled with people. A table against one wall was covered with a white paper tablecloth and dish after bowl after plate of food. Macaroni salads, Jell-O molds, a sliced ham, pies and cakes. Lines of paper-covered tables filled the remainder of the hall.

A flag and an upright piano stood at one end of the long room and along the walls beneath fading red, white, and blue bunting hung framed photos of youthful Sable veterans, the living and the dead. The crowd's air was quietly festive, relieved. Well, *that's* over.

Ruby helped DeEtta situate Jesse at one of the tables, out of the main flow of traffic, and joined the line near the coffee urns behind Silas Shea. People she hadn't seen since childhood nodded to her without surprise; she also noted how those same people avoided Silas, leaving him standing by himself in the midst of the crowd.

"Have you seen Carly?" Ruby asked Silas.

"Not yet," Silas said. "I expect he'll be here, though." Around her she heard patches of conversation.

"One thing about Mina; she always kept a clean house."

"You wait: Death always comes in threes."

"Save me a piece of that chocolate pie, will you?"

"Ruby." It was Wally Kentner. He held a cup of coffee, his eyes somber. "You remember Ford Good-light, don't you?"

Ford, Mina's high school sweetheart and first husband, had barely changed in the past nineteen years. Freckles still dotted his face. His sandy hair remained thick and curly. He wore a suit he might have worn to his wedding: wide lapels, flared pants.

Ford shook Ruby's hand and she winced as he pressed the area where the sliver she'd caught in Corbin's mill was still stubbornly embedded in her flesh.

"I'm sorry. Did I hurt you?" he asked.

"No. I caught a sliver earlier, that's all."

Silas leaned forward. "Let Enid remove it after the lunch," he said. "She's good at it; a steady hand."

"Thanks," Ruby told him noncommittally. As if she'd give Enid the opportunity to prod at her bare flesh with a sharp object.

"I'm sorry about Mina," Ruby told Ford.

He nodded. "It's been a tough couple of weeks for our son." Ford nodded toward the piano where three adolescent boys stood together, passing a set of headphones between them. Ford and Mina's son had Ford's coloring and Mina's small bones, a premature hardness around his eyes.

"But he has you."

"When they're that age they've positive they don't need a soul."

A man tapped Wally's shoulder and said, "Do you have a minute? I've got a term life question."

"Sure," Wally said. He waved his cup to Ford and Ruby and moved off with the other man.

Ford stepped closer to Ruby, his body tight, lowering his voice to confidentiality. "I heard you were the last person to talk to Mina."

"I think so. She phoned me in the middle of the night and was on her way to my cabin when she . . . when the accident happened."

"Mina never would have committed suicide," Ford said fiercely. "Carly's wrong about that."

"I agree," Ruby told him, wondering if Ford knew about Mina's supposed suicide note.

He glanced to his left and right. "She didn't accidentally drive off the road, either."

"Why do you say that?"

Ford shifted uncomfortably. "You heard me; it was no accident. When she married Corbin, she got more than a new husband. If I were you, I'd check into Corbin."

"Why should I check into anything?" Ruby asked. "It's up to the sheriff to investigate, not me. I moved to Sable so my daughter would have a quiet place to recover."

"Is that a fact? Mina told me she saw you snooping around Corbin's sawmill."

"You stayed in touch with Mina?"

Ford's eyes shifted. "We talked. I would have taken her back. She's the only . . ." He stopped and swallowed. "So why were you in the mill?"

"I was curious."

"Was there enough blood for you?" Ford asked, his voice rising. "Is that how you get your kicks, looking at death scenes? First Corbin's, and then isn't it funny how you turned up at Mina's?"

Suddenly Wally was beside them. He placed his hand on Ford's shoulder and asked softly, "You okay, guy?"

Ford shrugged off Wally's hand. "Yeah," he mumbled. "Sorry." And moved toward Mina's parents without another word to Ruby.

Wally looked after him. "He went on a weeklong binge when Mina left him for Corbin and I think something . . ." Wally snapped his fingers and shook his head. "Don't pay any attention to him."

"He implied Corbin was at fault for Mina's death."

Wally raised his eyebrows. "He'd blame anybody right now. A dead husband. Even you."

"Why me?"

"Because you talked to Mina last. Yeah, I know it doesn't make sense, but that's the way it is. My aunt was killed in a car wreck on her way to a hair appointment. For years Uncle Dan cut the beautician dead, claiming she shouldn't have scheduled the appointment when she did."

"*Did* Corbin do more than run a sawmill?"

"Not that I know of. I'm not exactly rumor central, but I think I'd have heard if he was involved in anything illegal."

A deeply tanned older woman stepped up beside Wally and slipped her arm though his, giving Ruby the once-over. Now *that* look Ruby understood completely, whether in San Francisco or Sable.

"Ruby, this is my wife, Susannah."

"Oh, so you're Ruby Crane," Wally's wife said, stressing the "you're" the way people did to let you know they'd already heard about you, and it probably wasn't good.

"It's nice to meet you, Susannah," Ruby said, smiling warmly and offering her hand. Once in a moment of naughtiness, Gram had told Ruby, "Always take the high road. At the worst, it gives you a greater height to look down from."

"Susannah's from Dallas," Wally told Ruby, patting his wife's arm.

The chime of silverware being tapped against a glass rang out over the chatter. The room silenced and Joe Asauskas, holding a table knife and water glass, announced, "Wally Kentner is going to lead us in a short prayer for Mina."

Wally Kentner lead a prayer? No one else appeared surprised, not even Father Dorman, who'd just come from presiding over the funeral mass. Susannah released her husband and bowed her head, inspecting her lacquered nails as she folded her hands.

Over the bowed heads, Ruby glanced around the room, not listening to Wally's sad voice and allowing herself finally to see who was there, recognizing one bent head after another.

Another person with unbowed head stood beneath the red, white, and blue bunting, surveying the room. It was Hank Holliday. Their eyes met and he nodded, a slow smile beneath damp eyes.

Ruby allowed herself a memory of Mina: at sixteen, standing on tiptoe to kiss Ford Goodlight.

"Amen," Wally finished.

"Amen," the crowd murmured, already closing in around the food table.

Enid Shea, after setting a fresh pan of rolls on the table, suddenly collapsed on a folding chair and threw her apron over her head. It was Mina's mother who gently pulled away Enid's apron and the two women rocked each other.

"Bet you never thought you'd see Wally Kentner leading us all in a prayer, did you?" a voice said close to Ruby's ear.

"Mary Jean," Ruby said. "I didn't see you earlier."

"There's nothing unusual about that, is there?" Mary Jean wore black, a bright blue scarf fashionably draped around her neck. "Do you like his Texas drawl, I mean doll?"

"I wasn't aware he was married."

"Mrs. Wally was Miss Alamo or something about a hundred years ago and never recovered. Be careful. I heard she's menopoisonous." Mary Jean absently fingered the old ice-skate scar on her chin and nodded toward the long tables. "Our daughters have discovered each other. That's Barbara."

Mary Jean's daughter sat in the chair next to Jesse. Jesse's lips were moving and Barbara nodded seriously, with no sign of indulgence or pity. Jesse's friends in Palo Alto had nervously visited the hospital once or twice, too uncomfortable to stay more than a few minutes, and had not been heard from since.

"Good. That's good," Ruby said, watching Barbara lean over and push back a lock of Jesse's short hair. "Will you and Barbara come over tomorrow?" she asked. "For dinner?"

"How about lunch? It's one of those teachers' work days and I'll take an extra long lunch."

"About eleven-thirty?" Ruby asked.

Mary Jean nodded. "This is Sable at its best, comforting one another."

"I talked to Ford," Ruby said.

"I saw you. He always hoped Mina would come back to him."

Ford stood by the piano lecturing his sullen son, the headphones and tape player in his hands, his mouth stern.

"Kids come at grief through the back door," Mary Jean commented. "Let's get something to eat. The food at these things is always good."

As they ate, Ruby kept glancing toward the door, waiting for Carly to appear. Georgia, Carly's wife, sat near Fran of Paulas's Drug Store, both their plates heaped high. On the table between them was an array of dolls made from clothespins: cowboys and Indians, even a buxom clothespin cowgirl.

"Color Festival entry," Mary Jean explained. "They do it every year. Last year they built a clothespin circus."

"I need some carpentry done on the cabin," Ruby told Mary Jean as she picked the olives out of a pale potato salad. "Someone mentioned a man named Zander but I can't find him in the phone book."

"You mean Lyle Zander?" Mary Jean asked.

"That's the name," Ruby told her. "Do you know him?"

"He's sitting right over there beside the Petree sisters."

Two tables over, next to the two elderly Petree sisters in matching blue pant suits, sat a big man in his late forties. He sat quietly, smiling, and Ruby noticed the plastic button at the base of his throat.

"Throat cancer," Mary Jean said. "Two packs a day. He doesn't like to talk in public."

Ruby couldn't take any more. She picked up her half-empty plate and said to Mary Jean, "We'll expect you tomorrow."

"Right. I'll bring you some applesauce. 'Tis the season."

Before Ruby could reply, she felt a hand on her shoulder. She turned to meet Enid Shea's resolute, tear-marred face. She held a blue-and-white first-aid kit.

"Silas told me you have a sliver in your hand."

"It's all right," Ruby said, pulling her hand behind her back. "I just haven't had a chance to take it out yet."

"Silas told me to do it," Enid said. "Follow me."

Mary Jean gave Ruby a tiny salute and mouthed "Good luck" as Ruby obediently followed Enid through the crowd to a quiet corner off the hall's kitchen.

"Sit down," Enid ordered, pointing to a straightback wooden chair.

"I can do this myself," Ruby protested.

"I doubt it or you'd have already removed it," Enid snapped.

Enid was not a big woman. She was blocky, without definition at her waistline, short-necked and plain-faced. Ruby had never seen her wear makeup. Her ankles were surprisingly dainty and her feet small—the one area of her body that was so feminine it approached lewd.

She set a chair opposite Ruby and pulled Ruby's hand into her lap. "This is going to hurt," she said coolly.

Ruby expected *that*. She didn't flinch at the size of the needle Enid held over a flaming Bic lighter from her pocket, not even when Enid squeezed Ruby's flesh into a ridge and jabbed the needle in what felt like two inches. She concentrated on Enid's bowed head, smelling the hairspray that held Enid's curls so tightly they might have been sculpted from plaster.

"There," Enid said triumphantly, holding up the needle for Ruby to admire the speared and bloody piece of wood. "That was a good one."

"Thank you, Enid," Ruby told her.

"You're welcome." Enid dabbed peroxide on the wound, watching with satisfaction as it frothed. "I don't approve of you, Ruby Crane," she said without looking up. "I never have, not even when you were a girl. You were a trial to your poor parents. You broke your mother's heart."

"You know that's not true," Ruby said. And if it was, her mother wouldn't have shared that fact with anyone, let alone Enid. Not only had her mother kept busy, she'd kept quiet.

"You ran away," Enid accused her.

"If she'd been stronger, that's exactly what she would have done."

Enid pursed her lips in frustration, then said, "I don't know why my husband has taken an interest in you, but I'm telling you, it doesn't extend to me."

"You're not accusing me of chasing Silas, are you?" Ruby asked.

"Don't be a fool. But with all your nosing around, if you get Silas into trouble, you'll regret it as long as you live."

"How could I get Silas into trouble?" Ruby asked.

Enid taped gauze to Ruby's hand and stood. "I'll make sure of it."

"I believe you," Ruby said, standing. "But—"

A door slammed and the crowded hall outside the kitchen suddenly went silent.

Ruby left Enid repackaging the first-aid kit and joined Mary Jean, who stood outside the kitchen door.

Sheriff Carly had finally entered the hall, his face solemn, eyes seeking through the crowd before he went directly to Mina's father. Exclamations were followed by a tight circle gathering around him and Joe Asauskas. Everyone in the room paused and watched, the air thick with dread.

"Something's happened," Mary Jean said quietly.

"Oh God, what else *can*?"

Mary Jean looked at Ruby with steady blue eyes. "Don't tempt the fates, Ruby."

Finally Carly stepped from the circle. He held up his hands as if the room weren't silent enough. "Mina and Corbin's house burned to the ground an hour ago." He paused for the gasps to subside and added, "The sawmill, too."

"Burned?" Ruby repeated.

"Not just dead, but erased from the face of the earth," Mary Jean said to no one.

Ruby looked around the room at the stunned faces. Erasure. Corbin, Mina, the dog, and now the physical proof they'd been members of the community. Vengeance of the most primitive sort. Erasure. What now: Sow their land with salt?

Ford moved purposely across the room toward Randy, Mina's son, and Ruby's first thought was, Yes, protect *him*.

The evidence of Corbin's and Mina's life wasn't all that was erased, Ruby realized. The proof of Corbin's tampered support and the straight-cut timber that confirmed Corbin hadn't been adjusting his guide pins had also been destroyed.

Chapter 16

"They're both dead and their house burned to the ground a few hours ago," Ruby said into the phone. "Their sawmill, too."

"Pretty severe," Ron Kilgore said. Ruby heard the soft *click-click* of computer keys as Ron took advantage of the moment. "What's the first husband like? Still carrying the torch?"

"He hoped she'd come back to him."

"Once the new husband was dead?"

"He didn't specify that." Ron Kilgore routinely zeroed in on the basest emotions as motivation: jealousy and misguided love. "Check that garbage first" was his credo.

"Think about it," Ron went on. *Click-click-tap-tap.* "Jealous number-one husband bumps number two into the saw, ex-wife declines number one's generous offer to forgive her her trespasses so he runs her off the road—head injury, am I right?—maybe bops her on the head with a rock to be sure she's dead, knows her so well he does a decent job faking a suicide note, then worries there's incriminating evidence in her house, maybe in the sawmill where he sliced up number-two husband so he burns down the house and mill. And waltzes away dusting off his hands. A job well done in the wild Midwest."

"Ford Goodlight, who is husband number one, was at Mina's funeral," Ruby told him.

"He paid somebody to set the fire."

"Word would get out around here."

"A device then. A slow burn, maybe. Oily rags, bad wiring, only a matter of time."

"I can't believe that."

"Then why ask me?"

"So you could play devil's advocate."

"I see." He paused. "She was a good friend of yours?" he asked.

"A very good friend," Ruby told him.

"That makes it tough."

"Oh," Ruby told him. "I didn't mention their dog was shot before Mina died. It was her watchdog. And an effective one, from my observation."

Ron was silent a moment. "That sounds too Gothic. People kill people more often than they kill animals."

"Not around here. They have official seasons for killing animals. Bow season opens in a week."

"What's a bow?"

Ruby made a raspberry into the mouthpiece. "The bow's the weapon, Mr. Big City. Men dressed like commandos skulk around the woods pointing their bows and arrows at deer, like Robin Hood."

"Sounds unsanitary. Be careful, Ruby. I trust killers who stick to human victims more than I do somebody who shoots a dog."

"I was in the sawmill."

"You already told me that," Ron said with his usual impatience.

"No. I mean yesterday morning, before the funeral."

The clicking stopped, followed by the sound of flesh against flesh. Ruby pictured Ron slapping his forehead. "What in hell for?" he asked.

"Two things. If the guide pins are misaligned, a saw cuts crooked boards. I was looking for crooked boards."

"And there were no crooked boards," Ron guessed.

"None."

"Maybe the sheriff took them."

"The boards were still on the belt. One had blood on it."

"What's number two?"

"The support Corbin leaned against because of his weak leg? It was there."

"I thought it *wasn't* there the first time you checked."

"It wasn't. But now it is. Or was."

"Somebody saw you in the mill," Ron said with certainty, "figured out what you were up to, and burned the place down."

"I don't think I was seen, but I did accidentally leave the lights on in the mill," she admitted.

"Did you drop your business card, too?"

"I'm *sure* nobody saw me. This has something to do with hardwoods."

"Who?"

"You know, hardwoods, the trees whose leaves fall off in the autumn. The hardwood they make furniture out of. Like oak and maple. Hardwood timber is mostly what Corbin was involved in. And it's a hot commodity in the county right now."

"You're not talking about crazed environmentalists offing loggers to set free wild baby saplings, are you?"

"If there are any rabid environmentalists in Waters County, they haven't exposed themselves."

"They've probably all been stuffed in the bogs."

"People here don't do that."

"Like they don't slice up citizens in sawmills? Talk to the sheriff."

"I have been, but . . ."

"You lack confidence in his sheriffly abilities, am I right? Is there a big mill around there, or just those podunk operations?"

"Northern Timber's the biggest," Ruby told him, already reaching for the Waters County phone book.

"Sniff around there. Men love gossip, too. There's always one guy who can't wait to spill everything he knows, especially to a beautiful woman."

"Why, Ron. How nice. You must miss me."

"Damn right. This place is a mess."

"I don't have any reason to visit Northern Timber."

"You're smart. Think of something."

"I'm going for a run," Ruby told DeEtta, who sat on the front lawn with Jesse, a card table between them, playing a simple game of War with a deck of cards used so often the cards had gone soft and gray-edged. Jesse slapped the table with each card with precisely the same force, in precisely the same sweaty circle on the tabletop, holding her hand flat overlong.

"Bye, Mom," Jesse said. "Bye, Mom," again.

Ruby ran east, her Nikes sending up little puffs of dust on the sandy soft shoulders. Past boarded-up cabins, past the house where the Vietnamese family lived, where a sleek black dog ambled to the pagodalike structure beside the driveway and barked halfheartedly at her.

She followed the curve around the lake, her breath coming harder. By the remnants of Fox Woods, where she'd first seen Mrs. Pink, Ruby stopped and bent forward, her hands to her knees, gulping deep breaths. She was out of shape.

A squirrel ran through the logging debris, scolding and chattering, and Ruby rose, looking at the devastation, wondering how a new forest could ever rise from such a mess. "Something went wrong there," Hank had said, referring to the way Corbin Turmouski had slashed and razed Fox Woods.

She knew how to get into Northern Timber.

"Glenn Wister's our timber buyer," the woman who answered the phone at Northern Timber told her. "I'll transfer you."

"I'll come out," Glenn Wister told Ruby heartily. "Give your place a look-see."

"I'd like to hear my options without the trees present," Ruby told him.

"I'll still have to come out to look it over. Two birds with one stone."

"And I'd prefer to meet in your office first," Ruby pressed, picturing this hearty man who was slated to be the grand marshal of the Color Festival parade. "Can you see me this afternoon?"

"How about in an hour?" he asked. "Will your husband be with you?"

"There's only myself."

"Gotcha," he said cheerfully, and Ruby pictured him rubbing his hands like a silent film villain over the widow trying to save the farm. "I'll be waiting. Coffee's on."

An hour gave her time. First, she drove to Mina's house. Cars and pickups were parked along both sides of the road two hundred yards before Ruby reached the site. A haze of bluish smoke hung in the air. Leaves were dusted gray with ash. Men and woman, whole families, hurried along the road toward the rubble, faces as eager as viewers of a really good horror movie.

Ruby had no intention of stopping, but she slowed to five miles per hour as she approached Mina's driveway and peered between the trees.

Fires were illusionary magic. Evil hat tricks. Now you see it, now you don't. As if she could blink twice and Mina's plain house would reappear; the sawmill rebuild itself from the ground up. How could the buildings just be *gone*?

But they were. A shockingly small pile of blackened smoldering rubble remained. The fire had burned fifty feet into the woods west of the house, and the trees stood stark and blackened.

Where Corbin's mill had stood lay a twisted black

mass of steel, unrecognizable, finally exorcised. The closest vehicle to the mill was blistered; the others still in military lineup, dusted with gray ash. Spectators quietly contemplated the remains, making mental crosses against the possibility.

A group of men, Silas Shea among them, stood between the house foundation and the twisted remains of the mill. The air around them was dusky, as if the group emerged from smoke. One of the men turned and looked at Ruby's passing car, then commented to the others and they all turned and watched Ruby pass by. She didn't speed up, nor did she look away. And neither did they.

Northern Timber occupied acreage on a paved road that was rutted from heavy machinery and loaded semis.

Four airplane hangar–size buildings were arranged in a rough rectangle surrounded by acres of logs piled higher than houses waiting to be sawn, freshly sawn boards banded by size and grade and lined in military rows, mountains of sawdust, yellow vehicles dwarfed by their tires.

The noise was deafening: clanking, whirring, the whining of saws and roaring of engines. The only vegetation near the smaller building marked OFFICE grew in a double bed–size plot beside the door. Bronze chrysanthemums and faded purple petunias. All else was dirt, driven over too often to bring forth even quack grass.

A radio talk show issued from the reception area, accompanied by the low roar outside. The rubber-matted floor was tracked with dirt, and a thin layer of dust that Ruby thought was probably impossible to eradicate layered all the flat surfaces.

"Yes?" the large woman at the desk asked. Her black

hair hung in ringlets, the same as a Victorian child's, and the whole time she dealt with Ruby she never missed a beat chewing her gum or moving her fingers across her computer keyboard. Ron Kilgore would have loved her.

"I'm here to see Glenn Wister."

"What's your name, honey?"

"Ruby Crane."

"He stepped over to the garage for a minute. Will Abel do?"

"Abel?" Ruby asked.

The woman with the flying fingers looked at Ruby in disappointment. "Abel Obert, owner of Northern Timber and our leader."

"I don't know . . ." Ruby began.

The woman paused with one hand long enough to pick up the phone, push a few buttons, and say, "Abel, there's a Ruby Crane to see Glenn but he's at the garage right now."

Abel Obert, dressed in the dark green of a garage mechanic, immediately appeared from down the hall. He was in his mid-forties, stoop-shouldered and loose-limbed, with glasses and indoor skin and a nervous walk, not at all what Ruby expected.

"Aren't you Phyllis's sister?" were his first words, followed by a flush that spread from his neck to his ears.

"Yes. Are you one of her old boyfriends?"

He laughed and pushed up his glasses, then took them off and rubbed the lenses with his fingers. "You can't believe *that*. What can I do for you?"

"I had an appointment with Glenn about my timbered property."

Abel nodded. "He's our buyer." He looked around the lobby as if hoping to be rescued. The black-haired woman concentrated on her computer screen.

"I can wait here," Ruby told him, motioning to the

orange Naugahyde chair beside a fish tank filled with artificial ferns.

He shrugged. "You could. Or if you want, I can give you the ten-cent tour."

She agreed and he led her out of the building and across the dirt toward the first building. "Hold on," he said, taking her arm as an oversized forklift lurched around them, driven by a bland-faced youth wearing headphones.

"We're cutting oak today," he shouted close to her ear. "Logs over sixteen inches. Then we send the rough boards downstate to be planed and kiln dried."

Ruby was in alien territory. Nothing resembled anything she knew. Men—she saw no women—wore ear protectors and hard hats and moved to the tunes of the machines, their faces emotionless, eyes on the logs and boards coming at them.

Motion and noise assaulted from every side. She followed the suddenly certain and agile Abel blindly between moving chains and rolling belts and the maw of an orange machine that screamed while it ground slabs into chips. Boards shot past, were grabbed and flung to another belt or another pile. She was drenched with sound, positive she'd never shake it out of her ears.

The mill was washed of color; walls of wood, floors of concrete; the clothing of the employees was worn to drab, paint had disappeared from machinery. The bark on the uncut logs dull brown. But then the saws screeched and the freshly cut boards swung past like gold being conjured from the depths.

Abel halted at the foot of a short staircase and patted the steel structure fondly. "Operator's booth," he shouted, pointing upward. In the booth at the top of the steps a man sat in a command chair operating a panel of buttons and controls.

Beneath the booth, directly in the operator's view, was the circular saw. A red laser beam flashed across a partially cut log and an instant later the log buzzed through the circular saw blade, separated along that exact red line.

There was no hand setting of logs here, no hip movement to turn a log, no eyeballing a cut. Only buttons and levers.

Movement and speed and sound. In narrow trenches built into the cement floor, a modified barn cleaner moved continuously, jerkily carrying sawdust out of the building. Everything clanking and turning and whining. Abel led her onward, pointing and smiling and saying words lost in the cacophony. No one looked up at their passage, their eyes wary on saws and boards ready to turn on them in a blink.

He stopped and pointed to a smaller saw with three blades. "My new edger," he said in her ear. "Slick, isn't she?"

Once, in her hurry to keep up with Abel, Ruby nudged up against a moving belt carrying narrow golden boards. She gasped, jumping back from the stealthy swishing touch on her pants. It was terrifying; it was exhilarating.

He pointed to three men pulling freshl.y cut boards off moving chains. "They're pulling green chain," he shouted.

"Off-bearers," she shouted back, and he grinned at her, giving her a thumbs-up sign.

They passed men stacking boards for an idling forklift and then exited through the huge doors into the daylight where, in comparison, the noise no longer seemed so deafening. Ruby caught her breath, relieved to be out of the building yet longing to go back inside and go through it again, slower. To figure it out.

"It gets in your blood." Abel was looking back at the operation, slowly nodding. "Once you get sawdust in your shoes, you never get it out."

"I believe you. That was oak?"

"Right." He pointed to a pyramid of long straight logs across the yard. "That's hard maple or you can call it sugar maple. We send it downstate for veneer. We're not set up to do veneer but you should watch them peel logs in a veneer mill sometime. That's a good show."

"Does this timber come from federal or private lands?" Ruby asked.

"Private. There's not much happening on federal lands anymore and the Forest Service quit cutting red oak in eighty-three. We have to scramble for hardwood. Can I show you our pallet mill?" Abel pointed across the yard to another building.

"Maybe another time. I didn't expect the saws to be so mechanized."

"Isn't everything?"

"But the saw itself?" Ruby asked. "Is the circular saw still the same as fifty or sixty years ago, despite the mechanization? Does it still have to be sharpened?"

"Sure. Some mills are turning to band saws for hardwood. Less kerf."

"What's kerf?"

"The width of the saw blade. The wider your saw blade, the more wood you waste when you cut. Most mills out West use band saws, even on softwoods; we're stuck in history." Abel absently picked up a chunk of tree bark and tossed it on a larger pile of wood.

"Are there still guide pins on circular saws and are they adjusted the same way?" Ruby asked.

"Definitely. You see some pins made of Teflon now to wear longer, but they still perform the same function. So you *do* know about sawmills?"

"Only the most basic elements."

"We're pretty basic ourselves," Abel told her, using his hands to demonstrate a small square. "A lot of operations would use us to blow their noses."

"So there's considerable competition?"

"You bet. Fewer trees, higher demand, more legal

hoops to jump through. Plus, everybody and his cousin wants the woods to stay the same; pretty. Pretty's got nothing to do with how Mother Nature works. Nothing stays the same," he said, reminding Ruby of Hank.

"Are you advocating clearcutting?" Ruby asked. They paused while a semi loaded with logs thundered through the mill yard.

"Mother Nature does it. If clearcuts were smaller and"—he smiled mischievously—"not cut in squares, who'd notice?"

"A lot of people," Ruby said. "They're downright ugly."

"So how do you justify what we're doing for the Kirtland warbler?" Abel asked.

"The bird? What are we doing?"

"They only live in clearcut or burned over jack pine forests. Once the jack pines reach forty, fifty years old, the bird disappears, dies out. So which do you protect? It's a juggling act."

"And we're new at it."

"Our balls are definitely not all in the air," Abel said.

"What about timber prices?" Ruby asked.

"All over the map. Right now, popple's not worth a cow's burp. Oak, hard maple, cherry. Black walnut. They're hot." He laughed.

"What's so funny?"

"The market. We're global." He pointed to a man in a white shirt and slacks walking toward the office. "That's Glenn. I'll walk you back."

"What do you mean by global?" Ruby asked.

He turned sideways so he could see her while he spoke. "A few years ago the Japanese discovered bowling. Do you know what bowling lanes are made of?"

"Hardwood?" Ruby asked feebly.

"Maple. The price of hard maple shot through the roof. If McDonald's decides to add a nice oak trim to the booths in their billions and billions of restaurants, then you can bet the price of oak does the same thing."

"Abel!" a man shouted from a smaller building. "That sprocket's the wrong size."

"Be right there," Abel called back. To Ruby he said, "We're getting a new gang saw next week. Stop by if you want to see it. Eight blades!"

"Thanks for the tour."

"Anytime."

Ruby watched Abel Obert hurry toward the smaller building, his face softened by gladness to be rid of her and back tinkering with his sawmill.

"Did Abel give you the nickel tour?"

Glenn Wister was in his mid-fifties, with narrow hands he moved with deliberation as he spoke. His eyes moved as precisely as his hands. She wondered which was natural: his happy-go-lucky conversation or his deliberate manner.

"Actually, he called it the ten-cent tour," Ruby told him.

A varnished slice of tree wider than Ruby could stretch her arms hung on the wall behind Abel, bearing more rings than the country had years.

He handed Ruby a paper cup of coffee. "Then he must have taken a liking to you. We met a week or so ago, didn't we?"

"Twice," Ruby told him. "Once with Wally Kentner and once with Hank Holliday."

"Right. Good to see you again. So you're interested in selling some timber around Blue Lake?"

"How did you know where the timber was?" Ruby asked.

"It wasn't hard to put together." He held his hands over his desk two feet apart, palms facing. He thumped the side of one hand down and said, "Ruby

Crane," then the other hand. "Crane cabin on Blue Lake."

"I have *no* plans," Ruby told him. "I'm investigating the possibilities." The coffee was bitter and there was only powdered creamer.

"This is a good place to start, then. I can swing by, look at your property, and give you a couple of options."

"For instance?"

"That depends on what your goals are. We can talk about it in detail once I see your trees. But we'll work for *you*."

"You're the first person I've spoken to," Ruby told him. "I'll want someone else's opinion."

He nodded and leaned back in his chair. "A second opinion is always a smart idea. You might talk to Silas Shea. He's a small operation but he's fair."

"I'm surprised a big company like Northern Timber competes with small mill owners like Silas," Ruby said.

"Abel started this company with a mill as small as Silas's. We're all after the same thing, big mill or little, and that's timber. Being bigger, Northern Timber can absorb a loss now and then that a small sawmill can't."

"How can sawmill operators like Silas stay in business, then, I wonder?" Ruby sipped her coffee, then set it on the low table beside her chair. Enough.

"There are men who prefer not to know where their next dollar's coming from rather than have to kowtow to a boss. Too independent. There's still room for the little mills in the business though, don't get me wrong. Some timber property's too small for a company our size to fool with."

"Corbin Turmouski appeared to be making a go of it," Ruby said casually.

Glenn shook his head and leaned back. "That poor son of a . . . Really bad luck. It spooks you when something that bad happens to a good man."

"Was he a good man?"

"One of the best. Solid. If he'd lived, he'd have had a mill this big within five years."

"Mina's funeral was today," Ruby told him.

"Yeah, I know. My wife went. I heard about their house, too." He shook his head gravely. "Carly thinks he has a murder case on his hands."

"You have to admit these two deaths are unusual," Ruby said.

"Freak incidents happen. A friend of mine was driving his parents to town a couple years ago. All three of them sitting in the front seat. You know where Sherman crosses Dodd? A kid in his dad's pickup ran a stop sign and hit them broadside." He slapped his hands together in one sharp clap. "My buddy walked away but his parents banged their heads together. Both of them dead, just like that."

Everyone had a story, a touch with tragedy for comparison.

"Did Corbin ever work for you?"

"Before he bought his own mill, he cut trees on contract for us now and then. I didn't have any trouble with him. His ex-wife raved a lot; she'd call here asking if he'd been paid. He was slow with child support, I guess."

"I didn't know he was married before."

"Four kids, too. He was a good logger."

"But slow with his child support," Ruby amended.

"You can't fault a man for that."

Ruby didn't agree but she kept her silence on *that* subject.

"Now Corbin and Silas," Glenn offered with more enthusiasm, tapping a pencil on his desktop. "*Those* two had feelings. Corbin would do anything to get a job instead of Silas. Silas has always operated on a shoestring but Corbin made it tougher for him. Then that forester, Holliday, came to town, and by the time he finished spinning his tales about the wonders of forestry management, the owner saw castles in the sky and Silas lost even more trees he thought were in the bag."

"So Silas Shea was losing jobs to both Corbin and Hank Holliday?" Ruby asked.

Glenn Wister blinked his eyes and Ruby could see him mentally tidying up, realizing how far they'd wandered from Ruby's timber project. He sat forward and looked into her eyes. "Back to business. This shop talk can't be very interesting to a little lady like you. When's a good time to look at your trees?"

As Ruby stopped her car before she pulled out of Northern Timber's driveway, she spotted two men lounging against a black pickup. One was Danny Greenstone, smoking a cigarette, wearing jeans and a tank top that exposed a red heart tattooed on his bicep.

When he saw Ruby, he stepped away from the pickup and began walking toward her car, his mouth moving in words Ruby couldn't hear, despite her open window.

When Danny was ten feet from her car, Ruby pulled onto the road and drove south, seeing Danny in her rearview mirror, watching her, his mouth still moving.

Chapter 17

Carly, his face tense, beckoned her into his office without rising from his chair. "Sit down, Ruby. A hell of a thing, isn't it?" His sleeves were rolled to his elbows; two cups of coffee sat on his desk.

"Do you know how the fire started?"

Carly nodded. "Gasoline and a match. Both buildings. We're lucky the whole woods didn't go up." He took a deep breath and folded his hands on top of the scattered papers. "What can I do for you? Has Danny been bothering DeEtta?"

"Did Lyle Zander give you a statement that he didn't request a rush job from Corbin?" Ruby asked.

"Have you met Zander?" Carly asked.

"I've seen him. I gather he has difficulty speaking."

"Not really. He's just embarrassed to have to hold his finger over his throat and whisper. But in answer to your question, all we know is that Corbin *said* he had a rush job. Maybe he was just determined to saw up the wood and used it as an excuse for Mina. I need something a little more concrete."

"I was in Corbin's sawmill this morning and I saw proof that there'd been tampering with his equipment," Ruby said.

Carly leaned forward, his eyes widening in eagerness as he asked. "What proof?"

She explained to Carly about the perfectly cut boards. "If the boards were straight, that meant the saw *wasn't* out of alignment so Corbin wasn't adjusting the guide pins."

Carly gazed off into the middle distance, his eagerness turning to disappointment. "Straight boards don't rule out an accident involving the guide pins. When I first left the service I worked in a sawmill up north. A log or a piece of wood can jam in the saw, and you'd better remove it as quick as you can before the blade heats up and warps."

"But would he have lifted the table beside the saw?"

"It depends on how the wood was caught. He might have to, to release the log easier."

"But I *know* the support wasn't there the first time I was in the mill."

Carly frowned. "Corbin's support? What are you talking about?"

Ruby explained the reappearing support while Carly listened, gravely nodding.

"So you were in Corbin's mill before today, too?" Carly asked.

"When Mina was alive."

Carly's brow was furrowed. "I'm curious, Ruby. How did you know what Corbin's support looked like, let alone whether it was there from one time to the next?"

"Silas described it to me. He said Corbin had a weak leg from polio."

Carly nodded. "He did. But now that the mill has burned to the ground," he said heavily, "there's no proof of whatever you saw inside."

"The remains of the support should still be there; it was steel."

Carly pointed his finger into his chest. "*I'd* expect it to be there. I've seen it myself. The fact that it was *missing* would be evidence. If I'd known earlier . . ."

Ruby gripped the arms of her chair. If he'd known earlier . . .

"Didn't you take photographs of the scene?" she

asked. "They'd prove the support was missing when Corbin died."

"We did. Hold on." He pulled a folder from his desk tray and opened it, a sick expression crossing his face for the briefest moment. He thumbed through a dozen photos, holding them so Ruby couldn't make out the details.

Then he closed the folder and clasped his hands over it as if weighting it down. "We didn't catch the corner where it stood in any of our shots," he said.

"Maybe one of your deputies will remember, or the EMTs."

"I'll ask, Ruby, okay? Be patient. You're used to things happening faster in the big city. We're doing our best and I promise you, we'll be just as thorough, if a little slower. Let us do our job, okay?"

"You're telling me to butt out?"

"You, of all people, don't need to be told that. I understand that Mina was your friend and you want answers, but right now, I don't have any and I'm as sorry about that as you are." Carly's face was sincerely sad, perplexed.

Ruby stopped by Bob's Store for milk. Bob's sat on a barren corner a mile from Blue Road, a single building with a wall down the center dividing the building into a grocery store and a bar.

Two cars and a motorcycle were parked in front of the bar half of the building, but she was the only customer in the grocery side. It was smaller than a 7-Eleven but packed with the necessities of life. On the floor near the entrance was a display of deer-hunting paraphernalia: buck calls, face camouflage, deer bait.

Next to the milk in the beer cooler were eight-ounce containers of sour cream, only on each lid was written in black marking pen: Night Crawlers. Ruby chose one of those, too.

As she skirted the display of day-old bread, the grocer came from behind a curtain, TV laughter trailing him.

"Ruby," he said, nodding. He was fiftyish, clear-eyed and clean-shaven, and Ruby had a hunch he didn't indulge in what he sold.

"Do I know you?" Ruby asked.

He shook his head. "I'm Bob. Ditka, like the football coach. I ask around when I see a new face. When you run a bar, it pays to know who's who."

"Do you work both sides of the business?" Ruby asked.

"Sometimes. The wife is tending bar tonight."

Ruby handed him a five-dollar bill. "Does Danny Greenstone frequent your bar?"

"He has lately. I see people more often after they lose a job. Damn shame about Corbin and Mina."

Since Bob had progressed from Danny Greenstone to Corbin and Mina, Ruby followed up the line of thought. "If Danny had gone to work that day . . ." she said.

He nodded sagely as he counted out her change from a till that didn't have a lock. "None of this might have happened."

"Did you know Corbin?"

"Not much. He wouldn't take the time to sit around in a bar. His wife came in a few times."

"Mina?" Ruby asked in surprise. "Alone?"

"That's right. She always bought a bottle of schnapps and took it with her."

A buzzer droned and Bob Ditka glanced at the door between the store and bar. "I'd better see what the wife needs."

Ruby picked up her worms and milk and left, wondering why Mina had chosen a bar on the other side of

Sable from her home. Because there were fewer people likely to know her?

After Ruby cleaned out a tangled mouse nest from beneath the stern seat, she and DeEtta carried the old aluminum rowboat from the garage to the shore of Blue Lake.

"It's pretty dented up," DeEtta said doubtfully.

"As long as it floats," Ruby told her. "Watch out for that tree root."

The only oars she found were a scabby wooden pair, one oar six inches longer than the other, the shorter one with a corner broken off the blade. "This'll be like walking with a peg leg," she told DeEtta as she settled the oarlocks into the sockets. "Now hand me the pole and worms and then we'll bring down Jesse."

"Should I stay?" DeEtta asked, handing Ruby the ancient child's rod and reel Ruby had found in the garage rafters.

"We'll be fine, DeEtta. We'll come in before dark and you're absolved of all responsibility. Go visit your sister."

DeEtta pulled at a reed growing beside the dock. "What if Carly told Georgia about, you know, Danny?"

"You've never told Georgia how Danny treated you?" Ruby asked in surprise. "But you're sisters," thinking even as she said it that she was a fine one to talk about the ideal relationship between sisters.

DeEtta shook her head.

"But she must have some idea, right?"

"I don't know."

"God, DeEtta," Ruby said in exasperation. "You'll never get out of this place if you can't face what's going on."

"Nobody's been divorced in our family since my great-aunt June in the 1920s."

"Daring, wasn't she? Does she still live on Becket Corners?"

"She's dead." DeEtta broke off the reed and stuck the end in her mouth. "She died in London."

"Do you think she cried into her pillow every night longing for dear old Sable?"

"My grandmother said she sent postcards every few months from all over Europe."

Ruby waited while DeEtta redigested that old family tale, then said, "Okay, let's bring down the fairy princess."

They settled Jesse at the stern end, propped by pillows, an orange kapok life vest dwarfing her slender body. Ruby dug the disparate oars into the soft lake bottom and they pushed off while DeEtta watched from shore, Spot by her side.

The lake was calm and Ruby rowed straight out from shore, pulling harder on the short oar. The oarlocks creaked and Jesse stared from one blade to the other, watching the oars rise and fall in the lake, the water cascading from the wood.

Ruby needed to think. Hadn't she also paddled out on Blue Lake the night before she ran away? That had been in a canoe and she'd known more back then. In her youthful mind the world was black and white and she'd seen only two choices: go or stay. A no-brainer decision.

Now life was far less certain, less binary.

Mina had been her friend and Mina was dead. Ruby tried to remember every word of their conversations, attempting to make sense of the words of a woman half crazed by grief. Or fear.

Ruby pulled on the right oar, turning closer to a scoop of shoreline filled with lily pads. "Shall we fish?" she asked Jesse.

Jesse thought for a few moments and slowly and solemnly replied, "I don't know how to be a fish."

"Neither do I, sweetheart. But maybe I can catch one."

The worms she'd bought were knotted together beneath the black dirt of their sour cream container. Overkill. She blocked Jesse's view of the operation and swiftly baited the hook, burying the hook's barb inside the squirming worm so it was completely hidden. Fish knew.

When she'd bit a pea-size lead weight closed over the line and attached the bobber, she cast sideways toward the lily pads, whipping the line too hard and landing it with a harsh splash.

Mina had died because she knew the truth about Corbin's death, and whoever killed her feared she was about to share that truth with Ruby. The suicide note hadn't been a wild spur-of-the-moment forgery. The words and letters had been deliberately, painstakingly formed, probably with a note in Mina's handwriting in front of the forger, perhaps tracing the letters. The killer had plotted Mina's death, with her watchdog dead and the suicide note already prepared.

Ruby slowly reeled in her line and cast it out again, a more graceful cast this time.

A heron suddenly rose up from the shore, squawking, its big blue wings audible as it flapped a hundred feet farther away from them and settled behind a dense growth of reeds.

"Was it a pelican?" Jesse asked, sitting up. Alert.

Jesse had loved the pelicans around Monterey. There'd been a stuffed pelican at Stan's house that belonged to her. Gone now.

"It was a heron," Ruby told her. "Like a pelican."

"A pelican," Jesse said. A faraway look came into her eyes and she recited, " 'The beak of a pelican can hold much more than its belly can.' "

Ruby's line tugged. She waited until the fish tugged

twice more, then gently jerked her pole upward, setting the hook.

"Got one," she told Jesse as she reeled in the zigging and zagging line. It was a perch, ten inches long. Ruby held its greeny gold body in her left hand while she worked the hook from its gaping mouth. Light shown through its gills, turning the inside of the perch's mouth translucent.

"Don't be so greedy next time," she told the fish as she leaned over the side of the boat and released it. The fish was gone in an instant, only ripples remaining.

She washed her hands in the water, then held one up to the sun at arm's length, parallel to the water, counting the fingers between the horizon and the lower edge of the sun. Fifteen minutes for each finger, forty-five minutes until sunset.

Jesse had cautiously put her right hand over the side of the boat, letting her fingertips trail through the water, her whole being focused on the sight and sensation.

Around the edges of the lake Ruby rowed, compensating for the short oar, smelling the heady incense of an autumn bonfire.

Why had Mina brought up the test-stealing incident in her phone call? Ruby had forgotten how she'd used a coat hanger to pry the lock on Mr. Wickler's door, the moment when the janitor stepped out to shake his dust mop. Had he pretended not to see them? Mr. Wickler wasn't a popular teacher.

She rowed through a thick settling of water bugs, sending them rippling off either side of the boat. Had Mina recalled the event for a particular reason? Had Corbin himself tried to steal something? Money? A timber contract? And had he been found out and killed for it?

Jesse sat up as they approached their dock, listening. Ruby heard it, too: muffled barking. She turned on the seat and scanned the pale shoreline among the shadowy trees, looking for Spot. Her last glimpse of the big dog had been as they'd rowed away, sitting on her haunches beside DeEtta.

Ruby pulled hard toward shore, sending the bow swishing and crunching onto the sandy beach as she leapt out and hauled the boat on shore.

The barking continued: steady, angry, coming from inside the cabin. Ruby stood ankle deep in the water and lifted Jesse out of the boat.

"I can walk," Jesse said.

"I know you can, but . . ." She stopped and set Jesse on her feet and then moved to the girl's left side.

It was a long slow walk to the dark cabin. Behind them, the remaining light gathered in the water and reflected back the sky. Around the lake darkness had fallen.

The cabin door was unlocked as she'd left it. Spot still barked, less angry but more insistent, from deeper in the cabin.

Spot was inside the bathroom and the door was closed. The dog whined and scratched frantically. "Good dog, good dog," Ruby called as she turned on the lights and settled Jesse into the chair, her eyes moving around the cabin, searching for disorder and mayhem.

Warily, she opened the bathroom door and Spot pushed past her, head and tail low. The dog ran from room to room, whining and growling. The bathroom was empty, in order except for the long claw marks where Spot had scratched the wooden floor and the door panel.

But how had she become locked in the bathroom? Ruby found Jesse's room in its normal tidy state. She ascended the steps to the loft and stopped.

This was the intruder's target; the lock on the metal cabinet where she kept her records and materials had been pried at, the frame around the padlock was scratched, and there was a fist-size dent in one door as if the intruder had vented his frustration at not getting inside.

Her light table was askew, her microscope still safe inside the cabinet. Her transparent grid plates sat out on her table. Anyone who didn't know her occupation couldn't tell from the items she'd left visible. Did they already know her career, or had they been idly searching?

Ruby's hands shook on the railing as she descended the stairs. In anger, not fear. Anger at the intrusion and defilement of her home.

Spot now leaned against Jesse's leg, head on her knee, as content as if she'd been the girl's trusty companion all day long.

Ruby reached for the phone to call Carly when she spotted the note leaning against the telephone. She didn't touch it. Instead she retrieved a sandwich bag from the cupboard and, with a pair of kitchen tongs, slipped the note into the bag, sealing it.

She laid it on her kitchen table and gently smoothed the plastic flat over the note. It was a quarter-page piece of plain white paper, two edges torn as if a page had been torn in half and then in half again.

"Mind your own business," the note read. Although it was printed, when she glanced at the spacing and placement of the words, her first thought was that the author was also the author of Mina's suicide note.

As soon as the lights went on in the little trailer, Ruby crossed the driveway and knocked on the door, saying "It's Ruby, DeEtta."

DeEtta threw open the door. "What's wrong?"

"Did you shut Spot in the cabin before you left for your sister's?"

"No. Why?"

"She was inside when we came up from the lake."

DeEtta swallowed and glanced into the dark night. "Do you think somebody was here?" she asked. "Inside your cabin?" Unconsciously, DeEtta pressed her hands against her breasts, continuing to peer into the darkness.

Ruby forced herself to laugh lightly. "No. Of course not. I left a window open. Spot's smarter than I realized." She noticed DeEtta's puffy eyes. "Are you okay?"

"Yes," she said, not sounding completely sure. "The job came through for Danny, the one with Wally's brother in Arizona."

"So he'll be leaving. I'm pleased for you, DeEtta. Really."

Back in her cabin, Ruby put the reluctant dog outside for the night. "Here's your chance to earn your keep," she said. "Don't let a soul near this place."

Then she locked the doors and tested the windows before she went to bed without calling Sheriff Carly.

Chapter 18

"Ask your local sheriff to send it to the state crime lab," Ron Kilgore said. "What's the name of that place: Boise?"

"Lansing. I've decided not to tell him about the note yet," Ruby said, glancing outside at a small flock of chickadees scratching beneath an oak, birds of winter.

"Why?"

"I have a hunch I should keep it to myself for a while."

"Somebody breaks into your house and you're reluctant to involve the sheriff? Is he a bad cop?"

"No, I don't think so, a weak one maybe. If I tell Carly, whoever's responsible will hear about it, and I prefer to see where this is leading."

"You call your sheriff 'Carly'?"

"It's an old nickname to distinguish him from his father, Carl, Senior. Admit it; it's more creative than 'Junior.' "

"Well, shucks, I'm impressed."

"I can't prove it but there are similarities between the MYOB note and Mina's suicide note."

"Weak or not, talk to 'Carly' when you think you're into the meat."

"I will. And I'm sorry I woke you up. I forgot about the time difference."

"No, it's time I rolled out of bed. The new receptionist starts today and I have to hide the bottles and take my dirty socks out of the desk drawers."

Ruby felt a tug of jealousy. She'd been Ron's first secretary, the person who'd organized his office. "Anybody I know?"

"She's from an agency. I had such good luck with you I requested another high school drop-out but they were fresh out."

"You just wanted someone you didn't have to pay a real wage."

"That, too."

After Ruby hung up she made herself a piece of toast. She'd been awake since four, stuck between awake and asleep when the devils danced in her head by madlight.

Mind your own business. Ruby heard the author's unwritten challenge: Mind your own business, *or else*.

DeEtta entered the cabin, humming "O Come All Ye Faithful."

"You seem happy," Ruby said.

DeEtta's eyes were shining. "I woke up this morning and it really hit me: Danny's leaving. He might even head for Arizona today. He promised Carly he'd go as soon as his car was fixed."

"Oh, joy to the world," Ruby said. "But I thought Danny bought a new motorcycle."

"Carly said he sold it to pay for car repairs." DeEtta's smile widened. "Then maybe I'll save my money so I can leave Sable. I want to see the ocean."

"Which one?"

"It doesn't matter."

Lyle Zander sat at a picnic table in front of a dome house in various states of completion, carving a duck decoy, completing it as he went, back to front, so that a duck of uncommon realism appeared to be backing out of a blank of basswood.

"My name's Ruby Crane," Ruby introduced herself, getting directly to the point. "I was at Corbin Turmouski's the day he died. He said he was doing a rush job for you."

The big man laid down his carving tool and shook his blond head. A tablet of cheap newsprint sat on the picnic table, a pencil beside it. "Not for me," he wrote in swift block print, penmanship stripped down for speed.

"It was oak, I think," Ruby said. "Wasn't he sawing oak for you?"

"Yes, but not a rush job," Zander wrote, underlining the word "rush."

"Supposing you *had* wanted him to do a rush job," Ruby asked. "Would you have phoned him or written a note?"

"A note," he printed.

"Thanks," Ruby said. She pointed to the decoy. "That's a beautiful mallard."

As Ruby pulled out of Zander's driveway, she wondered if that's what was in the folder in Mina's car: a note supposedly written by Lyle Zander. Mina knew Ruby was a specialist in forgery detection. Had she been bringing the note to her?

Glenn Wister grabbed a knapsack from his blue Northern Timber pickup and headed up the driveway toward Ruby's fifteen acres. "I'll be back in a half hour," he told her.

She watched him disappear into the trees and turned to see DeEtta in the cabin doorway regarding her with narrowed eyes.

"Are you going to cut the trees?" DeEtta asked.

"I'm only getting an estimate."

"Did you tell Hank Holliday?"

"I will," Ruby assured her. "Do you know Glenn?"

"The Color Festival committee made him grand marshal of the parade this year."

"So I heard. It used to be the mayor's job."

"Some people think Glenn *will* be the mayor, and maybe even a congressman someday." A mischievous look crossed DeEtta's face. "He does good works all over Waters County. I've heard he's getting even for being picked on as a nerd when he was young."

"He's not from here?"

"He wasn't *born* here, if that's what you mean, but he married one of the Barber girls."

Like an alien nation, you could marry into Sable and acquire all its attendant rights and privileges.

"I think we can help you," Glenn Wister told Ruby as he opened the door of his pickup and exchanged his knapsack for a black briefcase. He set the briefcase on the hood of his truck and unsnapped its brass latches.

"I see a lot of woods like yours," he said as he thumbed through brown file folders. "They've been ignored for years, become stagnant. The older the woods, the fewer the trees, and those old trees—they shade out every other little tree that tries to grow. Kills them."

"Are you saying there aren't very many valuable trees on those fifteen acres?" Ruby asked. "It hasn't been touched since my family bought it in the twenties."

"That's the problem," he said smoothly. "A lot of your trees have grown too large. Most mills can't handle big logs anymore, and there are defects in old logs like that: hollow spots, rot, cracks."

He set a single sheet of paper on the hood, angled toward Ruby. It was a contact. "But you wouldn't have to worry, *we'd* take the risk."

From another file folder, Glenn drew out a blue

piece of paper and laid it beside the contract. "Your biggest worry will be what to do with this."

It was a check, made out to Ruby Crane with the amount of several thousand dollars already typed in.

"You wrote me a check before you even appraised my trees?" Ruby asked incredulously.

"This is a generous offer. There isn't a mill around here that wouldn't agree. Plus we pay up front, before the first tree hits the ground. We take all the risk; if there's a hollow or rotted log, we're out the money, not you."

Ruby picked up the single-page contract while Glenn offered her an expensive pen. The contract contained her name and a property description along with a brief paragraph agreeing to the sale of her trees.

"This contract doesn't specify which size or species of trees you'd cut," Ruby pointed out. "Or whether you'd clean up the land afterward."

Glenn's voice softened; his words came faster. "Ruby, you've got a young girl's health to consider, too. This money would make life more secure for both of you."

"Is this what's called 'high-grading'?" Ruby asked sweetly. "Take the best and leave the rest?"

Glenn Wister's face flamed red. Calling a timberman a high grader, Hank had told her, was an insult that rated right up there with implying he wore pink underwear.

"Now, Ruby," he said. "I'm trying to do my best for you. But I'll tell you what: I marked your most viable trees with blue paint. Take a stroll through the woods and look them over." He handed her a can of black spray paint. "Any trees you don't want cut, cover the blue paint with this and I'll give you a firm offer on what's left."

"Can I keep this contract to look over, too?" Ruby asked.

Glenn gently removed the paper from her hands and slipped it back in his briefcase. "I'll bring it next time we chat. You can't keep this, either," he said in a teasing voice, picking up the check.

"I hope you're not making a mistake, Ruby," he said as he snapped his briefcase closed. "That would be a real shame."

Mary Jean Scribner was twenty minutes early, a victim of the Midwest habit of being early as opposed to the western penchant for not arriving until a half hour past the appointed time.

She carried two quart jars of applesauce, and her daughter, Barbara, was laden with a stack of cassettes and a portable cassette player.

"Ah! I can breathe," Mary Jean said, setting the applesauce beside the sink and fluffing her dark hair. "Fresh air, the lake." She nodded to Ruby. "Fresh friend."

"You sound like a woman who needs a change."

"Hah. I'll bet you don't even know when my period is."

"It gets that bad, does it?" Ruby asked, holding up one of the jars of beach sand–colored applesauce and seeing chunks of apple, flecks of cinnamon.

"Yes, it truly gets that bad. I've known people here so long I can't even tell you what they look like."

"Can Jesse and I go outside?" Barbara asked. She had dark hair like her mother, cut short, but a bolder girl than Mary Jean had been. "We can play our music louder out there."

Ruby started for the main room. "I'll get the wheelchair."

Barbara's nose wrinkled. "Do we have to? I can help her through the doors and we'll sit on the grass."

No, Ruby wanted to say, Jesse might fall. But instead,

she told Barbara, "Go ahead. Take the afghan on the back of the rocker."

"You're protective," Mary Jean observed.

"Wouldn't you be?" Ruby asked.

"*I'd* put a mama grizzly to shame. Let's sit on your porch."

They sat on the metal chairs, watching the two girls through the screen, both teenagers bent over the tape player.

"This is nice," Mary Jean said. "I've only been out here once besides the birthday party where I got this." She touched the skate blade scar on her chin.

Ruby couldn't remember. "At one of the parties?"

Mary Jean laughed. "No, Ruby Crane. You wouldn't have invited *me* to your parties. I came out alone one day when nobody was home. I swam off your dock."

"You never seemed like someone who'd trespass."

"I'm sure I didn't."

"Somebody was inside my cabin last night," Ruby told Mary Jean. "Whoever it was left me a note suggesting that I mind my own business."

Mary Jean tipped her head. "What did you do to attract their attention?"

"Mina was the closest friend I had in Sable, maybe in my whole life. I've asked a few questions, that's all."

"That's enough. In Sable, people gossip and they guess and they start vicious rumors." Mary Jean looked at Ruby over her raised iced tea. "But they don't openly ask questions. You're breaking protocol."

"Mina and Corbin are dead. Their dog was shot and their house burned. It's time *somebody* broke protocol."

Ruby hadn't told anyone except Carly and Silas about finding Mina's dog shot to death, and she was startled that no flicker of surprise crossed Mary Jean's eyes.

"But are *you* that person, Ruby?" Mary Jean asked.

"Who else is showing any serious interest? Carly's investigating but I sense he's not getting a lot of cooperation. Surely a sense of justice has filtered through the back roads to Sable."

"Don't make fun of your homeland." Mary Jean leaned back, resting her neck on the cool metal. "But you're right; I don't believe Mina's death was an accident. I might if it wasn't for the dog and the fire."

"You knew about her dog?"

"Everybody does. The word is you found its body stashed in the woods, and there are a few who think *that's* odd."

"I was picking flowers for Jesse. But I only told Carly and Silas about Pepper."

"Men spill it to their wives or their bar buddies. That's all it takes. The people of Sable are aware you have a few crumbs of information and that you're hunting for more. They're afraid of what you're up to."

"But why? Aren't they grateful *somebody's* looking for the truth?"

"In their deepest hearts, probably, but mostly they worry what else you might dredge up along the way. Everybody has secrets they'd sell their soul to the devil to keep hidden."

"Tell me about Corbin's and Mina's secrets," Ruby asked. "Was it a major scandal when Mina left Ford for Corbin?"

Mary Jean shook her head and looked out over Blue Lake. "That kept tongues wagging for months. Mina and Corbin were caught . . . what's that French term— you've been to college—*in* something?"

"*In flagrante delicto.* It's Latin and I only attended college illegally."

"Someday I want to hear how you did that." Turning toward the girls sitting on the lawn, she called, "Turn that music down a little, Barb," then went on. "Anyway,

Mina rarely left home afterward. I think being alone became a habit. People moved on to the next scandal but, by then, she didn't have many friends."

"Did Mina ever write you a note? A card maybe?"

"Not that I can remember. She hadn't sent out Christmas cards in years. Why?"

"I just wondered. Were you a friend?"

Mary Jean's face saddened. "In hindsight, not a very good one. Remember how funny and sharp she was? Later she used her sharpness to keep people out. It was hard to get close to her. There were rumors . . ."

"What kind?" Ruby asked.

"Are you sure you want to hear this? Mina and Corbin can't defend themselves."

"Don't speak ill of the dead, you mean."

Mary Jean clasped her hands between her knees. "Yeah." She looked up at the ceiling. "I feel like a rat dragging this up. A few months ago, rumors circulated that Mina was having an affair. She was seen *near* a motel with a man. Somebody else claimed they'd spotted Mina and her lover in the great out of doors, *in fragr* . . . doing it."

"Who was the man?"

"Nobody knew or else they chose not to say. That's why I suspect it's a rumor. Around here, a man involved in a scandal like that doesn't go unnamed."

"What about Corbin? Were there rumors concerning him, too?"

"No love affair rumors. He was wrapped up in his mill: visions of wealth danced in his head, I think. And of course, he and Silas Shea were always feuding, but nobody took that very serious."

"Until Corbin ended up dead."

Mary Jean shuddered. "Some people blame Silas but I don't believe it. The way they fought . . . like it was a sport. Blasting music at each other on loudspeakers and taking out ads against one another? That's more of a nyah-nyah-nyah quarrel, the way kids fight."

"The timber business is different here from what I'm familiar with out West," Ruby said. "It's been an education."

"From Hank the Hunk Holliday?"

"Is nothing sacred?" Ruby asked. An oak leaf twirled down from the trees, landing on Jesse's shoulder. It perched there, unnoticed, then fell to the ground.

"Not if we can help it. He's our Bachelor of the Month and you've raised local hackles by being seen with him, too."

"I like him and I like his ideas about managing trees and forests. I'd think tree owners would flock to him."

"It's still too radical. Who wants to admit they can't take care of their own trees? A tree used to be a tree, not a science."

"It's hard to believe you never left Sable," Ruby told Mary Jean.

"Do you mean because of my sophistication and worldview?" Mary Jean asked with an edgy tone to her voice. "Don't cut us short, Ruby. We have access here to almost everything you had in California. This is the information age, remember? Some of us choose to take advantage of it and others prefer not to. Provincialism is dead. Long live provincialism."

Jesse was in her room when Ruby left for Mabel's, worn out, Ruby thought, but happy. Mary Jean's daughter Barbara had left her an incomprehensible music tape.

"Think of it as progress," Ruby told DeEtta while they listened to the cacophonous music coming from Jesse's bedroom. Ruby wondered if the music was a comfort because it duplicated the sounds inside Jesse's head.

"You should buy her a tape player with headphones," DeEtta suggested.

Ruby took a break and walked through Sable. As she passed Wally's office, he stuck his head out the door. "Susannah wants to invite you and your daughter for dinner. She'll call you in a day or two, okay?"

"Fine," Ruby answered, wondering whose idea the invitation *really* was.

She stopped in front of St. Anne's, gazing up at the newly painted belfry. She hadn't been inside in years.

Mabel had said Father Dorman was turning homely old St. Anne's into a cathedral. Ruby pushed open the doors into the nave, curious, pausing to tap the closest holy water font with her fingernail. It was marble.

The air shimmered with streaming beams of color through new stained glass windows. There were new, statelier, high-backed pews of darkened oak, finer statues, Stations carved in relief.

Ruby's footsteps echoed hollowly and she paused, gazing around her. Long ago, the church had hired one of the last local Indians to paint the domed cove behind the altar a simple coat of flat blue paint. Instead, he'd spent days on scaffolding, a bottle of whiskey at his side, and in alcoholic inspiration created glorious banks of clouds from floor to domed ceiling. The splendored multilayered clouds of late summer, the clouds of imagination.

The committee hadn't requested art and wasn't about to pay for art. But when they discovered the Indian didn't expect a penny more, they let him alone, knowing a good deal when they saw it.

Now those clouds were all that Ruby recognized of

the old St. Anne's. They were as splendid as she remembered.

Footsteps sounded at the back of the church and Ruby turned to see Father Dorman, still rotund, his mouth pursed the way a man's did when he denied himself too much. He smiled and bobbed.

"Do you like our improvements?" he asked.

"I'm glad you kept the clouds," she said.

"Ah, yes, the clouds. They're our claim to fame. The Grand Rapids paper did a story on our clouds. The reporter called them Michelangeloish. I can't see it myself."

"What happened to the artist?" Ruby asked. "I remember watching him paint when I was little."

"I couldn't say. He probably died years ago."

"You've gained a few more wealthy parishioners since I left," Ruby said, pointing toward the new statues, the delicate gold-leaf work on the beams above them.

"People can be generous when their eyes are focused on higher goals." He paused and brought his hands together holily. "Seeing you here; does this mean you may join us Sunday? Your father never misses a Sunday."

"I have no plans."

"We gain strength to meet these recent tragedies when we join together."

"These 'recent tragedies' would be best served by solid police work, it seems to me," Ruby told him.

"I know you're frustrated with the lack of evidence."

"How do you know that?"

He smoothly went on. "We have to trust our local authorities. You were always . . . restive, Rubina, and now you're accustomed to the faster pace of a large city. The best course is to not impede the law's progress. You wouldn't want to inadvertently interfere with their investigation."

Ruby stepped away from him and into the aisle. "I have the feeling you're warning me."

"My child," he began.

"Excuse me. I have to get back to work," she said, and left the church, her steps echoing behind her.

Chapter 19

From the southwest, a wind blasted into Waters County, bending treetops, creaking the cabin, and sending flurries of autumn leaves in every direction, including circular. The blow was unpredicted and the afternoon was clear, blue-skied and crisp.

"Ten- to twelve-foot seas on Lake Michigan," the radio announcer warned gleefully. "Land gusts to sixty miles per hour."

DeEtta abandoned her twelve-foot trailer for the more solid cabin. "You never know," she said, carrying in three paperback mysteries and a bag of frosted animal cookies. "My niece, Little DeEtta, is spending the night with me. If the wind keeps up, could we sleep here?"

"The couch opens," Ruby told her. "How old is she?"

"Ten. I can make popcorn for all of us."

Jesse loved popcorn. She ate it now one deliberate kernel at a time.

Ruby said yes when Hank phoned and asked, "Can you get away for a few hours? I've got something to show you.

"Dress warm," he advised her before he hung up.

DeEtta gave Ruby a knowing smile. "You're going out," she said.

"For a while. Lock the door and keep Spot inside until I get back," Ruby told her.

"Sure. Bruce is bringing over Little DeEtta in an hour. He'll spend the evening with us."

"Make sure it's him before you open the door."

❖   ❖   ❖

Hank stopped at the end of Blue Road. Yellow leaves being blown from the aspens blew across the Cherokee and drifted against the banks of the road. "We can't get there until after dark," he told her. "So we'll take the long route."

"Why does it have to be dark?" Ruby asked.

"You'll see," he said, smiling.

"I used to strip the bark off birch trees and write notes on them," Ruby told Hank as they passed a grove of white birch trees standing at the edge of a swampy area.

"Birches are sixty-mile-an-hour trees," he said.

"What does that mean?"

"You can identify a birch when you're driving by at sixty miles an hour.

"Here's a forest Corbin cut," Hank said, stopping his Cherokee alongside the thin forest that held only a few tall trees. The forest rippled in the gale in currents and eddies, like wind over the lake. "In a year this will be so dense with aspen you won't be able to spit between them. You cut one aspen and a thousand come to its funeral. But see the trees left standing? No dings or breaks from being hit by falling trees. You destroy too much bark and the tree dies. The ground's not torn up and Corbin cleaned up the tops."

"Corbin logged the property alone?"

"He usually logged alone to save a buck, plus one other man who operated the skidder, to pull the logs out of the woods. Corbin prided himself on his speed. It takes a lot less time than you'd expect to mow down a forest."

"When did Corbin cut Fox Woods?" Ruby asked

"Last month."

"Abel Obert claims clearcutting isn't the horror we think it is."

Hank turned and gave her a long look. "Abel Obert, king of Northern Timber? You know him?"

"I toured his mill. I was curious about a bigger mill after seeing Corbin's and Silas's."

"Abel's a timber man to the heartwood," Hank said. "One of those apolitical single-minded types."

"Is he right about clearcutting?"

"Yes and no. It has its place: diseased forests, species regeneration. Not indiscriminate mowing down, but carefully managed, especially on hills and along waterways. But it gets bad press. People go into a panic when they hear the term."

"Is that like saying 'pretty is no way to judge the woods'?" Ruby asked, quoting Abel Obert.

"Right. Take a nice farm; now *there's* an example of removing a complete ecosystem, soup to nuts, and throwing chemicals on it besides. But put a white fence around it and stick in a few pretty horses and the same folks who decry cutting down trees lust after the farm. Who can figure?"

Signs picked out in the headlights vibrated on their posts and everywhere, leaves and bits of loose objects flew through the night.

"Okay, it's dark now," Ruby said. "What's the surprise?"

"You probably weren't aware of it," he told her, "but I've been on a few days' vacation from Sable. I'm returning tomorrow. I want to show you where I've been."

He swerved as a broken branch somersaulted across the road as effortlessly as a tumbleweed. "I didn't go far, except in state of mind."

The closer they approached Lake Michigan, the harder the wind gusted. Sand blew across the road like driven snow in their headlights beams, hissing against the Cherokee and building long low drifts on the pavement. "Just ahead," Hank told her.

He turned up a driveway of beach sand and stopped beside a low white cottage that hunkered next to a bluff that was hardly more than a humpy dune, anchored here and there by dune grass.

"Wait here," he told her. "I'll turn on the lights."

When he opened his car door, Ruby's ears popped as the winds swept inside, blowing her hair and scattering papers. But more powerful than the wind was the sound: the roar of waves that pounded like blood rushing in her ears; thundering punctuated by the splash of an out-of-sync curl of water. The night was dwarfed by resonance. And it was very close.

"That's the lake I hear," Ruby shouted. "I want to *see* it first. How near is it?"

Hank leaned close to her and said, "The other side of the bluff."

They struggled up the bluff beside the house, feet sliding on the loose sand, wind tugging at their clothes. Hank took her hand and pulled her to the top.

Above them the stars hung brilliant, the Milky Way as thick as cream. And thirty feet below them, the waves crashed against the shore, the crest of each wave flashing white as if the water's ferocity made its own electricity. A fine cold spray spattered her face and her clothes blew flat against her body. If it weren't for the anchor of Hank's hand, she'd be blown helplessly backward.

Long ago, when the winds blew, Ruby's quiet, timid mother had stolen every opportunity to escape to Lake Michigan. She'd paced and fidgeted until she dreamed up an excuse to flee the house, even lying to her husband, returning an hour or two later, windblown, smelling of water, her eyes content and the soles of her shoes golden with beach sand.

Ruby didn't know how long they stood in the wind and spray watching the hypnotic pounding of the waves, but when the spell was broken enough she felt the sand stinging her cheeks, she reluctantly turned from the water.

She slid on her heels down the bluff's loose sand and entered the cottage. The roar of the lake was a constant, even with the door closed. Ruby shook off her coat and looked around her. The cottage was a fourth the size of her cabin, sparsely furnished, a beach house. One all-purpose room with a bedroom on the side closest to the bluff.

"Is this a good getaway?" Hank asked.

"The best."

"I'll be sorry to leave it tomorrow and return to the reality of Sable," he said as he poured two glasses of red wine. "And watching my back."

Hank took a bag of potato chips from the cupboard and set it on the coffee table. "Sit down. I heard that was Mina's first husband you were talking to at her luncheon."

"His name's Ford Goodlight. He's raising her son, the teenager with the Walkman."

Hank nodded. "Everybody's sorrier than hell about Mina now but they could have been more compassionate after Corbin's death." His face tensed. "Why didn't any friends or relatives stay with her? Or at least get her out of that house? And that damn saw sitting in the backyard."

"She may have rejected their compassion," Ruby said, remembering the flowers rotting behind Corbin's sawmill. "Besides . . ."

"I know. I heard people didn't approve of the way she ditched her husband for Corbin, and . . ." He closed his mouth and raised his glass to his lips.

He'd heard rumors about Mina's affair, too, Ruby guessed. "Do you know who the man was?" she asked cautiously.

"No." He rolled his glass between his hands.

"I've been warned to mind my own business," Ruby told him.

He raised his head, frowning. "Who told you that?"

She explained about the note, the evidence that the intruder had snooped through her loft.

"It makes me certain that she was bringing me information regarding Corbin's death and she was killed to keep her quiet." Ruby told him about her visit to Lyle Zander and her suspicion that Mina was bringing her a note supposedly written by Zander.

"There had to have been more than just a note. I can't believe Mina would have driven to your cabin in the middle of the night for that. Have you talked to the sheriff?"

Ruby nodded. "Carly tells me I'm too impatient with the slower processes of the rural world. But he agrees, I'm sure of it. And now the evidence in Corbin's sawmill has been destroyed by the fire."

Hank lightly put his arm around Ruby's shoulder. "What evidence in the sawmill?" he asked.

Ruby told him about the straight boards, which might belie the theory of the misaligned guide pins, and Corbin's missing and then mysteriously reappearing support. "Which Mina lied about Corbin removing," Ruby said.

"Maybe."

"Carly said the straight boards didn't prove anything, that Corbin may have been trying to remove a piece of wood jammed between the blade and the guide pins."

"That's a possibility. People lose limbs too often trying to unjam a blade."

The windows rattled in a strong gust of wind and Ruby listened, thinking how some sounds became so familiar they became a comfort, like passing trains and waves, recalling the way Mina had listened to Corbin's saw.

"What would it sound like if a headsaw was jammed by a piece of wood?" she asked Hank.

"What do you mean?"

"The noise of the saw. I know what the saw sounds like when it's running and when it's sawing through a log, but does it sound different if it's jammed?"

Hank frowned. "It does. The saw sounds . . . tortured, not at all the businesslike buzz it has when it cuts wood."

"I don't recall a tortured sound coming from Corbin's sawmill the day he died, only logs and then . . . nothing."

"Ruby," he said thoughtfully, "this whole investigation *may* be better left to the sheriff. You're taking on Waters County like a one-woman police force."

"I think better when I work alone."

"Maybe, but this could be dangerous. Let me nose around a little . . ."

Ruby turned toward him. The wine was warming and she felt the first waves of relaxation.

His hand moved to the back of her neck and Ruby leaned against it, certain what she was doing, the signals she was sending.

We're not kids, she thought. I know what I want.

Hank took her glass from her hand and set it on the coffee table. He smiled and enclosed her in his arms, kissing the top of her head. She felt his heartbeat beneath her ear.

"I've been looking forward to this," he said.

"Oh, yeah? For how long?"

He laughed. "Since the moment I saw you with Enid Shea's cream cheese frosting on your chin." He stood and took her hand, nodding toward the bedroom.

"Wait a minute," Ruby objected. "These are modern days. Do you have protection?"

"That depends on how many times we do it."

"First we'd better make sure you can find me under all these clothes."

He slipped his hands beneath her sweater, shirt, and turtleneck and slid them up her back. His hands were warm, light on either side of her spine, and Ruby's skin shivered.

"How am I doing?" he asked.

"I think you've got it," she said, leading the way toward the bedroom.

Later, wrapped in blankets and drinking hot chocolate instead of wine, Ruby said, half seriously, "It might have been so good because of the waves crashing in the background. All that crescendo is inspiring."

"I'm willing to test your theory," Hank said. "How about tomorrow night in my hovel in Sable where the only accompaniment will be barking dogs and the occasional passing semi?"

Ruby curled inside the blanket, feeling her bare legs against her stomach, her skin still rosy and sensitive. For a brief while, she'd been on vacation, too. Death and injury banished for the duration.

The beach house was a squat little refuge, isolated and protected from wind and water. By tomorrow the wind would drop and Lake Michigan would be tame once again, showing its other, pretty, side.

"I don't mean to bring up bad memories," Hank said against her hair. "But why don't you and your father get along?"

"You've been talking about me again," Ruby said lightly. She curled against him. "You'd have to know my father. He believed my teen years weren't a phase; they were my destiny. In hindsight, I'm aware my grandmother's death undid me, but he didn't believe in excuses, either. All he could see was that I left his church, made trouble, swore I hated him, and accused him of killing my mother."

"I thought she died three years ago," Hank said.

"Only physically." Ruby sighed. "She kept a post office box in Pere so I could write to her. He forbade her: never more darken my door, that sort of melodrama."

Hank pulled her closer. "And your sister?"

"When the going got rough, Phyllis took our father's side. She and I tried to get together twelve years ago but it didn't work." Ruby paused, remembering herself and Phyllis accusing each other of, among other things, egotism, favoritism, and duplicity while two-year-old Jesse cried in her crib. "She writes to Jesse every month."

"Does Jesse ever ask about her?"

"She might when she's recovered more. I'm beginning to accept that she'll never be the old Jesse." Ruby felt the tears and turned her head. "But I expect her to become the complete new version."

Hank was thoughtful on the drive to her cabin, every little while glancing at her or touching her arm. They didn't speak but when he stopped his Cherokee beside her back door, he hugged her and said, "Call me day or night, Ruby," sounding too much like Ruby telling Mina to call her whenever she needed her.

The sky was still perfectly clear. O starry night. Trees above her swayed in the gusts, blocking and revealing the stars. Ruby took a deep breath. She felt good.

The Jeep's taillights disappeared in the trees and a figure moved near DeEtta's trailer. Ruby gasped and the bent figure scuttled forward.

It was Mrs. Pink. Her black clothing flapped around her body and with her staff she was a being who'd escaped from a dark fantasy. "I've been waiting and waiting and waiting," Mrs. Pink said, her raspy voice rising in agitation. "I need to tell you."

"What is it, Mrs. Pink?" Ruby asked. She didn't invite Mrs. Pink into the cabin, not wanting to risk waking Jesse or DeEtta and her niece. She moved from the cabin toward the garage. "Come in out of the wind."

"No," Mrs. Pink said, shaking her head. "I need to tell you about the men who came into the woods today. With paint."

"It's all right," Ruby told her. "It was a man I asked to look at my trees."

"Not him. Other men. On your land and on my land. *Mein* Frank is afraid. What are they going to do?"

"When did you see other men?" Ruby asked.

"This afternoon. I followed them from your land to mine. They're painting the trees."

Mrs. Pink had seen Glenn Wister in Ruby's woods and woven a fantasy around him, spreading his influence from Ruby's trees to her own.

"What are you going to do about it?" Mrs. Pink demanded. "You said we were good neighbors."

"In the morning, Mrs. Pink," Ruby assured her. "I'll take care of it in the morning. It's too dark to see tonight."

"Don't you have a flashlight?" Mrs. Pink demanded.

"Not one that's bright enough to see every tree in the woods. I'm going to bed now, Mrs. Pink," Ruby said. "Why don't you go home and I'll see you tomorrow."

"You won't forget?"

"No. I promise."

"Then I'll wait at my house for you to bring me the news."

Ruby unlocked her cabin door and went inside. The cabin smelled of popcorn. The couch had been opened and on it lay Jesse and Little DeEtta, who truly looked like a smaller DeEtta: round-faced, sturdy, plain brown hair. Both of them asleep.

DeEtta sat in the rocker reading one of her paperback mysteries. She looked up and waved her fingers at

Ruby, then pressed a finger to her lips and pointed to the two girls.

Ruby surveyed the open couch, the scattered magazines and cards and stuffed animals, the sleeping girls and the dog poking its nose from beneath the bed, DeEtta with her books and package of cookies on her lap. This wasn't a fortress; it was a summer camp.

Chapter 20

True to her word to Mrs. Pink, as soon as Ruby finished breakfast she walked up the driveway and across the road to inspect her own wooded acres. She looked for Mrs. Pink's black figure lurking behind the trees, making sure Ruby was being the "good neighbor," but there was no sign of the old woman. The capricious wind was gone and the morning was clear and still, cool.

Fifty feet into the woods stood an oak banded with red paint and Ruby came to a halt, frowning. Hadn't Glenn Wister been carrying a spray can of *blue* paint? The oak wasn't as thick as a power pole, and Ruby scraped at the red paint with her thumbnail; it didn't flick off the way old paint did.

She zigzagged through the woods, discovering more oaks and maples, a few beeches marked with both blue and red bands of paint, smaller trees banded with red paint but not blue. Only straight trees were marked, trees with branches beginning at least fifteen feet above the ground. The gnarled maples, the double-trunked oaks, the popples—even those that were thick and straight—were untouched by either red or blue paint. What did it mean?

Ruby turned around and walked back to the cabin, kicking at the leaves. Who else had been in her woods?

DeEtta was drizzling pancake batter into fat snowman shapes in a frying pan for her niece and Jesse, who both sat on the sofa bed in their pajamas, looking at comics, Little DeEtta speaking animatedly, Jesse scowling.

"Did Glenn Wister return yesterday after I left?" Ruby asked DeEtta.

"I didn't see him." The edges of her pancake bubbled and she expertly flipped it over.

"I'm going to Mrs. Pink's. I'll be back in twenty minutes," she said, and grabbed her car keys from the peg beside the door and one of Carol's gift jars of applesauce.

On the front porch of her house among all her bird feeders and birdhouses, Mrs. Pink sat intently eyeing the road, her hands folded in her lap. Waiting for her, Ruby was sure.

"I brought you some applesauce," Ruby said, setting the jar on an upturned crate beside Mrs. Pink.

"Did you make it?" Mrs. Pink asked, tapping the glass with an overlong fingernail.

"No. It's better than I could make."

Mrs. Pink nodded without argument. "Did you find the marks on my trees?" she demanded. "Where the men were?"

"Not yet, but I saw mine. Did you recognize the men?"

"Just men. They look alike to me." Mrs. Pink pointed across the road. "In there. Follow my mushroom path." She made shooing motions. "Go look now and tell me what you find."

Under Mrs. Pink's watchful eye, Ruby crossed the road where she'd indicated, stretching across the ditch. No path was visible among the fallen leaves, but Ruby spotted a foot-high ceramic statue of a ballerina in faded pink tulle leaning against a tree. Her nose was missing and one of her arms was sheared off at the shoulder; the other arm pointed gracefully into the woods.

Ten feet in the direction the ballerina pointed, Ruby

sighted a worn narrow path into the shady forest. It had begun as a deer trail, she guessed, from the way the path followed the line of least resistance.

Farther along the trail stood a mossy wooden carving of an antique horse hitch, a rusty metal ring hanging from its mouth. In the stand of red oak surrounding it, every tree bore the same red band as the trees in Ruby's forest. And more red-banded trees were visible beyond those.

Because of the time she'd spent with Hank, Ruby knew these trees were more marketable than hers. There was more hard maple and much of it was straight, unblemished. Above her, the leafy canopy was thick as the trees pushed skyward for light.

Ruby turned in a circle, wondering who the marks belonged to. Silas? If every tree marked with red paint was cut, this forest would be decimated and desolate. Nothing left but the smallest and the weakest.

"What are they doing?" Mrs. Pink asked, rising stiffly from her chair when Ruby emerged from the woods. "That's my trees. *Mein* Frank hunts there."

Hunts or haunts? Ruby wondered. "I don't know," she told her. "But I'll find out. I'll come back as soon as I have an answer."

"I'm not leaving this spot until I see you again," Mrs. Pink told her, pointing her gnarled finger toward the floor of her porch.

Ruby drove home, puzzling over the marked trees. When she reached her driveway, a blue pickup was parked across the entrance, blocking her way into the cabin. When the driver saw Ruby, he jumped out instead of moving his truck.

"You're blocking my driveway," Ruby said, opening her car door.

"I'm Chuck Baylor of Fogg Timber," he said, smiling. A small man with a lean and muscular body, his blond hair had receded halfway back from his forehead. He was tanned that deep brown that took months to fade.

"I'm not familiar with Fogg Timber," Ruby told him.

"We're over in Berry County. We don't do much work over here—yet."

Spray cans lay among the ropes and tools in the bed of his pickup, some stained with red paint.

"You marked trees in my woods," Ruby accused him. "Who gave you permission?"

He held up scarred hands and soothed the air. "Now, now," he said, "I was only trying to help."

"You were trespassing."

His voice deepened, ardently sincere. "No, no. I'm giving you another option. I heard Northern Timber was in here and I wanted to show you what *we* could do for you. I'll walk it with you, advise you how to get a better income out of your woods. You won't regret it."

"That's still trespassing. The only thing I want from you is your absence. Please move your truck so I can go home."

"Now, lady," he said. "You don't want to be taken advantage of. I hate to see that happen to a woman alone."

She remembered something Hank had said. "If you're serious," she began, watching Chuck Baylor's eyes light up, "talk to Hank Holliday. He's the forester who's managing my timber property."

Baylor's demeanor changed from conciliatory to pugnacious. The smile disappeared. "You're making a mistake working with that asshole," he said. "Holliday'll promise you a Garden of Eden and you'll end up with zip. No money and a bunch of overgrown, worthless, hollowed-out trees. I can't tell you how many times I've seen it happen. Zip."

"Please move now, Mr. Baylor," Ruby said. "If you're not gone by the time I'm back in my car, I'm calling the sheriff."

Ruby's hand was on her door handle when she remembered Mrs. Pink's marked trees. "And stay away from Mrs. Pink's property down the road, too," she told him.

Hitching himself into the driver's side of his truck, Baylor paused, puzzled. "I don't know any Mrs. Pink."

"The trees you marked two miles to the east, across from the lake."

"That's a legitimate job," he said. "That's why we're here. It doesn't belong to any Mrs. Pink. Some guy in Chicago owns it." He slammed his door and started his engine with a roar, then pulled away, spinning his tires and leaving Ruby in a dusty cloud.

The only time Chuck Baylor had sounded honest was when he denied knowing Mrs. Pink. She'd taken for granted that Mrs. Pink owned the land where her "mushroom trail" wandered. Could the old woman be confused?

Little DeEtta was gone and DeEtta and Jesse were performing arm exercises in the main room: lifting wrist weights, squeezing a rubber ball. Ruby phoned Hank's house, although she was certain he'd still be in his beach house, but he answered on the second ring.

"Late start," he said. "I'm just dropping off my gear. What's up?"

"Do you know Chuck Baylor of Fogg Timber?"

Hank groaned. "Not personally. He's an aggressive timber cruiser. I've heard you'd better count your fingers after a conversation with him."

"I have all ten, but he marked trees in my woods without permission."

"He's been known to do that."

"He marked trees on Mrs. Pink's property, too, but he claims the land belongs to a Chicago owner and he's logging it legitimately."

"I carry a plat book for the county. I'll bring it out and we can look it up."

"Do you have time?" Ruby asked.

"Yes." He paused. "Definitely. I'll be there in fifteen minutes. I'm looking forward to it."

While she waited for Hank, Ruby took over Jesse's walking routines. Jesse was unconcerned by her weak left side and wasn't particularly motivated to give up her wheelchair. Jesse had progressed to a one-pound ankle weight on her left leg. Although she began each session pitifully dragging her leg, making Ruby feel like a thirteenth-century torturer, by the session's end she was standing straighter and pulling her foot forward with more strength, doggedly working until Ruby called it quits. "Remember," the doctor had warned, "she'll adapt to whatever she's allowed to."

The phone rang and DeEtta answered, then held the receiver out to Ruby. "Todd," she mouthed.

"Hi," Ruby said, realizing she hadn't thought of Todd in days. Not once. She leaned against the table, her back to DeEtta and Jesse, bringing Todd's face into focus.

"How's life in the wilderness?" he asked, and they chatted about their respective lives. Ruby asked Todd bright cheerful questions about his work, realizing the nudge of remorse she felt was precisely because she felt none.

"Ruby," he said quietly as their conversation wound down. "What's going on?"

"What do you mean?"

"You sound different." He paused. "Have you met someone?"

Ruby took a deep breath. "I have. I can't say it's going anywhere, but . . ."

". . . you want to explore the relationship with this guy and see where it leads and you think of me warmly and you hope we'll always be friends, right?"

"My thinking isn't that slick," Ruby told him.

"But am I right?"

"If you're determined to reduce a complicated situation to black and white, I guess so," she admitted reluctantly.

"I knew this would happen," Todd said. "You shouldn't have gone back there."

Hank opened his plat book to the page containing Mrs. Pink's property. "M. Pink," it read. M: Mary? Margaret? Ruby hadn't ever heard Mrs. Pink's first name, had childishly never considered she had one.

"What exactly am I looking at?" Ruby asked him.

"Each page is a township in the county. Six miles by six miles, listing the owner of every piece of property. The plat book comes out once a year, so a few pieces of property will have changed hands."

Notes were scribbled throughout the plat book in Hank's writing: acreages, new owners, notes to himself. She wasn't surprised by his readable but economical penmanship, half print, initial letters begun in midstroke.

He put his finger to the narrow strip with Mrs. Pink's name on it. "According to this, she only owns the piece on the lake where her house sits, down to the water."

"But that can't be right. D. Townsend owns across the road? I've always believed that was Mrs. Pink's property."

"If you want, we can check at the courthouse. They record the property's history back to the first owner."

Ruby took him to her woods across the road and pointed out the blue and red bands, explaining how she'd contacted Glenn Wister in an attempt to discover more about Corbin Turmouski. He looked at her, opened his mouth and closed it again.

"Is this high-grading?" Ruby asked.

"Well, they've marked only the best trees, which is all

they'd be interested in." Hank circled the trees, scanning their trunks, calculating from one tree to the next. "No consideration here of the effect on the trees left standing."

He stopped in front of a maple with only a red band. "See how Fogg Timber marked smaller trees than Glenn did? This tree is only twelve inches DBH."

"What's DBH?"

"Diameter at breast height. It's a standard measurement. Remember your high school math? Pi? Roughly, you measure around the tree at breast height and divide by three. That's DBH. Fogg's more desperate than Northern Timber. The less timber available the lower the standards." He shook his head. "Back in the 1800s, they took hardwood with a DBH of forty-eight inches. Think of it."

Beneath a beautiful but economically unprofitable maple tree, Hank put his arms around Ruby. She leaned against him, wondering if Todd was right. Todd was a kind man, a gentle lover. But sadly, she realized there'd never been this sharp sense of *wanting* with him.

In the Waters County Register of Deeds office in the hundred-year-old brick courthouse, Ruby gave the gray-haired clerk the description of the property across from Mrs. Pink.

The woman looked from Ruby to the slip of paper. "This isn't your property," she said, pushing her glasses against the bridge of her nose. "You're farther down the lake."

"That's true, but I'd like to know who owns this property, please," Ruby said.

The woman took the paper to a card file, then pulled out a giant liber and flipped through the pages. She jotted on the paper and handed it back to Ruby.

"D. Townsend, Chicago," it read in the woman's handwriting, her *w* and *n* connected by a straight horizontal.

Ruby handed the slip back to the clerk. "May I see the complete record?"

"I really don't have time to write it all down," she protested.

"You don't need to," Ruby told her. "I'll examine the liber myself. I believe the deed history is a matter of public record, isn't it? I *can* look at it."

Wordlessly, the clerk retrieved the record book and fussily set it on the counter.

The first owner in 1856 had marked the deed with an X, the last owner listed, D. Townsend, Chicago, had signed with a leftward leaning signature, as left-handers often did. And between the first and last owners, there was no owner named Pink.

Ruby leaned back. "So the property never did belong to Mrs. Pink?"

"Afraid not," Hank said. "This should be up to date unless the property's been sold recently and the deed hasn't been recorded yet."

She flipped through a few more pages in the giant liber, glancing at other property deeds. Not only were deeds recorded but any other legal matter concerning the land: easements, building permits. "Look," she said to Hank. "Here's a logging contract for this property."

"We try to keep a complete history of information pertaining to our properties," the clerk interrupted, reaching for the liber. "Are you finished?"

Ruby reluctantly gave up the liber, curious how the conditions of the filed logging contract compared to the contract Glenn Wister had offered her.

Outside the courthouse, Ruby said to Hank, "I'd like to follow through with this, just to find out who the actual owner is. Wally Kentner has a monopoly on real estate at that end of the county. Let's stop by his office."

"The deeds clerk knew you," Hank said, nodding to a passing man dressed like a farmer.

"She knew about me," Ruby told him. "But I didn't recognize her. Word gets around fast."

"I bet half the county knows where you were last night."

"But hopefully not what I was doing."

"Give people credit for having some imagination."

Wally was away from his office, attending a meeting in Pere. "You probably passed him on the road," Mary Jean told them, casting speculative looks between Ruby and Hank.

When Ruby explained Mrs. Pink's claims about the land, Mary Jean nodded. "I know the piece. I think Wally approached the owner about selling but it was never listed for sale if I remember right. Just a second and I'll get the file."

"Look," Hank said while they waited, pointing to a Detroit newspaper. "News from the outside world."

Only a month ago, Ruby had read the San Francisco paper every morning. And listened to CNN before she went to bed. But that was before Jesse's accident and the implosion of their world.

"Here it is," Mary Jean said, opening a file folder and discreetly hiding pages of print with the edge of the folder. "David Townsend, Chicago."

David Townsend's signature at the bottom of what appeared to be a photocopy of the deed in the courthouse was as Ruby remembered it: crabbed and leftward-leaning.

"Seeing the forest logged will be hard on Mrs. Pink," Ruby said.

"I hate it when things like this happen," Mary Jean

said, closing the folder. "Changes are hard on old people. My grandmother still can't believe the old drive-in movie's been torn down. She loved drive-ins. My father used to take her every Thursday night."

When Ruby was finished explaining the land situation, Mrs. Pink's eyes filled with tears. "*Ja, ja,*" she said, rocking back and forth. "I remember now. It was so many years ago I forgot. I didn't have the money to buy it. I wanted it. The mushrooms."

"I'm sorry, Mrs. Pink."

"Who will cut it? Not Turmouski, thank God." She paused. "But he wouldn't cut my mushroom woods like he did that other one."

"Do you know why he cut Fox Woods so severely?" Ruby asked.

"Do you mean like . . ." She made slashing motions with her hands. "Because of what she did there. She ruined the land."

"What did she do there?" Ruby asked gently, trying to keep Mrs. Pink focused, wondering who "she" was.

Mrs. Pink pushed her index finger in and out of her closed fist in an obscene gesture. Ruby suddenly understood.

"Who was the man?" she asked.

"That one who smiles and sells all the woods. And he's got money now, too."

"What's his name?"

"I promised I wouldn't tell," Mrs. Pink said, and she stubbornly closed her mouth so tightly she appeared toothless. "She brought me schnapps."

"That's all right," Ruby told her. "You don't have to tell me. Be sure to come over for coffee soon."

It wasn't necessary for Mrs. Pink to say another word because now Ruby knew: Corbin Turmouski had destroyed Fox Woods in a rage. He'd left the property so badly scarred and mutilated the signs of his anger would linger for years. And all because those trees had witnessed his wife, Mina, having an affair with Wally Kentner.

Chapter 21

Wally waited in the same booth they'd shared a few days ago, a cup of coffee and a piece of apple pie in front of him. From wooden speakers in the Knotty Pine's ceiling, Frank Sinatra crooned about his way, loud enough to muffle conversation at surrounding tables.

Wally was relaxed, the top button of his white shirt undone, the ghost of a tie still circling his neck.

After the waitress brought her a cup of coffee, Wally said, "On the phone you sounded like you had urgent business."

With an apology to the deceased of the world and hoping she wouldn't charge her dead friend with lying, Ruby said, "Do you remember how close Mina and I used to be?"

"Inseparable," Wally said, smiling.

"We shared a lot of secrets," Ruby said, looking steadily into Wally's eyes.

"That's what good friends do," Wally said. He dipped his spoon into his coffee, giving it half a stir.

A woman entered the Knotty Pine and a tan mongrel slipped in at her feet.

"Peggy, out!" the waitress commanded, and the dog skittered on the tile floor and slunk back outside.

"When I returned to Sable," Ruby told him, "Mina and I rekindled our friendship. We didn't have much time but we caught up on our pasts: our marriages and children and love lives. Before she died, she told me about . . ." Here, Ruby nodded toward Wally.

He sat very still, gazing at her but his eyes gone distant, his face slackening.

"Who else knew?" Ruby continued. "Besides Corbin? Did you tell the sheriff?"

It was a calculated risk that paid off. As Wally gave a disbelieving shake of his head, Ruby glanced down so he missed the triumph in her eyes.

"She told you?" he asked.

Ruby didn't answer.

"It was a terrible mistake," he said in a low voice after glancing around the cafe. "We both knew it and we both wanted out as soon as it began." He clasped his hands together on the table, nudging away his partially eaten pie. "There'd been a spark between us since high school."

"I don't remember it quite that way," Ruby told him.

"Maybe it was only from my perspective," Wally conceded, "but I never made a move toward her."

"She approached you?" Ruby asked.

Wally shook his head. "In July the owner of Fox Woods contacted me about logging his property. I don't usually get involved in logging but I hoped he'd list the property with me if he decided to sell, so I arranged to meet Corbin at Fox Woods for an estimate. He got tied up and sent Mina to tell me he'd be late."

"And you started an affair that day?"

"No, Mina and I only talked . . . but it was the beginning. She and Corbin were having problems. Susannah was in Dallas for a month taking care of her mother. Mina was lonely and I . . . I don't know. I guess I still had a serious thing for her; maybe I always will. It was stupid and wrong and . . . a grievous sin."

"At what point did you decide it was sinful?" Ruby asked. "After the first time? The third?"

He winced, turning troubled eyes toward her. "We

got carried away, Ruby. Like kids, remember? In the end, we called it quits because we both felt too guilty." Wally turned his coffee cup in a circle, one finger on the handle.

"Were you still having an affair when she died?" Ruby asked.

"No. We ended it a few weeks after it began."

"After the night you made love in Fox Woods, shortly before Corbin cut it?"

Wally raised his head, his eyes wide. "Did Mina tell you that?"

"No," Ruby said. "Corbin did."

Wally's mouth fell open. "Corbin? That's impossible. He didn't even know you."

"He didn't tell me in words but he was enraged over some incident pertaining to Fox Woods. He didn't simply log the property; he butchered it like a madman."

"I'll pay for my moral failure all my life," Wally said. "Only God knows how Mina is paying."

"Who else knew about the affair?"

"No one." He stopped. "Except Susannah. She doesn't know the name of the woman but I confessed I'd been unfaithful. I owed that much to her."

"Did you feel better after you told her?" Ruby asked. "Did it lessen your burden to shift it onto her? Is she carrying it well?"

"That's not fair, Ruby," Wally said, leaning against the booth's high back. "Susannah and I are partners. She deserves my honesty. How would you have felt if one of your husbands had been unfaithful and kept it from you?"

"I've only been married once, Wally. I'd prefer my husband wallow in his 'moral failures' by himself rather than drag me into it so I could kiss it and make it all better."

"Maybe that lack of honesty is what doomed your marriage," Wally suggested.

"It's moot now, isn't it?" Ruby asked. Her coffee cup was empty. Was the affair and Corbin's knowledge of it what Mina meant when she said, "I lied to you about Corbin and our marriage"?

"So why did you want to talk to me?" Wally asked. He laughed shortly. "You're not intending to blackmail me, are you?"

"I'm trying to understand Mina's and Corbin's deaths. I promised Mina I'd help her."

"Mina's dead," Wally reminded her.

"I still plan to figure out what happened."

Wally's voice rose and one of the men at the counter stopped his coffee cup partway to his lips. "You're not thinking *I* had anything to do with her death, are you?"

Ruby didn't answer and Wally sat silently, watching her.

"The fire was arson," Ruby finally said.

"I know. Some people believe it was a ploy to hide a burglary. During Emma Snyder's funeral last year, her house was robbed. The thieves backed up a moving van in broad daylight. Cleaned out the place."

He held his hand out to Ruby. "Can't we forget this? The deaths have been a nightmare for the whole town. I think about Mina every day, despising myself and worrying I *did* contribute in some way to her death. It may be hard to believe that Mina and Corbin were both my friends, but they were. And Mina . . ." He straightened his shoulders. "Allow me to put that single mistake with Mina behind me. I was wrong and I know it and it'll haunt me for the rest of my life."

Ruby pretended not to see his hand, and he dropped it palm downward on the table with a thud. "You're as stubborn as you always were, Ruby, blaming and holding grudges. The world isn't as open and shut as you see it. I didn't act alone in that affair. The sexes are

liberated, did you forget? Mina bears just as much
blame as I do."

"Except she's dead."

"And every person in this town is damn sorry about
that, nobody more than me. But nothing will bring her
back. The rest of us have to continue living. Earn a
wage, be kind to our spouses and parents and children."
He tipped his coffee cup, looked into it, and said softly,
"Let it go, Ruby."

"When I know the truth," Ruby told him.

"You already do," Wally said heavily. "You just can't
accept it."

"You're supposed to call this number," DeEtta said
the instant Ruby stepped into the cabin, handing her a
slip of paper. "The woman said it was urgent."

Ruby held the paper to the light from the kitchen
window. She didn't recognize the phone number but
the 505 area code was New Mexico, she remembered
that much. She'd expunged Phyllis's phone number
from her address book years ago, but who else's could
it be?

"Jesse and I'll go skip rocks in the lake so you can talk in
privacy," DeEtta said with maddening accommodation.

Ruby sat at the kitchen table and rubbed her temples,
kicking off her shoes beneath her chair.

At least her sister was still safely in New Mexico and
not stalking the streets of Sable.

When their mother died, it hadn't been Phyllis or
their father who'd called Ruby; they'd coerced Father
Dorman into phoning her the next morning, after all
the arrangements were in motion, as if Ruby were a dis-
agreeable afterthought.

The refrigerator clicked on and Ruby stood and
pulled the pitcher of filtered water from the top shelf.

Why should she call Phyllis? Let Phyllis phone again on her own nickel.

The glass began to sweat immediately after she poured the cold water. She drew the letters *HH* on the side with her finger, retracing it with the diligence of a teenager. Hank Holliday.

She sat again, her thoughts shifting to Mina and Wally Kentner. He'd loved Mina since they were teenagers, that was no secret. Mina and Ford Good-light had been the class couple beginning in ninth grade. Mina had been friends with Wally—buddies— but her romantic attention had been on Ford and Ford alone.

But she'd "outgrown" Ford Goodlight, and obviously Corbin had lost his charms, as well. Who else had entered and exited Mina's life besides Wally?

Wally was wrong; Ruby didn't see the world as open and shut. But maybe her vision of Mina *was* skewed. Mina was frozen, a mixture of being seventeen and lost in grief, while in Ruby's mind, Wally had grown into the adult who'd taken advantage of young Mina. Ruby *didn't* know the Mina who'd lived between childhood and Corbin's death.

The phone rang and Ruby reached for it, her thoughts still on Mina.

"I knew you wouldn't call me back."

"You didn't give me a chance," Ruby said. "I just came home."

"Then you were in the middle of talking yourself out of it."

"What makes you think I'd have to convince myself?" Ruby asked.

"Fun-ny. Why are you cutting the woods by the cabin?" Phyllis asked. Hearing Phyllis's voice reminded Ruby of hearing her own on a recording. Familiar and uncomfortable.

"Who says I'm cutting the woods?" Ruby asked.

"Who do you think? You don't live in a vacuum back there. Dad told me."

"This *is* my land and my cabin, Phyllis."

"Only because Mom was delusional when she wrote her will. Cutting those trees is criminal. You know how Dad loved that place. It'll kill him."

"Did he happen to mention how many have to fall before he'd die or was he just making conversation?"

"God, Ruby, you are so self-centered it's sickening. Can't you forget it? You've got the cabin."

"Would I have it if Mom hadn't sent me a copy of her will?"

Phyllis was silent.

"Would I?" Ruby prompted.

"I don't know. Now what about the trees?"

"They're none of your business."

Phyllis sighed. "Is the Indian tree still there?"

Ruby had forgotten about the Indian tree, a twisted and dead elm with a distorted trunk that they'd once believed signified an Indian princess was buried beneath its tangled roots. One summer she and Phyllis had delivered weekly offerings of graham crackers and licorice to its base, convinced they were appeasing the princess's wandering spirit. Dine in.

"Probably; it doesn't have any economic value."

Phyllis jumped on that. "Are you cutting the trees for money, Ruby? If you need money, I'll write you a check. How much?"

"I don't need money, Phyllis." She didn't offer Phyllis the truth: that the trees would come down only over Ruby's dead body. Let her father sweat on that one for a while.

"Why didn't you tell me about Jesse's injury?" Phyllis demanded. "I had to hear it second-hand."

"It was only a few weeks ago."

"You obviously still get a thrill out of keeping secrets.

Jesse's my *niece*," Phyllis, who couldn't have children, said. "How is she?"

"She's improving every day."

The silence was awkward; Ruby heard their breaths countering one another's. Exhale to inhale, opposing as always.

"Don't cut the damn trees," Phyllis said, and hung up.

Chapter 22

Ruby drove to Silas Shea's without advance warning or invitation, her entrance ticket on the passenger seat: a moderately expensive box of chocolates from Paulas's Drug Store.

But first, she stopped in front of the remains of Mina's and Corbin's house and mill, gazing through the trees at the meager debris. Corbin's yellow vehicles were gone and despite the charred trees near the foundations, it looked as if the forest had already advanced, filling in the breach.

A movement near the house foundation caught Ruby's eye; she gasped as two deer broke from the trees and leapt across the road. She stared, transfixed.

The deer were silver. No: gray, from head to hoof. Apparitions gracefully bounding in front of her. Ghost deer, tails flagging, heads raised and dark eyes luminous.

Gray puffed from their bodies as their hooves touched the earth and Ruby realized the deer weren't gray or otherworldly; they were covered in ash.

She turned her car around in a policeman's turn, the way her uncle Mack had taught her: back up, go forward.

The red chickens were taking sand baths in Silas's driveway, scratching dirt beneath their wings and over their backs, ignoring Ruby as she got out of her car and approached the back door.

She knocked, immediately hearing noises from inside:

the thump of furniture, TV voices, no-nonsense foot-steps approaching the door.

"Ruby Crane," Enid said without any welcoming smile, her eyes narrowing, standing with the door open just wide enough to hold her body.

"I wanted to thank you for removing the splinter," Ruby said, presenting the box of chocolates with one hand and holding her other palm toward Enid to show the cleanly healing wound.

Enid took the box of candy and squinted at the pink spot on Ruby's palm. "Did you put hydrogen peroxide on it?"

"Twice a day," Ruby assured her.

Enid nodded. "It'll heal all right, then."

"May I come in?" Ruby asked.

Enid opened the door and Ruby stepped into the kitchen/living area. A partially crocheted afghan in autumn colors lay on the sofa.

A grocery list was pinned to a strawberry pin cushion on an end table. Ruby glanced at it before she sat in a padded rocker. Flour, minimarshmallows, Cool-Whip, pistachio pudding mix, words well formed and correctly slanted, the girlish hand of a woman who hadn't betrayed the orderly lessons of third grade.

On the television, four women shouted at the hostess of a talk show. Instead of turning the television off or down, Enid raised her voice.

"That's a beautiful afghan you're making," Ruby told her, seeing the crochet hook in the tightly ridged stitches.

"It is," Enid agreed. She sat primly on her sofa, hands to her knees, waiting stolidly without anticipation. A woman in the dentist's waiting room.

"I just saw two deer near Mina's," Ruby said. "They were covered with ash."

Enid nodded. "They roll in ashes to kill their fleas."

"I thought they were ghosts."

Enid snorted. "Ghost deer," she said, shaking her head.

Offering her second apology to the dead, Ruby said, "Mina was my friend, Enid, and I know how she felt about you. She told me about the carrot cake you baked after Corbin's death and how you visited to offer comfort."

Enid briefly raised her wrist to her nose. "I tried," she said. "Why did you come here?"

"I don't believe Mina killed herself," Ruby said.

"Of course she didn't," Enid snapped as if Ruby were a very dim woman.

"Who killed her?"

"If anybody *did*, we'll never know it. But she didn't commit suicide."

"I intend to find out," Ruby said.

"You won't."

Between words, Enid pressed her lips into a narrow trembling line.

"I know Mina and Corbin were having marital problems," Ruby tried.

Enid snorted. "Who on earth told you that? They were devoted to each other."

"But Mina had an . . ." She stopped herself in time. Of all people, Enid would be the one who was aware of Mina's affairs, who would have ferreted out every unsavory detail. Enid gazed steadily into Ruby's eyes. There was a message there Ruby couldn't read. A fierce defensiveness.

Suddenly Ruby realized Enid's expression wasn't defensive; it was protective. "Mina confided in you, didn't she?" Ruby said in wonder, only half asking. Had Mina been that lonely?

These two women, both without close friends, shunning or shunned; had they come together in desperation, Mina shyly sharing her thoughts and fears with stern Enid? And had Enid reciprocated?

Enid picked up her afghan-in-progress, studying an

auburn row of stitches. "Whatever Mina told me, it died with her. I wouldn't betray her now."

"You loved Mina," Ruby said quietly, lower than the screaming women on the television, remembering Enid's incomprehensible breakdown at the luncheon.

Enid laid down her afghan and rested her hands on her lap. "Other people's children can be closer than your own," she said, and Ruby strained to hear her over the television. "Once you push a baby out of your body, it spends the rest of its life trying to prove *you* were the accident. You wait. You'll see."

Ruby sat forward. "But someone's responsible for Mina's death—and Corbin's—they must be brought to justice. Certainly you believe that?"

"There are many kinds of justice. 'Vengeance is mine, sayeth the Lord,' " Enid quoted from the Bible.

" 'With a little help from my friends,' " Ruby quoted from the Beatles.

"And you've appointed yourself assistant to the Good Lord?" Enid asked, sitting up ramrod straight, her back not touching the couch.

"The position seems to be vacant," Ruby told her. "Mina asked for my help. She never let *me* down when we were growing up, and I intend to do this much for her."

"It's not your place," Enid said, her voice stern and unyielding.

"What about the house fire?" she asked. "Carly said it was arson. Did you see anyone that day?"

"I was at the hall, setting up the luncheon."

"What about Silas?"

"Ask him. He's in the good barn." Enid said "good barn" as if it were a title, like the "White House" or "the lake."

Shuffling sounded from the next room and Ruby turned to see an ancient woman in a loose paisley house dress, a few cottony wisps of hair clinging to her head, peering curiously in at Enid and Ruby through thick glasses.

"Do you want to watch TV, Mother?" Enid asked, nodding toward the blaring television.

The woman shook her head and waved a hand in disgust toward the TV set, then shuffled out of sight.

"When you removed my sliver," Ruby said, "you warned me not to get Silas in trouble. How could I do that?"

Enid folded her afghan and stood, making moves to end Ruby's visit. "When people stir a pot, a lot of innocent folks can get burned."

"Even when death is involved?"

"Everyone dies and there are always unexplained deaths. This is *my* house, Ruby. You can't come in here making demands. I'd like you to leave now." Enid pointed to the door, ushering Ruby toward it.

"Please help me, Enid," Ruby pleaded. "Tell me what you know about Mina and Corbin. Who were their enemies?"

"I've told you all I can," she said. "Talk to Silas if you want to. Go in through the red door."

Ruby walked down to the "good barn," trailed by two red-and-brown hens. The red door Enid spoke of was in a concrete addition to the original barn. The door stood open, an unlocked padlock hanging from the hasp. Ruby stepped inside the bare room, once a white-washed milk room. "Silas?"

There was no answer. She stepped through a second open door into a gloomier room without windows, the only light a rectangle from the milk room doorway behind her. After the bright sunlight she couldn't see. "Silas?" she called again.

Again there was no answer. She couldn't discern what was in front of her or around her, only the gloom and the silvery reflection from a spiderweb. She spread her arms and touched cool metal.

She froze at a soft movement in the dark, then took a step backward without turning around, backing into the milk room and out into the bright sunshine where the two hens clucked companionably.

A few seconds later Silas emerged from the milk room, wiping his hands on a rag and smelling of epoxy. "Ruby," he said, "I thought I heard my name. Come on in here."

He flicked a switch on the wall and the dark second room was filled with light. It was a storage room that held dusty milking equipment, automatic milkers with teat cups like torture machines, rusting containers of bag balm and disinfectants.

And through the next door was a large room brightly lit by banks of shoplights. In this room the walls were painted white, tools hung neatly on pegboards above workbenches. The wooden floor was spotless.

"What do you think?"

Ruby stood in the doorway, staring. Because what Silas was working on, what stood so brilliantly fresh and new as if it had escaped through time, was a partially constructed airplane of wood, wire, and fabric.

"It's beautiful." Ruby walked around the plane. One wing was covered with sailcloth, the other a frame of fragile lengths of wood. Ruby touch the plane's wing and the gossamer structure shuddered. "What is it?"

"A Blériot monoplane. My dad started it in 1922. He gathered most of the materials back then. See these ash struts? Hard to find wood like that now. I work on it when I need to relax."

Ruby thought of herself, calming her own frayed nerves by sewing Gram's quilts, work so intense that worries and fears were *forced* to recede. Silas's airplane was like that.

Country music beat softly from a radio on the workbench against the wall.

"Why do you keep a gun in here?" Ruby asked, nodding to a silver pistol lying beside the radio. It was a dull and worn .22, a cowboy's gun with pearl handles.

"Raccoons; they sneak in once it begins cooling off. They could make short work of this plane."

Ruby thought a mouse would have difficulty sneaking into the tightly sealed room.

"I brought Enid a box of candy for removing my sliver," Ruby told him.

"Tempt her off her diet, eh?"

"I didn't know she was on a diet."

"Always is."

"I also asked her about Mina," Ruby continued. "I want to know the truth."

Silas leaned against the workbench. "The truth," he said. "That sounds dramatic."

"You knew about Mina's affair with Wally Kentner," Ruby said.

Silas gave Ruby a long cool look. "It's history, Ruby. There's no reason to drag it up now."

At the mention of history, Ruby unexpectedly heard Mina's voice retelling their history test–stealing episode in high school, when they'd broken into Mr. Wickler's car. Ruby had suffered no remorse but Mina had felt guilty and confessed. "You almost killed me," Mina had reminded Ruby. You almost killed me.

Had Ruby been examining Mina's tale from the wrong angle, interpreting it as a message regarding stealing? Maybe Mina's point, if there was one, wasn't that tests had been stolen but that Mina, ashamed, had confessed and Ruby had "almost killed her."

If Mina had been attempting to communicate information about Corbin based on that juvenile misadventure, did she mean Corbin had been involved in dirty business? Had he confessed—or threatened to blow the whistle? The jig's up.

"Was Corbin involved in anything illegal he could have exposed to the police?"

"Such as?" Silas asked. He returned the epoxy to a row of cans beneath his workbench.

"I don't know. Timber? Drugs? Money? Mina implied—" she began to say, then stopped.

"It's easy to turn the words of the dead into the Holy Grail," Silas said as he wiped off the spotless bench top. "We look for secrets. Most of the time there aren't any."

"But was he?" Ruby asked again. "Did Corbin have financial problems?"

"If he did, I wouldn't know. Corbin was close-mouthed."

"I met Chuck Baylor from Fogg Timber," she told Silas.

"From Barry County? How'd you meet him? Be careful. He'd steal a hot stove."

"He trespassed on my land and marked trees he hoped to cut."

Silas laughed briefly. "Without your permission, right? He gets a lot of jobs that way. I didn't know he was cruising timber in this area."

"He's cutting a forest across from Mrs. Pink's."

Silas frowned. "Are you sure?"

"Mrs. Pink thought the property belonged to her so we . . . I, checked the deed for her. The owner lives in Chicago."

Silas fingered the scar over his ear. "You know that for certain?"

Ruby paused, realizing she was about to spill the fact that Mary Jean had shown her Wally's private files.

"Chuck Baylor said so," she said. "He must have had a contract."

Silas nodded distractedly.

"Are you familiar with that forest?" Ruby asked him.

He smiled at Ruby as if he'd forgotten she was there. "Not really. It concerns me that another logging outfit is moving into the area. There's not enough timber to go around as it is."

Mrs. Pink stood at the swampy end of Ruby's driveway, on the public side of the moat. Ruby braked and rolled down her window. Mrs. Pink, dressed in her usual black, held her staff in one hand and a polished wooden cane in the other.

"How are you, Mrs. Pink?" Ruby asked.

Mrs. Pink thrust the cane through Ruby's window. "This is for your girl," she said.

The cane was thick but light, ash maybe, like the Blériot's struts. The handle was bent instead of curved, carved flatter so the hand had a more natural—and more sure—grip.

"This is beautiful," Ruby said, examining the cane. "Thank you. Did it belong to your husband?"

"I don't know who it belonged to," Mrs. Pink said, "but now it belongs to your girl."

An older full-size brown car sat beside Ruby's cabin, the driver sitting inside, his head hardly higher than the steering wheel, wearing a gentleman's hat.

Ruby parked behind the car and turned off the engine, then sat just as still as the driver in front of her, her hands white on the steering wheel. She'd last seen that car in the cemetery.

The kitchen door banged open and DeEtta ran outside, her round face agitated, her hands clasped together at her heart.

"Ruby," DeEtta began.

Ruby waved her to silence and slowly and deliberately climbed from her car, carefully closing the door. "Where is he?" she asked.

"Down by the lake."

Ruby passed the car without glancing inside, taking in the scene by the dock: Jesse and Ruby's father facing each other in lawn chairs, leaning toward one another, their heads at the same pitch, looking like family.

"How long has he been coming out here?" Ruby asked DeEtta.

DeEtta wrung her hands, stammering. "S-since the day after Corbin died. I—"

"You're fired," Ruby said, and walked down to the shore, straightening her shoulders, smoothing the rage from her face, concentrating on a confident stride.

Her father looked up and Ruby's pace faltered. He wasn't diminished by age or ravaged by illness as would have befitted poetic justice. He was . . . mild.

A small smile played around his thin lips and he studied her curiously. His thick white hair was freshly combed, his collar buttoned; he was dressed for visiting. His eyebrows were white now, too, and when his smile relaxed, his face sagged into an old man's.

"Ruby," he said, lifting one of his trembling big hands. "You raised a beautiful daughter."

"You have no right to come here," Ruby told him.

"I'm getting to know my granddaughter."

"It's a little late," Ruby said.

He nodded in agreement. "We have to make up for lost time."

Ruby sat on the grass between her father and Jesse and rubbed her arms, suddenly cold.

"You destroyed my mother," she said, speaking calmly the words she'd once screamed at him as a teenager, her rage now undone by the sight of her father sitting before her, somehow stripped of all his old power. "I'll never forgive you for that."

An agonized expression settled over her father's face.

He wiped his mouth with a white handkerchief. "A man needs years sometimes to make sense of what he's said and done."

"You *hit* her," Ruby said quietly. "You humiliated her. And when I challenged you, you tried to make my life as hellish as you'd made hers."

He lowered his head. "I was wrong." Words she'd never heard from his mouth.

"If it hadn't been for Gram . . ." she said, still unwilling to let it go.

He heaved a deep breath, the sound ragged and unhealthy. "You were her favorite, over Phyllis, over your cousins." He paused. "And over her own children."

After a long silence, Ruby knew he'd said all he was capable of saying about the past.

"You're stirring up a lot of people, Ruby," he said.

"Are you warning me to mind my own business, too?"

"No," he said slowly. "I'm not. Silas Shea has been my friend for fifty years, and now he's gone in a direction he had no intention of going."

"In the timber industry?" Ruby asked.

Her father nodded. "It's like walking into a burdock patch. In five feet, you're covered with stickers. Everybody sees them clinging to you."

"So people in Sable *are* aware of what Silas has been involved in?"

"Most. They were able to close their eyes until . . ."

"Until Corbin and Mina died," Ruby finished. "Tell me what Silas has done."

Ruby's father lifted his cane and tapped it into the ground. "Silas is my friend."

"I'm your daughter."

He gazed at her for overlong and she sensed him making his choice. "It'll take an outsider to end this," he said.

Ruby nodded and bowed her head. *She* was the outsider. She felt her father's hand briefly touch her shoulder. "Albert's probably tired of waiting. Jesse and I have a date in two days."

After her father left, Ruby helped Jesse walk back to the cabin. "Will Grandpa come back?" Jesse asked.

"Yes, sweetheart. He will."

DeEtta sat at the table, her face drawn. "He wanted to see her. He said Jesse was like you. Am I really fired?"

Ruby looked out the window at the empty driveway. "You can stay," she said.

"Hah!" Ron Kilgore gloated when Ruby told him Wally had admitted having an affair with Mina. "Didn't I say to look for hanky-panky?"

Ruby and Jesse sat at the kitchen table after dinner, Ruby compiling a grocery list while Jesse copied words from the *Waters County Proclamator* onto a sheet of lined paper with her left hand. Slowly and awkwardly, her hand heavy on the paper. She wore her new headphones unconnected to any music. It was DeEtta's idea, to help block out distractions, and it worked. Only the louder sounds made Jesse raise her head.

"You did say that," Ruby told Ron. "But something about Wally's confession doesn't ring true."

"Give the feeling some credence, then. I believe in that stuff."

"You sound like a Californian."

"To the toes of my feet."

Ruby hung up and watched Jesse laboriously draw out the word "feasibility," her left hand and wrist twisted above the word, the side of her hand smeared with pencil as she dragged her hand over the words she'd already completed.

Jesse crossed her *t* right to left, the way lefties frequently did, feathering the left side. But not always, making it difficult to determine the handedness of a subject from his penmanship alone. Ruby hadn't noticed whether David Townsend, the owner of Mrs. Pink's "mushroom property," had feathered the left, a habit she usually noted. Sometimes, with a ballpoint pen, the lip of the pen left blots of ink at changes in strokes, as in the cursive *m*, giving away handedness.

Jesse was naturally left-handed. Ruby was convinced that, if only her daughter had been right-handed, her recovery would be faster.

Chapter 23

"Carly said Danny left for Arizona yesterday," DeEtta said. She stood beside the couch folding towels she'd taken down from the clothesline.

Jesse sat at the table, concentrating on dividing mixed vegetables into like components around her plate: peas here, corn there, carrots over here.

"He asked me to join him," DeEtta added

"Are you considering it?" Ruby asked, catching the softer note in DeEtta's voice.

"No." She folded the last towel and laid it on top of the stack. "He wants to change," she said uncertainly.

"Just wanting to change doesn't make it happen."

"I've never been to Arizona," DeEtta said wistfully.

"Don't confuse the two issues. Visit Arizona on your own. Don't use a bad relationship to escape Sable. Work through your problems first."

DeEtta raised her eyebrows at Ruby, a smile widening her face.

"Okay, okay," Ruby said. "Learn from my mistakes."

"Maybe I want to make my own."

"The eternal cycle," Ruby grumbled.

As Ruby left the post office after mailing a package for Mabel, she spotted Hank in the parking lot, leaning against the front fender of his Jeep, smoking a cigarette. "I was driving by and saw you go inside," he said.

He dropped his cigarette and ground it into the

gravel, then picked up the flattened butt and slipped it in his jeans pocket. "I'm down to one a day," he said. "On good days none. I plan to puff my last on Thanksgiving, after stuffing myself with turkey and gravy and two pieces of pumpkin pie à la mode."

"That's very ceremonial."

"After twenty-two years, it's the least I can do. Hop in. I'll drive you to Mabel's."

The Color Festival carnival was being erected downtown and Sable's main street was cordoned off. Hank waited for a woman driving past on a tractor, bags of groceries tied behind the seat, then pulled out, following the detour signs around the construction. The skeleton of the Ferris wheel frame was half assembled, rising above the bustle.

"Big day tomorrow," he commented. "First day of the Color Festival and opening day of bow season."

"We probably won't see another deer until Christmas," Ruby said.

"They'll head into the swamps," Hank agreed. "Be sure and wear orange if you go near the woods. By the way, I asked about Zander and his note-writing rather than talking. Sometimes his wife calls and gives messages for him."

"He said he would have written a note," Ruby reminded Hank.

"It could be he doesn't want to own up to having any part in Corbin's death, even if it was coincidental."

"Maybe. I discovered who Mina's affair was with," she told Hank. "Wally Kentner. That's why Corbin cut Fox Woods the way he did; he saw them together there."

Hank whistled through his teeth. "I thought Kentner and Corbin were friends."

"According to him, they were. Who's more convenient than your friend's wife?" Ruby asked. "Can I ask you something?"

"Shoot."

"Have you been involved in any forestry management contracts with out-of-area owners?"

"Just the job that got me here and an Indiana man planning to leave a healthy forest to his grandchildren. Why?"

"But there seems to be a high rate of timber being cut from land owned by people who don't live here."

"Profit takers," Hank commented.

When Ruby didn't answer, he said, "You're thinking hard, Ruby. What's this about?"

"I'll tell you if I'm right," she told him.

"Still trying to go it alone, I see," Hank said as he stopped the Cherokee in front of Mabel's studio. "Rest on your laurels and pull the wool over your errors."

"The precepts of a successful career."

"Can I take you to dinner tonight?" Hank asked, lightly touching her chin. "I know a little unpopular place on Wall Lake where the food doesn't come in plastic baskets."

"Candles?"

"Oil lamps."

"I'm won over."

"We could test your theory about lovemaking and the roar of waves afterward." He kissed her lightly and said, "I'll be back at five-thirty."

"Our local sheriff stopped by to see you this morning," Mabel said when Ruby entered the studio.

"Did he say why?"

"He might have. Whatever he said it didn't hold my attention. Carl Junior's definitely not Carl Senior."

"That's what I've heard."

When Mabel returned to her darkroom, Ruby called Mary Jean at Wally's office.

"How about a walk?" she asked.

"I'm definitely ready for *that*," Mary Jean said. "The carnival's going up outside my window and I feel like I'm caught in a construction nightmare."

"Is Wally there? Can you meet me in an hour by the old Ford dealership?"

"Sure. Wally's not here. We're closing the office for two days so he can bow hunt. Who drops in to buy real estate during the Color Festival, anyway?"

Ten minutes before she was scheduled to meet Mary Jean, Ruby left Mabel's studio and walked a block off the main street toward downtown, her bag over her shoulder, past houses that hadn't changed in a hundred years except for new coats of white paint.

The clank of machinery and the rat-a-tat-tat of hammers wafted over the quiet streets, echoing between houses. Sounds as familiar as autumn.

Ruby entered the main street beyond Wally Kentner's office, pausing near a group of restless young boys and pretending to watch the bustle of Color Festival activity, turning slightly to see Wally's office door.

Canvas-and-plywood stands were being erected on either side of the barricaded street: St. Anne's Bingo, the Jaycee's Pie House, the Lutheran's hot dog stand. Carnies erected the slicker and dirtier carnival booths: ball tosses, shooting galleries, video arcades. And in the center, the carnival rides: the slowly evolving Ferris wheel, the merry-go-round platform and Tilt-A-Whirl frame.

"Hey, baby," a man in colorless clothing on a spidery arm of the Octopus called to Ruby. She ignored him and one of the young boys beside Ruby said, "He's talking to you, lady."

"But I don't have to answer him," Ruby said.

The boy shrugged and nudged a friend, pointing to the bosomy depiction on a ride still packed on a flatbed trailer.

Mary Jean emerged from Wally's office and headed toward Porter and First without looking Ruby's way.

Ruby waited until Mary Jean reached the corner before she rapidly walked down the sidewalk to the office, the rear of rising booths on one side of her, buildings to the other, the sidewalk transformed into a shaded and narrow alley.

As she'd hoped, Mary Jean had left the door unlocked. Ruby glanced toward Paulas's Drugs. The Knights of Columbus blanket roulette stand blocked Fran's view of the office.

"Wally?" she called, to be sure.

When there was no answer, she removed a pair of disposable gloves from her bag and pulled them over her hands. Mary Jean's computer was still running, the monitor turned off. She flicked on the screen and found herself already in the office program. It took only a few seconds to type in the two addresses she was interested in and jot down the file numbers.

Suddenly the phone beside Ruby jangled and she caught her breath, not moving. Once, twice, three more rings before the answering machine picked it up. Ruby exhaled, exited the program, and turned off Mary Jean's monitor.

The gray metal file cabinet in Wally's office where Ruby had seen Mary Jean retrieve the other file was locked. "Damn," Ruby said, tugging vainly on the top drawer. Where would Mary Jean keep the key?

Ruby almost discounted the brass key that dangled from the fishing pole of the wooden figure on top of the cabinet as too obvious. But she'd read Poe and tried it anyway.

The lock popped out and the doors slid open soundlessly. She quickly found the files and didn't glance at the papers inside the folders but slipped both into her bag, checking her watch. Six minutes.

She relocked the cabinet, returned the key to the fishing pole, and glanced around the office to ensure she'd left nothing out of place, then removed her gloves and shoved them in her bag. A piece of cake.

Holding the bag close, she left Wally's office onto the busy carnival site. She'd taken two steps when she heard her name called.

"Ruby. Are you looking for me?"

It was Wally, dressed in jeans and a flannel shirt, a hammer in his hand.

"Hi, Wally," Ruby said brightly. Lying was so easy. "Mary Jean and I are meeting for a walk but I think we mixed up our rendezvous point." She held out her hand. "I was short in the Knotty Pine yesterday."

Wally switched his hammer to his other hand and grasped hers. "It's okay. I deserved it. We have to move forward; start from today and don't look back."

"Which of these booths do you belong to?"

"The Chamber of Commerce elephant ears stand." He laughed. "Politically fitting, eh? Are you coming to the festival?"

"Probably on Sunday. Mary Jean said you're taking a couple of days off to bow hunt."

He nodded. "Up near Gaylord. I'll be back to man the booth Saturday morning."

"Kentner," a man wearing a tool apron called. "Did you take my hammer?"

"Coming," Wally said, holding the hammer above his head. "See you, Ruby."

Mary Jean stood in front of the boarded-up Ford dealership, an MSU sweatshirt over her dress. A light breeze blew her dark hair across her cheek. "I was beginning to think you forgot," she said when she saw Ruby.

"I got caught up with a couple of last minute problems. It looks like the festival will be birthed on time."

"Listen," Mary Jean said, tipping her head.

Ruby did and heard the faint sounds of drums and wind instruments. "The marching band," she identified.

"Yup. Practicing. That takes me back." She fingered an imaginary clarinet.

They walked from street to street, sometimes through ankle-deep leaves. Ruby, aware of the folders she carried, kept her elbow over her bag, holding it close to her body.

"Oh, look," Mary Jean suddenly said, stopping.

Ruby raised her head. She'd been so engaged she hadn't noticed where they walked. Unconsciously, in footsteps and compass headings patterned during ancient times, she'd followed her old path home. She and Mary Jean stood at the sidewalk leading to the front door of her father's house, where Ruby'd grown up. She stared at the house; it was smaller than she remembered, shabbier. The wooden swing that had hung on the porch for thirty years was still there, the shades closed on her old room.

"Let's go back," Ruby said.

At five-fifteen, Mabel left, heading for the carnival site, her photo equipment over her shoulder, her face as avidly focused as a hunter's.

Ruby watched her disappear, then removed the folders from her bag. She laid the top page from the first folder on the glass and pushed the button. Nothing happened. "Add toner," the words on the panel blinked in yellow.

Toner? Ruby checked the cupboards and closets, finding one empty and inky orange container. She hadn't ordered toner. There wasn't any. She couldn't run the photocopy machine.

When Hank still hadn't appeared or called by six o'clock, Ruby phoned his rental house. There was no answer. She called DeEtta but Hank hadn't phoned the cabin either. "Is everything all right at home?" Ruby asked her.

"Jesse and I are putting together that new jigsaw puzzle you bought her, the one with all the colors."

Ruby was reduced to washing coffee cups in Mabel's darkroom sink, her impatience turning to anger at Hank, when Sheriff Carly entered the studio. Perspiration shone below his receding hairline.

"Mabel said you were here earlier," Ruby said, wiping the cups with a paper towel.

"Yeah. I saw your car out front." He was uncomfortable, glancing just to the left of her eyes, slapping his cap against his leg. Ruby set down the cup, filled with foreboding.

"What's happened?" she asked. *Jesse.*

"Holliday asked me to tell you he couldn't make your date."

Ruby crossed her arms and waited. Not Jesse.

"He's in the hospital."

Still she said nothing, though her heart pounded. It was another of Ron Kilgore's strategies, to allow the person providing the information to tell it his own way, to say more than he intended.

"He was in a fight out in the woods and the doctor's keeping him overnight."

"How badly is he injured?" Ruby asked.

"Bruises, sprained wrist, maybe a broken jaw. He drove himself to the hospital."

"And you've picked up the men who attacked him?" she asked.

"He hasn't identified them yet. He asked to see you."

Ruby picked up her bag. "I'll go right now. Is this connected to the earlier vandalism?"

Carly frowned. "He hasn't reported any vandalism. I read the logs every night and I'd remember."

"Why would you remember?" Ruby asked.

"Holliday's a controversial man and, to be honest, I *expected* an incident or two."

"If that's true, then you have an idea who's responsible, right?"

"Only in a general manner. I'll know better when Holliday can talk."

Carly walked with her to her car. His cruiser was parked behind the Pinto, the windows rolled down and his rifle visible. He opened the driver's door for her. After she'd buckled her seat belt, he didn't close the door but waited beside her car, his face a study.

"Is there something else you're not telling me, Carly?" Ruby asked.

Carly frowned, then leaned down and spoke in a low voice, as if someone might be listening. "Be careful, Ruby, okay? Will you do that much?"

Hank, wearing a pale-blue gown, was propped up in bed watching the TV news. His face was swollen, one eye closed and darkened, an ugly bruise at the base of his throat. His left wrist was bandaged and pressed close to his body. He nodded gingerly when he saw Ruby and she kissed the top of his head, the only spot that looked safe.

"Can you talk?" she asked.

He pointed to a pencil and pad of paper on the table that was swung across his bed. She moved it so he could reach it with his right hand, reminding her of Lyle Zander.

He wrote, *Can I have a rain check on dinner and . . . ?*

"Definitely," she said. "Who did this?"

They wore masks, Cute, huh? Good news though: My jaw's not broken, just damn sore.

"Did they say anything?"

No, not one single word, only grunts and squeals.

Ruby pulled her bag closer to her body. "Carly said you didn't report the other vandalism."

Hank looked as sheepish as possible beneath his injuries. *Tattling would be a bad business move,* he scribbled. *Being macho.*

"And look where it got you," Ruby said lightly, her thoughts racing in other directions.

Tear off this page, Hank wrote. *Be careful.* Those words he underlined, as well.

Ruby nodded and tore off the note, plus the three pages beneath it.

Chapter 24

Ruby drove too fast from the hospital toward her cabin, silently cursing the aged and slow-moving Cadillac that pulled in front of her, forcing her to pass on the right, tires throwing up gravel, a flash of pale startled faces through tinted glass.

The sun set behind her and as in fairy tales Jesse had once avidly listened to, Ruby raced darkness for the safety of home. The long roads had never stretched so distant, the sun had rarely slid beyond the horizon so quickly. Beside her, tucked between the seats, was her bag containing the folders from Wally's office.

Who had attacked Hank? Was the assault meant for him alone, or was Ruby included in that warning? It wasn't only the note-writer who'd advised her to mind her own business; half of Sable had suggested she butt out. She shook her head; if so many people hoped to deter her, then obviously she was heading in the right direction.

She turned onto Blue Road as the sun disappeared and the sky turned dusty. A fat woodcock flew up from the shoulder of the road, darting erratically in her head-lights. She caught a glimpse of its long bill before its crazy flight pattern carried it into the trees.

She pulled the Pinto close to the cabin, uncertain what she'd expected, relieved to see Jesse and DeEtta through the windows of the lighted cabin. Above her, the leaves rattled in a slight breeze, a bird tittered.

"I thought you were going out to dinner," DeEtta

said. She and Jesse sat on the floor, dominoes standing on end between them in an S-shape curve.

"It was canceled. Any calls?" Ruby asked as she bent and kissed Jesse's forehead.

"No. Well, there was one but when I answered, whoever it was hung up."

Ruby drank a glass of milk, standing. Listening, wary, eager to be upstairs in her lab.

"I guess I'll go across the driveway now," DeEtta said, rising from the floor.

"You can spend the night here if you want to," Ruby told her.

DeEtta looked puzzled. "No, thanks. Should I put Spot out?"

"I'll do it after Jesse's in bed."

Ruby built up the fire to a heated roar—Little pig, little pig—and read a chapter to Jesse from *The Wind in the Willows*. Jesse leaned against her arm, intently listening while Ruby held her thin hand, longing for the girl to snuggle, to giggle at Toad's antics. But Jesse was content; she accepted cuddling but rarely initiated it.

Over the sound of the logs hissing in the fireplace, Ruby heard the ticking approach of a car and stiffened, turning to watch Spot's reaction to the invading engine. Spot stood and ambled to the door without any show of concern.

"Here, sweetie," Ruby said to Jesse, placing her daughter's finger on the line where she'd stopped reading. "You can read by yourself for a while. Begin right here."

Headlights shone through the kitchen window, two blinding eyes that revealed nothing, then switched off, leaving an instant's glow. A car door slammed and the beam of a small flashlight bobbed toward the cabin. Across the driveway, the blinds on DeEtta's trailer window separated. Ruby grabbed the file folders from

Wally's office and shoved them into her cupboard behind a row of canned soup.

"Who is it?" Ruby asked when the knock came.

"Enid Shea."

"Enid?" Ruby whispered in surprise.

Enid stood in the doorway holding a plate of cookies. "These are for your daughter," she said stiffly, thrusting the plate forward. "I put in M&M's instead of chocolate chips. Young people like M&M's."

Ruby took the warm plate. "Thank you. Jesse will love them." After a moment she said, "Would you like to come in?"

Enid wore red plaid pants and a powder-blue nylon jacket, its lining printed with teddy bears. Her eyes hastily took in the cabin, then settled on Jesse.

"Can I take your coat?"

"I can't stay," Enid said, and approached Jesse, a nervous smile on her face. Ruby was used to that—people who yearned to do the right thing but weren't sure what that entailed—and thought nothing less of Enid for it.

"How are you, Jesse?" Enid asked, bending low and speaking loud, as if Jesse had a hearing problem.

"I'm fine, thank you," Jesse replied, calling forth well-learned good manners. "How are you?"

"Fine. I brought you some nice cookies."

Jesse glanced at Enid's hands and, not spotting any cookies, frowned, Enid's words too abstract. Ruby set the plate on the coffee table and placed one warm cookie in Jesse's hand. Jesse carefully picked out the M & M's and lined them in a row on her leg.

"God love her," Enid said.

They chatted, performing the tense preliminaries. Inconsequential talk about the autumn colors, how the bow hunters were poised in their camps waiting for daylight, and how deer blinds dotted the woods like guardhouse sentries.

Finally, when Jesse closed her eyes, although Ruby

doubted she was asleep, Enid said, "I've been thinking about our talk yesterday, about Mina."

Ruby nodded, wondering if Silas knew his wife was here.

Enid took a cookie from the plate and balanced it on her palm. "You're the only one who's asking serious questions," Enid said. "Everyone else is prepared to let it go."

"What did Mina tell you?" Ruby asked gently.

Enid returned the cookie to the plate, then wiped her nose with a tissue she pulled from her sleeve. "You have to understand: Mina was all alone out there. She didn't have any real friends. Corbin adored her, but that's not the same as friends. Once in a while, we talked. I know that sounds peculiar to you, Ruby; Mina and me being friends." Enid leaned forward. "It wasn't her fault."

"What wasn't?" Ruby asked.

"About the affair; it *was* with Wally. You see, Corbin was so much older than Mina and he was convinced she was perfect. He couldn't get over how lucky he was. But every dime went into that sawmill. He thought she was just as dedicated to it as he was, that he was doing it for her."

"And Wally was younger and wealthier," Ruby provided.

"She wanted to end it with Wally." Enid's hand absently moved in imitation of crochet work. In, up, and over. In, up, and over. "But Wally threatened to tell Corbin."

"So Mina continued the affair?"

Enid nodded. "For a while. She didn't love Wally. She wouldn't have left Corbin for Wally."

"Corbin found out anyway," Ruby said. "He saw them together in Fox Woods and that's when he destroyed the forest, right? Do you think Wally killed Corbin?"

Enid abruptly jerked her head as if the thought had never occurred to her. "No. Of course not."

Ruby covered Jesse with the quilt from the back of the sofa, then she sat back and crossed her arms, regarding Enid. "You're not telling me the whole story."

Enid's narrow eyes widened; her hands stilled. "That's what I know," she said.

Enid was frightened, it was so strong Ruby's skin goose-bumped with it. "Did you hear that Hank Holliday was attacked in the woods this afternoon?" Ruby asked. "He's in the hospital."

"Will he be all right?"

"In a few weeks. You're afraid for Silas, aren't you?"

"No. Silas isn't involved."

"Not involved in what?" Ruby asked.

Enid was caught off balance. Ruby suspected that Enid, by her own assessment, didn't lie; she might embellish and gossip, but dishonesty was territory she rarely and clumsily traveled. A spark of sympathy flashed for this woman who'd never been a friend.

"Not involved in what?" Ruby asked again. "Tell me what's going on, Enid. What were Corbin and Silas involved in?"

"It wasn't anything serious, not like you're thinking," Enid said. She bit her lip and said in a rush, "Corbin and Silas agreed to bid low on timber jobs, that's all."

"Agreed with who?"

"Each other."

"So when there was property with trees to be cut, they'd agreed to both offer a low price?"

Enid nodded. "That way they made more money on the timber later, when they sold it. Everybody believed they were enemies so if Silas made the first low bid, they'd ask Corbin and if Corbin's bid was low, too . . ."

"Then the owner believed the bids were legitimate. Price-fixing."

Enid nodded.

"How long have they been doing this?" Ruby asked.

"Since Corbin opened his mill."

"That seems fairly innocuous for the consequences," Ruby said.

"I don't know what that means," Enid said, flushing.

Ruby ticked off on her fingers. "Corbin and Mina are dead. Their house was burned, their dog was shot. What do these crimes have to do with Corbin and Silas agreeing to fix their prices?"

"That's all I know," Enid said. "Make what you want of it."

"When did Corbin change his mind about being involved?" Ruby asked.

"This summer—" Enid stopped and raised her hand to her mouth.

"After Fox Woods?" Ruby asked.

"Don't ask me any more questions," Enid pleaded with Ruby. "I have to go home now." She stood. "I shouldn't have come."

"I'm grateful for this, Enid, truly," Ruby told her.

"You're going to keep looking for the reasons Corbin and Mina died, aren't you?" Enid asked, and Ruby couldn't read whether Enid was hopeful or fearful, perhaps both.

"Yes. If I don't have to, I won't mention what you've said tonight."

"What I wish for most of all, Ruby Crane," Enid said, taking a deep breath. "I wish you wouldn't say anything bad about Mina. She made a mistake, that's all. She paid for it. We all make mistakes."

Enid lightly brushed her hand across Jesse's hair as she rose to leave.

"Be careful driving home," Ruby told her. "Lock your car doors."

Enid glanced sharply at Ruby but said, "I will."

❖   ❖   ❖

Ruby sent a reluctant Spot out into the night. It was cold; the weather report predicted frost in the lower elevations.

In the distance, a dog broke into fierce barking, the determined baying of one animal on the trail of another. Spot joined in with a single comradely woof from close to the house.

Price-fixing between Corbin and Silas? Enid had told the truth, even if it was only the partial truth. And despite what she claimed, Enid *was* afraid for Silas.

The night felt edgy, as if a storm secretly gathered over the lake. Ruby sat on the couch waiting for Jesse to fall into a deeper sleep and pulled the quilt to her chin, leaving the light by the bookcases burning. She sat up when Jesse sighed, held her breath when a dry leaf skittered down the roof, gasped when the dying coals shifted in the fireplace. Her ears rang from listening.

Finally, she heard Jesse's delicate snores and rekindled the fire, then removed the folders from the cupboard and carried them up to the loft.

She preferred to work by natural light enhanced by artificial bright light, but now she switched on all the wattage in her lab, including the light table and mercury lamp, even her bedside light.

She set the folders side by side in the middle of her table and opened them, studying the documents pertaining to two pieces of property: Fox Woods and Mrs. Pink's mushroom woods.

The deed for David Townsend, the owner of the mushroom woods, was a copy of the land deed filed at the courthouse. Beneath the deed was a logging contract with Fogg Timber signed by David Townsend less than two weeks ago.

Ruby glanced between the crabbed, leftward-leaning signatures of the two documents, instantly seeing the crime, excitement rising. She laid the copy of the land deed on her light table and then, directly on top of it, she placed the logging contract, matching signature over signature. She couldn't help smiling. There was always a slight variation in every signature a person made. Never were they absolutely identical, as these two were.

She studied the logging contract and noted the studied "drawn" lines of the signature. She was certain it was a forgery. Beneath the signature was the September date two weeks ago in the same left-leaning penmanship. Although the penmanship in the actual signature appeared left-handed, the drag line of the ballpoint pen on the right side of the upstroke in the 8 of September 18 showed that the author was more likely right-handed.

The logging contract was a single paragraph, a vague agreement with Fogg Timber for a "stock reduction of D. Townsend's trees." It could mean anything, from cutting down a single oak tree to clearcutting. Ruby looked through the remaining papers in the folder: a land description, an aerial photograph of the property, and, finally, a computer printout containing a brief factual description of David Townsend, seventy-six, retired coal miner. That was curious.

Spot began barking outside and Ruby stood and looked out the loft window, seeing only darkness. Clouds obscured the moon. Finally the urgency left Spot's voice and she quit barking altogether.

Ruby returned the papers to the folder and set it aside, then reached for the Fox Woods property.

First, she discovered the same documents: the deed, another vague logging contract, this time with Corbin Turmouski, signed by Pauline Cassette of Columbus, Ohio, in a graceful looping signature, including the date a month ago. Ruby knew before she tested them, that the signatures would be identical.

But besides the printout of Miss Pauline Cassette's particulars: sixty-eight, retired schoolteacher, there was also a penciled notation that Pauline had died only a week after signing the logging contract. Stapled to the printout was the photocopy of a check from Corbin Turmouski to Pauline Cassette, dated after her death.

Ruby sat back, thinking, then pulled both logging contracts from their folders and began a study of the dates beneath the signatures.

For such a precise study, Ruby used her transparent grid, placing it over each date to judge the subtleties in letter height and slant. The capital letters of the month she gave a cursory glance. Forgers usually paid the most attention to capital letters; tending to trip themselves up in the small letters in the body of the words; it was there that a forger's lifelong habits couldn't be denied.

Relationships between heights of letters rarely changed, no matter what type of fancy maneuvering forgers attempted. These relationships were so inconspicuous they had to be measured.

In the date beneath Pauline Cassette's name, the connection between *s* and *t* in August dipped beneath the baseline of the other small letters. The same was true between the *p* and *t* in the word September beneath the Townsend signature.

Letter by letter and number by number, Ruby examined both dates, noting the feathered tail of the comma after the numerical day, the unusual heavy pressure on the 9s in the year, as if the writer were uncomfortable with their formation.

Then she compared the photocopy of the mind-your-own-business note and Mina's suicide note to the dates. While there were similarities in spacing, she needed more samples to conclude that the two notes were written by whoever authored Pauline Cassette's and David Townsend's signatures.

What she *did* have, Ruby decided, leaning back, setting down her pencil, and flexing her fingers, were two forged signatures and two sets of dates, all written by the same person.

Ruby noted David Townsend's address on another piece of paper and put it in her pocket before she locked the folders holding the contracts inside her metal cabinet.

The clock above her desk read 3:30. Fully dressed, Ruby stretched out on her bed in the warm loft to rest her eyes.

She opened them to broad daylight and the sound of running water. She sat up and rubbed the stickiness from her eyes. It was nine-thirty in the morning.

DeEtta sat at the table with an untouched piece of toast in front of her. Jesse was slowly eating her precisely laid out breakfast by herself, just as DeEtta had promised she would. Oatmeal in the center, orange juice at two o'clock, toast at ten, and two spoons beside her bowl.

"I overslept," Ruby said. "You made coffee. Thank you, dear girl."

"I saw your lights on late so I let you sleep." DeEtta's eyes were red as if she'd spent the night awake herself.

"Thanks." She mussed Jesse's hair. "Good morning, sunshine."

Jesse said, "Good morning, sleepyhead."

"Was that Enid Shea who was here last night?" DeEtta asked, tearing the crust off her toast but not eating it.

"Yes," Ruby said.

"Oh."

Ruby poured herself a cup of coffee and sat beside the telephone. She smoothed the slip of paper from her pocket and dialed information for Chicago, Illinois. "May I have the number for David L. Townsend?" she asked the male operator.

After the mechanical voice gave her Townsend's phone number, she dialed it while DeEtta hovered nearby, once dropping a spoon that clattered on the wooden floor.

"Is Mr. Townsend in?" she asked the elderly-sounding woman who answered.

There was silence and Ruby asked, "Ma'am? Are you still there?"

"David died last week," the woman said, her voice going flat. "It was his heart."

"I'm very sorry," Ruby told her. "I apologize for bothering you."

"Why did you want to speak with my husband?" she asked.

"It doesn't matter now. I was curious about land he owned in Michigan."

"Oh, we haven't been up there in years. Can you call back in a few weeks?"

"I will. Thank you, Mrs. Townsend. I'm sorry for your loss."

Ruby sipped her coffee, trying to fit the details together, turning them this way and that and adjoining them reluctantly like the most stubborn of interlocking jigsaw pieces.

"I have a fizzy stomach," DeEtta told her. The toast still sat on her plate, uneaten, the crusts torn off and shredded. "Is it okay if I go lie down for a while?"

"There's some Pepto-Bismol in the medicine cabinet," Ruby told her.

"No thanks," DeEtta said, kneading her stomach. Her face was grayish, the snap faded from her eyes.

"How long have you been feeling like this?" Ruby asked.

"Since last night, something I ate. I'm better now, though. If I sleep a little longer . . ."

"Wave a white flag if I can bring you anything."

It was seven in California but Ruby dialed Ron Kilgore's number. A new message came on the machine, a woman's voice more officious than Ruby's, precisely enunciated.

"Pick it up, Ron," Ruby said after the beep. She waited until a minute had elapsed and the machine cut her off, then she redialed his number but only reached the machine again. Ron's wife might have taken him back. More likely he was working on acquiring Mrs. Kilgore number four.

She called Hank's hospital room. It rang four times and was routed to the nurse's station.

"He checked out an hour ago," the nurse told Ruby. "A friend picked him up."

"Who was it?"

"I couldn't tell you. A man."

Ruby tried Hank's house but there was no answer, no answering machine, either. She cleared away Jesse's breakfast, confused. Hank had asked her to take him home from the hospital. Why hadn't he called her?

Glancing out the window as she washed the breakfast dishes, marking time until she called Ron again, Ruby gasped in shock.

A man dressed in khaki camouflage warily advanced on the cabin. Accenting his one-piece camouflage suit were dulled black boots and a green stocking cap. His face was completely obscured with green, brown, and black blotches.

Ruby stood before the sink, frozen. The enemy has landed. Make no sudden moves.

Then she realized he wasn't packing a military rifle but a hunting bow, and remembered: Today was the first day of bow season.

Wiping her hands on a dishtowel, she left the cabin and approached the man who nodded to her, waiting in the driveway, the tip of his bow resting on his boot.

"Hi," he said. With all the paint she couldn't read his expression but saw the flash of straight white teeth and judged him friendly. A quiver of neon pink plastic-feathered arrows hung on his shoulder. His bow had two strings and an electronic sighting apparatus at midpoint. Not exactly like Robin Hood.

"Can I help you?" she asked. She smelled an artificial apple odor emanating from his clothing.

"I got turned around, I guess," he said, the teeth flashing in embarrassment. "I'm camped with a buddy on his lake lot. We got in late last night and into the woods early this morning so I didn't take too good a notice of the driveway."

"Try farther east. There are some vacant lots over there."

"Okay," he said, looking at the cabin and down toward the water. "This is a pretty place."

"Thank you. The land across the road is private," she told him. "No hunting."

"It's not posted," he said.

"It's private property."

He shrugged. "You should post it then."

Ruby watched him walk back up her driveway into the trees. Within a few steps he faded eerily into the woods, invisible.

Chapter 25

Ruby dialed Ron Kilgore's number twice more without success. Hank's number she tried three times without an answer, unease mounting. Where could he have gone in his battered state besides home?

"Would you like to go outside?" Ruby asked Jesse.

"Outside of the cabin, to sit beside the lake," Jesse said. More and more, Jesse struggled to make each statement completely accurate. Taking a bath wasn't simply taking a bath; it was running warm water in the bathtub and sitting in it to wash herself clean. She built each idea from the bottom up, creating a tidy and complete picture.

With Spot circling them, Ruby helped Jesse maneuver with her new cane to the shore of Blue Lake, her sweater now topped by a bright red shirt of Ruby's. Ruby wore a red scarf around her neck and had tied a sporty red bandana around Spot's throat. The dog was nervous, too edgy to sit still, her eyes on the woods where, Ruby guessed, invisible hunters stalked the wily deer.

Bow season lasted until Christmas but the main flurry of activity took place the first week. It was a statewide event, but minor compared to November 15, the day rifle season began, when even the schools closed.

DeEtta's trailer was silent, the blinds closed, and Ruby pictured the woman inside, curled in sleep.

"How's this?" Ruby asked, settling Jesse in the sagging lawn chair facing the lake.

"This is nice," Jesse told her. "I like the trees." She pointed to the yellow and scarlet trees reflected from Blue Lake's surface.

Ruby slipped out of her sandals and walked along the cool damp sand, her heels sinking in the soft earth.

She might not reach Ron, but as soon as she heard from Hank, she'd present the forged contracts and her written reports to Carly. This evidence wouldn't disappear like the straight-sawn lumber and Corbin's support had. Once she had standards to compare to the dates on the contracts, the criminals could be charged.

Beside Jesse, Spot growled and her ears perked forward. The dog's hackles rose and she took two wary steps toward the cabin, her head high, sniffing.

"What's the matter, girl?" Ruby asked. "More of our friendly hunters?"

But Spot's growls turned more menacing. She bunched her muscles and was off like a shot, fur rippling, racing toward the cabin. No, toward DeEtta's trailer, her tail and head low, barking fiercely. Ruby watched, puzzled. A moment later she heard DeEtta scream.

"Stay here, Jesse," she warned her daughter. "Don't move and I'll be right back."

She ran after Spot. The dog crouched in front of the trailer, barking and snarling. The trailer door was flung open as Ruby reached it.

But it wasn't DeEtta who emerged; it was the bow hunter, dressed in his camouflage and face paint.

"What are you doing . . . ?" Ruby began and stopped, taking a single step backward. This man wasn't the bow hunter at all; it was Danny Greenstone, his hair tousled, his camouflage suit unzipped enough to show a V-neck T-shirt.

It happened so quickly but at the same time every movement and action was as precise as slow motion. Certainly there was time to stop him.

Danny leveled his hand at the menacing dog. Spot didn't hesitate, her teeth bared and hindquarters gathered to leap. But then Danny's hand recoiled; there was a simultaneous flash and retort and Spot collapsed to the ground, whimpering. And that quickly Danny turned the gun toward Ruby.

A grunt sounded from behind Danny. DeEtta, her mouth taped and hands behind her, threw herself against him.

"DeEtta," Ruby cried.

Without taking the gun off Ruby, Danny punched DeEtta in the stomach and pushed her inside the trailer, where she collapsed on the floor, moaning. Danny locked the door from the inside and then pulled the knob off the door, leaving just the useless rod. He did it with such ease Ruby knew it wasn't the first time he'd locked DeEtta inside. He slammed the door, then turned the outside knob, testing it.

Ruby knelt beside Spot. The dog's eyes showed white with pain. Blood smeared her ruff, darkened her bandana, and spilled onto the dirt. The shot was low in her shoulder; it might be all right; Ruby couldn't tell. Knowing better than to touch the wounded animal, she whispered Spot's name and the dog closed her eyes, panting.

"Get up," Danny ordered Ruby.

"What in hell are you doing?" Ruby asked, not moving from Spot's side. "Shooting dogs and beating up women? Are you stupid or is this just one of your better days?"

"Get up, I said," he ordered again, more shrilly, brandishing the gun.

Ruby obeyed. Jesse still sat in the lounge chair, facing the lake like an innocuous Wyeth painting. If Ruby could get out of this, Jesse might never be the wiser. She had to keep Danny's attention away from Jesse.

"I thought you were in Arizona," Ruby said.

"That's what you were supposed to think."

"What's wrong? You didn't have enough money to leave?"

"I had the money, all right." Danny's voice rose unsteadily. "You city bitches think every country guy lives on bottle deposits and food stamps."

"If you get excited, they get excited," Ron had once commented regarding a hysterical and ultimately dead hostage victim. Ruby lowered her voice, attempting to smooth it over the hammering of her heart. Danny was nervous, frayed and unpredictable.

"Tell me what you want, Danny," she urged him, "so I can take care of DeEtta and the dog."

Jittery energy emanated from Danny's body. His eyes cast wildly around him. "I want what's locked in that metal cabinet; the one upstairs in your cabin."

"The cabinet?" Ruby asked, surprised. "What's in it?"

"You tell me."

"If I open the cabinet for you, will you leave? Go to Arizona or Timbuktu or wherever?"

"Maybe. But DeEtta's coming with me."

"You can't take her, Danny. Will you keep her tied up and locked in so she doesn't run away? What kind of life is that?"

"She's my wife." He jerked the gun toward the cabin. "Let's go."

"You'll be disappointed," Ruby said. No sound came from inside DeEtta's trailer, not even moaning. Ruby reluctantly left Spot and led Danny toward the cabin. "I don't have any money," she told him.

"I already told you I don't need money."

"Then who's paying you to do this?" As soon as she said it, Ruby knew it was the truth: Danny wasn't this original a thinker.

Danny didn't answer. He walked close to her shoulder, smelling of alcohol and cigarettes, and although she couldn't feel or see it, she was conscious of the gun aimed into her body. Don't move, Jesse, don't move, she prayed silently.

Inside the cabin door, she reached for her purse hanging on the wooden wall peg.

"What are you doing?" Danny asked, panicked, jabbing the gun into the small of her back. She winced but didn't cry out.

"The key to the cabinet's in my purse. I carry it with me."

"Dump it on the table."

She did and the contents of her purse clattered in a jumble on the tabletop.

"God, what a mess. You women are all alike," Danny said, pushing aside her compact and notebook to pick up two quarters. He flipped open her wallet with one hand and removed the bills and shoved those in his pocket, too. Then he pushed a ring of keys toward her. "This it?"

"One of them is," Ruby said.

"Okay. Pick it up and let's go."

"I know about the forged logging contracts," Ruby said as she took her first step up to the loft.

"What logging contracts?" He sounded genuinely ignorant.

"The contracts you're being used to hide," Ruby amended. "Did you forge the signatures?"

"Nobody's using me."

"Who paid you to stay away from Corbin's sawmill the day he was killed?" she asked.

"I was sick."

"What was it worth to shoot Mina's dog?" she persisted. "A hundred bucks? Two hundred?"

"Shut up," he growled, pushing the gun into her back, and Ruby did.

In her lab, Danny waved his free hand toward her desk and equipment and asked, "What's all this stuff for, anyway?"

"I do graphic arts," Ruby told him as she sorted through her keys and he nodded, perfectly accepting.

She unlocked the cabinet and opened both doors wide. Danny pulled out her stereoptic microscope and Ruby winced as he dropped it on the table, knocking it on its side. He leafed through her forms and envelopes, dropping them to the floor where they spread like wastepaper. She held her breath as he thumbed through her file folders of cases, including the folders from Wally's office, but he glanced at them without interest.

"Where's the recording?" he demanded.

"What recording?" Ruby asked.

"They told me . . ." And he stopped.

"Someone told you I had a recording of you?" Ruby asked. "Did it implicate you in Mina's death?"

"I didn't touch her," Danny said, his voice rising shrilly again. He shifted from foot to foot, the gun wavering between Ruby's head and heart. "It was in here; where'd you put it?"

"Danny, I never had any kind of recording in this cabinet, and how in hell *could* I have a recording of you?"

"You stole it."

Ruby shook her head and leaned against her lab table. "You've been tricked, Danny. You've been set up by someone who wants to get inside this cabinet without touching it. Your fingerprints are all over the cabinet, the equipment, my papers. You've done the dirty work and now you'll take the blame for the whole mess. You cleared the way for Corbin's death; you shot the dog. Did you burn the house, too? And Mina, did you run her off the road?"

Danny's narrow eyes grew wilder. A tic jumped in his cheek. He slammed one of the cabinet doors so hard it flung itself open again and more papers slid to the floor.

"All I was supposed to do was pull in front of her car

when he called and get out of there. How could I know she was going to die?"

"When who called, Danny?"

Ruby steadied the rage that blurred her vision and made her heart pound beyond any fear. She had to get Danny out of there, away from the cabin and Jesse. When he didn't answer her question, Ruby continued. "Nobody'll believe a punk like you. You're a drunk and a wife abuser. Wife beating's not a popular sport anymore. If you're caught, you'll end up behind bars until you rot. That's what they're counting on. If I were you, I'd get out of Michigan—fast."

"I didn't know anybody'd die," Danny said. "It wasn't my fault." He looked longingly at the loft steps, as if Ruby were the one with the gun and he desired nothing more than to escape the barrage of her words.

"Did you sign any papers, Danny?"

He shook his head, swinging his whole upper body. "It wasn't my fault."

Ruby dared to take another step closer to Danny, a step closer to the gun. "Who paid you to pull in front of Mina's car? Who was it?"

Suddenly there was a poof of wind past Ruby and Danny rose in the air. It was almost comic, this man in paint and camouflage, his arms outflung and the gun clattering to the floor. He folded inward and crumpled next to Ruby's cabinet.

Ruby spun around to face Wally at the top of the steps, holding a pistol with a silencer attached to it. He, too, was dressed in camouflage, only his face was unpainted. "Kids like that irritate the hell out of me," he said. "Always whining about not getting a fair deal."

"Wally," she breathed. "What are you doing?" Was Danny dead? He didn't move, made no sound.

Wally stepped over Danny to the open cabinet. "I'm protecting my interests," he said. He quickly sorted through the files Danny had already jumbled, selecting the two folders Ruby had taken from his office. He held them up and said, "Unlawful entry isn't very polite."

"You can destroy the logging contracts but that won't make any difference," Ruby said.

"It will if you're not around."

"Someone else will stumble over the truth."

"I doubt it. These contracts are legitimate."

"They're forgeries, executed after the signer's deaths, then backdated. The families will discover what you've done."

"And if they do, won't they be happy to discover there's a little extra bonus: a check already made out to the dearly departed."

"But not written for a fraction of the amount the trees were worth, right? David Townsend and Pauline Cassette aren't the only out-of-state landowners whose signatures have been forged, are they?"

"We can chat some other time," Wally said. "Now let's go see your little girl."

Ruby's heart dropped. "Don't you dare hurt her."

"Let's go," he said, waving the gun for her to descend the loft ahead of him.

Chapter 26

Stay calm, Ruby told herself. For Jesse's sake.

Jesse looked up as Ruby and Wally approached. Her forehead creased at the sight of a stranger until Wally said, "Hello, Jesse. You look pretty today."

"Thank you," Jesse said, and turned back to watching the bright autumn colors circling Blue Lake.

"Wally," Ruby said in a neutral voice. Sometimes it was the tone Jesse heard more than the words. "You're not alone in this scheme, are you? Corbin and Silas were involved, too. And what about Glenn Wister?"

"Don't try to figure it out, Ruby," Wally warned her. He set the folders on the grass, weighting them with a rock.

She persisted, anything to keep his mind off Jesse. "I already know about the price-fixing. That was easy money until Hank Holliday came to town and started wising up the property owners.

"But then you concocted a plot to log off land that belonged to out-of-staters. You researched their lives, ascertained what kind of families they had and whether they kept close tabs on their Michigan property. And when they died, you assigned Corbin or Silas to log the property immediately while you forged a logging contract you then dated *before* their deaths."

"You could never leave anything alone," he said. "Always poking around and asking questions. If you hadn't been Mina's friend . . ."

"What would have happened?" Ruby demanded.

"Would she have fallen in love with you instead of Ford Goodlight? Or Corbin?" A thought stabbed Ruby's mind and she rejected it. No, Wally couldn't have.

"You're the one who was inside my cabin," Ruby accused him. "You wrote the mind-your-own-business note. And Mina's suicide note. Of course," she said, picturing how it was done. "You must have had a note or letter from Mina, written when she was happier, at the beginning of your affair. That's why the writing was larger, more open; you traced letters of the alphabet directly from her note, stroke for stroke. It wasn't as clumsy as most tracing, but you gave yourself away—people never construct a letter of the alphabet exactly the same each time they write it."

"Aren't you the expert," Wally said.

"Yes," Ruby admitted. "I am. Did you write a note in Lyle Zander's hand, too? Telling Corbin the job had to be rushed? That way you knew exactly when Corbin would be working in his sawmill."

Wally waved his gun toward the dock and that's when Ruby noticed the dented aluminum boat tied to the end of the dock, floating high and empty.

"What are you going to do? You can't get away with this. It's broad daylight."

Wally shrugged. He opened the gun and examined the chamber, then closed it. He didn't point it at Ruby or Jesse but into the ground, the way the kids who won their certificate in firearms class carried their guns.

"I'm still trying to understand how this all comes together," Ruby went on in a conversational tone. "The price-fixing, the attack on Hank, the logging." She paused. "Mina's and Corbin's deaths."

"Deaths," Jesse whispered, turning to look at Ruby.

"Do you see the ducks?" Ruby asked, pointing at the pair paddling near the thicker reeds. Jesse frowned, watching the ducks that cautiously swam in circles, black eyes alert to the humans on shore.

"Did you shoot Danny because he could have incriminated you?" Ruby asked. "Did Danny threaten to tell Carly how you paid him to stay home from Corbin's mill that day and to run Mina off the road? Did he shoot Mina's collie, too?"

"You forget Danny's in *your* house, Ruby," Wally said calmly. "He pushed his wife around and you made a big noise to the sheriff, a real little rabble-rouser for women's rights. You threatened to kill Danny if he set foot on your property again. Danny mouthed that around himself."

Jesse scowled, trying to take in the conversation, but she showed no fear, only concentration. Her eyes moved from face to face as each spoke. Ruby stood beside Jesse, one hand on her daughter's shoulder.

"Who killed Corbin and Mina?" she asked.

Wally gazed at Ruby steadily, unwaveringly, and Ruby stepped back, swept by sorrow: sorrow for herself and Jesse.

Wally's eyes were cool, detached, the kind of expression Ron Kilgore claimed was deadly. He showed none of the nervousness or near hysteria that Danny had exhibited.

"Did you kill Corbin?" she asked.

"No," Wally answered with calm certainty. "He fell."

"Because you removed his support. You were there that day, making sure it happened."

Wally didn't answer.

"But Mina," she whispered. "You killed Mina. Danny said he pulled out in front of her and drove away. So she swerved to avoid him but the accident didn't kill her, did it?"

An emotion finally kindled deep in Wally's eyes and he glanced away over the water of Blue Lake. "Corbin told her everything."

Ruby heard a car engine but it was too distant. "Corbin learned of your affair with Mina and threatened to reveal your land scams even though he'd be implicating himself. All he cared about was ruining you, getting even. Mina knew the entire scheme and she was tired of the lies. She was bringing me a copy of one of the logging contracts the night she died, and maybe a note from Zander that you'd forged. After you killed her, you removed them from her car."

"If she'd only stayed out of it . . ." Wally said softly.

"But that's not the real reason you killed her. Once Corbin was dead, you thought Mina would turn to you. You loved her all your life, that was no secret. But Mina rejected you completely, even when she was free, didn't she?"

"That's enough," Wally said, his eyes hardening again. He waved his gun toward the dock. "The two of you," he said. "On the dock."

"Why?"

"Jesus Christ, Ruby. Will you just do what I say?" He raised his gun, pointing it directly at her head. Ruby helped her daughter stand, placing the cane in Jesse's right hand and using her body to block the girl's view of Wally's gun.

"Come on, sweetie," Ruby crooned. "Come with me. It's okay."

They crossed the soft sand and stepped onto the wooden dock, with Wally a step behind them.

"All the way to the end," he said.

The aluminum boat bobbed on the water before them. Ruby scanned the shore for hunters or weekenders, anyone.

"Forget it," Wally said, guessing her thoughts. "Nobody's paying any attention. Hunters sure as hell aren't stalking deer in the lake. Even if they looked right at us, what do you think they'd see? A nice little family enjoying their dock."

Ruby supported Jesse as they crossed the broken board and stopped three feet farther down the dock.

How could the water be calm, the trees so bright and colorful beneath autumn-blue sky? It should be storming, the lake wind-lashed, lightning on the horizon.

"All the way to the end."

"Not until you tell me why."

Wally gave a single harsh laugh. "You're in no position to make demands."

"Then shoot us right here. That might get some attention."

"I'm not going to shoot you, Ruby. You're going swimming. You were a weak swimmer as a kid, I remember. No strength in your arms. If I can remember that, other people will, too. All those times we went swimming and you pooped out. Remember the night I dragged you out of the river because you couldn't fight the current? I don't imagine that's changed."

It hadn't. "But Jesse?" she asked.

"You'll have to try and save her, too," Wally said. "It might wear you out, though."

"Please, Wally. Let me take her to the cabin. You can do anything you want to me, but let Jesse go."

"No thanks. It wouldn't be as convincing."

"You saved my life once and now you're going to take it?"

Jesse began to rock her upper body. Ruby didn't know how much the girl comprehended, but it was getting the better of her.

"What's wrong with your kid?" Wally asked as Jesse's head bumped rhythmically against Ruby's chest.

Ruby didn't answer. She put her hand over Jesse's cane and suddenly lifted her head and peered behind Wally, startled by a black shape approaching the shore.

As Wally glanced behind him, Ruby jerked Jesse's cane from her hand, feeling the solid strength of the wood. She swung the cane against Wally's right shoulder, connecting wood to flesh with a sickening thump. Wally staggered and grunted, reaching for his shoulder, but Ruby hadn't struck him hard enough to force him to drop the gun.

The gun wavered and swung toward Ruby's chest. Ruby gripped the cane with both hands and lunged toward Wally, pushing the rubber-tipped end into his sternum with all her strength, sending him flailing backward. His foot slipped into the space left by the missing board, and he dropped into the hole to his thigh, his face lengthening in shock. He struggled futilely, then placed the palm of his free hand on the dock and tried to pull himself from the hole, the gun now pointed at Ruby's foot.

Still using both hands, Ruby slammed the cane against Wally's right wrist, stumbling with the force. His hand shuddered and his fingers unwillingly relaxed. They both grabbed for the gun, Wally grasping with his undamaged left hand, but the pistol splashed into two feet of water and swiftly sank to the amber lake bottom.

Neither of them said a word. The sounds across the peaceful lake were of grunts and a hard object meeting flesh.

Wally swiped at Ruby's leg with his outstretched left hand and she jumped back, feeling the brush of his fingertips against her skin. He grunted and threw himself forward, pulling all but his foot from the hole.

Ruby swung the cane against Wally's head. He cried out and Ruby swung again. And then again. Blood poured from Wally's nose and a fire raged inside Ruby. She wanted him to bleed; she wanted him in agony and terror; she wanted Wally Kentner to die.

He cowered, one foot still in the space between the boards, fighting to protect his head while he twisted out of the path of the battering cane.

Ruby grew aware of a voice calling to her. Still holding the cane over Wally's head, she looked up. Mrs.

Pink stood on the shore, pointing behind Ruby. "Your girl," she called. "Your girl."

Ruby whirled around and saw Jesse teetering on the end of the dock, her balance askew, about to fall into the lake.

She dropped the cane and ran frantically to her daughter, grabbing Jesse's arm as her foot slipped off the wooden boards, sending her toward water that was over her head.

Jesse dangled as Ruby held her by one thin arm, and then she jerked her daughter toward her, both of them tumbling backward onto the dock.

Wally had finally extricated his leg from the gap and now sat unsteadily on the edge of the dock, hands to his bent and bleeding head. The gun glinted in the shallow water beneath him and Mrs. Pink walked into the lake to her thighs, her black clothes swirling around her. She bent down, plucked out the pistol.

"Don't move," Mrs. Pink told Wally, aiming the dripping pistol at him. "I will kill you dead."

He shook his head.

Ruby clutched Jesse gratefully to her heart and carried her off the dock. "Believe her," she murmured to Wally, nodding toward Mrs. Pink.

"Mrs. Pink," Ruby said, looking at the old woman's drenched dress and arms. "Give me the gun. Go to the cabin and dry off. Hurry."

"*Ja, ja,* or I'll catch my death. Here, you take the gun."

"Get up," she told Wally, pointing the wet gun at him. "Walk ahead of us toward the cabin. Hurry up."

Wally stood unsteadily, wiping at blood that dripped down his cheek to his neck, and stumbled from the dock to the shore. The pants leg of his camouflage suit was torn and blood darkened the mottled cloth.

"Raise your hands," Ruby told him. She lifted Jesse in her arms, holding her to her left side, the gun in her right hand trained on Wally. He limped ahead of them, one palm to his bleeding head.

"Did you see DeEtta Becket?" Ruby asked Mrs. Pink. "Where is she?"

"In her tin box," she said, shivering so hard her teeth chattered. "I told her to stay quiet. *Mein* Frank said I should go in your cabin and call the sheriff so I did it."

"What did you tell the sheriff?"

"I lied so he'd believe me. I told him you broke your legs and I couldn't help you."

Ruby heard the sound and looked toward the driveway. "Oh, God," she whispered. She recognized the flatbed emerging from the trees. It was Silas Shea's truck and it was coming fast, jouncing past the cabin and jerking to a stop on the rough lawn. Ruby held the gun on Wally and clutched Jesse tighter. She couldn't hold off both Wally and Silas.

"Keep walking," she told Wally, who'd grown more alert with Silas's arrival. "Stay in front of me."

Silas swung down from the truck and Ruby moved the gun between the two men. "Keep back," she warned Silas.

"Are you all right?" he asked Ruby. His face was grim, his eyes shadowed. "Did he hurt you?"

"I said stay back," Ruby told him.

"Ruby, I didn't—"

Suddenly Wally broke away and sprinted toward the trees behind DeEtta's trailer. Silas pounded after him, snaring Wally's arm and wrapping him in a bear hug before he'd gone twenty feet. "No you don't," he said, and roughly shoved Wally back toward the cabin.

"Let me take Jesse," Silas offered. "It's okay. Enid told me she was here last night. I can help you."

Ruby studied Silas. He'd aged in the past days, gone smaller than that first day when he'd canoed across Blue Lake. Wally stood with his back to her, muscles gathered as if anticipating another chance to escape. She had no choice but to trust Silas.

"Can you see to DeEtta in her trailer?" Ruby asked him. "Mrs. Pink called the sheriff. And Spot's been shot; I don't know how bad it is. Oh. And Danny Greenstone's up in my loft. He may be dead."

Silas's mouth dropped open. "You've been busy."

With Wally leading the way and Ruby aiming the gun at his back, Ruby helped Mrs. Pink and Jesse into the cabin, glancing at the steps to the loft before putting Danny out of her mind.

She pulled a kitchen chair into the middle of the main room. "Sit down," she told Wally.

"Let me go, Ruby. It was all an accident."

"I've never encountered an accidental forgery," Ruby told him. "And don't mention Mina or you may not live until Carly gets here."

Ruby tied a length of clothesline around Wally's hands and feet, feeling like an actor in a TV show, which reminded her to check Wally's pockets for weapons. She pulled a Swiss Army knife from his hip pocket.

"Ruby," Wally said. "I—"

Ruby jerked on the clothesline and Wally winced. "Whatever it is, I don't want to hear it," Ruby told him. "It's going to give me great pleasure to testify against you."

She found towels and dry clothes for Mrs. Pink downstairs and helped her change in Jesse's room. "You were heroic, Mrs. Pink," Ruby told her.

"*Ja*, but don't tell *mein* Frank."

Ruby heard the faint groans from the loft above them about the same time she heard the comforting wail of approaching sirens.

The ambulance took both Danny and Spot, the dog lying on a stretcher beside Danny. "The vet's along the route to the hospital," the blue-jeaned EMT told Ruby. "We'll drop her off."

DeEtta accompanied them, reluctantly consenting to a precautionary examination only after they agreed to let her ride up front instead of in the back with her husband.

"Danny surprised me last night when I left the cabin," DeEtta told Ruby. "He said if I told he'd hurt Jesse."

"Don't think about it," Ruby told her. "Come back when this is over."

"Can I?" DeEtta asked, her face brightening. "Do you mean it?"

"Yes."

Sheriff Carly circled Wally, who was still tied in the chair. "You went too far, Kentner."

Wally raised his head. His hair had fallen forward and was sticky with blood, "You idiot," he jeered. "You never would have figured it out on your own."

"Looks that way, doesn't it?" Carly agreed affably.

"But you knew," Wally snarled from his chair, briefly struggling against the clothesline that bound him. "The whole town knew. They decided to take the 'contributions,' the new football field, the ambulance, and the clock downtown. All those pretty statues in the church." He sniffed. "Payoffs so they wouldn't ask too many questions. Where'd they think the money came from?"

"Then Glenn Wister *is* involved?" Carly asked.

Silas entered the cabin at that moment and answered for Wally. "Glenn's not involved in the forged logging contracts," he said. Ruby could discern in the cautious tone of Silas's voice that whatever Glenn's involvement had been, it would be unprovable, nothing the local population wouldn't forgive and forget before an election.

"And only one person was involved in the deaths," Silas added, nodding toward Wally.

"I'll take Wally to the car," Carly said. "And then I have questions for you, Silas. Why don't you come with us?" he asked amiably while he untied Wally's ropes and hoisted him to his feet.

Silas nodded. "After I take Mrs. Pink home. I'll follow you. I know the whole story."

"Give me your word you'll be in my office in an hour."

"You have it," Silas told him.

"He's in this up to his neck," Wally said. "Whatever he tells you will be a lie."

"I didn't kill anybody," Silas said.

After Carly led Wally from the cabin in handcuffs, Silas leaned over Mrs. Pink, who wore Ruby's yellow terry-cloth robe and a pair of Jesse's Snoopy socks. Mrs. Pink had one timid arm around Jesse, who leaned against her side.

"I'll take you home in a few minutes, Mrs. Pink."

"I'm not going in your truck," Mrs. Pink said huffily.

"Do you want people to see you dressed like that?" Silas asked her.

Mrs. Pink fingered the yellow robe. "Maybe once I'll ride in your truck," she amended. "If I can have my door open."

"Whatever you want."

Ruby poured two small glasses of whiskey and gave one to Silas.

"Thanks," he said with no mention of his stomach. "I meant to tell you; I picked up Holliday at the hospital."

"Where is he?"

"Enid's taking care of him. It was her idea."

There was a story Ruby wanted to hear.

"You aren't involved in the deaths?" Ruby asked Silas. "Is that the truth?"

"It's true. I swear it."

"Then what happened?" Ruby asked.

Silas sat down heavily, his shoulders slumped. "I may as well tell you; practice for telling Carly—or a jury."

Ruby nodded and leaned against the log wall, listening.

"Enid told you the truth," Silas said. "Corbin and I—and Glenn—agreed to agree on the logging prices. We had the county pretty well sewed up. It was an agreement among friends, making sure we all stayed in business." He took a gulp of whiskey, grimacing.

"Agreeing to price-fixing was one thing, but Wally got involved and he was greedy. At first, Wally told us when timbered acreage was coming up for sale before it hit the market, and we'd buy it, log it off, and all three of us share in the timber profits. It was easy money. Then Wally cooked up the forged land contracts. He said it was foolproof. If the family came around and asked questions, one of us had a contract and a signed check ready for them. Glenn didn't want any part of it. He'd been careful and Wally didn't have a hold on him."

Ruby sipped her scotch, letting it burn on her tongue before she swallowed. "But Corbin wanted out?"

Silas nodded. "We both did, but by then we were in up to our necks. Wally held the trump card. When Holliday came to town, Corbin hoped he'd blow the scheme wide open, or at least wise up the landowners so Wally would be forced out of business. Corbin saw Wally's tricks as a threat to his plans for a big business. Holliday would take the heat, not Corbin."

"But then Wally and Mina had an affair."

Silas's face saddened. "Corbin didn't care about the repercussions after he saw them in Fox Woods. He was determined to put Wally out of business and he didn't care who got hurt, even if it was himself. He threatened to go to the law with the whole story."

"So Wally got Danny drunk, maybe he paid Danny to remove Corbin's support. Did Wally push Corbin?"

"I don't believe he did. Without noticing his support was missing, Corbin was bound to fall. He probably leaned the way he usually did without even looking. It would have been an automatic gesture."

"But why did Mina lie?" Ruby asked. "Why did she say Corbin removed the support himself?"

"My guess is she was still trying to protect Corbin. If Wally threatened to discredit Corbin's memory by exposing Corbin's part in the scheme or even the affair."

"But Corbin was dead."

"Mina wasn't thinking clearly," Silas said.

"Until she decided to tell me the true story in the middle of the night. Wally killed her. Wally said Corbin told her everything: about the price-fixing, the land sales. Did you know that?"

Silas nodded. "She told Enid."

"Didn't you realize Mina was in danger?"

"I knew she and Wally were lovers," Silas said, downcast, rubbing his big hands together. They swished like fine sandpaper. "I never suspected he'd hurt her."

"Is Abel Obert involved?" Ruby asked, remembering the owner of Northern Timber and his proud ten-cent tour.

"Not Abel. He was too absorbed in running his mill. He turned the timber buying completely over to Glenn."

Ruby thought for a few moments, swirling the scotch in her glass and holding up the glass to gaze at the amber liquid, finally seeing the truth.

"You used me, too, Silas," she said quietly. "Just like Corbin hoped to use Hank. You asked me to look for the support in Corbin's mill, hoping I'd blow the scheme wide open, that I'd be curious enough to finger Wally and somehow you'd escape this mess. I was expendable, wasn't I?"

Silas lowered his head. "That's harsh, Ruby."

"But it's true, isn't it?"

"I didn't realize the danger you'd be in. I tried to tell you to quit snooping around but you wouldn't listen."

"You're in trouble, Silas."

"I know that. This is the end of an era anyway. Waters County was a pocket of ignorance. If it hadn't been Holliday who began changing the logging methods, it would have been somebody else."

"Changes are inevitable," Ruby said.

"Once this is over it'll put me out of business."

"I think you put yourself out of business," Ruby told him.

Chapter 27

Ruby brought Hank Holliday to her cabin the day after Enid released him from her house. He spoke through clenched teeth, fascinating Jesse as completely as if he were a ventriloquist's dummy.

"I wouldn't miss this to manage a forest full of veneer maple," Hank said, holding up the front page of the *Waters County Proclamator*.

They sat in the metal chairs on her front porch. Autumn was in full power, the trees completely turned and their colorful leaves drifting across the ground, rattling dryly whenever the breezes blew. A gold-and-bronze world. The air was sharp, the odor earthy and final. Winter waited beyond the horizon.

Ruby watched DeEtta and Jesse walk by the water, kicking leaves, Jesse moving slowly but on her own, using Mrs. Pink's gift cane. Ruby's father sat in a lawn chair near the dock, his face to the sun, turning to watch Jesse each time she raised her voice.

"You'll probably be called as a witness," Ruby told Hank.

"It might not be necessary after Danny finishes singing his songs."

"But Wally was the instigator of . . ." Ruby pointed to his black-and-blue face.

"That little episode is the least of his problems.

I hope that girl has sense enough to go through with the divorce," Hank said, nodding toward DeEtta.

"She's already filed," Ruby told him. A late mosquito had bitten her shoulder and she slipped her hand beneath her leg, determined not to scratch the bite.

"Will she be staying here?"

"For a while, but she's aching for a new beginning, away from Sable; I've talked to Ron Kilgore and he's agreed to hire DeEtta; his new secretary is way too organized for his tastes."

"So a nurse's aide would suit him better?" Hank asked.

Ruby laughed. "He thinks an 'unspoiled' country girl is exactly what he needs."

Hank nodded toward the shore and Ruby's father, who held out a hand to Jesse. Ruby tried to remember a time when her father had been as tender to her. "Are you and your father making progress?" Hank asked.

"After twenty years, it isn't going to happen overnight," Ruby told him. "But he loves Jesse. She begins special classes in Pere next week."

"Big step," Hank commented. "She's improved in the short time I've known her. Kids recover more quickly than adults, I think; our bodies really want to be healthy." He touched her hand. "So you'll stay?"

"Until summer, at least," Ruby told him, moving her chair closer to his. "It depends on what Jesse will need. And you? Do you intend to stick it out in Sable?"

"Sure. Once this case is settled my forestry consulting services will be more in demand. Talk about free advertising."

"Do you think Wally will get the punishment he deserves?" Ruby asked, knowing in her heart he could never be punished enough to suit her, never enough to pay for Mina's death.

"He may. With the trial scheduled here in Waters County, it'll be a true trial by his peers." Hank pulled on the waistband of his pants. "Enid Shea stuffed me full

of food. It'll take me a month to get over the three days
I spent with them."

Ruby nodded. "She brought me a carrot cake
yesterday."

Enid had appeared at the door, peevish and defensive. "You can bring that plate back sometime," she'd
said. "And you could bring your daughter, too, if you
want to."

"She's a prickly old bird," Hank said. "Her softer side
only comes out in connection with food."

"She's frightened for Silas," Ruby told Hank, "but
Carly said he's cooperating. Silas and Danny are the
keys to what really happened."

Hank turned in his chair. "Mary Jean wasn't
involved?" he asked.

Ruby peered through the screen. "She says she wasn't."

"But you don't believe her?"

"Danny claimed people in Sable knew, that they
closed their eyes and didn't ask any questions." She
pulled her legs onto the seat of her chair. "Mary Jean
told me Wally investigated out-of-area owners as poten-
tial buyers and sellers, and it's hard to believe she
wasn't suspicious."

"She might have delved deeper," Hank said.

"This is a small town," Ruby said. "We try not to
snitch on each other."

"You said 'we,'" Hank accused her, smiling.

"It was accidental," Ruby told him. "Completely."

"Right," he said.

Jesse's voice reached Ruby's ears and she sat forward,
watching her daughter carefully lay her cane on the
ground. Then DeEtta threw an armful of leaves over
Jesse's head and the girl held up her hands as if snow
were falling.

Match wits with the best-selling

MYSTERY WRITERS

in the business!

Match wits with Richard Jury of Scotland Yard. And solve these cunning murders by

___ The Anodyne Necklace	10280-4	$5.99
___ The Deer Leap	11938-3	$5.99
___ The Dirty Duck	12050-0	$5.99
___ The Five Bells and Bladebone	20133-0	$5.99
___ Help The Poor Struggler	13584-2	$5.99
___ I Am The Only Running Footman	13924-4	$5.99
___ Jerusalem Inn	14181-8	$5.99
___ The Man With A Load Of Mischief	15327-1	$5.99
___ The Old Silent	20492-5	$5.99